The Lion and the Leopard

Brian Duncan

The Lion and the Leopard
Brian Duncan

ISBN: 978-0-9915032-1-6
(Also available for Kindle)

Design and layout by Lighthouse24
Interior maps and charts by Philip Laino
Cover photos courtesy of Peter Charlton
(except “Two Nurses” licensed from Alamy)

In memory of
my aunt
Catherine (Kay) Bracken
author of
'Antiquities Acquired'
and
'Roman Ring'

EAST-CENTRAL AFRICA, 1914-18

Author's Note

This is a work of fiction, although its background is historical. *The Lion and the Leopard* is the third in my trilogy of historical novels set in Southern Africa. It brings together Martin Russell, the main character in *The Settler*, and Alan Spaight, the main protagonist in *Lake of Slaves*, as well as members of their families.

The setting is the First World War campaign in East Africa, when the Allies fought the Germans from the first days to the very end. 'The Lion' in the title refers to the symbol of the British South Africa Police (BSAP), and 'The Leopard' refers to the symbol of the Nyasaland Volunteer Reserve. Both units played a prominent role in the campaign; I had the privilege of serving as a reservist in both of them – much later, of course!

This was a largely forgotten campaign of the 1914-18 war. My story covers the southern region, where units of the German *Schutztruppe* (Defence Force), commanded by Colonel Paul Emil von Lettow-Vorbeck, invaded Nyasaland (now Malawi), Northern Rhodesia (now Zambia) and Portuguese East Africa (now Mozambique). Allied forces tried in vain to defeat von Lettow, but he proved a wily and indefatigable opponent. The suffering and death were dreadful; over 100,000 troops and porters are estimated to have died.

My grandfather went to Nyasaland in 1922 as General Manager of the railway. When he retired in 1936 he bought a farm near Zomba, which my father took over in 1947. I have based some of the background to this book on recollections of my times on the farm. I was fortunate to visit many of the locations portrayed in this book, over a long period (1947-1986), including the length and breadth of Nyasaland. I sailed on Lake Nyasa and visited Lake Tanganyika. I toured Abercorn (Mbala), the Kalambo Falls, and Mbeya with friends Roger Harris and John Collyer, and made several excursions to the Copperbelt and Elizabethville in the then Belgian Congo. I also met, as a schoolboy, two men, Geoff Thorneycroft and John Ness, who fought in the 1914-1918 war (the Thorneycrofts had the farm next door to ours, in Nyasaland).

I relied for background information on many books, including *Tip and Run* by Edward Paice, *Murray's Column* by Tony Tanser, *Cinderella's Soldiers* by Peter Charlton, *My Reminiscences of East Africa* by Paul Emil von Lettow-Vorbeck, and articles in the Nyasaland/Malawi Journal. Any historical inaccuracies are my fault alone!

I have written some ChiNyanja words in this novel – the official name of the language was changed to ChiChewa in 1968. My spellings are based on my memories of the language, from when I spoke it over sixty years ago; current spelling may be different. At that time, and earlier, the term 'European' was used for white British and Germans in the war theatre, to distinguish them from 'Africans.'. However, the term is not appropriate for Rhodesians and South Africans. 'Native' was used for indigenous people (another 'n' word was commonly used, but I have avoided it). *'Bwana'* - equivalent to 'sir' or 'mister' - was the common salutation for European men, in both ChiNyanja and ChiSwahili/KiSwahili. *'Dona'* – equivalent to 'madam' or 'mrs' and derived from Portuguese - was used for European women.

I'm truly grateful to Dr Anne Samson, author of *World War I in Africa: The Forgotten Conflict Among the European Powers* for checking the historical background for me; any errors are my fault. She has helped me with suggestions for background reading. I'm deeply grateful also to my partner Tessa and my daughter Caroline for patiently reading the draft and making helpful suggestions. I'm also grateful to Peter Charlton for answering my questions and generously allowing me to use photos from his book. Many thanks to Lynn Leonard for checking my German. Philip Laino made my sow's ears sketches into silk purse maps with great patience. Doug Heatherly has also been infinitely patient and helpful when making the cover and formatting the text. Both Phil and Doug earlier helped me with *Lake of Slaves* and I'm very fortunate to have found them.

THE RUSSELL AND SPAIGHT FAMILIES

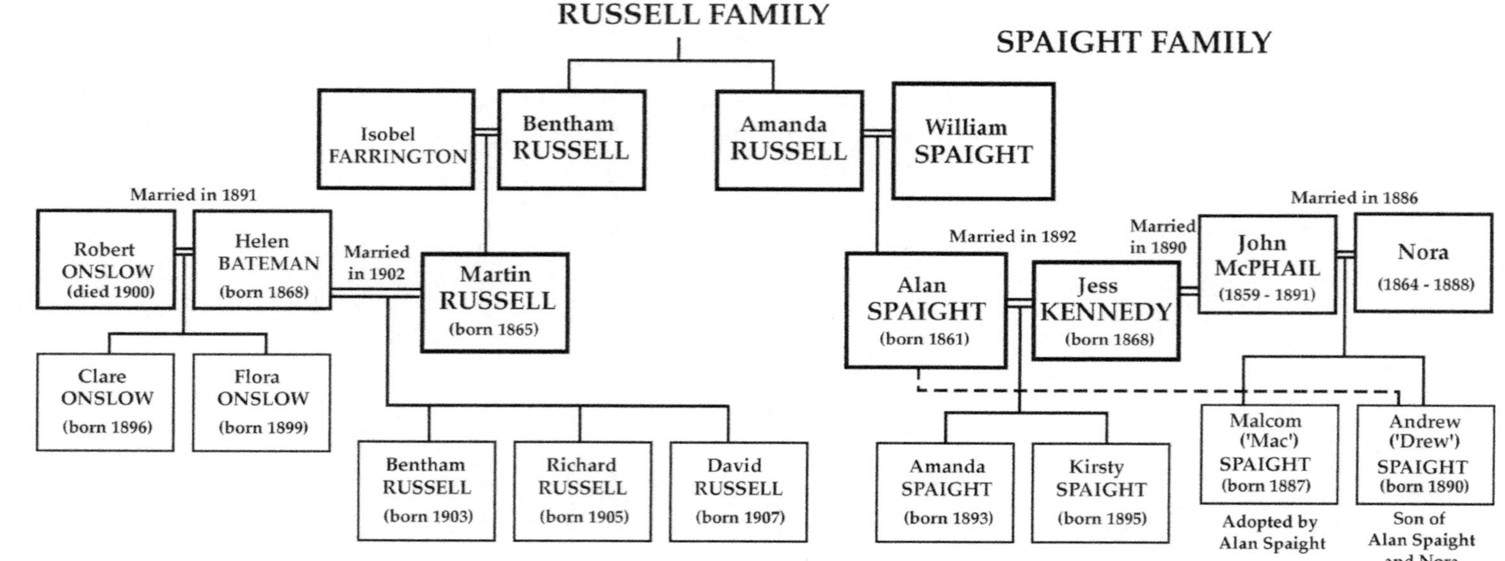

1

Long Valley Farm, Salisbury, Rhodesia - June 1914

Martin Russell's birthday ought to have been a joyous occasion. His loving family surrounded him, and his farm prospered. Yet a dense cloud hung over him, casting a shadow over his thoughts: the imminent prospect of war in Europe, with its threat to Southern Africa, and to his family.

His wife Helen invited only family members to the party, with one exception. They gathered at his farm 'Long Valley,' eight miles east of Salisbury, the capital of Rhodesia. It was July, mid-winter, and the vast dome of sky held no clouds, arching above, clear and pale blue, the air crystalline and cool, five thousand feet above the level of the far distant sea.

Martin lounged in a comfortable cane chair on the lawn, his long legs stretched out, savouring the ebbing warmth from the late afternoon sun. A monolithic figure, his tall body was hardened by years of physical activity, skin browned by the African sun, fair hair thinning and, as if to compensate, a short Van Dyke beard, streaked with grey. His forehead and upper cheeks were blotched with sunspots as were his long bony arms.

Forty-eight today, a prominent figure in the country, recognised by almost all the Europeans in Rhodesia, and many Africans. Usually quiet and contemplative, he could be outspoken when moved by perceived injustices; some thought him a trifle pompous. His character and war record ensured his election to the Legislative Assembly. Many thought he was a Pioneer, one of those who came to Mashonaland in the 1890 Column sponsored by Cecil Rhodes' Chartered Company. In fact he was a 'follower,' having entered the territory a few months later.

Beside him were two Ridgeback lion hounds: Gregor the old grizzled dog, and Suzi, his second mate; two of their last litter were out running with the farm manager. Martin put his hand down to fondle Suzi's ear, and she uttered a small groan of contentment. I ought to feel like that, he mused, instead I'm deeply anxious.

A huge lawn spread in front of the house, dry now, since water was too precious to use on it. Even so, the grass was soft and springy. Beds of roses near the house were now dormant and pruned back. Around the perimeter of the garden grew tall indigenous trees, mostly *msasas,* with some jacarandas and flamboyants nearby; they would flower in October – spring. The trees were so tall and majestic that they seemed to create a great arboreal cathedral, a scene that Martin never tired of admiring. It was his haven from the daily problems on the farm and the stresses of national politics.

He was proud of his large property, purchased in 1892. He started living in a temporary pole and *dagga* house – so practical and pleasant that instead of destroying it, he retained it for guests. He built the main house soon after, using kiln-fired bricks set on stone foundations five feet high. Both houses were thickly thatched with tall *hyperrhenia* grass. Wide verandahs surrounded the main house to catch the breezes in summer. The spacious rooms inside were tall-ceilinged, with windows netted to keep out mosquitoes. A large kitchen complex spread behind the house, and next to it wood burning boilers providing ample hot water to the bathrooms.

"Are you alright, darling," asked his wife Helen, touching his shoulder lightly as she moved past, a tall, stately, fair-haired woman. "Not worrying about war threats, I hope."

She was desperately worried about the looming war in Europe, knowing that her husband would want to be involved, and fearing that her children might follow him into whatever conflicts might develop. Her father had been an officer in the British army, and she knew how easily and quickly a war can spread its deadly influence.

Helen went up to the verandah and returned, stepping slowly and gracefully, leading three servants dressed in spotless white uniforms carrying trays with sandwiches, *samoosas* and cakes. She walked over to Martin and placed her hand on his shoulder again, sensing that something troubled him.

"Alan will be here soon, so I decided to bring the food out."

He looked at his pocket watch. Four o'clock; where were they?

His thoughts were interrupted by a high-pitched twittering call – a pennant-winged night-jar. Being nocturnal, it would be difficult to see, but he recognised the characteristic call. He reached for a small pair of binoculars hanging on the chair near his hand, then put them down and watched Helen instruct the servants as they placed plates of food on trestle tables draped with linen cloths, spreading light muslin covers to keep flies off the food.

Her former slim figure was filling out with middle age. She wore a long cotton dress, and would soon cover her shoulders with a shawl, for the cold winter evening. Noticing him watching her she smiled. She had a calm capable even-tempered manner.

"Put it over there!" A high-pitched command.

Martin moved his gaze across the lawn to his three sons, who had brought a croquet set from the house. Bentham, known as Ben, was the eldest, now eleven, named after Martin's father. Tall for his age and tow-headed, he was already taking charge, pointing to the places where the hoops should be stuck in the lawn, ordering his brothers around.

Richard, nine, and David, seven, were following instructions, but their father knew they would feel resentful of their elder brother bossing them around. The boys had grown up on the farm. They wore khaki cotton shorts and shirts, and sandals, oblivious of the cool air. Typical Rhodesian schoolboys, they helped on the farm, loved to hunt and fish, and enjoyed riding and all the other sports on offer.

Ben came over to his father, fuming. "They're so stupid! They can't put the hoops in the right places."

"They're younger than you. Tell them nicely."

Martin thought many times in the preceding months that his sons would be lucky to escape this war that was coming – unless it was an unusually protracted one. The American Civil War had dragged on for four years, and the Boer War for three; surely this one would not last as long.

"I'll take you boys on," called a deep voice with a drawling Australian accent.

The three boys shouted in glee, gathering round the tall bent figure of Tom Ellsworth. The only non-family person present at the birthday party, he was Martin's closest friend. They met in 1890 and later formed a partnership to mine for gold on the farm, and later in the Mazoe Valley; a fruitful venture that made both men wealthy.

Suddenly the dogs started up, their ears pricked, Suzi growling. Martin saw a car at the far end of the driveway and knew it must be his cousin Alan Spaight with his two daughters. Barking furiously the dogs ran forward until Martin called them off; they returned, waving their tails. The large Vauxhall that Alan had hired drew up near the garage, and he stepped out with his daughters.

"Is it three years since we last met?" called Alan, strolling up to shake his cousin's hand.

He was an inch taller than Martin, but more wiry. His hair was so pale blond it was almost white, as was his clipped beard, sprinkled with grey hairs. His eyes were pale grey-blue, sunk deep below pale bushy eyebrows; something aquiline about his appearance.

"It was in Johannesburg," Martin replied, "when we were on our way to England - you were returning."

Martin kissed both Alan's daughters on the cheek. Amanda, known as Mandy, was slightly taller than her sister, with long blonde hair tied in a pony tail. Many young men in Salisbury had fallen in love with her; she was reputed to have turned them away in droves. She wore her nurse's uniform with a jaunty white cap perched on her head.

Kirsty put her cheek forward. Slightly shorter than her sister, she was dark haired, with a rounder figure, and dimpled cheeks; the more serious of the two she was said to be her sister's gatekeeper, outspoken and argumentative.

Martin called to his sons and watched proudly as they advanced, felt hats clutched in left hands, to shake hands with Alan. They regarded him with curiosity, and Ben asked boldly, "How did you come from Nyasaland, Uncle Alan?"

He smiled. "I came by train. I hear you go to my sons' old school in Salisbury."

They nodded, and said, in a disjointed chorus, "Prince Edward School."

"*'Tot Facienda Parum Factum'*," recited Alan.

The boys grinned, and Ben added, "The school motto, sir."

"I saw it again today, when I was in the town, on the blazer of one of your fellow pupils. Who will translate it for me?"

The younger boys nudged Ben with their elbows, and he piped up. "'So little done; so little time left'. It was a saying of Mr Cecil Rhodes."

"Quite so." Alan laughed. "My Latin is very rusty, but I learned some of the language at school – in England."

Helen came forward to meet her guest. "Good to see you again, Alan, So you're taking the girls home with you. We're going to miss them."

She invited everyone to help themselves to the sandwiches, *samoosas* and cake. They encircled the trestle tables, the children jostling and anxious to fill their plates, knowing they should hold back until the adults helped themselves.

Martin waited in line beside Alan. "I'm sure the girls are glad to have you escort them on the journey back to Nyasaland."

Alan laughed. "I suppose so, though perhaps they would have preferred more interesting company. As you know, my sons did the journeys on their own - every year, when they came here for boarding school, but they always travelled with people we knew."

Martin introduced Tom Ellsworth, adding, "Tom's mining expertise helped us to finance the farm in the early years."

"Not mentioning that it was Martin who staked me when I was prospecting." Ellsworth, tall and taciturn, spoke with a slow Australian drawl. "I was living on mealie-meal – *sadza* – and not much else."

Martin laughed. "Now he dines at the Salisbury Club on the finest steaks." He asked Alan, "How long can you stay?"

"Only a couple of days, Martin. My journey's a bit complicated because of taking the two yearling bulls with us. By the way, I'm most grateful for your gift of the Mashona. It's I who should be giving something to you, for all the hospitality you and Helen have given to our children over the years."

"You'll like the Friesland too. Mandy and Kirsty have named it Hans." Martin had bought him on Alan's behalf, from a dairy farmer at Marandellas."

"I'll have my work cut out looking after them on the journey."

"No doubt the girls will help you."

"They will." Alan sighed. "They're looking forward to going home, but they're nervous of malaria fever – after those bad doses they caught on their way here two years ago. At least we now know that mosquitoes carry the disease, and we can take extra care to prevent the damned things from biting us."

—•—

Martin and Alan sat together on a bench at the edge of the lawn. The young people played croquet, the click of the wooden balls echoing across the lawn, mingled with cries of elation, disappointment and laughter.

"It's strange," Alan mused, "that we are both second husbands, and have adopted the children from our wives' first marriages. Now, your two daughters have retained their father's last name, haven't they?"

"Yes, in order to inherit from his estate. They now own a manor house in Essex and some farm land, with a tenant – his rent payments do little more than maintain the property. I gather your stepsons have taken your name."

"After their grandfather died. The old man was a teacher and left them several hundred pounds – but when he died the boys wanted to change their last name to Spaight – besides, Drew is my son."

"And looks like you."

"Your step-daughters could be yours."

"I suppose so." Martin sighed. "Well, cousin, I think we're at the end of an era. Your children have grown up, and the girls are returning home. That's good news. But I'm afraid we'll soon be embroiled in a war, and it's not of our doing."

"I fear you're right, Martin. At least your sons are too young to be called up. But you and I are still young enough to fight, and my sons are old enough. What really worries me is that Mandy and Kirsty are talking about serving. Their mother will do her best to stop that."

He paused, looking at the croquet players. "What about your girls, Martin? I hear that Clare has started at nursing school."

"We have misgivings," Martin replied, "but she's a free spirit and very determined. Flora is quite different – seems happy to stay at home and help her mother."

"But Clare could be called to serve as a nurse – if there's a war?"

"We won't allow it."

"You may have no choice."

—•—

2

Khundalila Farm, Zomba, Nyasaland – June 1914

Jess Spaight walked down to the buildings where the farm animals were kept. She was in charge of Khundalila while her husband Alan was away in Rhodesia; of all the farm activities she was more interested in the animals than the crops. Her sons Mac and Drew looked after the tobacco and maize, so she could concentrate on the small dairy herd, the beef cattle, and the sheep.

A short and slightly stout Scottish woman, with dark hair, she moved easily and confidently. She had lived in the country for twenty-seven years and raised four children. She missed her two daughters, but her spirits were lifted when she reminded herself that they would soon return from Rhodesia, escorted by her husband.

Milking was in progress in the byre, a low thatched building made from bush poles, with walls of sun-dried mud bricks, and a cement floor graded so that water flowed away when it was washed. As she approached she could hear the cows munching, and the metallic ring of milk squirting into the buckets.

There were eight cows, local humped *Bos indicus*, crossed with an imported Jersey bull. Their yield was modest, perhaps a gallon and a half from each per day at the peak of their lactation period, but the high butter fat content enabled Jess to make plenty of cream, butter and cheese, which she sold to the growing numbers of European residents of Zomba.

Walking into the byre she greeted Adam, the assistant farm manager, a tall young African in his mid-twenties.

"*Muri bwanje*, Adam," she said in ChiNyanja – the traditional greeting, "Are you well?"

"*Ndiribueno, dona; zicomo*. I am well, madam. Thank you." He dipped at the knee and clapped his hands gently together in traditional respect for an elder.

"Is everything well?"

"*Inde, dona.*"

She walked round the byre with him. He was supervising the two milkers, making sure that they washed both their hands and the cows' udders, then massaging them to encourage the milk release. Milking was hard work; Jess had trained the men herself, using her experience from her uncle's farm in Scotland.

The milk from each cow was taken to a separate room, where it was weighed and emptied into a churn, then left to cool to room temperature. When the cream had risen it was put through a mechanical separator, the handle wound by a young African, separating thick cream and leaving the skimmed milk to be fed to the calves and lambs; some of the cream was made into butter.

Jess moved on with Adam to look at two calves in a small enclosure; they came up to her and licked her hand. In the same yard were half a dozen weaned lambs, gambolling with each other. The main flock of thirty sheep had gone out to graze. They were a native breed with fat tails, originally brought to this region by Arab traders.

Another thatched shed was for pregnant cows, separated from the main herd. Alan was experimenting by using bulls of exotic breeds, such as the neighbour's Jersey, and a Shorthorn from another farmer. The calves from these crosses were quite large and sometimes caused birthing problems for the small native cows.

Returning to the dairy Jess poured cream into bottles and wrapped one pound blocks of butter, which she took to Zomba every day; they were sold on commission by the town grocery store. Once it had cooled, the farm milk was poured into small metal cans with lids that could be padlocked, each belonging to a town customer. Each can had the customer's name painted on it. A servant would bicycle out to the farm, collect the full can, and leave an empty one to be collected next day. Jess's customers required different amounts of milk on different days, so she had to be meticulous in filling their orders.

Refrigeration was a constant interest on the farm. Alan and his sons experimented, but so far their most efficient system was to wrap the milk containers in cloth soaked with alcohol, which they obtained by fermenting waste products. The evaporation from the cloths reduced the temperature of the milk.

Jess returned to her house at nine o'clock. It stood on a rocky knoll overlooking the Likengala River, the design similar to the Russell house in Rhodesia, a long single-story red-brick building with a thick grass-thatch roof, raised on a stone foundation and surrounded by deep shady verandahs, intended to keep the house cool during the hot summer months. In the winter, when nights were cold, wood fires warmed the living rooms and bedrooms. Two wings had been added as the children grew up, so they could each have their own bedroom and bathroom.

A guest cottage stood at one side, built for Jess's mother, Marge Kennedy, who had died two years earlier. On each side of the main house were two huge trees, one a wild fig, the other an acacia, and near the river stood several stately *mbawa* trees.

Living on the farm with Jess were her two stepsons, Mac and Drew. When she first came to Nyasaland in 1887, Mac was a baby, the son of Dr Andrew McPhail and his wife Nora. Jess was employed by the McPhails as the child's nanny, needed because Nora was a trained nurse and worked all day with her husband at the hospital. Meanwhile, Jess fell in love with Alan Spaight, who she met on the river steamer when they both came to the country, but to her dismay she discovered he was having an affair with Nora McPhail. The result was Nora's second son, Andrew, known as Drew. When Nora died from puerperal fever, Jess married Dr McPhail, and became the step-mother of the two boys. A year later McPhail died of malaria and Jess then married her true love Alan Spaight; they had two daughters, Amanda and Kirsty.

—•—

Drew was at the breakfast table when Jess entered the dining room; he stood up and kissed her cheek. Tall, fair and athletic, he was now twenty-six. The family all knew that he was really Alan's son, and most people now assumed that he was, particularly because there was such a strong physical resemblance; few local people knew nor cared about the circumstances. Several of the young women in the territory were in love with him, whereas his dour and brooding brother seemed to either fascinate or repel them. He was in many ways a younger version of Alan, and excelled at rugby and tennis, but was more interested in studying wildlife. He was also shy and lacking confidence, so Jess thought. She nick-named him 'Drew the Dreamer', because he was inclined to disappear into his own thoughts. His family had grown used to it, but his girl-friends found it distracting. Looking at him now, she wondered if he would ever surprise her and choose a spouse.

"Everything alright at the dairy?" he asked.

She nodded. "How about the grading?"

"Plodding along. I hope Pa will approve. I feel quite nervous, but Goodwill says we're doing a good job."

Drew was in charge of the tobacco grading while his father was away. Every cured tobacco leaf had to be sorted by position on the plant, size, colour, and degree of blemishes; typically there might be up to twenty grades on any day. The leaves were then baled and sold to the Imperial Tobacco Company in Limbe, about forty miles away. The company would penalise a farmer for poor grading by paying a lower price. Alan had a reputation for being one of the best graders in the country.

A few minutes later they heard a motor-cycle come to the front of the house, followed by clumping footsteps, then the sound of running water in the bathroom as Mac washed his hands. He came into the room, nodded to his mother and brother, and sat down heavily. Malcolm, known as 'Mac' was the more serious of the brothers, now twenty-eight, dark and frail, with a pronounced limp, the result of a childhood riding accident which had also crippled his left arm. When he needed to use it he wore a contraption of his own making, with rods and springs to strengthen it. He had an aversion to horses and other animals after the accident, instead giving his attention to all things mechanical, especially motor-cycles and cars. The family nick-named him 'Mac the Mechanic', because the Africans on the farm had given him the same name. Shorter than Drew, and slightly built, his left arm withered and twisted; his whole body seemed distorted. He pushed back his black unruly hair with hands ingrained with dark stains from motor grease.

"Well, dear?" said Jess. "How has your day been – so far?"

He waited while a servant placed a bowl of maize porridge in front of him. "The pump at the river has broken down again. I have to cut a new leather washer. If that doesn't work we may be short of water until I get a replacement from Blantyre." He poured cream on his porridge, and bent to spoon it into his mouth, frowning.

"I'm sure you can fix it, dear," said Jess.

Mac grunted.

"I have some news for you two," Jess went on. "H. E. wants to come out for a shoot."

His Excellency – 'H.E.' – was the Governor of Nyasaland, Mr George Smith, not yet knighted, though everyone knew it was just a matter of time before he got his KCMG.

"He has visitors, a lady from England and her daughter. He wants to bring the girl here for the shoot, so I invited them for lunch, and then I thought we could organise a beat for *nkwali* and guinea-fowl."

"Ma, I don't want to be involved," said Mac, in a petulant tone. "I want to work on my bike – it's the only chance I have."

Jess knew that Mac hated to participate in any social activity, so she did not argue with him and turned to Drew.

He was frowning. "I don't like organised shoots. For one thing, as you know, the guinea-fowl fly very short distances, and usually find a perch in a tree. And the *nkwali* fly so low there's a real danger of shooting one of the beaters."

Jess sighed. "I don't want to turn him down. Your father values the Governor's friendship..."

"I could take them for a walking shoot," suggested Drew. "We've done that with H. E. before, and he seemed to enjoy it."

—•—

The Governor's car swept into the driveway in front of the house, a large Wolseley, with a splendid crown on the number plate. He drove himself, and beside him was a young woman, fair-haired, pretty and petite. The Governor was above medium height, heavily built, clean-shaven and jovial. He was greeted at the steps by Jess and her sons, and introduced the girl as Emily Fountaine, on her first visit to Africa.

She wore casual clothes, suitable for an afternoon on a farm with walking and shooting, but somehow contriving to look smart. Her white blouse was crisply ironed, and her culottes were in perfect fashion. Her fair hair was pulled back into a small pony tail.

They sat on the verandah before lunch. Drinks were served: beer for the men, and lime squashes for the ladies.

"How are you enjoying your visit to Nyasaland?" asked Jess of Emily.

"Oh, very much, Mrs Spaight," she said, in a refined, rather haughty voice. "My only regret is that my father is not with us. He has important matters to attend to in Cape Town."

"Emily's father is a Major-General and has been posted to South Africa to assist the High Commissioner," added the Governor, by way of explanation.

"These are worrying times," said Jess, wishing that Alan was here to be host and carry this conversation.

"Indeed." Smith looked out across the garden, admiring, as he always did, the array of flowering shrubs, surrounding a green lawn that he knew was irrigated from the river. "It seems quite likely that Britain will be drawn into war. The consequences are far-reaching."

"How will it affect us here?"

Instead of answering himself, the Governor turned to Drew. "What do you think, Drew?'

"Me? Er." Drew had been admiring Emily Fountaine while she looked out at the garden. He knew she was unattainable and probably not the sort of girl he liked, but she was undeniably striking. "Well, sir, our problem will be German East, I suppose. Pa says there are three thousand European settlers there, and almost all of them will volunteer to fight."

"How many European soldiers can this country raise?" asked Emily, for the first time looking at Drew in the eyes. He is incredibly handsome, she thought, and he can at least utter, when asked a question.

"We think perhaps two hundred," answered Drew in an apologetic tone.

"Well surely that means the Huns could overrun this country."

"We'll get help, of course," said the Governor. "The Rhodesians can raise a couple of regiments, and South Africa will support us."

"Are you sure about that?" asked Jess. "It's only twelve years since we were fighting them – in the Boer War. They might not wish to come to our aid."

Smith frowned. "Hm. We'll have to see, Jess. My guess is that Botha and Smuts will bring them onto our side."

They were joined by Mac for lunch; he frowned at his plate for most of the meal. At the Governor's suggestion, they did not talk any more about the war. Instead he questioned Jess about the early days in Nyasaland, partly for the benefit of Emily, but also because he genuinely enjoyed hearing her stories.

Jess said: "I came out in 1887 as a young girl, with my parents; my father was recruited by the Church of Scotland Mission in Blantyre, as a lay farmer. He saw the opportunity and bought land. A few years later he helped my husband Alan to buy this farm – next door. When my parents died I inherited their farm, so we have two, side by side. We started growing coffee, but had to give it up, and now we grow tobacco – and we have some cows."

The Governor said to Emily, "Jess supplies us with milk, butter and cheese too."

"I do admire you," said Emily in a slightly condescending tone. "It must have been quite difficult in those days."

"It was. We had no roads, to speak of. No telegraph or electricity. There was a lot of sickness from malaria and dysentery. Our biggest problem was the farm labour. The local chiefs wanted us to pay them for the right to use their villagers as labourers. Then we had raids from the Angoni..."

"They are the warlike tribe from the highlands in the centre of the country," explained the Governor. "They're an offshoot of the Zulu tribe."

"We also had raids from slavers," continued Jess. "They would come from Portuguese territory to the east, and our labour would vanish in terror."

The Governor took up the story. "Jess's husband was one of those who helped Sir Harry Johnston to put down the slave trade – twenty years ago."

Although she found the stories interesting, Emily hoped that this visit to the farm would give her an opportunity to ride and shoot in the countryside. Brought up in a hunting-shooting-fishing family she thoroughly enjoyed the sports, partly because it gave her the opportunity to mix with men. When they were drinking coffee on the verandah after lunch she talked to Drew.

"Mr Smith says you're a naturalist – you know a lot about the animals here."

Drew laughed in a self-deprecatory way. "I am interested in the wild life. I've had a lot of help from others, including Pa and our African farm manager, Goodwill."

"But you do shoot animals?"

"Only for the pot. I have no problem shooting guinea fowl for us to eat, or an antelope for the Africans to eat. But I would never shoot an animal as a trophy."

Oh dear, thought Emily, you would not mix easily with my family. "What about fox hunting?"

Drew looked at her carefully, wondering if he could detect aggressiveness in her tone. He guessed that she came from a social class in England that enjoyed fox hunting. "I've heard that it started as a means of controlling fox numbers – they were regarded as vermin..."

"Still are."

"But it's become a national sport, hasn't it. Certainly the prey is uneatable, as Oscar Wilde said."

"So, if you came to England, would you not participate?"

"Probably not."

She sighed. "What are we going to do this afternoon?"

"I think the idea is for you and the Governor to have a nap, and then we'll have tea at half past three. After that we'll go out to look for green pigeons and guinea fowl."

Emily thought it quaint that she was taken to a guest room and left to nap for a couple of hours, but she knew that the Governor relished the rest at weekends. Besides, even though it was mid-winter, it was quite hot outside.

They were in the guest house, a thatched bungalow with two bedrooms, separated by a living room. Each bedroom had its own bathroom. Emily lay on the bed, a four poster with a mosquito net, and thought about Drew.

He was awfully appealing, and somehow vulnerable. She felt much less confined here in Zomba, with her mother absorbed in her friendship with Mrs Smith. The Governor and his wife were easy-going, relaxed in their habits. They did not even dress for dinner unless there were other guests.

She fell asleep and was woken by a knock on the door.

"Time for tea, Emily," called the Governor.

She tidied her hair and her clothes, and put on a cool linen jacket the colour of avocado.

—•—

After tea the visitors and Drew climbed into the Spaight's Wolseley, a model similar to the Governor's, but modified to carry more luggage. The two Ridgebacks, Ranter and Lolloper, jumped into the open boot, excited and delighted to be taken out for a shoot, tongues lolling, panting in anticipation.

The dusty road towards Lake Chilwa bisected the two farms, each a thousand acres in extent. Drew turned onto a side road leading down to the Likengala River. The open forest was mostly *miombo*, mixed *Brachystegia* and *Uapaca* species, with occasional *mukwa*, acacia and fig trees. The ground cover was sparse dry grass, just enough to provide cover for small birds such as francolins (*nkwali*).

"At this time of year the guinea fowl like to stay near water," Drew explained. "They drink at least twice a day. Also, there's a fig tree along here that's a favourite of green pigeons – would you like to try for them?"

"Surely we can't shoot them in a tree," said Emily. "It would be unsporting, wouldn't it?"

"I would clap and you shoot when they fly up."

Drew parked the car in a patch of shade; they climbed out and checked their guns. The Governor had a twelve-bore and Emily a twenty-bore, each with No.6 shot. Drew carried a twelve bore, but with SSG cartridges in both breeches.

"In case we encounter something heavier," he explained.

"Such as?" asked Emily.

"Wild pig – or a leopard."

"A leopard?" she raised her eyebrows.

"There are plenty of them around, aren't there, Drew?" asked the Governor.

"At least one pair in every thousand acres, sir, I estimate, judging by reports from other farmers."

"What about lions?" asked Emily.

Drew was somewhat put out by her way of speaking; she seemed almost disdainful. "I doubt there are any resident prides now – on the Palombe plain, although there would have been when my father first came here." He broke his shotgun and checked the cartridges loaded in the breeches. "Now there are villages everywhere, and more cultivation. The antelopes that lions feed on have been driven out or shot out. Of course we do get the occasional lions looking for prey at this time of year – like our cattle."

"Oh dear." Emily said it jokingly; she did not seem overly concerned.

They walked slowly, the hounds at heel, towards a rocky rise where a massive fig tree crowned the top, and soon could see several dozen green pigeons feeding on the fruit, chattering and squabbling, their detritus littering the ground below.

Drew led the Governor and Emily from tree to tree, cautiously approaching until they were about fifty yards away. The only sounds were the crickets, and the pigeons in the tree; also the hounds beside them, panting, and occasionally pausing to moisten their tongues.

"We can now move into the open," he said quietly. "If they do not fly up when we're twenty yards away, I'll clap."

They advanced slowly, but the pigeons seemed so absorbed in their eating that they paid no attention.

"I'm going to clap now." Drew waited while the others raised their guns, and then gave a short loud clap.

The pigeons rose together, their wings clattering, a milling cloud of parrot-green, outraged, frightened. The visitors fired both barrels and Drew saw two birds fall. He sent the hounds to point them, and followed to where they waited proudly.

"There you are," he said, presenting the birds to the visitors. "The African green pigeon."

"Beautiful colouring," said Emily. "What are they like to eat?"

"Excellent," replied the Governor, "but much less meat than an English pigeon."

"Would you like to try for a guinea fowl, sir?" asked Drew.

"By all means, Drew. Lead on."

"We must be very quiet, so that we can hear them. I will then direct you forward. The birds usually rise together and fly to a tree. Because they're heavy, they don't waste energy flying forward from cover to cover, like francolins do. So they look for a tall tree. You will have to take your shots at the first flight."

The two visitors nodded, and he noticed a faint smile on Emily's pretty face. Leading them down a path towards the river, he kept the hounds to heel and listened for the ticking-cackling sound that guinea fowl make when they feed. He knew there was a large flock in the vicinity, and guessed that the birds would be within a couple of hundred yards of the river.

Sure enough, he heard an alarm call, a different tone from the more contented cackle of feeding birds. The second time he was able to pinpoint the direction, and pointed for the visitors to move forward, keeping together. He walked behind them, restraining the eager Ridgebacks.

Suddenly a great noise erupted as the flock of guinea fowl – over a dozen birds – took flight, crying in alarm. The visitors fired two shots, but Drew could not see whether they had scored a hit. Most of the birds flew to a grove of *mbawa* trees near the river, where they perched, indignant, calling to each other in protest.

"I think I hit one," said the Governor, breathing hard. "What about you, Emily."

Shaking her head, "I was too slow."

Drew sent the hounds forward and Ranter discovered a wounded cock bird thrashing in the grass. The young man picked it up and wrung its neck skilfully, then held it up for the Governor.

"One of the pellets hit in the shoulder, so it could no longer fly." He showed it to Emily. "A fine cock bird. See his bright blue neck – to attract the females."

She looked at the dead bird with interest. "Yet in our species it's the female that has to do the attracting."

"What would you like to do now?" Drew asked. "You can take a pot shot at the birds in the trees, but it's almost impossible to move them, even by clapping."

"I don't want to do that," said Emily.

The Governor looked at his watch. "It's nearly five thirty. It'll be dark by six. I suggest we go back. My wife wants us back in Zomba in time for supper."

—•—

When they said their farewells, Emily reached up to kiss Drew on the cheek as she thanked him.

"I would love to ride here with you," she said. "We have two more weeks before we set off home."

They agreed that he would fetch Emily from Government House in three days time.

That night, at supper, Mac said to his brother, "I don't know what you see in that flipetty little thing."

"Who, Emily?"

"Yes. She's so precious. What do you think, Ma?"

Jess could not help smiling. "She does seem to be a little princess." She knew Mac's antipathy was rooted in jealousy.

Drew thought a great deal about the girl, and wondered whether she liked him. But she would soon leave the country.

—•—

3

Long Valley Farm, Salisbury, Rhodesia – June 1914

Helen came towards her guests and held up a hand diffidently. "It's time for the birthday cake. Gather round."

Martin watched her light the candles on his favourite chocolate cake. Too many, he thought – forty-eight. Tactfully she'd used four larger single candles for the decades, and then added eight smaller ones. Even so, it was an impressive conflagration. He invited his two younger sons, still excited by these things, to blow out the flames.

"I propose a toast to my cousin," announced Alan. "And to absent family and friends. I know that Jess and my sons would like to have been here."

"And my parents," Martin added, "and yours."

They drank a toast in good South African wine, and Martin said, "I would like to thank you all for helping me to celebrate my birthday. Alan, it gives me particular pleasure to have you here – we have enjoyed getting to know your daughters these last two years – and your sons before that."

They waited for him to say more, so he added: "In a couple of days, Alan, Mandy and Kirsty will set off back to Nyasaland. I wish we could go with them – we have long wanted to visit their country. One of these days we'll get there."

—•—

After the tea party, when the young people went back to their game of croquet, Alan watched his daughters with love and admiration. He had missed them greatly during the last two years and looked forward to taking them home. He was proud of the independent spirit that led them to make the arduous journey from Nyasaland to Rhodesia, and then to study hard for two long years. Of course they'd had each other for company, but they were strongly bound with their family and must have sorely missed their mother and their brothers.

Even allowing for a father's pride he thought they were gorgeous girls, Mandy tall and willowy, moving with the grace of a dancer, her face calm in repose but quick to animate, blue eyes flashing and wide mouth smiling. She could be wilful, he knew, but she was loyal and generous.

Her sister was shorter and more curvaceous, dark and olive-skinned, much like her mother Jess, quick to express her opinions, more soulful, slower to smile. She seemed to have more inner strength than Mandy, who was inclined to be emotional.

Thoughts of the impending war returned to fill him with anxiety, fearing that his sons and daughters would be drawn into the conflict. He and Jess would try to restrain them, but there was bound to be a surge of volunteering. Besides, he intended to join too, and that would make it difficult to prevent the others.

And what would service entail? It could be argued that he had already done his fair share: with the British army in the Sudan, and then the slave war in Nyasaland. They had been hard times, dreadful conditions, friends and colleagues wounded and killed; he himself had been wounded. Even so, he could not stay away from the war that was to come.

Before supper they all came out onto the verandah and sat in an elongated ring, adults on cane chairs, children on wicker stools. The servants brought hissing paraffin lamps and served drinks. Ben sat with his brothers, occasionally jostling each other in friendly rivalry. Clare and Flora sat behind them, elder sisters, trying to make sure their brothers behaved.

Tom Ellsworth asked, "How did you come to settle in Nyasaland, Alan?"

"I was a soldier first," he replied. "After Sandhurst I was commissioned in the British Army – went to the Sudan. Then I was seconded to a Sikh regiment – served two years in India. I had a disagreement with my colonel and resigned my commission; found a job with the African Lakes Company in Nyasaland – have you heard of them? It's a Scottish trading company. We call it Mandala – the African name. It was originally set up to support the missionaries, and to open a road from the north end of Lake Nyasa to Lake Tanganyika – named the Stevenson Road, after the Scottish merchant who provided the funding. Anyway, I went out to Nyasaland in '87, to work for Mandala as a trader. But I never had a chance to do much work because I was involved in the anti-slavery wars..."

"You mean, even though you were a civilian you had to fight the slavers?" asked Ellsworth.

"Yes. In the early scraps we fought them off." Alan laughed, remembering the bizarre defence of Karonga, when a few white men and their local supporters were surrounded by slavers with several hundred armed mercenaries.

"It must have been a difficult campaign – in such a remote area."

"It was. We were plagued by malaria, and the logistics were awful – there were no roads. In fact, without the little steamships on the lake it would have been impossible."

"So when did you start farming?"

"I left the trading company after a year – bought land near Zomba – started growing coffee. Did quite well for about ten years – then had disease problems. At the same time prices fell – over-production in Brazil – so we switched to tobacco."

"Is it a good crop for you?" asked Martin.

"It's a great export crop because it has a high value for its weight. Have you tried growing tobacco here?"

"No. As you know, flue-cured tobacco needs sandy infertile soils, so that the nutrients can be controlled. On these red soils the tobacco plants grow rank and the quality of the tobacco is unacceptable..."

"You could grow Burley air-cured tobacco, or fire-cured tobacco."

"Possibly."

—•—

When Helen called them in to supper they sat at the big dining table, except for the three Russell boys, placed at a side table within reach of their parents' discipline. Alan admired the heavy wooden furniture and plantation shutters. Looking at his host, he thought that Martin had developed a gravitas in both physical appearance and demeanour. He was thicker now, more stolid, slower in his movements, his face more graven. His step-daughters seemed to reflect their parents: Flora was quieter than her cousins, like her mother she said little unless invited. In contrast, Clare was more vivacious, and joined in conversations about every topic, more aware of current events.

After supper the three men sat on the verandah. A hurricane lamp burned on the floor near the main entrance to the house; the light penetrating only a dozen yards into the surrounding dark. Between them a bottle of Scotch whisky stood on a low table, and beside it a bucket of ice. They wore bush jackets over their sweaters and smoked pipes as they gazed out into the cold dark night.

Attending them, a dark figure sitting on the verandah steps, was Moses, the Russell's senior house servant. Educated at a mission school in Nyasaland, he was clean and fastidious, short and stocky, muscular, and always cheerful, a feature that attracted Martin at their first meetings, and now endeared him to the family.

Now, he came forward and said. "Do you need anything else, sir? May I go now?"

"Thank you, Moses. I think we have everything we need."

"*Zicomo*, Moses," said Alan, a simple 'thank you' in ChiNyanja.

"*Zicomo, bwana*." Moses nodded, smiling, and left them.

"How did you find him?" asked Alan.

"He was recruited from Nyasaland to work on the mines in South Africa. Then he came here to work on my mine, which is where I found him – by chance. He's well educated – a good man – taught me ChiNyanja – so that I can communicate better with the men from Nyasaland in my labour force, about a third of them."

They sipped their whisky and looked out at the dark night. Then Martin broke the silence. "I was talking to a South African friend at my club yesterday. There's trouble brewing in South Africa. Have you heard? It seems that General Hertzog wants to break up the Union. He objects to all the bureaucratic paraphernalia of the Union, and its dealings with the British Government, whereas Botha and Smuts are happy to be more pragmatic and get on with developing the country.

"Do you think Botha was right to expel Hertzog from the Government?"

"I do, because he was speaking publicly against the Government policy. You cannot keep a member of the Cabinet who speaks contrary to its policies – at least on major issues. Of course, Botha was aware that Hertzog and others might start an opposition party, and, sure enough, they formed the National Party."

"How much support do they have?"

"A lot, apparently – most of it in the rural areas. But those country Boers are important, obviously."

"Do you think there could be a revolt – a rebellion?" asked Alan. "Presumably a lot of them are anti-British, and perhaps even pro-German."

Martin sucked on his pipe as he thought. "I still correspond with friends down south. Yes, there is a real possibility of a rebellion. The Boers are still organised in commandos – as they were during the war with the British. Many of the rural commandos would support the rebels."

"Where would Rhodesia stand if there was a civil rebellion in South Africa?"

"We think it would be unwise to become involved in a neighbour's domestic dispute. Jameson and Rhodes made that mistake when they instigated the Raid in '96..."

Tom Ellsworth interjected. "If the legitimate government of South Africa requested assistance surely the Chartered Company would provide support? In a case like that they would ask Whitehall, and the British would give them the nod."

Martin stood up and started pacing. "Milton will do nothing without the support of the Assembly. You see, Alan, we have a majority of elected members in our Legislative Assembly. That means the Chartered Company officials can no longer dictate to us. But Milton, as the Administrator of Rhodesia, would have to defer to the British Government before taking any action – on external affairs. I've no doubt that the elected members would vote for action, but Milton would still have to get permission from Britain."

Alan re-lit his pipe. "What if war breaks out in Europe? We would find the Germans facing us on the battlefield – here in Africa. We would be held in a pincer. It's South-West Africa that would concern you Rhodesians – on your western border. I doubt their East African colony would trouble you."

"But Northern Rhodesia and Nyasaland have boundaries with German East Africa. Also, we would all feel obliged to support Britain in a war against Germany in Europe as well."

"Our priority must be Africa," replied Alan, his voice rising, so that the dogs stirred. "This is where are homes are. We have to protect them, first and foremost. Would we be expected to go to Europe?"

"Most Rhodesians wouldn't hesitate," Martin retorted quickly. "We would be the first to go to help Britain."

Alan shook his head. "I suspect you would be more useful here, defending this part of Africa. There are so few of us in Nyasaland. We're very aware of the threat from the Germans to the north of us, but I doubt we could recruit more than a couple of hundred able-bodied Europeans, outside essential occupations. Also, we're a Protectorate, not a Colony. Whatever we do is dictated by the British Government..."

—•—

Martin invited Alan and Tom to go with him to check on a cow that was about to calve. It was so cold they had to go back for thick jackets. Before they walked the hundred yards to the farm buildings they re-lit their pipes.

"If war breaks out," said Alan to Tom Ellsworth, "what will you do?"

"I'd be considered too old, I suppose."

Martin laughed shortly. "Perhaps I would too, though I would like to do something useful. I don't wouldn't want a desk job..."

"If they did take you on what rank would you have?"

"Major, probably. I would be quite senior, so not expected to go on patrols – or that sort of thing. We have a Commandant, Colonel Edwards, and several part-time Majors, myself included."

"Then what sort of job would they give you?"

"I don't know, Alan. Perhaps a company to command. And what about you? What would you do?"

"I would like to be actively involved. Like you, I would hate to have a desk job."

They had reached the byre and what Martin called the 'maternity ward'. The cow seemed comfortable, chewing the cud, her large moist eyes reflecting the light of the hurricane lamp.

"I hope we'll all see each other again." Martin laughed. "I don't mean that we'll survive, although that's desirable, but that our service would bring us together."

—•—

Mandy and Kirsty Spaight shared one of the guest rooms. Their beds were barely a yard apart, so they were able to whisper to each other.

"The men seem certain that war is coming," said Kirsty in gloomy tones. "I wonder how it will affect us."

"It's exciting in a way..."

"What do you mean?"

"It will throw our lives in the air, and who knows where we will land up."

"But think of all the fighting and killing. It would be awful, wouldn't it?"

"Of course. Perhaps it won't come to that. They might negotiate a peace."

Kirsty sighed. "Father says that the generals have to have their wars. It's what they live their lives for."

—•—

Martin lay beside his wife. All was silent in the house, except for the chirping of crickets and the occasional owl's hoot. He turned to her, noticing in the almost dark that she lay on her back, her eyes open.

"Darling, thank you for my birthday party," he said.

"You enjoyed it?"

"It was good to have Alan here – and Tom."

"They're good men." After a pause, she added, "You talked a lot about the threat of war. It can be rather depressing."

"It's on our minds most of the time." He paused, listening to her breathing. "It may seem odd to you, Helen, but I almost wish it would come..."

"That does seem strange."

"You see, the war in South Africa was a sort of defining period in my life. The war against the Matabele was short and severe, but the three years in South Africa were..."

"And you want it to happen again?"

"In a way, I suppose so. But I'm glad that the boys are too young to get involved..."

"But you will?"

"I would have to. I could never sit here and do nothing, or spend the time shuffling papers on a desk."

Helen laughed quietly. "So you want a second defining period in you life? You're lucky, my love, that your wife comes from an army background. My father used to talk to me about these things. I can imagine him nodding agreement with your sentiments, and urging me to be understanding."

He leaned over and kissed her.

—•—

The following day was June 29, 1914. Martin rode into Salisbury with his cousin. At a station siding they put the two young bulls in the railway truck that would take them to Beira. One of them was Martin's gift to Alan, a young Mashona yearling bull named Shiva. The other was the same age, but larger, named Hans, a Friesland, the South African version of a Holstein. Both animals were in peak condition, but nervous in the unfamiliar surroundings, eyes wide and shifting constantly.

Alan purchased some agricultural materials at the Farmers' Co-op: seeds and chemicals, packed in crates; the two men supervised their loading onto the train. They adjourned from the station to Meikles Hotel for lunch, and Martin bought a copy of the Rhodesia Herald newspaper. The headline read, *"Crown Prince Ferdinand Assassinated"*.

The two men sat on the verandah of the hotel, looking out over the square, and studied the news together. Carts and wagons rumbled by, and the occasional car puttered with them. The winter sun warmed them; it was a contented atmosphere, in contrast to the momentous news.

In portentous tones Martin said, “The Austro-Hungarians will probably move against Serbia, and Germany is bound to support them. But Russia supports Serbia. France has a treaty with Russia and will likely become involved against Germany. What will happen next? I think Britain will have to support France, and that will pit us against Germany. It’s a strange chain of alliances – or misalliances. We’ll be at war before the year is out, Alan. Mark my words!”

—•—

4

Rhodesia to Nyasaland – July, 1914

The train pulled out of Salisbury station, heading east. The little group of the Russells receded into the dusty distance, standing on the station platform, waving handkerchiefs that were now little scraps of white fluttering above them. Mandy wondered when she would see them again.

"I wish they didn't live so far away," she said to her sister. "They're such a dear family. One's own relatives are so special, aren't they?" She felt her eyes smarting with tears that she dabbed away as they welled up.

The train gathered speed as the busy chuffing of the steam engine changed to a steady throb. Mandy and Kirsty had made this journey, in the opposite direction, two years ago, but they remembered little of it – both of them were recovering from malaria fever and bundled up in blankets, feeling sorry for themselves, far from home, with the prospect of two years' study in a strange country.

"We're qualified nurses now," Mandy said, and Kirsty smiled at her sister's *non sequitur*. "We can go anywhere in the world and we would get a job."

"I don't want to go anywhere else," said Kirsty. "Salisbury was alright, but I prefer home, don't you?"

Mandy thought about it. "Zomba is much quieter – a bit of a backwater?"

"You'll miss all the Salisbury parties. You're a party girl, Mandy, let's face it."

"Perhaps. We had a lot of fun."

Kirsty mused, "I wonder what will happen if there's a war with the Germans. It's scary, especially when you think about how awful the Boer War and the Crimean War were. This one could be worse, because they have bigger and better weapons – like machine guns."

"If it happens, I hope we can stay together." She gave her sister a hug.

They went to the dining carriage, where their father and another man were smoking pipes and in deep conversation. The two men looked up as the girls entered, then resumed their conversation about growing coffee. Mandy found it all rather tedious – when they weren't talking about coffee growing it was about the war; endless discussions about alliances and treaties, about armies and invasions.

The train rattled and rumbled on, past Ruwa, where they had friends who grew tobacco. The rolling open savannah was serene under a cloudless sky, the earth dry as a biscuit, covered with sparse grass the colour of honey. The *kopjes* were piles of granite boulders, like ancient castles collapsed into untidy heaps.

—•—

When the train stopped at Marandellas they all clambered out and went to look after Hans and Shiva. The two young bulls were in good form, rolling their eyes, and licking hands with their abrasive tongues. Alan made sure they had enough food and water before the train headed on for Rusape, where they stopped again and made another visit to the bulls.

All the way from Salisbury the train followed the watershed, at an altitude close to five thousand feet. Near Rusape massive granite monoliths towered hundreds of feet into the pale blue sky. The Salisbury-Umtali road ran beside the railway line, and they could see occasional ox wagons and donkey carts, whose occupants waved as the train rumbled past. A few motor cars had been brought to Rhodesia, and they saw two of them – Model-T Fords – like toys jerked on the end of a string, as they bumped along the dusty road.

The train reached Umtali by late afternoon, a sleepy little town of tin-roofed bungalows, tiered among trees in the hills. Here they would spend the night while the locomotive took on more water and coal, and wagons were shunted into new configurations. A pony cart took the passengers to their hotel for supper. When the girls went to the wash-room they were horrified to see how cinders had worked into their hair and clothes; there was nothing they could do but laugh.

After supper, while the sisters went to their room, Alan walked back to the station and visited the two bull calves. Later, he went to the bar for a nightcap before retiring.

Mandy could not sleep because she found the whole journey so exhilarating. She wished she could see more from the window of the room, but it was too dark – there was no moon. She pulled on her dressing gown and went out onto the balcony porch, flinching at the cold night air.

—•—

The train set off for Beira on the following afternoon, headed east from the mountains towards the coastal plain, and would have been able to gather speed if it were not for the condition of the track. They could feel the brakes being applied, especially when going round bends. Valley walls crowded them, draped in luxuriant vegetation, echoing with the cries of birds returning to roost. It was soon pitch dark. Sparks snorted from the funnel of the locomotive like fireflies. The beam of the great headlight on the locomotive lit the way ahead, to warn the driver of line breakages and rockfalls, as well as wild animals.

There were two sleeper compartments, one for Alan, the other for the girls, with up and down bunks. Mandy and Kirsty said goodnight to their father and locked themselves in, then undressed and tried to wash from the tiny metal basin, standing unsteadily as the carriage rocked. The water sloshed around, so it became a wet flannel event. They had to brush the cinders off the bedding, but could still feel the grit in the sheets.

—•—

After crossing a flat plain of sparse grass, reeds and vast swamps, the train reached Beira by late afternoon. The port, near the mouth of the Pungwe River, was the most important in the Portuguese territory. Even so, the town was merely a motley collection of single-story houses roofed with clay tiles, and sheds of rusty corrugated iron.

The travellers took a donkey cart from the station to the Grand Hotel. The name was misleading; it was a modest, rambling building, smothered with bougainvilleas, and surrounded by scrubby grass, constantly invaded by ants, and sand from the beach. A saving grace was the wide verandah looking over the Indian Ocean. Sitting out there in the evening, Alan drank iced beer and the girls sipped lemon squashes, while served curried prawns and roasted peanuts by a smiling African waiter.

As the sun set Alan told his daughters about the stormy coast of Africa, where the opposition of winds and currents created enormous waves that could swallow up a ship in seconds. The reefs and beaches were littered with the remains of ancient sailing vessels that had foundered.

"Fortunately for us, we now have steam power to hold the ship's head into the wind and to move away from the hazards of the coast."

"But what if the engines fail?" asked Kirsty, typically inquisitive.

"They are quite reliable, but, if they do, we throw out a sea anchor and hope to ride the storm."

He told them how the early Portuguese explorers found several entrances to explore the mighty Zambesi River. "It was Vasco da

Gama who was the first European to find the river. At that time there was an outflow at Quelimane. He named it the *Rio de Bons Sinais* – which means the River of Good Omens. There were four other places to enter the river, but sand bars reduced the draft; even at high tide the waves were intimidating. About a hundred years ago the outlet at Quelimane silted up. The Portuguese never discovered the best alternative route – it was found in 1889 by Daniel Rankin, a British explorer based at Quelimane; he heard about it from a local planter. That was two years after I first came out here. It's called the Chinde channel, and has a deeper draft than the others; also it's easier to navigate. The British have a concession at Chinde where passengers and freight are trans-shipped from ocean-going vessels to river steamers."

"Why didn't the Portuguese discover that channel?" asked Kirsty. "They had three hundred years to find it."

Alan laughed. "When you get there you'll understand. It's flat marshland – a typical delta – with no landmarks, which is one reason it's so difficult to navigate into the river. Sometimes ships spend hours, or even days, trying to find the right channel."

Mosquitoes were everywhere, and the girls were nervous about contracting malaria again. When their father first came to Africa in the 1880s people did not know that the malaria parasite was carried by mosquitoes. Now everyone knew that each bite from the insect might infect them with the disease. They spread citronella oil on their skin, and covered themselves with clothing so that only their faces and hands were exposed. Kirsty was the most concerned, having suffered badly when she had fever; she wore a hat with a net coming down over her face and neck, like a bee-keeper.

—•—

Two days later they sailed from Beira in a rusty tramp steamer headed up the coast to Chinde. There were four other passengers: a Mr and

Mrs Roberts, who were missionaries destined for Blantyre, Roland Benting-Smith, a Captain in the Devonshires, and Mr Van Zyl, who was travelling to Nyasaland to recruit labour for the mines in South Africa.

"I'm going to Zomba," said Roland, or 'Roly' as he liked to be called. He was long, lanky and awkward, with a haughty, drawling voice and a loud laugh. "I'll be attached to the King's African Rifles, but hope to be made ADC to the Governor."

"How were you chosen?" asked Alan.

"Wheels within wheels," answered the young man, with an air of mystery. "My father is a retired army officer and has a good friend who knows the Governor..."

"We know the Governor quite well," said Alan. "Perhaps we know his friend."

Roly looked rather uncomfortable. "Actually, sir, my father's friend is General Fountaine – he has been given a post in South Africa – he's attached in some way to the High Commissioner. It's his wife who's a friend of the Governor's wife – if you see what I mean." He rolled his eyes.

Mandy thought he seemed lonely, having travelled on his own since leaving Cape Town. Quite confident and cheerful, he soon attached himself to the Spaight party, attracted by the two girls.

It was a great relief for Roly to meet such congenial company. On the long voyage from England he tried to find out more about his destination, but his companions all wanted to question him about the military implications of the simmering cauldron that was Europe. What were the ambitions of the Kaiser? Was the British Army prepared for war? Could the British and French generals work together? He did his best to give them considered answers, but wanted to hear about Africa.

He had spent a few days with the Fountaines in Cape Town, where he renewed acquaintances with the family. He had not seen Emily since they were school children and was intrigued to hear that she had just returned from a visit to Zomba with her mother. He found her rather diffident about discussing their trip, although she assured him he would enjoy the place.

Mandy was intrigued by the young army officer. He differed so much from the men she had encountered during her two years in Salisbury. His aristocratic accent was quite strange, and he seemed to know a lot about the world in general. He was able to join in conversations on a wide range of topics, when her Salisbury friends would have been tongue-tied.

She was flattered by the young officer's obvious attraction to her. "What do you think of him?" she asked her sister.

"He's a rather overbearing young man," replied Kirsty. "Not my type ..."

"Why not?"

Kirsty pondered. "I suppose because I don't think I would be comfortable with his family and friends. They would be too socially superior... stuck up. You know he went to Eton."

"That doesn't mean he's our social superior."

"Perhaps not. Anyway, Mandy, you can have him.

—•—

All eight passengers sat together to dine in the cramped wardroom. The ship's captain sent a message saying that he could not join them because he was busy on the bridge. A Goan steward, resplendent in a stained white uniform, served a simple meal of curried chicken and rice, followed by fresh fruit from the market in Beira.

"I trust we will not have curry at every meal," said Mrs Roberts, a small, thin and grey woman, stooping like a wet bird. "Spiced food does not agree with me. I wish I could lend a hand in the kitchen."

"It's called the galley, dear, and you might die of heat-stroke," said her husband with a patient small smile; he was large and florid, constantly wiping his face with a large handkerchief.

"Personally, I would not mind curry for every meal," said Roly in his loud languid way. "My father was stationed in India, and my mother learned to make it in many different varieties – meat, fish, eggs, vegetables..."

"Curry was often used to disguise meat that had gone bad," said Kirsty, provocatively.

Mrs Roberts put her knife and fork down with a grimace.

Above them a fan circulated unsteadily, merely stirring up the humid air. Through the portholes they could glimpse the heaving sea and receding coastline.

"I understand that you've lived in Nyasaland for some time," said Mr Roberts to Alan, who then explained how he had gone out to the country. "So you have lived there for twenty-seven years," Roberts went on. "You must be one of the longest serving expatriates there."

"True," said Alan, "but I serve no one but myself." Everyone laughed, and he went on. "I bought land to farm after I'd been in the country for just a year."

"For beads and calico?" The missionary's tone was mildly disapproving.

"No. The land belonged to the Crown, so to speak. I had to pay for it. Even so, it was not expensive."

Mr Van Zyl said, in his thick South African accent, "What are my chances of recruiting labour?"

Alan laughed wryly. "You will be competing with us farmers. We don't like it when you fellows come round with your wallets bulging."

"Can anyone buy land?" asked Van Zyl. "I used to farm myself, in the Free State."

"You must remember that Nyasaland is a Protectorate. Almost all the land belongs to the local African people, under the protection of the British Government. However, Crown Land was purchased in the early years of the Administration – some of it designated for European settlement and being farmed now. There's a market for that land, just the same as in South Africa."

"Is it good farming country?"

"Oh yes. The rainfall is quite reliable, although droughts do happen. The soils are fertile. Our main disadvantage is distance from markets. You see, we're landlocked. Virtually the only route for exports, and imports, is by rail, then ship – to South Africa and Europe. It's costly, and not very reliable."

"I know we're headed for Chinde," said Roly, "but where exactly is it?"

Alan answered in his slow deliberate way. "It's really just a small settlement with a jetty on the bank of the Zambesi River, where it spills into the ocean..."

"It's a little corner of hell!" interjected Kirsty.

Her father raised his hand in mild reproof, and continued. "We change onto a paddle steamer to go up the Zambesi to the tributary Shire River, and then up to Chindio, the railway terminus that opened this year. Eventually the railway will go to Beira, but that means crossing the Zambesi, and it's a mighty big river to bridge."

Van Zyl said, "You could take the goods across the river by barge."

"Yes, and it's being planned now. But that adds to the costs – taking the goods off the train at Chindio, loading them on barges, unloading on the south bank, and then putting them on a train that will run to Beira."

Mrs Roberts interjected. "So, on this journey can we take the train all the way from Chindio to the Shire Highlands?"

"Yes," Alan replied, "to the terminus at Limbe, near Blantyre."

"Is there no railway to Zomba?" asked Mr Roberts. "Why is that – it's the capital?"

"Simply that there's not enough traffic to justify extending the line. Mind you, a war could change that!"

—•—

5

To Nyasaland – July 1914

That evening Roly wrote a letter to his family in England.

...The coastal steamer dropped me at Beira, which is a somewhat derelict port – hot and fly-ridden. My hotel – The Paradiso – was rather basic, and nothing like paradise. The staff were willing but seemed un-trained. After a day I was glad to get on the next steamer for the voyage to Chinde.

My fellow passengers have lifted my spirits somewhat. There is a British settler, Alan Spaight, with two pretty daughters, returning to their farm near Zomba. I hope I will see more of them during my service in Nyasaland. There are also two missionaries, who I fear will find conditions in Africa rather trying, though one has to admire their optimism. Also, a South African intending to recruit labour for the gold mines – a decent enough Boer type. We all get on quite well, and Mr Spaight can tell us where we are and where we're going.

I must admit that I got rather despondent after leaving the Fountaines in Cape Town – even wondered if I was doing the right thing. I did not see much of the General, because he spent most of the time at the High Commission. Mrs Fountaine and Emily tried to entertain me, and I had to buy some clothing and equipment. They had been to Nyasaland for a visit and spoke highly of the place, though they said it was very cut off.

Now I feel more cheerful, and I look forward to seeing the true Africa. So far we have seen no wild animals, only sea birds. But Mr Spaight promises that there will be some game viewing when we voyage up-river. I'm looking forward to using my faithful Purdeys again.

The food is not bad – lots of curry and rice, which I like, but I suspect is to disguise suspect ingredients. At any rate, I'm at no risk of starving. The choices of drink are limited to beer (cold in bottles) and gin and whisky – no wine.

Well, I will close this now. My next will be from Zomba.

—•—

The ship entered the Chinde mouth of the Zambesi River at dawn next day. At the jetty they all disembarked and boarded a much smaller paddle steamer. Although it was midwinter the sun beat down with fierce intensity; all metal objects became too hot to touch. The outlook was not inspiring: mudflats and reeds, and river water stained rusty brown with mud and algae. Swifts darted across the sky in their ceaseless hunt for insects. A few cormorants hung their wings to dry, roosting on stumps.

Alan concentrated on unloading the two bulls, and took them to their crate on the steamer; the animals were soon installed with water and bedding. Meanwhile the girls supervised a gang of porters carrying their personal baggage to the paddle steamer, giving instructions in fluent ChiNyanja, understood by many of the porters. They were accompanied by the gallant young officer, anxious to be helpful, but feeling handicapped because he could not speak the language.

The voyage up river was uneventful, the scenery of flat marshland enlivened by a great variety of bird life. Most spectacular were the fish eagles with their haunting raucous cries.

They spent that night on the steamer. The cabins were cramped and hot. Supper was served under awnings on the deck, where mosquito nets had been draped. The meal was a familiar curry and rice, which raised a heavy sigh of resignation from Mrs Roberts.

Alan said, "Not much has changed on this part of the journey, in the twenty-seven years since I first came here. The mosquitoes are as ferocious as ever."

"Is there no way they can be controlled?" asked Mrs Roberts. "A predator perhaps?"

"At least we now know that they carry malaria," added her husband, "so that we can take precautions."

"They say you can spread oil on the surface of the water, to stop them breeding," said Roly, "but obviously the areas are too vast. My parents say the best way to avoid malaria is to prevent a mosquito from biting you."

"Quite right," added Alan. "One has to be very conscientious."

"We also have tsetse flies in Nyasaland," said Kirsty, deliberately provoking the missionaries. "They carry sleeping sickness in humans and *nagana* in livestock."

"Will they affect us?" asked Mrs Roberts plaintively.

"They could kill you," replied Kirsty, raising one eyebrow.

"Generally it's not a problem in the highlands – in Blantyre," replied Alan soothingly "The main habitats for the tsetse flies are in the lower altitudes, where there are forests, and plenty of wild animals. The flies like to rest on tree trunks in the shade – they don't like open savannah. Also, there are reservoirs of parasites in the wild animals, which are immune to *nagana,* so there is less risk of infection where there are fewer wild animals."

Mr Roberts said to his wife, half jokingly, "Do you wish you'd stayed in Scotland, my dear – where the only problems are the midges?"

—•—

Roly found it difficult to sleep. The captain gave permission for the men to spend the night on deck if they wished, so he rolled up his bedding and carried it outside. Lying on the deck in a warm breeze he could look up at the star-filled sky and watch the constellations wheeling above. The engine rumbled below, and the paddle-wheels rhythmically churned the water at the stern. The shores were invisible in the dark.

He was awake at first light, looking up to see Alan Spaight on the foredeck using binoculars to scan the shore. Here the Zambesi River was over a mile wide and surrounded by marshland. When Roly borrowed the binoculars he saw only the fringes of tall reeds alongside the river banks.

The voyage up the Shire was uneventful, the scenery of flat marshland enlivened by a great variety of bird life. Reaching Chindio at midday they moored at the jetty to disembark. Hordes of native labourers gathered to unload the steamer and transfer the goods to the train, which stood in a siding nearby.

Alan had arranged for his African farm manager, Goodwill, to meet them at Chindio, to assist him with the two young bulls. He was tall and sombre, with white salting his short curly hair. When he was introduced, Roly was surprised at the African's fluent English, until Alan explained that he had been educated at a mission school.

"They are fine animals," said Goodwill admiringly.

"Let's hope they sire plenty of healthy offspring," said Alan. "We can sell the males from Shiva to African farmers to improve their stock, because they should be hardy enough to cope with our climate. It remains to be seen whether we get strong crosses from Hans; it may be that the exotic blood makes them too weak for African conditions."

"Like the European settlers?" asked Goodwill.

Alan laughed. "You could say that."

Roly helped the two girls to settle into their reserved carriage on the train. He found the heat very oppressive; the light breeze seemed to bring only hot air from the floodplains around them. He was perspiring profusely, while the girls fanned themselves, excited at the prospect of starting the last leg of their long journey, and scarcely noticing the heat.

"Will I see the true Africa now?" asked Roly, wiping his face with a large handkerchief. "Lots of sweating smelly natives, ha ha."

Mandy and Kirsty looked at each other and said nothing. They were sitting in the dining car, where a uniformed African steward had brought them lime squashes.

"We think this is Africa," said Kirsty. "Perhaps you mean the open savannah, teeming with wild animals – the picture book Africa. But this is also the true Africa. There are so many different climates. It's not always hot like this, Roly. In the Shire Highlands, where we're going, the winter nights are cold – we need fires."

"How do the natives cope with the cold; they seem to have no clothes – to speak of?"

"They have fires too. They make a big fug in their huts, full of smoke."

Alan came in to join them, and drank most of his lime squash at once. "Well, the bulls seem happy. We gave them banana leaves, and Goodwill will make sure they have plenty of water. They caused quite a stir – the local Africans admire them."

"*Nyama*," said Kirsty. She turned to Roly. "That means meat in ChiNyanja. "Synonymous with 'food'."

"Mr Van Zyl says the Africans will eat anything that moves," said Roly, "and even a few things that have stopped moving."

—•—

When the train rumbled out of Chindio by late afternoon, it passed through flatlands before turning north to run parallel to the Shire River. As on the river steamer, they were the only European passengers. The sleeping berths were similar to those on the train from Salisbury to

Beira; the upper bunk hooked up during the day so that one could sit on the lower bunk, as if it was a settee. If the windows were opened hot air blasted in, carrying cinders from the locomotive, so they relied on electric fans to stir the air within the compartments.

While waiting for the girls, Alan stood in the corridor looking out of the window. The train was passing a huge area of swamp land, and a couple of hundred yards away was a herd of about thirty elephants. He took his binoculars out of the capacious pocket of his jacket to watch the herd.

At that moment Roly joined him and he pointed to the elephants.

"There you are, Roly. See that old gentleman, with his harem of cows and youngsters. He has a fine pair of tusks."

"How has he escaped the ivory hunters?"

"Partly luck, I suppose. Also, this area of swamp is very difficult for hunters. It's full of crocs and mosquitoes. Mind you, he's the sort of male that they look for. His tusks must weigh close to a hundred pounds each."

"They look very long. What's the maximum size?"

"The record? The Natural History Museum in London has a pair that weigh over two hundred pounds each tusk; they're eleven feet long."

"Heavens, that's twice the size of those. How can the beast hold its head up?"

"They're immensely strong – you'll find out. Ah, here are the girls."

They assembled in the dining car at sundown; it was rather sparse compared to the one on the Rhodesian train. The African staff, dressed in white uniforms and smiling, were less experienced, but did their best to serve efficiently, steadying themselves as the train swayed. The other four passengers sat at a table next to Alan's party; conversation between the tables was almost as easy as if they were sitting together. Coffee and tea were served at the end of the meal, and Van Zyl brought out a bottle of good South African brandy which he shared liberally.

Alan could tell that his daughters were excited, knowing that they were on the last lap of the long journey. They had not seen their mother and their two brothers for two years. Their eyes were shining and they could scarcely sit still.

The young British army officer was full of questions. "Did you go up the Shire by steamer, sir – when you first came to the country?" he asked eagerly.

"Yes, I boarded the *James Stevenson* in Chindio, and met Jess – now my wife – and her mother Marge."

He could remember the occasion as if it happened today. Jess was only nineteen then, straight out from Scotland, eager and wide-eyed, excited at the prospect of a new life in a strange land.

"It was slow work in the paddle steamer," he continued, "going upstream against the current, trying to avoid the sandbanks. This is a much easier journey."

Mrs Roberts swatted a mosquito away from her cheek, and Alan said, "I trust you are wearing citronella."

She nodded and smiled. "Of course – the perfume of tropical Africa."

"So, how far could you go up the Shire River?" asked Roly.

"As far as the base of the Murchison Cataracts – the depot for the African Lakes Company – Mandala – for whom I first worked. The company unloaded their steamers there, and used porters to carry all the goods up to Blantyre. There was an alternative track, alongside the Cataracts to the Upper Shire – which is the way the porters used to carry the bits of the steamers now used on Lake Nyasa. They were taken in pieces up that track and re-assembled at the top of the rapids."

"The early missionaries must have had tremendous hardships," mused Mrs Roberts. "It's so much easier for us."

"Yes, it was tough for them," Alan replied. "The local people were not belligerent, but there was plenty of inter-tribal fighting – and theft. Livingstone and his companions were constantly losing personal possessions to local villains. And it's not surprising; the natives had next to nothing. They were ravaged by famine and disease, raided by Angoni warriors and slavers..."

Roly asked, "Why was slavery so prevalent here, so long after it was abolished in Europe and the United States?"

Alan looked out of the window. Cinders from the locomotive flew back like showers of stars, and he wondered how often they started fires in the bush, which was tinder dry at this time of year.

"This part of Africa belonged to no one except the local tribes. The British were pushing north from the Cape, the Portuguese held the eastern coast, the Belgians were probing from the Congo, but in '87, when I first came out here, the vast central area, from the Limpopo River to Lake Victoria, was virtually *terra incognito* to the Europeans..."

"The Arabs had explored into the interior?" asked Mr Roberts.

"Of course. The Arabs had been trading into the interior for several centuries, and by the mid-1800s they'd established trade routes for their commodities – ivory and slaves – which had good markets in the Persian Gulf, India and further east. All they had to do was to get the tusks and the slaves from the interior to the coast. Then they could be shipped away by sea in *dhows*."

Van Zyl poured more tots of his excellent Cape brandy. "Was there no one to stop them?"

Alan let the fierce liquid slide down his throat; he could feel it course down into his belly. "The only people who could have stopped them were the Portuguese. They opposed slavery in theory, but in practice turned a blind eye to what was going on. In fairness, there were very few officials on the ground, and they connived with the slavers."

"The British wouldn't have liked that," said Roly.

"No, but it was a roaring trade – some estimated that ten thousand slaves started the journey to the coast every year, but only a third reached the markets. Livingstone saw what was going on, and publicised the horrific practices..."

"The missionaries were disgusted," said Mrs Roberts. "

"They were, but they could do little to stop it. The British Navy had a squadron of frigates based in Zanzibar to intercept slave *dhows*, but ninety per cent evaded them."

"Pa was in the slave wars," announced Kirsty proudly.

"I was sent to Karonga, at the north end of the Lake, soon after I arrived, in '87. There was a half-caste slaver named Mlozi and we fought him and his henchman for four years without any real success..."

"And Pa was wounded by a bullet," interjected Kirsty. "Show them."

Mandy got up and playfully tried to peel back her father's shirt at the shoulder, while he protested, knowing that there was now only a patch of puckered skin.

"Several of us were wounded," he said, "and a couple of Europeans were killed – and about a dozen African *askaris*. Then Harry Johnston, the first Commissioner of Nyasaland, brought in a contingent of Sikh soldiers from India, under the command of a Captain Maguire..."

"Indian soldiers? I had no idea..." said Roly. "Did they have any heavy weapons?"

"They had a couple of mountain guns and a Maxim machine gun, and that tipped the scales – sadly, not without losses. Maguire was killed, and several Sikh soldiers too, but in another four years the slaving was virtually eradicated."

"Father was made a CB," said Kirsty proudly.

"What's that?" asked Van Zyl.

"Companion of the Bath," she replied, and they all laughed.

"Of the Order of the Bath," corrected Roberts gently. "An important honour, and I'm sure well deserved."

"I was a soldier without a commission or a rank," Alan said. Wanting to change the subject from himself, he added, "By the way, Van Zyl, I hear that some of you Afrikaners are looking for another fight?"

Van Zyl looked surprised. "That is true, Mr Spaight, but I doubt they will start a rebellion. If they do, it will certainly fail..."

"Why are you so confident of that?"

"Most of us have had enough of fighting – it's only twelve years since our war with the British ended. We want to get on with our lives in peace."

"Will South Africans support Britain if we have to fight Germany?" asked Alan.

Van Zyl shook his head. "I really don't know, Mr Spaight. Some will want to, others – the National Party – will be opposed to us getting involved."

"I hope the pro-British forces prevail."

—•—

During the night the train left the course of the Shire River and started winding up the valley of the tributary Ruo, the boundary between Nyasaland and Portuguese East Africa. Alan had difficulty getting to sleep and stood in the corridor thinking about all the materials for the railway that were brought along the very route they had followed – the metal sleepers, the rails, and the cement for the bridges and buttresses – all came by ship to Chindio. The construction was hampered by the scarcity of labour, since recruitment for the mines in South Africa had taken many of the able-bodied natives.

Roly had a cabin to himself. He lay on his bunk smoking a last cigarette, thinking about the day's events. Admiration for Alan

Spaight grew during the evening conversations. He was the epitome of the colonial pioneer. He seemed to know a great deal about everything, yet was modest in offering his opinions. Roly watched him tending to the young bulls, and talking to the staff on the ships and on the train, both in English and ChiNyanja. He had a way with the local people, praising them and joking with them, never behaving as a superior being; giving instructions rather than orders. Roly also admired Alan as a former soldier now involved in the government of the country, impressed that he had been awarded a CB, not bestowed lightly.

He knew that he was extremely lucky to have fallen in with the Spaight family. They had already given him a wealth of information about Nyasaland. Furthermore, they invited him to come and stay with them on their farm, only five miles from Zomba, where he would be stationed.

He mused a great deal about the two girls. How different they were: Mandy so lovely and graceful, but perhaps a trifle flighty; Kirsty more serious, but also pretty in a dark Celtic way. He idly conjectured about what his family would think if he married one of them. His father was a retired colonel who had served in India and in the Boer War. His mother was the daughter of a senior civil servant, a Whitehall mandarin. The Benting-Smiths were not aristocracy, but they were certainly upper class. Would they look down on these colonials?

He had been told that his tour of duty would last for about three years. However, a war would upset any normal timetable. He might even be recalled to Britain. It would be a pity to turn round and go back; he was finding Africa rather exciting.

—•—

When the British passengers assembled for breakfast the train had left the Ruo valley and was winding its way slowly up through hills into the Shire Highlands. Although they looked for wild animals there were only a few small antelopes, difficult to spot. The vegetation had changed from savannah grasslands to what Alan called *miombo – Brachystegia-Uapaca* forest. The trees were not tall because the soil was shallow and rocky, but their shade was dense enough to prevent much undergrowth.

Reaching the Limbe railhead at midday they were met at the station by Mac and Drew, Alan's two sons. It was two years since they last saw their sisters, and they all embraced fondly. The Spaights said farewell to the missionaries and drove to Ryall's Hotel in Blantyre in their dark green Wolseley car, a 1912 24/30 M5 model, imported in the previous year, It seated four comfortably, and Alan had added a waterproof baggage holder at the rear. The girls had not seen the car before and circled it, admiring its shining trim and gleaming head-lamps. The large spare wheel was fastened outside the driver's side door.

Roly was surprised at the number of houses and shops in the town, although it was tiny compared with most in South Africa. It was now the commercial capital of Nyasaland and sprawled among low hills at an altitude of three thousand feet. Alan told Roly that he did not care much for Blantyre; it seemed to him rather downhearted. Though smaller, Zomba had been selected in the very early days of the Protectorate as the capital, and Blantyre had the air of a rejected suitor.

—•—

When they reached the hotel Jess Spaight was standing on the verandah, a charming and cheerful woman, with dark hair and brown eyes. She was deeply in love with her husband and overjoyed to have him back, after an absence of three weeks. She also rejoiced to see her two daughters again and could not restrain her tears as she greeted them.

The two years of parting had been difficult for her. She was anxious in case one or both of the girls might marry a Rhodesian and be lost to her. She was also afraid they might contract malaria fever again, without her to nurse them. Yet here they were, looking healthy and happy.

"I'm really surprised there's no railway line to Zomba," said Roly, as they sat on the verandah of Ryall's Hotel, with cold shandies and beers.

"Not enough freight traffic," answered Alan. "We would like a connection, but it's not justified yet. Perhaps if there's a war..."

"What's the Governor like, sir?" asked Roly, imagining a tall long-nosed aristocrat, laden with gold braid.

The sons nodded to their father, who answered cautiously. "George Smith? He's a good man – in his mid-fifties – very popular with us Europeans. He's an administrator, whereas his predecessor, Bill Manning, was a former army officer..."

"And a friend of Pa's," interrupted Mandy.

"As was the first Governor, Sir Alfred Sharpe," added Kirsty. "He was best man when Pa married."

Am I supposed to be impressed? thought Roly. He guessed it was a small pond, where the senior settler families were important fish.

"Smith is not a personal friend, but I've come to know him well, mainly through my membership of Legco. He often invites me for informal discussions about issues affecting the settler community. Also, we've taken him duck shooting on Lake Chilwa several times, and he seems to like it."

After supper Jess and her daughters went to their hotel rooms, while Drew and Mac went to take care of the two young bulls in the African Lakes Company livery. Alan and Roly sat on the verandah drinking whisky nightcaps; Alan smoked his pipe, and Roly a cigar.

"What will you do if there's a war, sir," drawled Roly.

Alan pondered. "I would like to serve – do something useful. I'm a Major in the NVR – the Nyasaland Volunteer Reserve – but my age is against me. I hope they won't give me some sort of desk job. I'd hate that."

"You seem to have a lot of valuable local experience."

"I suppose so. We old hands know how to look after ourselves in the bush."

"Do you think the Germans will attack – invade Nyasaland?"

Alan shrugged. "They might, Roly. We could have a real fight on our hands."

—•—

In bed with Jess, Alan told her about his conversation with Roly. "You know, sweetheart, I think I must have enjoyed the campaigns against the slavers, even though it was often very gruelling. Two decades of peace have been pleasant, and..."

"You never hesitated to go off to the fighting, but did you 'enjoy' it?"

"Of course 'enjoy' is not the right word. It was stimulating, exciting. I think it was the camaraderie, more than anything, that made it worthwhile. I met some fine men – Maguire, Lugard, Nicholl, the Moirs, Johnston..."

She laughed softly. "My dear, are you preparing me for what might come? Do you want to become involved in this new war that might come?"

"I do..."

"Haven't you done enough? Surely it's time for the next generation?"

"Mac and Drew? They're certain to volunteer – or be called up – although they might not take Mac because of his disabilities. Men of their age will bear the brunt of the fighting."

Jess sighed. "I dread them going off like you used to, never knowing when you would come back."

"You know, Mandy and Kirsty might be called up, too. There's bound to be a great demand for nurses."

Jess started to sob. "I couldn't bear it."

—•—

Next morning Alan drove Jess and the girls, and Roly, in the Wolseley. Meanwhile, Drew and Mac, assisted by Goodwill, loaded the two bulls into padded crates in the farm's lorry; they would travel at a slower pace that than the others, to avoid jolting the young bulls.

Roly was surprised at the high quality of the road between Blantyre and Zomba. It had a tar 'macadam' surface, and was the longest single stretch of it in southern Africa. There were places where heavy storms could wash the road away, though it was not a problem now, in the dry season. Gangs of labourers employed by the Public Works Department were constructing culverts and making other road improvements.

The Spaights stopped at intervals to point out landmarks to Roly, including the estates owned by Europeans. Chiradzulu Mountain was straight ahead of them, while to their right, about forty miles away, was the magnificent Mlanje massif, rising in isolation from the plain to a height of nearly ten thousand feet. Ahead, blurred in blue haze, was Zomba Mountain, their destination.

By noon they reached the Bruce estate, where they had been invited to have lunch with old friends, Andrew and Flora. During the meal they discussed the looming war and its implications for them. Austria-Hungary had declared war on Serbia, and it was thought that it was only a matter of time before France and Germany would become involved.

"I don't think the Germans up north will bother us, do you?" asked Andrew Bruce. "Most of them are settlers like us. Surely they won't want to leave their farms?"

"There are far more of them," said Alan. "Three thousand, I think. They've been adding to their regiments of trained *askaris*, whereas we've wound down our regiment."

"Do you think they would attack us?" asked Roly, looking at his host with hooded eyes.

"Some people think they will. If they can secure Lake Nyasa it would give them a transport route to the south. I suppose we should not be complacent..."

"But what strategic value would that have for them – to invade south, I mean?"

"Not a great deal," said Alan. "But it would tie up British resources. We and the South Africans would have to stop them. We would have to divert troops here that could be used elsewhere – in Europe."

—•—

After they had argued to and fro for about twenty minutes, Alan changed the subject, turning to his host. "What can you tell me about John Chilembwe?" he asked. "I hear that his sermons are becoming quite seditious."

He turned to Roly and explained. "Chilembwe is an African priest, who was trained in America and is reputed to be against the European settlers. He has a church near here."

"I'm not too concerned about him," said Andrew, who was inclined to bluster. "He dresses and behaves like a European himself, so I don't think he would harm us. I have a couple of my men keeping an eye on him. If he tries to raise a rabble I'll hear soon enough."

"If you're here," said Flora Bruce sourly. "If there's a war you may be called up."

"Then, my dear, it will be up to you to inform the Governor."

Alan did not reveal that he had his own informer, his farm manager Goodwill, who had a friend, a disciple of Chilembwe. This man had told Goodwill something about the seditious activities of the priest, probably not appreciating its importance.

—•—

The Spaight party set off again at two-thirty, Alan driving, with Jess sitting beside him. Roly sat with the two girls on the back seat. They reached Zomba at four, and parted from him at the King's African Rifles barracks, where he was greeted by Captain Charles Barton, the senior British officer in the territory.

The KAR was the only military unit in Nyasaland, and had traditionally recruited its askaris from local men. Currently the first battalion (1/KAR) were in the Northern Frontier District of British East Africa, north of Nairobi. The second battalion (2/KAR) had been disbanded in 1911 as an economy measure. Many of the askaris from this battalion travelled to German East Africa and joined army units there. Indeed, there were so many of them that the Germans used British bugle calls and commands.

The only KAR troops remaining in Nyasaland in 1914 were a company of askaris in Zomba, and another at Fort Maguire; most of these men were recruits undergoing training. Two other companies were on leave, and could be called up, if required.

The only other military unit, the Nyasaland Volunteer Reserve, a small and exclusively European outfit, with sections in different districts, had emerged through rifle shooting competitions, but in recent months added more serious military flavour to their training.

—•—

The Spaights continued their journey, passing through Zomba and turned east towards Lake Chilwa, reaching their farm *Khundalila* half an hour after parting with Roly. The girls were ecstatic to be home after their long absence.

"I don't ever want to leave again," said Mandy.

"Me neither," added her sister, but she knew it was unrealistic. "We might have to leave the farm, but not Nyasaland."

The family was greeted by Adam, Goodwill's son, and assistant farm manager, who had grown up on the farm. The servants also greeted them warmly; they had known the family for many years. Three Ridgeback dogs surrounded them, jostling for their attention.

The two girls ran out to the stables to see their beloved horses and came back half an hour later.

"They remember us," announced Kirsty.

"You should have seen them," added Mandy. "Snorting and stamping. They knew at once who we were."

Alan said, "I'm not surprised. They may not be as intelligent as dogs, but..."

"Oh, we knew the dogs would remember us," chorused the girls. The two Ridgeback lion hounds were now their constant companions, gazing at them lovingly.

They congregated on the deep verandah for a drink before supper. It was growing dark quickly and night sounds were emerging – a crescendo of crickets, pigeons and doves roosting, a cow lowing from the byre, and, in the far distance, the yelp of a jackal.

Alan left to warn the night watchmen to be aware of hyenas. Jess went to the kitchen to check the preparations for supper.

"It's so good to be back," said Mandy. "This is such a special place."

"And being with our family," added her sister.

When Alan and Jess returned they started talking about the war.

"It's been twenty years since we had war of any kind in this country," said Alan, in somewhat gloomy tones. "I suppose it was too good to last."

"Perhaps it will all fizzle out," said Jess, " – after they rattle their sabres and shout at each other."

"And if not?"

"Then we could be in for a hard fight."

—•—

Philip Laino

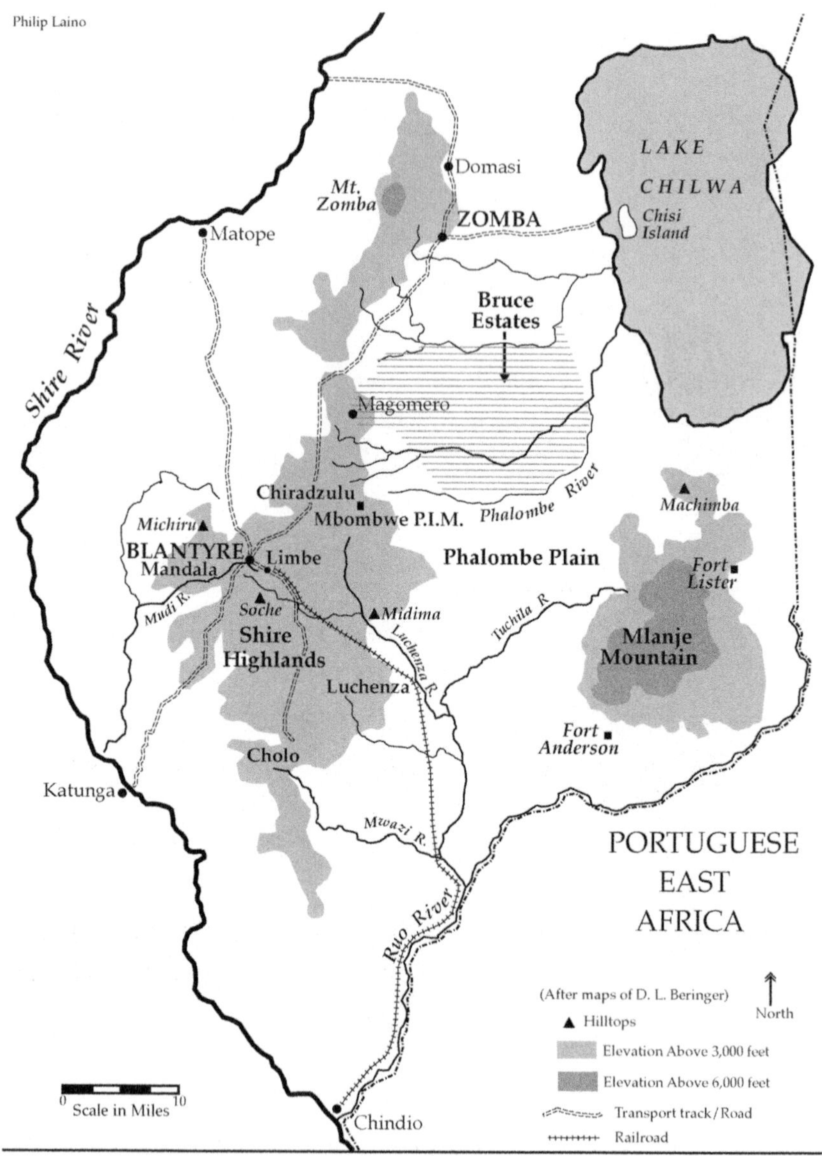

NYASALAND — SHIRE HIGHLANDS

6

Zomba, Nyasaland – August 1914

As a member of Legco, Alan was entitled to see most of the confidential telegrams that came to the Chief Secretary's office. He went into Zomba almost every day and was shown into a quiet office where he read the files. On July 27 Hector Duff joined him, and tea was served.

"I see the German newspapers are suggesting their government should not be obliged to support Austria," said Alan.

Duff smiled. "Yes, but the Germans cannot allow Austria to be defeated. Their perceived threat from Russia is too great."

"So, do you think war is inevitable?"

"The French Government seems to think so, and the German war machine is mobilising as we speak." Duff sipped his tea. "Interesting, Alan – the French can send radio signals to St Petersburg from the Eiffel Tower."

Alan read another telegram. "It says here that the German Government requested our neutrality if they do not attack Belgium and France. I'm glad that offer was rejected."

—•—

"How are your family?" asked Alan, as he walked with Goodwill round the farm buildings; they spoke in both English and ChiNyanja.

"Very well, thank you, sir," replied Goodwill. He was almost as tall as Alan, powerfully built, his hair grizzled, his expression solemn. "The young *donas* are looking well."

"They are, and glad to be home. How is the school?"

"Good, sir." The farm school was Goodwill's pride. He had helped Alan to start it, and became the first schoolmaster; when it expanded Alan made him the principal. The pupils were children of farm labourers from *Khundalila* and other neighbouring farms.

"It's good to be back." Alan sighed contentedly. "We must start the seedbeds soon."

It was now spring and they would sow tobacco seed in beds, near the river; the seedlings were later transplanted into the fields, at about the time of the first rains, in November.

"I hear there may be a big war in Europe," said Goodwill diffidently.

"Yes, Goodwill. It seems certain now. The British may become involved, because they have alliances with other countries. What's important for us is that the Germans to the north may become our enemies. They may attack us."

"We have few soldiers to defend ourselves."

"True. We'll get help from the South Africans. The British may send soldiers too."

"My people fear the *WaGermani*. They are said to be cruel people."

Alan laughed. "Where did you hear that, Goodwill?"

"Sir, we have heard about the rebellion in German East Africa. The German *azungu* killed many people and destroyed their crops."

"Ah, so I have heard. The Germans said they were attacked and had to defend themselves."

"Perhaps." Goodwill smiled. "But we hope they will not come here."

Alan tried to conceal his surprise that Goodwill held these sentiments. "It is said that there were spirit mediums that encouraged the local people to attack the German settlers – the Africans said the *azungu* bullets would turn to water – that's why it was called the *Maji-maji* Rebellion. Isn't *maji* the Swahili word for water? Do you think anything like that could happen here, Goodwill?"

The African frowned as he considered his reply. Although he had not yet confided in Alan, he was becoming more and more concerned about the preaching of John Chilembwe. "I have not heard of any spirit mediums that are against the *azungu*. Even so, it might happen."

—•—

On August 3, when Alan again went to the Chief Secretary's office; Hector Duff was away at Government House, but his young secretary sat Alan down and brought him his cup of tea.

"I suppose you've read all these, Emma," he said.

"I have, sir, but you know it's all a bit above my head. I know it's awfully serious. That's why Mr Duff has gone to see H.E."

Alan wondered how much she imparted to her family; she was the daughter of the Deputy Director of Public Works. Of course, he thought, it would not matter much. All the really top secret files were kept in Duff's safe.

Much of the news in the despatches would be reflected in the Nyasaland Times tomorrow. The Germans and the French had mobilised their armed forces. It seemed just a matter of time before war would be declared, despite the protestations of the politicians.

—•—

Roly Benting-Smith arrived to have lunch at *Khundalila,* riding on a handsome chestnut charger, allocated to him by the KAR. He was an accomplished rider, having ridden to hounds in England.

He was greeted by Alan, Jess and the girls.

"What a delightful place," said Roly, obviously much impressed. "The garden is amazing, better than the one at Government House, and that's beautiful enough. You evidently have ample water to lavish on the lawns and flower beds; it's all so green and lush."

Before lunch Alan took Roly for a ride round the farm. Parts of it were irrigated, using a canal that drew water from the Likengala River. One of the secondary canals took water to a reservoir near the house, and from there it was pumped up to a circular brick tank at the highest point of the knoll whence it fed sprinklers for the lawns and flower beds around the house.

"That little village – over there – is where the servants and the permanent labourers are housed," explained Alan, pointing to the cluster of small brick and thatch houses. "Each one has a single large room and a kitchen; the toilets are long-drops – much the same as we have, but theirs are outside. They have a piped water supply – not normal for farm labour, but it's much healthier. That long building is the primary school. When the children reach the age of about ten, they go to the mission school in Domasi."

"Is that usual," asked Roly, "I mean to have a farm school?"

"No. Nor is it usual to have brick-built houses for the labour. Grass huts are the norm..."

"But wouldn't the native worker feel more at home in a grass hut?"

"Ask them, Roly. They'll say they prefer the brick house. It might be the status it confers. I think I was the first in the country to start a farm school, but there are others now. I thought it would help to attract and retain a labour force, and it seems to have worked. I have fewer problems with workers than the other farmers in the district."

"Are those tobacco barns?" Roly pointed to the tall brick buildings.

"Yes; we copied the design from the Americans – from Virginia. Each barn stands alone because of the fire risk. The tobacco leaves are hung to dry with heat from flues on the floor of the barn. Hence the term 'flue-cured tobacco'."

They dismounted and tethered the horses. Alan showed Roly the inside of a barn, which was not being used at that time of year. "The heat comes from furnaces fuelled by firewood. As you saw, we maintain large stacks of wood. We have to be very careful of fire. During curing, when the tobacco leaves are dry, they're highly inflammable."

Alan led his visitor to the sheds. "We grow fifty acres of Virginia tobacco, and we have eight barns. Each curing cycle takes about a week; then the barn is unloaded and the cured leaves are laid in a pile – called a 'bulk'. After a few weeks in the bulk, the leaves have a more pliant texture, like chamois leather; the aroma is nice and sweet. We grade the leaves and bale them for sale to the Imperial Tobacco Company in Limbe."

"That sounds like an awful lot of leaves to handle."

"It is. We transplant about six thousand plants to the acre, so that's 300,000 plants on my fifty acres. Each plant has a dozen or so leaves, so that's three to four million leaves, and each one has to be put in a grade..."

"Good Lord! How many labourers do you need to do that?"

Alan laughed. "A lot. During harvest and grading we have about sixty or seventy part-time workers – we're not as efficient as Americans; our work rate is much lower. That's in addition to twenty permanent labourers. The casual – temporary – workers come to us from November until the end of July."

"Where do they live?"

"In nearby villages; they walk to work. When I started the farm in '88, we had great difficulty finding labour because the chiefs and headmen used to demand bribes and other inducements to let us use their people. Also, in the early days the villages were raided by slavers and Angoni warriors, so the labourers would all flee. Of course none of that happens now."

"Is your tobacco used to make cigarettes?"

"Most of it – in Britain. Some other types – sun-cured and air-cured – are grown by the Africans – and go into pipe blends."

"And cigars?"

"Cigar leaf was grown when the first British settlers started farming here. It's still grown, on a small scale, but not the quality of Cuban leaf. You know, Roly, we grow more flue-cured tobacco than any other country outside the United States, although I think the Rhodesians will soon overtake us."

"I remember you said you grew coffee when you started the farm," said Roly.

"That's right – I'll show you."

They mounted their horses and Alan led the way from the tobacco sheds. Some of the fields were fallow and sown to pasture grass, while others had been ploughed and were now bare, the sandy soil exposed in neat furrows. Further on they came to a five acre plantation of coffee trees, in the shade of silver oaks. Their glossy dark-green leaves contrasted with the pale yellow-beiges and biscuit-browns of most of the winter vegetation on the farm.

"This is all that's left of our coffee plantation," said Alan. "I've kept it for our own use, and for friends. You never know when there might be a change in the market. Fifteen years ago we had a hundred acres of coffee on this farm, and seventeen thousand acres in the Shire Highlands..."

"What went wrong?"

"We had disease problems – particularly a bug called the Antestia beetle. At about the same time there was over-production in Brazil, and world prices fell sharply. So we looked around for something else. Some of the planters turned to cotton, but I never liked the crop so I didn't try it..."

"Why didn't you like cotton?"

Alan shrugged. "It's very prone to insect attack. Also, the farmer sells a raw product of fairly low value. It's the ginners and spinners who make the money. Anyway, I switched into tobacco as soon as I could make the bricks and build the barns and sheds. Several of my near neighbours are managers of estates belonging to a large company. We help each other a lot, and we get seed and technical information from the Americans."

"Do the Americans grow tobacco here?"

"No, but a couple of men from Virginia came here in '02. They only stayed for one year, but they started us off."

They rode back and Alan stopped to talk to Goodwill, dismounting and introduced him to Roly.

"You remember Goodwill. He met us at Chindio. He has worked for me since I started the farm. That's twenty-six years, isn't it, Goodwill?"

"Yes, sir."

"He was taken from his village as a slave. I think you would like to hear the story, Roly, but we'd better get back for lunch or I'll be in big trouble."

He turned to Goodwill. "We need to talk. Let's meet tomorrow morning."

While they walked back to the house, Alan said, "He's a good man. His father was an Angoni sub-chief, and his mother an abducted Nyanja girl. When his father died, he and his sisters fled with their mother back to their former Nyanja village. The children were educated at the Presbyterian mission at Domasi, near Zomba. When he was about twenty he was captured by an Arab slaver and taken to the Indian Ocean coast. He and his companion were chained on a *dhow*, which was wrecked in a storm, but they managed to escape, and walked back to Nyasaland."

—•—

Over lunch Alan was amused to see that Roly was still captivated by the two girls, but particularly Mandy. He would gaze at her, then realise that his attention might be too obvious, and would start a line of conversation before returning to glance at the girl. Alan had seen many young British officers during his years in the Army. He tried to assess whether Roly was different, or had any special qualities.

They started a conversation about nick-names, Alan explaining that the Africans who worked on the farm had names for the Europeans, which they used among themselves.

"Mine is *Woyera*, I suppose because my hair is so pale it's almost white. Jess's name is *Dona Kalata*, because she's always writing notes to people." He laughed.

"I have to," Jess retorted. "Otherwise you forget."

"And Mandy?" asked Roly.

"She's *Dona Chikasu*," answered Alan, "I think because she often used to wear yellow dresses and shirts."

"Mine is *Dona Carvalho;*" said Kirsty, "*carvalho* being the ChiYao word for horse, I guess because I spend so much time with the horses."

"And Drew?"

"He's *Kutchera*," said Alan. "The word means a trap for birds. When he was a small boy he was always making traps to catch birds and animals. It's interesting how the Africans noticed these things."

"I wonder what name they would choose for you," said Mandy, looking at Roly provocatively; *Talika*, perhaps."

"What does that mean?"

"Tall. Or ...what do you think, Roly?"

He shrugged. "Perhaps something to do with me being a soldier? By the way, I went to church this morning. Is that where you married, Mrs Spaight?"

She smiled. "No, Roly. It hadn't been built then. We were married at the mission church at Domasi."

"Both marriages," said Kirsty.

Jess laughed shyly. "You see, Roly, I was married to a Dr McPhail before I married Alan."

Roly already knew this, but nodded politely. "I'm surprised how small Zomba is. Somehow I expected a town more like Blantyre, but it's quite tiny isn't it? Perhaps the smallest capital in the world."

"I suppose so," said Jess. "When we first came here there were less than a dozen white people, so we think it's grown a lot. It must seem very small and provincial to you. Anyway, I'm glad it's not like Blantyre – not my favourite place."

"Why is that?"

"Too hot and dusty."

Kirsty added, "She doesn't like the commercial area, but we have to have one somewhere. Those Indian stores are so useful. They stock material for making clothes, and all sorts of spices."

Sitting out on the verandah after lunch, Alan smoked his pipe and Roly a cigar, while Jess served coffee, ground from their own beans. The Ridgebacks curled in contentment at their feet. Although it was winter the breeze that wafted along the verandah was warm, and the sunshine outside had a bright intensity.

Roly wondered if he could live on a farm like this. He admired the Spaight family, who seemed so well adapted to the local conditions. But despite all the attractions it was so far from friends and family. The place was remote, far removed from the immediacy of Europe, and even the cities and bustle of South Africa.

"You have an enviable way of life." he said, rather haughtily. "A large comfortable house, dogs and horses, servants to attend to your needs. You grow most of your own food. You can hunt and shoot, play tennis and cricket and rugby football at the Club..."

"It is a good life," said Alan, nodding. "What do you think, sweetheart?"

Jess looked up. "I like it. There's not much to trouble us – except a few creepy-crawlies..."

"Oh, Ma!" chorused her daughters.

"Well, there are snakes and scorpions. There's always the risk of fever, which is why we try to make sure we're not stung by mosquitoes. You must be careful, Roly."

The conversation turned to events in Europe. "It seems," said Roly, "that everyone is waiting to see what the British Government will decide."

"They must support the French, surely," said Kirsty. "Otherwise, what's the point of having an *Entente Cordiale*?"

"Well," said Alan, "as you know, a lot of people think we should not become embroiled."

At that moment a government messenger arrived on a bicycle, nervous of the dogs, who barked and sniffed him until Alan called them off. The man wore a khaki uniform and a fez cap with a scarlet tassel, and his dark skin was beaded with sweat. He handed over a letter which bore the official seal of the Chief Secretary.

Alan opened the letter. "It's a request for me to attend a meeting at Government House tomorrow. I suppose you know about it Roly?"

"I heard they were planning to have one. I was told to stand by."

Kirsty said, "The dogs of war are baying."

—•—

7

Zomba, Nyasaland – August 1914

Alan drove to Government House in Zomba. The African guard at the gate knew him well, and they exchanged pleasantries in ChiNyanja while he signed the visitor's book. Another uniformed guard waved him up the driveway, where he parked next to other cars, near the porch. Entering the front hall he met the senior officials who made up Legco, the country's legislative council: the Chief Secretary, the Attorney-General, the Financial Secretary, and the heads of the larger government departments. Roly Benting-Smith stood at the Governor's side, resplendent in his regimental uniform.

The men all moved into the meeting room and sat down around a large polished table. Place names indicated where they should sit; each man had a notepad and pencil, and a tumbler of water. His Excellency, Mr George Smith, Governor of Nyasaland, came in to sit at the head of the table, a square-faced, middle-aged man with greying hair. He had a commanding presence.

Flanking the Governor were the most senior civil servant, Chief Secretary Hector Duff, and Roly, who was taking the minutes. At the far end of the table were Alan Spaight and Andrew Livingston Bruce, the non-official members of the Council, appointed by the Governor. Beside them sat a uniformed officer, now introduced.

"I've invited Captain Barton to our meeting," said the Governor, "as the senior KAR officer in the country. I'm sure he is well known to you."

Everyone at the table looked towards the young army officer, sandy-haired and moustached, who looked bashful and serious. His commanding officer was on leave in England, and he was nervous about the responsibility being heaped on his shoulders.

"I have also invited Captain Benting-Smith, seconded to us from the Devonshires. He arrived a few days ago to be my ADC. Welcome to our council, Roly."

Roly smiled languidly as he nodded and looked around the table; he felt distinctly uncomfortable, disadvantaged by his lack of knowledge of the country. The serious expressions on the faces of the Council members did nothing to reassure him. It was as if he was being scrutinised by an array of colonels and generals, all strangers.

"Gentlemen," the Governor continued, glancing at a sheet of paper, "it seems we are at war."

Smith looked around the table and wondered how they would cope. Nyasaland was about the least important possession in the British panoply, so did not attract the cream of colonial civil servants. Nevertheless, knowing them all, he expected they would do a workmanlike job.

"Yesterday, German forces entered Belgium, and His Majesty's Government issued an ultimatum to Berlin, which expired at 2300 hours GMT. This meant a declaration of war. I have called you here to make plans for action. I've been requested by Whitehall to supervise the conduct of the war in this country. As you know, Commander Rhoades is the senior naval officer, but he's at Fort Johnston, and I've instructed him to remain there to await orders. Captain Barton represents the army – the KAR, of which we have only two companies available." The Governor sighed heavily, as if to suggest that he was much displeased about this paucity of soldiers.

"The Nyasaland Volunteer Reserve is called up for active duty, and all NVR commissions are hereby gazetted. Major Spaight, you are now the *de jure* commander of the NVR. As a former British Army officer, and with more military experience in this country than any of us here, I will be relying on you to help me. I want you to be my Military Attaché..." He gave a short laugh. "Your being a member of Legco is just an added advantage."

The Governor then turned to Benting-Smith. "Roly, although you were intended to be my ADC, I believe I can manage without one for the time being. You can be more useful working with Captain Barton. As a regular army officer you are more valuable than most of the volunteers. We need you in an active role."

He then turned back to face the solemn faces around the table, and gestured to a large map on the wall behind him. It had been hurriedly prepared and hung by Roly, on the instructions of the Governor.

"Gentlemen, we now need to agree on the disposition of our meagre forces. My main concern – and you can disagree, if you wish – is that the Germans will invade from the north. Of course they may have other objectives – perhaps attacks to their north against British East Africa. I've discussed these matters before with Major Spaight. The Germans already control Lake Tanganyika with their gunboats, and we think they will at least try to capture the Stevenson Road and Lake Nyasa. That would give them control over the north-south transport system through the whole of central Africa."

The Governor stood up to show the locations on the map and to emphasise the gravity of his words. "If Captain Barton concurs I want the two KAR companies to station themselves up here – in Karonga – to prevent the Germans from gaining control of the Stevenson Road." He muttered, almost to himself, "God knows, it's a pitiful force..."

Barton coughed politely and interjected. "With respect, sir, the Huns could circumvent Karonga by using the lake."

The Governor nodded. "True, Barton, and that is why I intend to order Rhoades to take our gunboat, the *Guendolen,* to destroy their *Hermann von Wissmann*. It's smaller than our *Guen*, and the only vessel they have on the lake – of any consequence. It's vital that we do this, so that we have total control of Lake Nyasa. Do we know where the *Wissmann* is?"

Roly cleared his throat and tried to speak calmly. "Rhoades telegraphed today, sir. He saw the ship about a week ago at Sphinxhaven – he says that's on the eastern shore of the lake, about a hundred miles from the northern end – so roughly thirty to forty miles across from Nkhata Bay." He stood up and went over to the map, pointing diffidently at the spot.

"How long would it take Rhoades to get there?" asked the Chief Secretary.

The Governor turned to Alan. "What do you think, Alan? The *Guen* can do about five knots with a full load, in a hurry? So about forty hours?"

Alan nodded. "Yes sir, but there's a problem. The only weapon on the *Guen* is a three-pounder Hotchkiss, and I've heard Rhoades say the shells in the PWD store at Fort Johnston are ancient. A lot of them may be duds."

Barton coughed politely and looked around the table. "There's another problem; we don't have a gunnery officer. I've had some training, but..."

The Governor groaned. "This is becoming a pantomime! You're telling me we have a gunboat with only one gun – and no one knows how to fire the thing! Damn it, what's the point of having a gunboat if we don't know how to fire the bloody gun?"

Barton tried to speak soothingly. "I agree, sir. But no one thought the ship would ever be used as a gunboat again – when anti-slaving operations were over. Actually, Rhoades can fire the gun, at a pinch, but his job is to command the ship, and steer her. I know a young RNVR man in Cholo. I'm trying to find him, to see if he knows the Hotchkiss."

"What's his name?" asked Smith, a trifle testily.

"Gavin Henderson," replied Barton. "I think Mr Spaight – Major Spaight – knows him."

"Alan?" The Governor was plainly irritated that his strategic war meeting had descended into discussion about finding a young man who might know how to fire a gun.

"He works on the Williamson's tea estate in the Cholo area – plays rugby for Cholo," said Alan. "We could contact him by telegraphing the DC there."

"Let's do it," growled the Governor, nodding to the Chief Secretary, who left the room.

Alan said, "Going back to the gunboats, sir, I do agree that control of the lake is crucial. But do we have to destroy the German ship? Couldn't we capture her and use her ourselves?"

"What do you think, Barton?" The Governor looked at the Captain, his eyebrows raised.

"I agree with Major Spaight. In theory we should do that." Barton sighed heavily. "In practice it might not be so easy. We could send some KAR men on the *Guen*."

"We have to try. Go on, Alan."

Alan continued. "I expect reinforcements will be sent from Rhodesia, but they also have to contend with the threat from German South West Africa. Whitehall will have to weigh up the competing threats and decide where to send their forces. If the Rhodesian troops do come here we need to provide transport and accommodation."

The Governor nodded. "Also, you should know that the South African Government has offered Britain all the help it can provide. I've asked the Chief Secretary to set up a task force to prepare for the arrival of support troops." He turned to Roly. "Captain, I want you to go north with Barton and the KAR contingent. That way you can support the company commanders, and you can send me bulletins."

Roly gulped. "If you say so, sir."

The Governor then turned to Alan. "I want you to go to Fort Johnston to supervise the embarkation of the *Guendolen.* You must also mobilise the other lake steamers and organise the movement of out troops north. Mobilise the NVR, and you and Barton can decide on their disposition. I recommend you use most of them at Karonga." He wiped his forehead with a handkerchief. "Do you expect that there'll be any objections from your men? Most of them are planters, aren't they?"

"It's about the best time of year for them to go away, sir – not that any time is a good time. The problem is they won't know how long they'll be away. If this war drags on until the rainy season it'll be very difficult for the farmers – not only planting their crops, but leaving their families alone and unprotected."

—•—

As soon as he returned to the farm Alan explained to his family what the Governor had said about the need to gain control of the lake, and about the search for Gavin Henderson. They were gathered on the verandah, waiting until the servants had brought drinks and *patsagolas* before talking. Drew was playing tennis in Zomba, but the two girls and Mac joined their parents.

"I've met Henderson at NVR functions," said Alan, "and I saw him play rugby for Cholo against Zomba – a very strong forward, built like a bullock. He came to Africa for adventure – a couple of years ago."

"We've met him, too," said Mandy, "just before we went to Rhodesia – at parties in Blantyre. Kirsty fancied him..."

Kirsty rolled her eyes. "You do talk rubbish. He's nice enough, but... Well, he's a long way away."

Alan said, "We sent a message to the DC in Cholo, asking Henderson to come to Zomba. I suggested that he could come to stay with us."

Jess produced a letter, with a flourish. "This came by messenger today – I was waiting for you to return, sweetheart. It's from Dr Sanderson. He wants Mandy and Kirsty to become full-time nurses at the Zomba hospital..."

"That's wonderful!" enthused Mandy, bouncing in her chair.

"Why did he ask you – and not us?" asked Kirsty. "We're adults, aren't we?"

"I suppose because I'm a friend. He possibly thought that your father and I would have to give permission."

"Where would we live?" asked Kirsty, now sounding more enthusiastic.

"There's a house in Zomba that you can use. The matron lives there, but there's plenty of room for you. It's too far for you to go into town from here every day." She paused, and her eyes welled with tears. "No sooner do you come home that you're off again."

"Well, we won't be far away." Mandy went over and hugged her.

"I'm not sure if we want to share a house with the matron," said Kirsty. "But we might be sent to the front."

—•—

Gavin Henderson rode into *Khundalila* late that afternoon, on a battered old motor-cycle. He was greeted by Alan, and shown into the house. The young man was of medium height, powerfully built – the muscles in his arms and thighs bulged – clean-shaven, with fair hair... He was weary after the long ride, but soon realised that he was being welcomed into a friendly family.

He was struck by the good looks of the two girls and remembered meeting them two years before. They shook his hand with confidence and offered him something to drink. He chose a lemon squash and was taken to the guest cottage where he bathed and changed into clean clothes. Rejoining the family he was seated in the living room and given a cold beer.

"How do you feel about being recruited for action?" asked Alan.

"Frankly, I'm honoured, sir, but I don't know much about what's happening."

"It's confidential." Alan told him about the planned expedition to destroy the *Wissmann,* and watched Gavin's expression as he listened eagerly, sitting upright on the edge of his seat.

"Do you think you'll be able to fire the Hotchkiss?"

"Oh yes, sir. It's really quite simple. My concern is about the ammunition being sub-standard."

Alan nodded. "We'll have to do some test firing on the lake."

"Tell us about yourself," said Jess.

Gavin smiled diffidently. "My family live near Lymington, in Hampshire. We have a forty-five foot ketch that we've sailed in home waters since I was a child. We've been to the Baltic several times, because we have friends there..."

"Germans?" asked Alan.

"Yes. We've known them for many years, through sailing." He sipped his beer. "I went to Cambridge and studied agriculture. While I was at the university I joined the RNVR. When I graduated I decided to go out to German East Africa – our friends in Kiel had cousins there. I went to Moshi – near Mount Kilimanjaro – four years ago, to work on their coffee estate. After a couple of years I thought I would come here to see this country. I found a job on a coffee and tea estate, with the Williamsons at Cholo."

"Do you want to farm yourself – to buy a farm?" asked Jess.

"Oh yes. But I don't have the capital. I've saved a little, but not nearly enough to buy an estate. My parents have offered to help me..."

"We used to grow coffee," said Mandy. "But we switched to tobacco when the coffee price collapsed."

Gavin nodded. "It doesn't seem like ideal coffee growing conditions round here. The Williamsons told me that the climate in the Zomba area is too dry – the rainy season too short."

"I agree with that," said Alan. "It's better suited to tobacco."

"I seem to remember that it's against your religious principles to grow tobacco," said Kirsty.

Gavin blushed. "Did I tell you that two years ago?"

"As I remember."

The young man twisted his large strong hands. "You see, I think tobacco is a narcotic – and dangerous, with bad effects on health."

Kirsty continued. "So tea and coffee are stimulants, but not narcotics?"

"Precisely."

"So what do you think about us growing tobacco?"

Gavin looked stricken, and Jess came to his rescue. "I think that's unfair, Kirsty. This young man is a guest in our house, and you're subjecting him to a sort of... an inquisition."

Kirsty smiled, but did not look apologetic. "I'm sorry. Let me change the topic. So do you speak German fluently?"

Gavin smiled shyly, pleased that the younger sister had relented. He remembered that she was the more serious of the two girls. At dances she had preferred to sit and talk, while her sister scarcely left the floor.

"I spoke it quite well before I went to Moshi. Living with the German family there improved my fluency..."

"So you could be a spy?" pursued Kirsty.

He shook his head vigorously. "Definitely not. I wouldn't want to. I know I could be caught out. Just imagine a German who spoke English fluently coming here. You could easily trick him to find out whether he was really British."

"How?" both sisters chorused.

Gavin thought carefully. "By asking about his background – the schools he went to – that sort of thing..."

"But he might have lived in England."

"True – and that would make it more difficult."

"You've lived in Germany," said Kirsty.

"Yes, but not for long enough to know the things that a German would know."

Alan cut in. "I expect you could be very useful to us, Gavin. You could act as an interpreter, and you could question prisoners."

"I suppose so." The young man sighed. "It's so sad that our two countries are at war. I like the Germans. We have cultural differences, of course, but we have common roots."

—•—

Gavin left next day to meet with Captain Barton in Zomba, and moved into the KAR cantonment to stay. When the two girls were alone with their parents they explained their determination to go to Fort Johnston or Karonga if the Germans invaded. Everything they'd heard about the war plans convinced them they would be most needed on the northern border.

Alan shook his head mournfully. "This is a man's affair. I would be very unhappy if you went there and got involved in the fighting."

"There are women there already," said Kirsty, "like Mrs Webb, the Resident's wife. We wouldn't be fighting. We would be at the rear, tending the wounded."

"Well, that's as maybe," said Jess, "but it doesn't mean that you should go."

"We're trained nurses," argued Mandy. "When we were at nursing school they told us we might have to go where there was fighting. It's happened ever since nursing started – remember Florence Nightingale?"

Jess started to weep, and Alan put his arm round her. She said, between sobs, "I can accept the idea of you nursing in Zomba, but this is too much."

"We could at least go to Fort Johnston," replied Kirsty in a consoling tone. "The wounded will be brought there first. I know Dr Sanderson – the District Medical Officer there – I like him. I'm sure I could work for him."

That night Alan and Jess discussed the matter and decided that they could not prevent the girls from going north. "What bothers me most," said Alan, "is what the German *askaris* might do to them – if they were captured."

"It doesn't bear thinking," said Jess.

—•—

"It could complicate the logistics," said Captain Barton, when the proposal was raised at the next planning meeting. "All the transport and accommodation is geared to moving men. I respect the Spaight girls' desire to help, but..."

"You'll need nurses, Barton," said the Governor. "If the Huns invade and there's a battle there'll be casualties – isn't that inevitable? The doctors will need help."

Barton looked uncomfortable as he nodded.

"There are already two women in Karonga," said Roly. "Couldn't they do the nursing?"

"They're not trained nurses," said Alan. "They're just housewives. I dare say they would be helpful, but... I think their presence proves that we could have women nurses there too. Look, I don't want my daughters to be at the front, but it should not be a purely male preserve."

—•—

8

Fort Johnston, Nyasaland – August 1914

Next morning, a contingent of officers set off from Zomba in a KAR lorry, consisting of Major Alan Spaight, Capt Barton, Capt Benting-Smith, Sub-Lt Gavin Henderson, and Volunteer Mac Spaight, NVR. Also making the journey, by mule and on foot, were Lt Beaumont and twenty KAR *askaris*.

Mac was in the group because of his expertise with the lorry, and transport in general. He was in charge of NVR transport, and inordinately proud of the Thorneycroft 'J' four-ton lorry. It was one of only a dozen motor vehicles to enter the country and was far sturdier than the more common Model 'T' Fords, which had to be strengthened to cope with local conditions. Even so, this was the first journey of any consequence that the lorry had taken.

Mac's main problem was transporting the petrol. It came in four gallon tins, packed in pairs in wooden crates; the lorry used a gallon for every twenty miles. The journey to Fort Johnston was over eighty miles, so it would consume at least eight gallons for the round trip. He had been sending crates of petrol to Fort Johnston for the last two days, by mule and donkey. Now, he was content to take only one crate on the lorry, but was concerned about the fire risk and insisted that the passengers refrained from smoking on the vehicle.

They travelled north on the dusty road that skirted the eastern foot of Zomba Mountain, leading to Domasi, where they stopped at the mission. They spent half an hour exchanging greetings with missionary friends, drinking their fill of water and fruit juices, and smoking pipes and cigarettes. Thereafter, the road deteriorated as it wound through hills to the escarpment of the Shire Valley, where they stopped for Mac to check the oil and water.

Alan took Roly and Gavin to a rocky outcrop with a panoramic view over the Shire Valley. The air was hazy with wood smoke, and the Kirk Range was only just discernible in the far distance.

"Named after Livingstone's doctor," said Alan, pointing at the distant mountains. "There's the Shire River. You won't see the water, because it's almost dry, but the greener vegetation along the banks shows the course. Our road leads to Liwonde, where there's a crossing. To our right – upstream – the river comes from Lake Palombe, and further, from Lake Nyasa."

"Sadly for us there's not enough water in the river now for the steamers to operate, so it's Shanks' pony – or wheeled transport, like the Thorneycroft. You see, from here on we can't use oxen and horses for transport because the valley is infested with tsetse flies – they transmit *trypanosomiasis* – we call it 'tryps' – sleeping sickness. Donkeys and mules seem to be somewhat resistant, either to the flies or the parasite – perhaps both."

"What about those who can't walk?" asked Roly. "Such as returning wounded?"

"In former days we Europeans used to travel in man-carried hammocks called *machilas*, which we can use for the wounded. So, if we don't have a motor vehicle we'll walk with a convoy of porters."

Gavin said, "I heard that two more Thorneycroft lorries are on their way here from England."

"That's true, but we have to make better roads for wheeled transport. And we need a system of supplying the petrol to fuel them."

"So what is sleeping sickness?" asked Roly.

"It's called *nagana* when it affects animals. It's a blood parasite, transmitted by tsetse flies – rather like malaria is carried by mosquitoes – seems to affect domestic animals like cattle and horses more than sheep and goats. I think it's because the flies go for softer, less hairy animal coats..."

"So humans would be the most enticing?"

"Yes. Be careful not to be bitten. The tsetse looks like a horse fly, but the bite is worse. Its wings are crossed on its back. I'll point one out to you."

—•—

They descended slowly into the broad flat valley, with savannah forest stretching as far as the eye could see on both sides of the track. The lorry ground along, with Mac frequently changing gear to negotiate dips and hollows. Some small stream beds had been filled with brushwood after the rains ended, to make their crossing easier. Dust rose in clouds around them, and they were soon coated with it.

At midday they reached the Shire River. Normally, it would have been over a hundred yards wide and flowing strongly. Now, it was little more than a stream, flowing below steep banks, among rocky pools. On the far side was a large village of several hundred grass huts, the home of Chief Liwonde.

There were no barges here, but some enterprising local men had roped together a half-dozen dugout canoes, with a crude platform of planks on top. Mac was able to drive the lorry down the bank and across a ramp and fasten it securely on the platform with chocks and ropes. The ferry men paddled the makeshift boat across the remnants of the river.

Alan explained to Roly and Gavin that the Shire River was the only outlet from Lake Nyasa. The volume of outflow had declined for several years, and was now only a fraction of what it had been.

"At first we thought the water was being blocked by sand bars where the river flows out of the lake – there are masses of reeds there. But that would cause the lake level to rise, and it hasn't – in fact the reverse. We now think the lake level, and the river outflow, are controlled by the balance of rainfall on the lake surface, and evaporation. We seem to have had a series of years when evaporation has been greater than rainfall. Hence the level of the lake has fallen, and the river has virtually ceased to flow."

Barton pointed at a pool downstream. "I say, look at that – a croc!"

Sure enough, the sinister outline of eyes and nostrils drifted on the bottle-green water, a menacing reminder of the dangers facing them if their contraption capsized.

On the far side Mac drove off the ramp and the lorry wheezed up the bank, and then onto to the track that wound for another twenty miles along the river's west bank to Lake Palombe.

When they reached this small lake, all they could see was a vast expanse of *Phragmites* reeds. After stopping in the shade of a baobab tree Alan explained. "The overflow from the big lake flows into this little one, and from here into the Shire River. This lake's about fifteen miles long and ten miles wide – very shallow – I think a maximum of only ten feet deep. Good *chambo* fishing they say!"

Roly asked, "What happens if there's no overflow – I mean from the big lake, like now?"

Barton chipped in. "They say that there were periods in the mid-1800s when Lake Palombe dried up, presumably because there was no overflow. There's not much water in it now."

They stopped again where the track was close to the shore and walked onto a tiny sand beach. A light breeze cooled them as it swept over the rippled lake surface. A flock of pelicans took flight, and in the far distance a couple of dugout canoes were being poled slowly towards them. Alan presumed they were fishermen.

"Are there crocodiles in here?" asked Roly in a nervous tone. "My father warned me not to go near any water."

"Quite right," replied Alan. "The rule is – where there's water there's a crocodile. The exceptions are on the mountains, like Zomba and Mlanje, and in large open water, such as Lake Nyasa."

"So might a crocodile emerge from this water and ...?"

Alan looked at the young officer, wondering if he was pretending to be nervous, or was genuinely cautious. "It's possible, Roly. Perhaps we ought to move away."

—•—

They continued their slow progress north for another ten miles, reaching Fort Johnston, at the southern end of Lake Nyasa, by mid-afternoon.

"The fort was built in 1891," explained Alan, "at the height of the slave wars. It was designed by Captain Maguire, who named it after the first Commissioner, Sir Harry Johnston."

The fort was about a mile south of the Lake, where a harbour had been created, surrounded by dry docks and warehouses. Dominating the harbour was the 350 ton steamer, the *Guendolen.*

"There she is lads," said Alan. "Named after Lady Gwendolen Cecil, daughter of the Marquess of Salisbury, and a pint for anyone who can tell us why the spelling of the name is different. I think it must have been a quirk in the Public Works Department documentation."

The ship had fore and aft masts, and a funnel amidships; it was painted white. Between the funnel and the foremast, on the top deck, was a broad awning to give shade, and there were awnings along the side decks as well.

"She looks more like a tripper ship than a gunboat," drawled Roly.

"There's the Hotchkiss!" announced Gavin. "I wonder how they've fastened it down. Kicks like the devil."

Mac parked the lorry at the docks, and started to check the engine. The others strolled over to the *Guen* and walked up the gangway to meet Commander Rhoades, who was supervising the stowing of ammunition for the Hotchkiss three-pounder. A stocky man with red hair and a pointed ginger beard, he greeted them enthusiastically, pumping their hands with a firm grip.

"Glad to have you aboard, Henderson," he said to Gavin, giving him a long appraising look. "God knows we need an officer who knows one end of ship from the other."

He pointed at the pile of shells on the deck. "I have no idea how many of these will work. There's more in the shed."

"Have you fired the gun yet?" asked Gavin.

"Not yet – waiting for you." He waved his visitors to the central awning. "Time for a drink, eh?"

They sat around a folding table under the main deck awning. The flat surface of the lake glared and shimmered in the late afternoon sun; a cooling breeze ruffled the awnings. The scene was so peaceful that thoughts of war and fighting were incongruous.

"What do you know about the German ship?" Alan asked Rhoades, while accepting a cold bottle of beer.

"I know her well, Spaight. Been aboard her several times." He released a short burst of laughter. "You see, Captain Berndt – her commander – and I are old friends. When we're at port together we down a dram or two."

"And where is the ship now?"

"That I don't know. Last time I spoke to Berndt – a couple of months ago – he said she was due for some repairs. They have a slipway at Sphinxhaven – a crude affair. It's near the northern end of the lake. Of course, she might be anywhere now."

"How can we find out where she is?"

Rhoades swigged some more beer and wiped his moustache, then belched. "The local fishermen know. Once we get within about fifty miles of her, we'll get good information from them."

"Won't they warn the Huns about us?" asked Barton.

"Not if we don't dawdle in our approach."

Roly coughed as he prepared to enter the discussion. "I know nothing about naval matters, Commander, so please bear with my questions. If you were to confront the *Hermann von Wissmann* in open water, how would you fare?"

Rhoades opened his mouth to reply, and then hesitated. Amused at the army officer's upper class accent, he was about to say something facetious, but decided against it. He stroked his red beard while he chose his words. "Difficult to say, Captain. The *Wissmann* is smaller and slower, but she's more manoeuvrable. Our gun is larger, but it's slower to fire – and we have dubious ammunition. Shooting a gun from a ship is a hit and miss affair – unless there's a dead calm the movement of the ship upsets the best aim. Imagine firing artillery while there's an earthquake going on." He chortled and opened another bottle of beer.

After a short silence, Gavin asked: "How do you propose to neutralize the *Wissmann,* sir?"

Again Rhoades hesitated before replying, watching the others with small rheumy eyes. "We must take her by surprise – if possible while she's lying in harbour. That means we have to move quickly, and hope she's still on the slipway at Sphinxhaven. We need to take on wood fuel and food supplies at Kota Kota – that's ten hours steaming from here – and again at Nkhata Bay – another, say, eight hours. The southern boundary of German East Africa begins roughly opposite Nkhata Bay, and we then ought to find the *Wissmann.*"

"The Governor says you must have the support of some soldiers," said Alan.

"Why so?"

"Well, if you find the *Wissmann* in port, she could be protected by local German land forces – they might have moved some troops there. We're suggesting a dozen KAR *askaris*, under the command of Lt Beaumont."

"Yes, I see." Rhoades gazed out to the north, and Alan wondered if he resented these orders. "Very well. Now, we have a lot to do before we go into action. We must test the ammunition, and we need to put some armour around the vulnerable parts of the ship."

—•—

The officers stood in a semi-circle beside the Hotchkiss gun – Alan, Rhoades, Roly, and Barton. They were joined by Beaumont, the young KAR officer who was to be in charge of the *askaris* on the *Guen*. Looking over the side they could see Gavin supervising two Africans who were about to carry boxes of shells from the quayside. One of them hefted a box onto his shoulder; the other had difficulty lifting his. Without hesitation, Gavin picked up a box in each hand, using the rope handles, and started up the gang-plank.

"Christ, that man's strong," muttered Beaumont.

"The boxes weight seventy pounds each," muttered Rhoades.

Gavin and the African sailor arrived, sweating profusely, and placed the ammunition boxes on the deck, aft of the gun, which was mounted on a stout pedestal. The six feet long barrel was slender and pointed over the prow.

"It weighs about a three-quarter ton," said Rhoades. "Slows us down somewhat."

The gun could be manually swivelled round, as Gavin demonstrated, in a 360 degree arc, and the elevation could also be wound up or down. Each shell weighed about five pounds and carried a high explosive charge.

"What's her range?" asked Barton.

"I've been reading the manual," answered Gavin, patting a worn buff booklet. "About seven thousand yards maximum, but effectively two thousand – say a mile."

"You'd have as much chance of hitting a ship at that distance as I would leaving a bottle of whisky unfinished," growled Rhoades.

—•—

Gavin selected a small rocky islet about three hundred yards away. Its huge boulders were covered with white streaks of cormorant excrement; he was assured that it had no human habitation. Moored to the jetty fore and aft, the *Guen* rocked gently in the wavelets coming into the harbour. These motions seemed to magnify as Gavin sighted the Hotchkiss, the foresight gyrating around the pile of rocks. He pulled the firing lever and nothing happened.

Looking over his shoulder he noticed Commander Rhoades' anxious expression. Cautiously opening the firing chamber he extracted the shell. There was a clear indentation at the end of the cartridge, where the firing pin had struck, yet the propellant had not exploded. He could see no evidence of corrosion, yet the chemicals must have deteriorated with time. Picking up another round, he examined it, slid it into the chamber and gently clanged the breech closed.

This time the report came almost as an anti-climax. The Hotchkiss rocked back; a puff of gunpowder smoke drifted off the ship, and Gavin watched for the shell to land. He guessed that it would fly over the islet, and soon saw the tell-tale splash a couple of hundred yards beyond.

"Let's compare the cases," suggested Alan.

Gavin held them side by side, the dud and the second that fired; there was no discernible difference. The indentations from the firing pin were identical, and neither cartridge showed any sign of corrosion.

"Try two or three more," growled Rhoades.

Gavin fired three more times. Two shells worked, the first and last, one short and one over the islet; the second shell was a dud.

Rhoades clawed at his beard. "Forty per cent duds! We may have to board the *Wissmann* with *askaris* after all." He turned away in disgust.

—•—

Next morning Gavin was greeted on deck by Rhoades who had an African sailor beside him, a man who looked to be in his late forties or early fifties, his short curly hair grizzled. His wide mouth, when it smiled showed large strong teeth. He wore the uniform of the *Guen*, white duck shorts and short-sleeved shirt, with a small white cap.

"This man is our bosun," said Rhoades. "His name is Kawa – a good man, as you'll discover. He has some tales to tell, and I hope you and Beaumont will find time to listen to them."

Gavin shook hands with Kawa, using the traditional palm-thumb-palm grip, and could feel the African's strength. "I would like to hear your stories," he said.

"Whenever you wish, *bwana*." Kawa grinned, his voice deep and full of good humour.

Near midday Gavin was talking to Beaumont when he saw Kawa nearby and called to him. He introduced the boatswain to the KAR lieutenant and they shook hands.

"Tell us about the slavery and the *Domira*", said Gavin, as they moved into the shade of an awning.

Kawa started speaking in slow clear English. "I was captured by slavers when I was a young man. My parents were fishers on the lake – they were captured too. We were taken across this lake in a *dhow* – then marched to the coast. My companion was Goodwill – he now works for Mr Spaight in Zomba."

Gavin nodded. "I've met him."

"When we reached the ocean we were put on a *dhow*, in chains, but we released ourselves – secretly. The *dhow* hit a reef and sank – we swam to the shore. Then we walked back to the lake..."

"Heavens! How long did that take you?" asked Beaumont.

"About four months, *bwana*. It was dangerous – the local people could have sold us back to the slavers." He sighed. "When we reached the lake we turned south and were taken across Lake Chilwa by a fisherman. We walked to Zomba and were sheltered in the mission at

Domasi. Mr Robertson found this job for me and I have worked for Mandala since then."

"On the *Domira*?" asked Gavin.

"Yes, *bwana*. Later, we took the Indian *askaris* to fight Chief Makanjira – his village was on the far side of the lake." Kawa's eyes widened as he told his story, and his words tumbled out. "We went up a creek – then Captain Maguire took some Indian *askaris* and fought with Makanjira's men, but they were driven back. The Captain was killed – and several *askaris*. Then my skipper, Mr Keiller, talked with Makanjira's men. A group of us went to the village, but we were betrayed and all were killed except me – I escaped, even though I was wounded. I came back to the *Domira.* It was stuck on a sandbank, but we freed her and got away."

"What an experience," said Gavin. "You were lucky."

"Yes, *bwana*." Kawa pulled down the collar of his shirt and showed them the scars of his wounds. "Will it be different fighting the Germans?"

"Probably." Gavin pondered. "They have better weapons and more discipline. They have many *askaris* who are well trained – like ours."

"Perhaps I should stay on the ship." Kawa burst out laughing, joined by the two Europeans.

—•—

9

Sphinxhaven, Lake Nyasa – August 1914

The *Guen* got under way by late evening, as the sun dropped behind Dedza Mountain to the west. Stars emerged in the darkening sky, and a breeze from the lake, now tinged with the *Guen*'s smoke, was cool enough to make Gavin fasten his jacket buttons. Looking along the ship he could see a row of anxious faces; the *askaris,* sitting on the deck, dubious about their destination, and the means of getting there. The vast expanse of the lake must seem intimidating, he thought, with its legends of monsters, and, more recently, about slavers.

Beaumont stood despondently by the rail, watching the *Guen*'s prow slicing the lake surface. Yesterday he was comfortable in the fort near the shore, and now he was a supernumerary on a little steamer with one gun, looking for an even smaller steamer on seventeen thousand square miles of lonely water.

The *askaris* were good men, generally cheerful and willing, but Beaumont did not know enough of their language to communicate with them, and had to give orders through a mission-educated African sergeant-major. He had for companions Rhoades and Henderson, who spent most of their time poring over charts and discussing gunnery tactics, and Dr Sanderson, plucked from the hospital at Fort Johnston to be the expedition's medical officer. The fifth European was Jock Manning, a fitter from the Public Works Department, busy trying to weld armour around the gun emplacement.

Gavin spotted Beaumont and joined him. "Are you glad to be going into action?" he asked.

The lieutenant chose not to answer, but asked, "When do you think we'll get back to Zomba?"

Gavin laughed. "I wish I knew. I'd be surprised if we get back before the end of August. We're in God's hands." He noticed Beaumont's mouth drop open. "Surely you didn't think we'd be away for a few days?"

The KAR officer shrugged despondently. "It was a good life in Zomba. Too good to last. My fault for choosing to be a soldier. I should have been a pen-pusher…"

"I assure you all the pen-pushers are going to be in uniform."

"I suppose so." Beaumont smiled ruefully. "I say, Henderson, what's the difference between a ship and a boat? I called this – the *Guen* – a boat, and Rhoades gave me a severe look."

Gavin laughed. "It's all a matter of size, old chap. The *Guen* is large enough to be classed as a ship. You see, she has a boat on board – a dinghy. But the dinghy couldn't be called a ship. See what I mean?"

—•—

Alan spent the next two days in Fort Johnston organising transport for men and supplies to be sent by ship up the lake to Karonga. The British had at their disposal seven steamers, ranging in size from the *Guendolen* (340 tons) to the *Charles Janson* (25 tons). The three largest were built in the late 1890s and brought to the lake to help suppress the slave trade. In fact, not one of them had fired a shot in anger, since the slavers were defeated in 1895.

He spent much of the time drafting and dispatching orders by telegraph, on behalf of the Governor, requisitioning the ships for wartime use. The *Pioneer* arrived at Fort Johnston the day after the *Guen* left to go north. Alan helped to ensure that she was re-fuelled and took on supplies much faster than was customary. Captain Barton and a platoon of his KAR men boarded and set off up the lake for Karonga.

Meanwhile, Alan sent telegraphs to the African Lakes Corporation and the Universities Mission, ordering them to send their ships to Fort Johnston to collect more troops. He also sent messages to the District Commissioners at Kota Kota and Nkhata Bay to arrange for fuel and food supplies to await them at the ports. The wood fuel used by the steamers had to be cut from forests and hand-carried to the ports.

On the evening of August 10, Alan received a telegram from the Governor in Zomba asking him to return as quickly as possible. There was no reason given, nor any indication of what was in store for him. The journey was uneventful, in the Thorneycroft lorry, driven by Mac, and he reported at Government House by three in the afternoon.

Inevitably, a meeting was in progress, and he was ushered into it by the Governor's new ADC, who struck him as being so young that he ought still to be in school. A large map was spread over the table and the men around it were discussing the movements of the ships and troops.

Alan knew them all: Captain Stevens, his deputy in charge of the NVR, Hector Duff, the Chief Secretary, and other senior civil servants, including the Director of the PWD. The General Manager of Mandala was present, as was the General Manager of Nyasaland Railways. The Governor invited Alan to address the meeting.

"As you know, sir, the *Guen* is heading for Sphinxhaven to attack the *Wissmann*. All the other ships are being used to transport men and supplies to Karonga, to stem any land invasion attempts. If the *Guen* is successful, we will have free use of the lake to defend this territory."

Thereafter, the meeting discussed details about road and rail improvements that should be made for future troop movements.

At about five o'clock a telegram arrived with news that the *Guen* had reached Nkhata Bay. Rhoades had heard from fishermen that the *Hermann von Wissmann* was still on the slipway at Sphinxhaven. He planned to cross the lake next day with the aim of attacking the German ship the following dawn.

"Thank God we have a man like Rhoades to do this!" said the Governor. "Let's wish them well."

—•—

Rhoades spent much of the night of August 12th at the helm of the *Guen*, allowing Gavin to relieve him for short naps. The lake was calm and the night clear, a great vault of stars arching above, and reflecting as glittering sparks on the lightly-ruffled dark water. Gavin knew the lake was immensely deep, and it was easy to imagine monsters lurking beneath.

It was less that forty miles from Nkhata Bay to Sphinxhaven, and Rhoades steamed at half speed. The first dawn light was showing behind the hills ahead of them as the *Guen* made landfall south of the German harbour. When the ship was about a hundred yards from the shore the Commander turned to port and they drifted towards the rocky promontory that gave the harbour its name; with a little imagination one could see the shape of the Sphinx in the boulders.

Gavin busied himself with the Hotchkiss, making sure that a supply of shells was ready to hand. His pulse raced, and he was sweating despite the cool morning breeze. He could not forget the anticlimactic silence whenever he tried to fire the gun and encountered a dud round.

As soon as they passed the promontory the *Hermann von Wissmann* came clearly into view, her metal parts glinting in the dawn light. She was propped with wooden spars on a cement slipway – out of her element, awkward and vulnerable. Around the slipway clustered tin-roofed sheds and beyond them a village of grass huts belonging to fishermen.

Rhoades and Gavin had agreed that the best aspect for attack would be to rake the *Wissmann* fore and aft, rather than from the side.

This was because of the elevation problems with the Hotchkiss. The Commander steadied the *Guen* as best he could, pointing directly at the German ship at a range of about two hundred yards.

Gavin's first shot sailed high above the target, crashing with a shower of dust and foliage into the scrub beyond the village. Silence on the *Guen* as he re-loaded. The second shell was a dud, and he heaved it into the water in disgust. The third shot was high, the fourth and fifth were duds, the sixth was short and send a plume of water showering over the German ship. By this time they could hear shouts from the shore and saw Africans scurrying around the harbour buildings.

Gavin fired for at least five minutes, taking time to allow for the fore and aft rocking of the *Guen.* Finally, he was able to place a round near the *Wissmann;* it blew up one of the small ramshackle sheds up the slope, and led to more shouting. Two more dud shells followed. He wiped the sweat from his forehead and anxiously looked up at Rhoades.

The Commander wore a deep frown on his forehead, but merely nodded at Gavin, who muttered a prayer, asking God to make the shots tell, but not kill anyone. He bent back to the gun-sight. Carefully allowing for the movement he pressed the firing lever once more.

It was a direct hit. A couple of the wooden props fell away, and the *Wissmann* listed over to a 45 degree angle. A cheer rang out from the company of the *Guen*, and Rhoades clapped Gavin on the back.

At that moment they saw the stocky figure of a white man, dressed in baggy shorts, shirt tails hanging out, hurrying down past the crippled *Wissmann*, waving his arms and shouting. He made straight for a small dinghy, hitherto unnoticed, and started to row towards the *Guen*. It was Captain Berndt, Rhoades' erstwhile drinking companion.

He arrived, sweating and swearing, and was helped up onto the deck.

"*Gott verdomm!* What are you doing, Rhoades?"

Rhoades revealed that Britain was at war with Germany. It transpired that the German authorities had neglected to inform the commander of the *Wissmann.*

"So, I am your prisoner?" he groaned.

"I'm afraid so, Berndt." Rhoades put his arm around his friend's shoulders. "Come with me – we'll look after you well."

Meanwhile, Beaumont disembarked his platoon of *askaris* using *Guen's* longboat. Within a few minutes they were on the little beach and advancing up the slope to secure the harbour, although there was no sign of any opposition.

Having locked his German counterpart in a cabin, Rhoades took Gavin with him in the dinghy to examine the *Wissmann.* The shell explosion had created a hole about the size of a dinner plate just below the water line. They judged it would take a couple of days to repair the hole and drag the ship into the water. Furthermore, Berndt had said that there were some problems with the transmission mechanism between the boat's engine and her single screw.

"We can't stay here to make the repairs," said Rhoades. "We'll have to leave her here. That means we have to disable her."

He instructed Gavin to take the screw off the *Wissmann*, and to dismantle the steering gear, which would make it difficult to repair the ship without specialized parts. "We'll come to fetch her when we have more time."

By noon the *Wissmann* was disabled and the *askaris* were back aboard the *Guen.* Beaumont had spent the morning trying to get information about movements of German forces in the area. He'd had little success and was happy to be back, sitting under the awning with a cold beer, as the *Guen* headed to Nkhata Bay.

"So, Commander," he said, holding up the bottle to salute Rhoades. "To the victor of the first engagement of the war in Nyasaland."

Rhoades grinned. "To be pedantic, Beaumont – technically we're in German East Africa. By the way, I read that a gun crew in Australia fired the first Allied shots in the war, and the Royal Navy bombarded Dar-es-Salaam on August 8, so ours weren't even the first naval shots. And it wasn't a very glorious conflict, was it? At least there was no loss of life, and now we can use the lake without fear of attack – at least on the water."

—•—

10

Zomba, Nyasaland – August 1914

Roly invited Mandy Spaight to go up the mountain for a picnic, borrowing a Vauxhall car from Lt Beaumont, recently returned from the lake. He loaded it with food and drink, a ground-sheet and a blanket.

"Perhaps, you're overdoing it, old boy," suggested Beaumont, stroking his moustache. "Anyone would think you were planning to spend a month up there."

Roly shrugged. "I can always bring back the left-overs. Anyway, who knows what might happen. The road might become impassable, and we would be trapped up there."

"Wishful thinking. Her father would be up there in a jiffy."

Roly stowed some extra blankets in the boot, arranging them so that they prevented the tins and bottles from moving. "I've heard that a cold mist can come down on you without warning," he said.

"It's called a cloud. In effect you're up in the clouds." Beaumont kicked the rear tyre. "Anyway, I envy you. She's a smashing girl. I've danced with her a few times." He looked wistful. "Never had the courage to ask her out."

Roly found Mandy waiting at the Club, wearing a white shirt and linen jacket, and khaki culottes, with a wide-brimmed straw hat. She was excited at the prospect of driving up the mountain; it would be her first time in a car, although she had often been there on foot or horseback.

He drove the Vauxhall carefully up the road past Government House, and then to the entrance of the single track road up the mountain, built for engineers and labourers to construct the water supply and hydro-power system for Zomba. They waited a few minutes until it was ten o'clock, obeying the rule that up-going traffic started on the hour, and down traffic on the half hour, to prevent vehicles meeting head on.

Roly looked at his pocket watch and started forward with a surreptitious glance at his passenger. The sun was bright and the road dry. To their right they could see the town growing smaller as they gained height. Soon they could see only scattered rooftops. The road was cut out of the mountain side, the slope on the right so steep that it was intimidating; he concentrated hard to keep the car on the road.

Mandy was not in the least nervous, but she was still intrigued with this young officer, the first of his kind she had met. He was very attentive, which she liked, but sometimes he seemed rather arrogant. Tall, gangling, and uncoordinated, he still managed to move with purpose. Not handsome in the conventional sense – he had a slightly receding chin – his usual expression was good-humoured. She liked his confidence, as a capable driver, and had admired his ability as a rider.

After ten minutes they emerged onto the rim of the mountain's bowl and parked on a patch of cleared ground. The air was clear and cool, redolent of ferns and bracken. It seemed as if they'd been transported into a different world, alone, with only wild animals around them.

They walked to the edge of the escarpment to admire the view. Mlanje Mountain in the hazy distance, purple and brooding, rising starkly from the plain like a primeval wall. To the east, ahead of them, Lake Chilwa was a shining pewter disc, and beyond rose the low hills of Portuguese territory.

"There's the farm," exclaimed Mandy, pointing. "Do you see? There's the road that runs between our two farms, and there's the plantation of trees that we use for firewood for the tobacco barns. You can see the Likengala River – where the trees along the banks are darker green."

Standing close to her, to follow her directions, he caught a floral scent and vowed to himself that he would hold her in his arms that day. She had a reputation for being flirtatious, but there must be a serious side if she'd pursued a career in nursing. She was bold and courageous, as he'd seen when they rode together. His only concern was whether he could have a conversation with her, but perhaps that was not important – at least today.

Mandy turned and said, "Come over here."

He followed her and saw two flat gravestones, side by side, made with large stones cemented together. The inscriptions read:

Nora McPhail
Loving wife of John McPhail
Mother of Malcolm and Andrew
May 24, 1864-June 5, 1888

John McPhail
Loving husband of Nora and Jess,
father of Malcolm and Andrew
Feb 7, 1857-September 18, 1891

"Mac and Drew's parents?" he asked."

"They are Mac's parents, and Nora was Drew's mother, but his real father is Pa. Nora died of puerperal fever, after having Drew – so sad; she was only twenty-four; not much older than I am. Then John McPhail married Ma, and soon after he died of malaria – as so many did in those days."

"So...your father had an affair with Nora?"

She laughed. "Well done. You worked that out."

They walked back to the car and looked over the bowl of the plateau, a huge amphitheatre stretching for several miles to the further rim. They were the only humans in an area of tens of thousands of acres; it was too cold for Africans to live there. The upper slopes of the bowl were covered with open grassland, scattered with rocky outcrops. Lower down were patches of woodland and giant tree ferns along the streams that converged into dense forest in the bottom of the bowl.

"I think it's too steep to take the car further," he said. "If it rains this track would become very slippery. We should walk from here?"

She nodded agreement and helped him to open the boot, taking out the baskets of food; he felt embarrassed because there was so much.

"Goodness, you have brought lots!" She laughed. "We can't carry all this food. Let's select what will fit in two baskets. You can carry them, and I'll bring a groundsheet and a blanket."

They walked down the track for several hundred yards until they came to the stream. She knew that it flowed through the riverine forest to a cleft in the rim of the mountain where it tumbled over the edge. Government engineers had diverted some of the water to supply the town of Zomba.

Here the stream splashed through rocks, pausing now and then in small pools. The heath slopes reminded Roly of Scotland, where he had been taken trout fishing as a schoolboy.

"Is it safe to walk here?" he asked, imagining that there must be wild animals.

"Oh yes," said Mandy confidently. "We can walk upstream. I know there are some flat rocks – just right for a picnic."

A few yards upstream they found a rock the size of a billiard table, with the sparkling stream running past one end. When he spread the ground-sheet and blanket Roly felt the sun-warmth of its surface.

Mandy unpacked the baskets and spread out the food. "What a feast," she said, spreading a tablecloth.

"I hope there's something you like."

"Of course – lots."

There was bread, and a knife from the officers' mess, some ham and mustard, cheese, tomatoes, bottles of preserved olives and capers, salt and pepper, apples and guavas, a bottle of white wine, two glasses, a corkscrew, and white linen napkins.

While they ate Mandy told him how she and her sister decided to go to Salisbury to study nursing. "We could have gone to England, but it was so far away, and expensive. South Africa was an option, but in Salisbury we had Pa's cousin, Martin Russell, and his family."

In turn he told her how his family had strong connections with the British Army, so it was natural for him to go to Sandhurst and take a commission. "Apart from a stint in Canada, I haven't been overseas, until now. I was keen to come to Africa. You see, I missed the Boer War, but my father was in the First Boer War – he was at Majuba Hill..."

"When the British were defeated."

"Yes, they were. It was one of the reasons they started the Second Boer War, the big one. They wanted revenge."

"I'm surprised to hear you say that, as a British man."

He laughed. "I wouldn't have said it to that Boer chap – Van Zyl – on the boat."

She lay down on her back, looking up to the sky and the scattering of a few fluffs of cloud. A Battaleur eagle made elegant circles above. "Will you be in the army all your life?"

"I suppose so. I enjoy the life. I don't know what else I would do." He was still standing and looked down at her and a strong surge of physical attraction came over him.

Mandy was saying, "My father thought he would be in the army all his life. Then he had a quarrel with his colonel and had to resign his commission..."

"What happened?"

She turned her head to look at him. "You'd better ask him; I might give you a wrong version. Anyway, as you know, he became a farmer."

He lay down beside her, but not touching her. They faced each other, and he looked into her large grey eyes. When she smiled he felt himself dissolve. He put his arm over her and pulled her tight against him.

—•—

11

Zomba, Nyasaland – September 1914

Gavin moved into a mess for young officers in Fort Johnston, a house requisitioned for them because there was not enough room at the KAR mess. He was something of an anomaly in the gatherings of young men. They respected his physical strength and prowess at rugby, but were puzzled by his religious beliefs which led him to eschew tobacco and limit his intake of beer to one pint.

Later he paid a return visit to the estate at Cholo and said his farewells to the Williamsons, collecting a few articles of furniture, pots and pans for his new home.

Commander Rhoades gave him a variety of tasks, including commissioning and maintaining the small guns on the steamers, making an inventory of all ammunition, some of which was sent to Nkhata Bay, and training the boatswains in gunnery.

He was free for alternate weekends, returning to Zomba, where Roly Benting-Smith invited him to stay, sleeping on a folding camp bed in the spare bedroom. The two men had a common background in England, public schools and homes in the rural south.

Gavin sought out Kirsty at the hospital and waited while his message was delivered. He had bathed and wore a clean uniform of white shirt and trousers; his face and arms were sunburnt. The shirt epaulettes carried his sub-lieutenant's stripe. A combination of the heat and nervousness made him perspire, and he could feel the droplets of sweat dribbling down his back.

He now felt strongly about Kirsty, having recognised her qualities of steadfastness and intelligence. He much preferred her type to her glamorous but flighty sister. He lacked confidence when it came to meeting and talking to women, and it had taken much self-urging to bring himself to this place.

She appeared suddenly, wearing her nurse's uniform, and a small white cap perched on her dark hair. A curl of black hair was pasted on her forehead, which shone with perspiration. There were shadows around her eyes from lack of sleep, but she was smiling and seemed pleased to see him.

"I haven't much time, Gavin," she said. "We're very short-staffed."

"Will you come out with me?" he asked.

She looked at him carefully. "I have tomorrow afternoon off. What do you suggest?"

"Whatever you would like to do?"

She gave a short laugh. "Sleep." Then she saw his crestfallen expression. "We could go riding at the farm. You could stay in the guest cottage. My parents would like to see you."

—•—

Next day, at the appointed time, he rode up to the hospital on his motor-cycle and found her waiting, wearing a white man's-style shirt and the khaki jodhpurs that the Spaight girls habitually wore for riding on the farm. She was used to riding on the pillion with her brothers, but it was the first time Gavin had taken a girl on the bike. He liked having her arms tighten around him, and the feel of her breasts on his back.

At the farm they were greeted by the dogs, milling around them, sniffing and waving their tails. Alan and Jess came down the verandah steps, and Jess said, "Well, Gavin, you're the hero of the hour!"

Gavin blushed. "It's Commander Rhoades who deserves all the credit, Mrs Spaight. It was he who took us to the quarry and into position – all I had to do was fire the gun."

"You're too modest," said Alan. "It was great success. Everyone is talking about it. They say it was the first naval victory of the war."

Kirsty said, "Sorry, Gavin, I forgot to congratulate you yesterday."

He shook his head, embarrassed. "Hardly a naval victory. After all, the *Wissmann* was on the shore."

"Well," replied Alan, "it's had a great impact on the strategy of the war here – by giving us control of the lake. I expect you'll be going up to Karonga. You'll see Mandy there. We'll give you a few things to take to her." He shook his head. "I wish she wasn't so near the likely action."

"Have they heard anything about a possible invasion?" asked Gavin.

"Nothing, but it could happen at any moment – despite the success you fellows had at Sphinxhaven."

—•—

They rode along the farm track towards the *dambo*, Gavin on Mandy's horse. He had learned to ride with the German family in Moshi, but felt uneasy on a strange horse, and reluctant to reveal it to the girl.

Cicadas were starting their early evening chorus in the trees that fringed the grassland. The small herd of beef cattle and the dairy cows grazed under the supervision of a small herd boy with a long stick, who watched them apprehensively as they rode by. Kirsty looked to see that he was keeping the cattle away from the centre of the *dambo*, where it was too wet for grazing.

"You've lived here all your life, haven't you?" asked Gavin.

"Yes, apart from the two years at nursing school. We went to England four years ago, to see our grandparents, and all the aunts and uncles and cousins. We were away for three months. I don't think I would like to live in England."

"Why not?"

"I suppose because I felt a stranger there. What about you?"

"England is my home country, but I like Africa. I would be happy to settle here."

Kirsty sighed. "You know, Gavin, this war has really upset our lives. My sister finds it exciting, but..."

"We wouldn't be here now – together – if it wasn't for the war."

"Perhaps not, but you used to come over to Zomba for parties, and we sometimes went to dances at the Cholo Club – before we went to Rhodesia. I remember talking to you about sailing. You said you wanted to build a boat."

He laughed. "I built a 'Water Wag'."

"What's that?"

"A thirteen foot sailing dinghy."

She dismounted. "Let's walk down to the river."

Gavin followed suit and they led the horses to the bank that steeply fringed the Likengala River, where they tethered them in the shade of a tree and walked down the bank. Here the 'river' was only a stream, and the flow was decreasing as the dry season progressed. The banks were about fifteen feet high, densely shaded with tall trees, contrasting with the bright sunshine above. They sat on a thick dead tree-trunk, washed down in a flood and now straddling the water.

Kirsty took off her hat and shook out her hair.

"It's strangely peaceful here, isn't it? Quite different, obviously, to the plateau, but I like coming here."

He tried to summon up the courage to tell her that he was falling in love with her. She was observing him surreptitiously, suspecting he was too shy to speak.

"What will you do when the war is over?" she asked.

Relieved to be able to talk on another subject, he replied. "I would like to buy a farm here – in Nyasaland. But I don't have enough money. I think my father would lend me some. He thinks I'm safer here, though my parents are concerned about me settling so far away, because they would hardly ever see me."

"So you have no plans to return to England?"

"Only to see my family."

Kirsty sighed. "As I said, I don't think I could live in England. I would find the life too confining, too restricted by rules and regulations. It's so damp. I know all that rain makes it green and beautiful..."

She paused and held up her hand to indicate that they should be quiet. Then she pointed, and after a moment he saw something move on the far side of the stream. She moved slowly to be nearer to him, and whispered in his ear. "It's a water monitor."

Then he made out the shape of the great lizard, working its way cautiously along the bank. It was about five feet long, grassy green in colour, its head alert, beady black eyes searching, tongue flickering – a miniature dragon. They watched its ponderous progression down the stream bed.

"We've never seen a nest or babies," said Kirsty. "Drew has looked for them all his life."

"It's the first one I've seen. It must be difficult for them to survive the African hunters."

"Oh yes. They would kill it – though Pa won't allow them to kill on this farm. It's a small nature reserve. Probably the reason that monitor is here."

After a while, he said, "So you would be happy to live your life here?"

She nodded. "I suppose so. I'll be a nurse..."

"You'll marry."

"Perhaps, and have children."

Gavin looked at her with solemn intensity. "Kirsty, do you think we should be completely honest with each other?"

She drew back in mock surprise. "I suppose so, Gavin, why do you ask?"

He blushed and searched for words. "Well, I feel very strongly about you. I find you very exciting. I would like to be more demonstrative, but I don't want you to think that my intentions are impure."

She stifled a smile. "Do you mean you want to have a platonic friendship?"

"Oh no! I mean I..."

She waited, trying not to smile.

"You see, Kirsty, all the men are saying that they want to have... love affairs, before they go to the front and get killed. They say it would be awful to die without having had an..."

"Without having had sex?"

His face reddened. "Yes. But I think it's a sacred part of marriage, and... well, one ought to marry first."

She smiled as she looked up and saw his anxious expression. "So are you proposing to me, Gavin – so that we can get married and then have sex?"

"Not at all." He was mildly indignant.

"We hardly know each other. We haven't even kissed."

"I can put that right, now."

"Is kissing permissible?" She laughed and let him take her in his arms.

—•—

A week later, only Alan and Jess were at supper with Kirsty and Gavin. Mandy was with Roly at a party in the KAR cantonment, and Mac had ridden his motor-cycle to Blantyre. The servants had left, and Jess served the meal herself, while they talked about the war in Europe.

Later they went out to the verandah for coffee, so that Alan could smoke his pipe.

Gavin asked Alan, "What do you think the Germans will do now, sir?"

"I think they'll probe our defences to see how we react. I don't think they'll attack in strength. They are too few and too widely scattered – it's such a vast area, between their northern border and Lake Nyasa, and between the ocean and Lake Tanganyika. But we have the same problems – it will be just as difficult for us to attack them."

Alan paused to light his pipe. "We were discussing the other day the possibility of carving up German East Africa, to divide their forces into small units that wouldn't be able to communicate with each other." He sighed. "We concluded that it wouldn't be practical, because we don't have enough men, and the area is too huge."

"Perhaps we should talk about something else?" suggested Jess, and the men laughed.

Gavin coughed. "Mr and Mrs Spaight, I have a question to ask – a favour. I would like to marry Kirsty."

There followed a moment's silence. Alan knew that his daughter had grown fond of Gavin, might even love him. But the concept of them marrying had eluded him.

He said, "What do you say, Kirsty?"

"We would like to be engaged, Pa. I don't know if this is the right time to get married..."

Jess had a shrewder idea of the relationship between the two young people. She had spoken to Kirsty at some length about the risks of a love affair, especially during a war. Her daughter assured her that Gavin had strong religious principles and would not indulge in a pre-marital affair.

Now, Jess said, "Well, I have to agree with you." She looked at them with sympathy. "You see, at any time you could be sent to different fronts, live miles apart, have difficulty writing to each other, tempted by other people..."

"Ma!" interrupted Kirsty with disapproval.

"You may protest, but..."

"You could be unofficially engaged," said Alan. "Have an understanding – that you will marry when things settle down, when the war ends, which hopefully won't be too long."

"So, do I have your permission?" Gavin tried not to sound plaintive.

Alan looked at Jess, who nodded. He said, "You have our blessing, Gavin. I think this deserves a toast. We have some Drambuie, A small tot for you girls?"

—•—

12

Karonga, Nyasaland – August/September 1914

Karonga was the most northerly British settlement on Lake Nyasa, about twenty miles from the Songwe River, the border between Nyasaland and German East Africa. Once a focal point in the fighting against the slavers at the end of the previous century, it was now a sleepy administrative centre. Two rudimentary roads linked the settlement to the border, one alongside the lake, the other a couple of miles inland. The Stevenson Road linked Lake Nyasa to Lake Tanganyika. Both great lakes and the road between them were now of immense strategic importance.

A handful of British government officials lived in Karonga, three with wives. The District Commissioner sent a message to local planters, asking them to reinforce the numbers at Karonga; several of them rode there on bicycles. Meanwhile, the expeditionary force was steaming up the lake from Fort Johnston. The fleet, carrying five hundred men, consisted of *Guendolen, Chauncy Maples, Pioneer, Adventure* and *Queen Victoria,*

—•—

Roly stood beside Mandy at the rail of the *Guen,* awed by the immensity of the lake, and also relishing the company of the young girl. During the planning of the voyage he hoped that she would be a fellow passenger. She told him about the objections raised by her father, and her counter-arguments, that eventually prevailed.

The ship followed the Nyasaland shore, most of which was mountainous. After leaving the Kirk Range behind they passed the Nyika Plateau, mysterious, uninhabited, and unexplored by white men.

Mandy had proved elusive until this moment. For the first two days she felt sea-sick and stayed in her cabin, where the port-hole allowed just enough of the lake breeze to relieve the heat during the day. On the third day she emerged but kept to herself until she was sure the nausea had gone.

"Have you been on the lake before?" he asked her.

"Oh yes. Pa took us all up to Karonga three years ago. He booked cabins for us on the *Domira*. He wanted to show us the scene of his exploits in the anti-slavery campaigns."

"What is it like there?"

She smiled, watching his supercilious expression. "A tiny place, just a *boma* with a few officials and their houses – and that's about it. Strange that such a little place should be so important."

"Are you nervous about going there?"

"Nervous? No. Even if the Germans invade and defeat us, I'm sure they'll treat us honourably."

Roly nodded his agreement, but said nothing about his concerns about the African *askaris*. There were rumours that they might behave brutally to conquered white people, killing the men and raping the women. Images had revolved in his mind for days. Military children, like him, were weaned on stories of rebels, dervishes and mutineers, who slit throats, disembowelled, and otherwise destroyed the brave soldiers in colonial conflicts.

The calm surface of the lake stretched ahead to the horizon. To the west, tall mountains rose in grey and purple beyond the narrow smoky coastal plain. On the other side of the lake the mountains of German East Africa rose majestically – land of the enemy.

With customary confidence, Roly decided that the moment had come to reveal his feelings. He announced, "Mandy, I want you to know that I've fallen in love with you." He regarded her with solemn eyes.

She delayed her reply while she chose her words. "That's sweet of you, Roly, and I'm flattered..."

"But?"

"No 'but'." She sighed. "It's just that... Well, everything's in such turmoil, isn't it? We should not make declarations and commitments because we could be sent to places that are far apart..." She was quite surprised to have found words that concealed her misgivings. She liked Roly, and enjoyed his admiration, but knew that she was not in love.

"But we could still be..." Roly went on.

"Be what?"

"Engaged, or something."

"Are you proposing to me, Roly?"

"I would if I knew that you liked me."

She turned away, partly because she did not want him to see that she found his earnest approach amusing. "Of course I like you, but we don't know each other very well, do we?"

He straightened up, much taller than her. "We've been together for... about six weeks. We've seen quite a lot of each other – surely long enough to know our feelings."

"Let me think about it." She was relieved to see the boatswain, Kawa, approaching. "Oh, Kawa, *muribwanje*."

"Ndiribueno, dona; kaya enu?"

"Bueno, zicomo. I want you to tell the Captain about the slave battles."

—•—

The KAR contingent disembarked from the steamers at Vua because there were fears that the Germans might shell them if they moored at Karonga for an extended period. Only Mandy was permitted to remain on the ship, to save her the long walk to Karonga. The troops then trekked north, arriving weary and footsore.

A motley collection of brick buildings and grass huts spread out from the lake shore. On a slope above them was the African Lakes Corporation store and shop, low brick buildings with corrugated iron roofs. Near the top of a low ridge stood a red brick bungalow surrounded by tall *Brachystegia* trees – the home of Anthony Webb, the DC. His office was nearby, but discreetly separated from the Mandala shop, with half an acre of dried grass lawn in front. The roads and paths were outlined with white-washed stones, those markers much favoured by British administrators.

Webb emerged from his office as the two captains, Barton and Benting-Smith, approached. After introductions he invited them into his office and instructed an orderly to prepare tea. The two officers placed their pith helmets on chairs that lined the room.

"You must be weary after your march from Vua," said Webb, brightly. He was thin, of medium height, with a straggling moustache and a sallow complexion. "When we've had our discussion you can have baths and rest in the guest bungalow. Miss Spaight is being looked after by my wife – it's very good of her to come up and help here."

He explained that there were four other British officials stationed in Karonga, and when news of the war became known several other people in the surrounding area came into the town; among them two ladies. One of the resident officials was Dr Leys, a government medical officer, and Mandy would be working under him.

"Now let me show you the lie of the land." Webb walked over to a large map hanging on the wall behind his desk. Roly could see the northern end of the lake, with the villages along the shore marked. The hinterland was evidently sparsely populated, judging by the paucity of village names, and the thin network of lines indicating the tracks joining them.

Webb was proud of his map; he had embellished it with information gleaned from his trips around the district – going on *ulendo* – he called it.

"The northern boundary with German East is here – along the Songwe River. There's a large village – Kaporo – our northernmost..."

"Is there a District Officer there?" asked Roly diffidently.

Webb shook his head a trifle wearily. "No. There was, but I moved him south to Kirapula – here." He pointed out the spot on the map. "I judged that keeping him at Kaporo would invite the Germans to capture him. Mind you, I don't think they're ready for that. Only a few days ago my opposite number in New Langenburg, Herr Stier, sent me a message asking whether war had been declared!"

He opened a drawer in his desk and pulled out a sheet of paper, which he handed to Barton. It read:

> *Dear Mr Webb,*
>
> *I am not clear whether England is at war with Germany or not. I have tried to find out from Mbeya, but have had no replies. Please could you tell me what is going on."*
>
> *Yours truly,*
> *Stier,*
> *Administrator, Neu Langenburg*

"What did you tell him?" asked Barton.

Webb shrugged. "I wrote a note saying that the war was on – that's all. I've heard that about two dozen Huns came to New Langenburg, and several hundred askaris. That's why I sent my urgent message to the Governor, and I presume that's why you gentlemen are here."

Barton started drumming his fingers impatiently on the desk. "Yes, we'd better start fortifying this place. I'll need all your people to help. We'll build a stockade – like the slavers' stockades – with earth and timber. We'll need labourers to cut down trees and carry earth."

He turned to Roly. "I want you to go north – get information about what the Germans are doing. If they're preparing to invade, we need to know about it." Turning back to Webb he added. "Now their gunboat has been disabled they won't be able to come down the lake, will they?"

"Not in any numbers. There are a few small *dhows* and canoes, but..."

"That means they'll come down the shore road, through Kaporo and Kirapula. Going through the bush would be too slow. What do you think, Roly?"

"I agree, old chap. But what on earth would be the purpose of them invading – apart from a sort of propaganda achievement? After all, it's just a string of fishing villages – with due respect, Mr Webb."

The DC frowned. "I agree, Captain – they aren't very significant, nor is Karonga for that matter. But the Germans might march further south. If we don't stop them... within a month they could reach Zomba, and Blantyre, and then they would have conquered the country..."

"It wouldn't be so easy," interrupted Barton. "They would have to supply their troops, and the only efficient way to do that would be to use the lake, which is not an option for them."

Roly raised a languid eyebrow. "With dhows and dugouts?"

"Not really practical, is it? I suppose they might try." Barton smacked the desk with the flat of his hand. "Well, gentlemen, I suggest we get to work."

—•—

Roly kept trying to find opportunities to talk to Mandy, but she remained elusive. Dr Leys kept her busy, having discovered that she was a well-trained nurse with experience in anaesthesia, and much more useful to him than the other three willing but inexperienced women.

One evening Roly saw her hurrying along the path between the makeshift hospital rooms and the house she shared with Beatrice Empson.

"I want to speak to you?" he asked, trying not to sound brusque.

"Of course." She gave him a winning smile.

"I think an attack is inevitable, Mandy. I'm concerned for your safety."

She put her hand on his arm. "Roly, that's sweet of you. I'm concerned about you, too – after all, I'm here in the boma, but you have to go out on patrol."

"I just can't bear the thought of you being taken prisoner – if this place is captured..."

"Don't worry. Come."

She took him by the hand and led him down the path towards the lake. There were a few people at the jetty, where a dinghy from the Victoria was being unloaded. She took him along a path to a cove on the lake shore, which was reserved for the Europeans to swim. She moved cautiously, because hippos could come out of the water to graze, and might be aggressive if their path was blocked. They came to a small beach among the rocks. The place was deserted, and when they were hidden by an outcrop Mandy swung round to face him and wrapped her arms around him. He bent to kiss her and she responded without hesitation.

"I've wanted to do that for such a long time," he muttered.

She laughed. "You haven't known me for long."

"Long enough. If only we were in a normal situation..."

She smiled at his solemn expression. "What's normal? We're far from our homes. We have to make the best of where we are."

He was like the young men she had partied with in Salisbury, slim and pliant, confident, but uncertain what to say. She pulled away from him and said, "It's time we got ready for supper."

—•—

Roly wrote a letter to his parents. After asking after their health and his siblings, he wrote:

> *I am writing from Karonga, a small town at the north end of Lake Nyasa. We are expecting an attack from the Germans, but don't be alarmed. There aren't many of them, and we have a splendid little force here.*
>
> *I'm living in a small house that belongs to the District Officer, who has kindly given me his guest room. We officers all eat in a mess – simple fare, chicken and rice. It's the beginning of the rainy season now, so very hot and humid, with thunderstorms around. We were lucky to have a calm voyage up the lake – it can get very rough in a storm.*
>
> *We are a motley group here – some government officials, KAR officers (seconded from British regiments, like me), volunteers who are mostly European planters, and even a couple of RNVR officers on a lake steamer. Of course most of the soldiers are natives (called askaris), who are willing and cheerful. Apart from the NCOs they are not very well trained. We have Maxim guns, but no artillery, unless you count an old muzzle loader – like something from the Indian Mutiny!*
>
> *We even have a few women here, who will be nurses if there is any fighting. One of them is a girl named Amanda Spaight, who I met on my journey from South Africa – she and her father and sister were on the boat from Beira.*
>
> *I must end now and check our fortifications.*

—•—

For the next several days Captain Barton organised his *askaris*, supplemented by labourers recruited by the Resident, to fortify the centre of the town and the landing jetties. They erected an earth bank, on top of which they made a wall of vertical logs. A ditch was dug outside the wall, about six foot deep and five foot wide, the spoil going into the earth bank. This gave the log wall an effective height of ten to twelve feet, with platforms on the inner sides, enabling soldiers to shoot at the enemy while protected.

One morning Barton received a visit from Mr Webb who silently handed him a letter, written in English:

From: Captain von Langenn Steinkeller,
Military Commander, Neu Langenburg
To: Mr Webb, Resident Commissioner, Karonga

Dear Mr Webb,
I hereby warn you that my forces will soon invade Nyasaland. I respectfully request that you evacuate all European persons from Karonga to avert a massacre by my askaris.
Yours truly,
von Langenn Steinkeller

"What do you think of that?" Webb removed his solar *topi* and wiped sweat off his brow.

"We're not leaving," replied Barton gruffly. "It's up to you whether you stay."

"I'm staying." Webb took the letter back and turned away.

—•—

Before leaving on his patrol Roly said to Barton, "I say, old man, how am I supposed to find out if the Huns will invade?"

Barton looked at him with a hint of impatience. "We know they plan to invade – they wrote to us. What we need to know is when and where. The villagers along the border are bound to have heard something. You might be able to capture a patrol."

Roly dutifully departed and eventually approached Kaporo, the small fishing village where the Songwe River flowed into the lake. It took him the best part of two days to walk the fifteen miles, moving cautiously, in a compact group consisting of his batman, two KAR *askaris*, and three policemen from Karonga, who acted as guides. The latter had been chosen because they knew the terrain and the local language, ChiTumbuku. All were armed with Lee-Enfield rifles, except Roly, who carried a Webley revolver, and his batman, who had the officer's 12-bore shotgun in a canvas holster slung over his shoulder.

Their route followed the sandy lake-side track, winding through palm trees and reed beds. Now and then they encountered a cluster of huts belonging to fishermen, where the stopped to enquire about possible German patrols. They spent their first night at Kirapula, where the headman informed them that some shots had been fired across the Songwe River.

Roly was enjoying his role as scout. He suspected that Barton gave him the job thinking he was an effete desk soldier, softened by his sojourn at Government House. In fact, he had kept fit by swimming and playing tennis in Zomba. He always enjoyed shooting, and here he could down the occasional guinea fowl with his shotgun. The weather was pleasant, the days sunny and warm, the nights crisply cold. His batman, Jason, a former Mandala employee, was adept at making a comfortable camp.

Roly wore a khaki tunic and voluminous shorts, puttees wound round his lower legs, and leather boots. On his head he wore a large pith helmet with a broad brim; it was effective at preventing sun-stroke, but would not deflect a bullet. He had a pair of binoculars slung round his neck, and his revolver at his right hip. On his left hip was a tin water bottle with a canvas sheath. On seeing him depart, Mandy giggled and said, "All you need now is a cleft stick, for carrying messages across swollen rivers."

He got his first intimation of war from a group of villagers fleeing south from Kaporo on August 20. They gabbled about German's *askaris* burning huts and chasing women. Roly immediately sent one of the policemen hurrying back to Karonga with a message for Barton, then turned his group back for a more leisurely return. He had no intention of confronting the invasion single-handed.

On reaching Karonga he found that his news had galvanised the occupants into further efforts to fortify the *boma*. Barton sent more patrols towards the border, and two NVR scouts had narrow escapes from German patrols.

A captured *askari* told them that the main German force, commanded by *Hauptman* von Langenn-Steinkeller, had marched from New Langenburg – their destination Karonga.

—•—

Knowing that the Germans had no gunboats on the lake, Barton decided to make an exploratory voyage, taking Roly with him on the *Guendolen*. Thus Roly met Gavin Henderson again and chatted to him as the little steamer chugged north towards the mouth of the Songwe River and the border. They stood near the prow, feeling the rhythmic slap of the waves against the ship's hull.

"You must be happy to be on a ship," said Roly, envious of his companion's easy relationship with Commander Rhoades.

"Oh, I am. She's a great little craft – the *Guen*. All the lake steamers are. Mind you, I haven't been in a lake storm yet. I've heard they're ferocious."

"You must come ashore and visit us, old boy" said Roly. "You can stay with me in the DO's modest little house."

Gavin thanked him. "I would like to see Mandy and give her news of the family. By the way, Kirsty and I have decided that we'll get married when the war is over..."

Roly was stunned. "Do her parents know? Have they agreed?" He looked at the shorter, but much heavier, man, and envisioned him entwined with the voluptuous sister of the girl he loved.

"Oh yes. But it's not an official engagement. Kirsty's trying to get permission to come up here, but she's made herself too useful in Fort Johnston. Between ourselves, Roly, they're afraid of both sisters being killed or captured."

"And what about Major Spaight? What's he doing?"

Gavin laughed. "He's champing at the bit. Hates being tied up in red tape at Zomba. Wishes he could exchange places with you. Actually, I do think he's ideal for the job as H.E's military attaché."

—•—

Commander Rhoades kept the *Guen* well off shore because the lake was very shallow in these parts. They were able to identify the small settlement of Kaporo, and then the Songwe River, marked by the banana trees along its course, contrasting with the dry brown bushveld on either side.

Barton announced that he wanted to fire a couple of shells into the river.

"Can you see anything to fire at?" asked Rhoades, somewhat surprised.

"Who knows, they may be there. Let's see if we can ginger them up a bit," replied the laconic Barton.

The *Guen* was duly pointed towards the shore, and Gavin aimed the Hotchkiss. He fired three times – one shell was a dud. Meanwhile, unknown to the British, three German officers were moving a field gun across the Songwe River. They heard the boom of the *Guen*'s cannon, then one shell, soon followed by another, fell close by. The Germans fled, astonished, thinking the British knew where they were, and amazed at the accuracy of their fire.

On returning to Karonga, Barton discussed with Webb the possibility of forestalling the expected German invasion. They invited Roly to join them, in Webb's spacious but stuffy office.

"It occurred to me," said Roly, "that they may not be aware we've destroyed the *Wissmann.*"

Webb nodded. "True. We could send them a message. Then they'll know that no lake-borne support will come their way."

"More important," said Barton, "they'll know we can bring reinforcements up the lake without hindrance." He stroked his chin. "We could send a patrol under a white flag with a message for von Langenn."

"We should send a German speaker," suggested Webb, then added, "but if he was captured they could interrogate him."

"They could do that in English," Roly pointed out.

"An officer who understands German might overhear something useful."

"Gavin Henderson, on the *Guen*, is fluent in German," said Roly.

"Of course." Barton struck his left hand with his fist.

—•—

Gavin set off next morning, a burly figure in khaki shirt and shorts, with the same group that accompanied Roly on his patrol. He had the loan of the estimable batman Jason, instructed to ensure that the young RNVR sub-lieutenant was well looked after. Gavin was pleased to discover that he could converse with the policemen, who, as local men, understood ChiSwahili, the language he had learnt in Moshi.

They plodded up the dry sandy track, flanked with palm trees among sparse grass. One of the policemen strode in the fore, carrying a pole with a white flag; the poor man was not really aware of the danger. They were unarmed, except for Gavin, who carried a revolver.

As they trudged further from Karonga, Gavin grew apprehensive. He had been told about the German patrols, and presumed they would fire at the slightest sound of advancing enemy. Consequently, he ordered the men to talk normally and not act furtively. He expected that they would be seen first, and hoped fervently that the white flag would be honoured.

They were only eight miles north of Karonga when they heard a shout from ahead. "*Halt!*"

Gavin ordered his group to stop, then called out. "*Wer sind sie?* – Who are you?"

"*Legen Sie Ihre Waffen hin!* – Put down your weapons!"

Gavin slowly laid his revolver on a clump of dry grass, then looked ahead down the track. He could see no one.

"*Kommen Sie langsam nach vorn!* – Come forward slowly!"

Gavin took the white flag from the policeman and walked forward along the centre of the track. He had gone about thirty yards when two armed Germans emerged from the bush onto the road, followed by a dozen uniformed askaris. The Germans beckoned Gavin to approach.

"*Sprechen Sie Deutsch?*" they asked.

"*Ja.*"

They signalled him to come closer, then asked, "How do you speak German?"

"I'm British – I used to work for a German family on an estate in Moshi," he replied.

The taller of the two Germans broke into a smile. "What are you doing here?"

"I moved to Nyasaland two years ago. I was sent under the white flag to tell you that your gunboat, the *Hermann von Wissmann*, has been destroyed..."

He could see shock cloud their expressions, and continued. "That means that we have control of the lake. We ask that you should not invade this country, because we can bring more troops by ship. It would be a waste of your men to fight us here."

The tall German, who wore sergeant's stripes, took out a cigarette and offered one to Gavin, who refused it. The shorter German also took out a cigarette and the men started smoking.

"How do you know about the *Wissmann*?" asked the sergeant.

"I'm a naval lieutenant," said Gavin, pointing to the RNVR insignia on his shoulder. "I was on our gunship when we surprised the *Wissmann* at Sphinxhaven. Captain Berndt is now a prisoner."

The sergeant groaned and stamped his foot. "That is bad news for us. So? What do you wish to tell us?"

Gavin said, "I have a letter here, from Captain Barton." He handed it to the sergeant. "I suggest you return back over the border. We will go back to Karonga."

The sergeant nodded and stuffed the letter into a pocket without looking at it. Then he ordered his group to turn back. He waved to Gavin. "Farewell, Lieutenant. We may meet again."

—•—

Two days later, ignoring Barton's plea, Steinkeller's main German column marched south into Nyasaland. They had 22 officers, 270 African *askaris* armed with rifles, 40 mercenaries armed with flintlocks, and about five hundred local tribesmen armed with spears. Steinkeller was confident that their two field guns and four machine guns gave them more firepower than the British, and that they would soon capture Karonga.

After crossing the Songwe River they spent the night encamped at Kaporo. On the following day Steinkeller dispatched a column, under his deputy Lt Aumann, along the inland track, with thirty askaris and half the mercenaries. He then led his main force along lake shore track.

Meanwhile, the British in Karonga had been strengthened by a contingent of the NVR, brought in by the *Chauncy Maples.* Most of the fifty-five men were planters and government officials.

Capt Barton held a meeting in the DC's office, attended by his second in command, Capt Alexander Griffiths, Lt Philip Bishop, Roly Benting-Smith and Mr Webb. Although Webb considered himself the senior man, he was willing to defer to the young captain in the circumstances. Even so, he thought Barton sounded less than confident, and wondered whether one of the other officers would have made a better commander.

Benting-Smith was leaning back, ostensibly casual, but his fingers tapping nervously on the sill of the open window. Phil Bishop was studying a map on his lap, brushing away a persistent fly.

"As you know, Mr Webb," Barton started, "I have organised our force into three companies. Each of us officers will have between a hundred and two hundred men, and we'll divide the machine guns. My plan is to counter the German invasion. We'll meet them with force, on ground we know. We'll travel light so that we can move quickly. The heavier equipment will go north on the steamer *Vera* to Kaporo."

Ever since he heard rumours of Barton's plan, Webb's misgivings had intensified. "Er, I don't want to interfere, Barton; after all, you're the military commander. But do you think it's wise to divide our meagre forces?"

Barton looked surprised, then frowned, as if annoyed. "I certainly don't intend to wait for the Germans to attack. If they do, we'll either forestall them, or circle behind them."

"Don't you think you're leaving us rather few troops to defend Karonga?" Webb persisted.

Barton looked out of the window, as if making an assessment of the defences. "You have a strong position, but I intend to stop the Huns from reaching you."

Webb nodded, but looked unconvinced. He wondered how the army could have allowed this strategically important area to be defended by so few, under the command of an evidently inexperienced captain.

As it happened, Roly was thinking the same thing, glad that it was not his responsibility, but convinced that, if he was commander, he would have kept his entire force in Karonga.

He sought out Mandy to say farewell, eventually finding her in the clinic, where she was dispensing quinine. She handed the medicine to an orderly and came out onto the path, leading Roly for a stroll.

"You will be careful?" she said.

He laughed. "I'll try. I wish we knew more about how many of them there are, and where they are. Actually, I'm more concerned about you, Mandy." He bent to speak quietly. "I really wonder how wise it is for us to march out and leave so few of you here in Karonga."

"We'll be alright."

—•—

13

Karonga, Nyasaland – September 1914

"Forward march!"

Captain Barton ordered his men out of Karonga, following the narrow inland track. He reasoned – correctly as it turned out – that the Germans would use the more direct lake shore track. He intended to outflank them and take Kaporo from the west, but he did not know that the Germans were already on their way, and so the two forces passed each other unawares.

Roly walked within sight of Barton, expecting that his commander might want to consult him at any time. They left the track and picked their way through open forest, interspersed with scrub thorn brush. The grass was long but straggling, and easily bent down. The movement of the men created much dust and a loud swishing noise. The heat was oppressive, and he was soon bathed in sweat, irritably shifting his belt and pouches. His only weapon was the Webley revolver, in a leather holster at his side. He was glad of his stout puttees keeping the thorns out of his legs; the leather sweatband of his large pith solar helmet was soon saturated.

Barton preferred his own company, and Roly was happy to chat quietly to one of the KAR sergeants, who spoke good English.

"Slow going, eh, sergeant?"

"*Inde, bwana*. Easier if we were on the road." He was intrigued by the tall awkward officer, who spoke only a few words of ChiNyanja.

He suspected that the man was inept, and might prove a liability if there was a fight.

They came to a river bed with a few pools and a slow trickle of water. The men were permitted to break off and fill their water bottles.

Barton beckoned to the sergeant. "Is this the Kasoa River?"

The sergeant, who wore a pillbox fez and khaki shorts and shirt, shook his head. "Perhaps – I am not sure, sir." He called softly to one of the *askaris* and spoke to him in ChiSwahili. The man nodded, and so they confirmed that it was indeed the Kasoa.

"We shouldn't leave it too late to make a camp," suggested Roly, glancing at the sun, already low. Barton shook his head and signalled for the men to march on.

For another hour they tramped along, meandering through the trees and scrub, swatting at tsetse flies, and muttering about the heat. When Barton called a halt, near a small pool, he was answered with a collective sigh. The men quickly un-shouldered their weapons and packs before the commander could change his mind.

They were in the bush between the Kasoa and Lufira rivers. Exhausted from their day's march, they lay in a rough defensive square, with the porters in the centre. Within a discreet patch of open ground reserved for the officers, Roly's batman, Jason, built a small fire and made tea. Porters brought their ground-sheets and food, which Barton's servant unpacked, while Jason prepared a meal of boiled bully-beef and dried biscuits.

Roly was so hungry he did not care that the fare was so basic. He and Barton and Griffiths spoke little during their meal. Only when they lit up cigarettes and pipes did Roly start a conversation.

"The Huns will probably want to get back to their farms," he said, sounding less than hopeful.

"They won't be allowed to, surely?" said Griffiths. "They're not volunteers, they're conscripts."

"Yes, but they won't have much stomach for a fight. What do you think, Barton?"

Their commander had been thinking about something else. "I'm more concerned about their intentions now. Wish we had some cavalry to find where they are..."

"No chance of that," snorted Griffiths. "They'd succumb to the tsetse flies within days... besides attracting predators – like lions."

"Are there lions here?" asked Roly, trying not to sound nervous.

"Of course." Griffiths played with the naïve British officer's concerns. "This sort of bush is full of lions. You ask the natives." He called to Jason, who was cleaning the cooking dishes. "*Nkanga kuno,* Jason?"

The African looked up and nodded.

"You see?" Griffiths said to Roly. "One good reason to have the porters and askaris sleeping outside us." He laughed. "Mind you, they say that lions prefer the taste of white men. I suppose it's an exotic flavour for them."

—•—

Meanwhile, Steinkeller's main force was camped only two miles from Karonga, and Lt Aumann's column was only a short distance to the west. Barton had advanced north between the two German groups without either of them knowing. Karonga was the vulnerable nut, ready to be cracked.

Remaining in the settlement was Lt Phil Bishop, in command, assisted by Anthony Webb, and nine other European men, together with Mrs Webb, Mandy Spaight and Beatrice Empson. They were supported by forty KAR *askaris* and twenty African policemen. Their only artillery was the old muzzle-loading cannon, a veteran of the slave wars.

Several local Africans came into the *boma* during the night and told of encountering German patrols near the town. This news so alarmed Bishop that he decided to call a meeting of the Europeans; they gathered in the hall next to Webb's office.

Bishop knew that he had to be frank with them, but he did not want to frighten them. "I think an attack is imminent. I don't know if Barton's column can prevent it – they may even have been defeated or captured. My inclination is to concentrate our resources in the storerooms; they'll be easier to defend than this *boma*."

"I agree," said Webb. "We can place the *askaris* along the brick wall. The women can stay in the rice store, which will give them some protection."

"I would like to be more useful," said Mandy. "I can shoot a rifle as well as any *askari* – probably better."

Bishop groaned. "Mandy, I could never forgive myself if you were killed or injured in the firing line."

They agreed on Bishop's plan and hastily set up their defences in the walled traders' compound, where they spent an uneasy night.

—•—

That evening Steinkeller sipped coffee beside a campfire and listened to one of his *askaris*, who had been taught English at the mission in Chirenje, and was employed for his local knowledge. Short and thin, he was of an age that the German could not determine, especially as it was so dark on the edge of the clearing, ten yards from the fire.

"What is this place called?" asked Steinkeller.

"It is Kombwe, *bwana*."

"How far to Karonga?"

"It will take one hour, by walking."

Von Langenn lit a cheroot. "Do you know the road?"

"Yes, *bwana*. It is better to stay on this road, near the lake. On that side," he pointed inland, "is the lagoon. The men do not like to go there."

"Why not?"

"*Bwana*, there was a terrible killing there. Many of my people were killed in the lagoon and the swamp."

"Who killed them?"

The African replied in reedy fluent English. "It was the slave trader, Mlozi. My people are *WaNkonde* and we were being destroyed by this Arab man and his followers..."

The German held up his hand to interrupt. "When was this?"

"*Ee, bwana* it was more than twenty years ago. I was a child then, and I am thirty years old now."

"Very well, go on."

"My people moved to be near Karonga, because there were British men there – fighting the slave traders. My people camped near the lagoon – we were attacked by Mlozi's men. Some were killed by shooting, some drowned, many were eaten by crocodiles. My father and mother ran away. Ten years later the British caught Mlozi. They hanged him." The little man gestured graphically.

Steinkeller stroked his beard and thanked the *askari*. Then he said, "Why are you with us – the Germans – and not the British?'

"I was recruited by your people, *bwana*. If I was living in Karonga I would be with the British."

—•—

The Germans prepared to attack Karonga at dawn. They did not expect the town to be reinforced, even though they knew the *Hermann von Wissmann* had been destroyed, and lake steamers could use the lake without hinder. When Steinkeller heard that the defences were being strengthened he doubted the veracity of the news.

The column was organised with much shouting. Above the noise Steinkeller heard the chugging sound of a steamer on the lake. Hurrying through the bush to the shore he saw two British ships, one towing the other. Using his binoculars he saw the *Charlotte*, towing the *Vera*; both were taking Barton's heavy equipment north to Kaporo.

The temptation was too much. He ordered the two field guns towards the shore and started firing at the British boats. The sound of the gunfire carried to the defenders of Karonga, and to Captain Barton's forces in the bush.

—•—

On hearing the German guns Lt Bishop and his *askaris* rushed to their posts.

"They're attacking! Get to your posts!" the defenders shouted to each other.

Webb and the government officials joined the soldiers at the barricades. They waited nearly two hours before seeing movement in the trees north of the *boma*. The ground around the stockade had been deliberately cleared for a distance of about five hundred yards. There were gasps of surprise and fear when the German troops emerged from the trees.

"Fire!" shouted Bishop. "Aim carefully! Don't waste your ammo!"

The British were good shots and the German advance wilted under heavy accurate fire, retreating to cover.

"Can't we fire the cannon?" shouted Webb.

"Not that easy, sir," replied Bishop. "The gun crew has gone with Barton."

"Ye Gods! There must be someone who knows how to fire it."

Eventually some NVR men were able to get the venerable weapon into action. Its distinctive boom scared the German *askaris* and carried to Barton near the Lufira River.

—•—

At first Barton was dismayed, realising that the Germans had marched past him. He began to have doubts about his tactical decision, but there was no going back now. He was not pleased when Roly approached, heavily frowning, an ungainly figure in his huge shorts.

"I say, old man, shouldn't we get back to help them?" asked Roly, still convinced they should not have left Karonga in the first place.

"No. It would take too long. The men are exhausted. But some can go." Barton called to his second in command, Captain Griffiths.

"Sort out the fittest men, Alex, and lead them back to Karonga as quickly as you can. Take only light kit. Don't let anyone slow you down. Leave falterers by the wayside."

It took about ten minutes to select the men from many volunteers, and prepare them for the forced march. They took only rifles, ammunition and water bottles, leaving their packs and camping gear in a heap under a large kapok tree.

Meanwhile, Barton was heartened to hear continuing gunfire from Karonga. "They must be holding on," he muttered to Roly. "I'm going to set an ambush in case the Huns retreat – they might go back to the border for reinforcements. We'll go to the Kasoa River and dig in there."

"But they might not go back," countered Roly, somewhat confused by his commander's thinking. "Then what?"

"Well, they have to come back, sooner or later don't they?"

"If they capture Karonga they might stay and use it as their base."

Barton felt his spirits sinking. "I still think we should set up an ambush."

—•—

For three hours the Germans continued firing at the British defenders in Karonga. Only the accurate fire from the British *laager* kept them from advancing out of cover. Steinkeller tried to decide whether the distance was too great for a frontal charge, not knowing what weapons his opponents possessed. He suspected they might have Maxims in reserve.

Dr Leys was wounded in the hand by a bullet splinter, and one of Mr Webb's eyes was injured when a falling brick broke his glasses.

Mandy was frustrated, confined to the storeroom. “I should be out there at the wall,” she muttered, as she dressed Dr Leys’ wound.

“Don’t try to be the Amazon,” said the doctor. “Your value is here, and there’ll be more wounded – more serious than this.”

“We should have more nurses, Dr Leys.”

“I agree with that.”

The sudden clear sound of a bugle call carried from the German lines. Everyone in the British *laager* stopped talking.

“What was it?”

Someone cried out, “It’s ‘Fix bayonets!’”

—•—

14

Karonga, Nyasaland – September 1914

It took Griffiths only three hours to get back to Karonga along the road; on the previous day it had taken the column eight hours to cover the same distance through the bush. They arrived exhausted and drenched with sweat, but attacked at once, taking on the Germans from behind.

It was the deciding factor. Steinkeller was wounded, as were many of his askaris. He hurriedly ordered a retreat, but had to fight his way through Griffith's men. Trying to keep some semblance of order the Germans marched back to the Kasoa River. It took them two hours, and as they wearily started to cross the river bed they were met by blistering fire from Barton's men on the far bank.

A fierce fight ensued. Tired and dispirited, the Germans tried to find ways across the narrow river. The British had the advantage of firing from prepared positions, but Barton did not know the size of the German force, nor that they were retreating in disarray. Even now he feared that the defenders in Karonga had capitulated.

The KAR askaris were firing at the bush ahead, where it was assumed that the German force were in hiding. Concerned that they were wasting ammunition Barton urged his officers to keep the firing under control. He ordered fixed bayonets and an advance, only to encounter small groups of Germans sheltering in thick vegetation between small bare fields where local Africans grew their crops.

John Ness, one of the NVR volunteers, was probing ahead, sniping at the enemy from an anthill. He was a good shot and disabled a German machine gun team, but they regrouped and opened fire at him, wounding him in the chest.

Roly ran up to him, hunched and scared, appalled to see the patch of blood on Ness's shirt. He turned and called some askaris to carry the wounded man back to cover. It was his first experience of combat, of bullets flying at him.

"I hit a German officer," said Ness, grinning despite the pain from his wound. "Please try to get me his binoculars."

A short while later Roly found the body of the German and removed the field glasses that were hanging round his neck, as well as his Luger revolver. When he returned to his askaris he found them hunkered down and firing at any movement on the far side of the Kasoa. Hearing shouted orders he thought the Germans might be preparing to make a dash forward.

"Keep firing!" he instructed. "Anyone short of ammo?"

He could hear bullets crashing through the foliage of the trees and shrubs, making noise of disproportionate intensity. Wishing to move to a position where he could get a better view, he ran, stooping, his revolver held out in his right hand.

At that moment a bullet hit him on the jaw and he tumbled over, unconscious. His askaris saw him fall, and two of them hurried to his side, despite the spasmodic German firing. Seeing the severity of the wound, one of them ran, jinking through the trees, to find Captain Barton.

Meanwhile, Lt Napier, in charge of the *tenga-tengas*, was trying to prevent them from bolting from the battlefield. He explained that the noisy firing was from the British machine gun, not the enemy; nevertheless, some of them waded into the river, risking crocodiles, to hide under the water.

Napier saw the *askaris* searching for someone. "What's the matter!" he shouted.

"*Bwana* shot," said one of them.

Napier's immediate fear was that Barton had been wounded or killed, and that he would have to take over. He followed one of the soldiers to where a large uniformed body was lying in the undergrowth. Bullets were still flying as he crawled forward.

"Oh, shit, it's Roly," he muttered to himself. "Poor fellow."

He could see blood all over Roly's head and on his chest. Finding a limp hand and then the wrist, he searched for a pulse, but it proved difficult. Eventually he found it, his fingers slippery with blood. The pulse was weak and erratic.

He beckoned to the *askaris*. "Carry him back to the trees," he instructed.

They dragged Roly like a carcass through the grass and bushes until they were in the shelter of the forest, Napier wincing as he saw the damaged head lolling. Then two askaris carried the wounded man further to the rear; one holding him by the armpits, the other by his legs.

"We must make a stretcher," muttered Napier, reflexively cringing as a bullet ripped through the leaves of a shrub near him.

He ordered the soldiers to make a *machila* out of bush timber, while he tried to wash Roly's wounds with water from his canteen. The hammock-like contraption was more practical than a rigid stretcher, because two strong men could carry it in single file.

—•—

Eventually Steinkeller's men were able to force their way through the British lines and head for the border. Their losses were heavy; nineteen out of twenty-two German officers were casualties, as were a hundred *askaris* and many more irregulars.

Napier eventually found Barton, who was limping around in great pain from a wound in the thigh.

"Take charge, Napier," he grunted, "I'm weakening. How bad is Roly?"

"Looks bad. I think the bullet went into his jaw. He was bleeding heavily, but it seems to have stopped. His pulse is weak and unsteady."

"We must get him back to Karonga at once. Good idea to knock up a *machila.* Select the best team to run him back. I'll need one myself, but look after Roly first." Barton leaned against a tree, his face pale and drawn. "Make sure all the wounded are collected. Take care of them until we can get them to Karonga."

Napier gave the orders and came back to Barton later. "Roly is on his way. By the way, I've spoken to a couple of German prisoners – they say they reached Karonga but were attacked from the rear, and retreated..."

"That must have been Griffiths." Barton's voice was weaker now.

"It was a good show, sir. We virtually destroyed their force."

"We were lucky, Napier. Yes, we did well. Sorry to leave this mess to you."

—•—

Dr Leys frowned as he tried to examine Roly's wounds with sore and watering eyes. Roly lay on his back, unconscious, his face bruised and smeared with blood. He was white and still, like a cadaver. Mandy stood beside the doctor, tears welling, fearful that the wounds threatened the patient's life.

"Severe trauma," said the doctor quietly. "The bullet seems to have struck the jaw here – about mid way – broke the bone, then travelled along to the angle, breaking the external maxillary artery on the way. It exited at the angle – must have been spent when it hit him, otherwise it would have caused even more damage. Knocked him out like a boxer hit with an uppercut..."

He probed gently inside Roly's mouth. "Fragments of bone to get out – and his tongue has swollen."

He looked up at Mandy. "I have to move on. I want you to clean him up. Check the inside of his mouth for pieces of bone – we don't want him to swallow any. Make sure he doesn't swallow his tongue. I'll come back when I've seen some of the others."

She nodded and watched Leys stand up, wearily, and shuffle across the room towards another stretcher, his long white coat stained with blood. She wondered how long he could keep going. She turned and wiped Roly's face with a damp cloth, grimacing when she felt the floppy broken jaw bone. She could see the bullet entry hole and the torn flesh where it had made its exit, shuddering as she imagined the damage it would have caused. I have to keep him warm and quiet, she thought.

It was actually rather hot in the hospital shed, and certainly not quiet. More than a dozen wounded men were groaning as they were cleaned and probed, then bandaged and carried to another large shed, to recover or die.

Opening Roly's mouth gently she ran her index finger round inside, finding a couple of bone fragments. His breath was wheezing, and she thought the swollen tongue was blocking his trachea. Probing with her forefinger she opened the air passage. As she bent to feel his pulse a drop of sweat fell from her chin. Looking at his face she saw how bruised his eyes had become; there was no expression, no sign of consciousness. His pulse was weak.

She moved over to where Dr Leys was working on Captain Barton, and helped him dress the wound.

"How is Roly?" asked Barton.

"Shot in the jaw," replied Leys. "Haven't had time to examine him in detail."

"Will he survive?"

"Can't say, Barton. He lost plenty of blood. We'll get the wounded back to Fort Johnston – as soon as we can."

Leys and Mandy moved on to some Germans, one of whom had been wounded in the stomach; he was dying.

—•—

In the evening she sat with Roly, in the storage shed that was used as a recovery ward. He was still unconscious, but his pulse was steadier. Dr Leys found her there and put his hand on her shoulder; he knew she must be exhausted.

"Mandy, I want you to go back to Blantyre with the wounded men. They'll need a nurse to look after them on the journey."

"If you say so."

She wanted to go back south, without really understanding why. She wanted to watch over Roly, but there was no compelling sentiment about it. At least she would be with him when he recovered consciousness. She had no sense of abandoning the 'front', because there was general agreement that the Germans were unlikely to invade again, at least for a few weeks.

"We had fifty men wounded. I've selected a dozen who should be the first to go – with you. The others can follow later, or be treated here."

"How many were killed?"

"Thirteen of ours – five Europeans and eight *askaris*." He sighed wearily. "It was a nasty little battle."

—•—

Roly gained consciousness on the steamer a day after leaving Karonga. Mandy had gone to fetch drinking water and returned to see his eyes fluttering. He was lying on a thin kapok mattress on the deck, in the shade of an awning, where a light breeze cooled him. His head was swathed with bandages, like an Egyptian mummy, leaving little more than his eyes, nose and mouth in view.

She crouched beside him and took hold of his hand. When his eyes opened he glanced around fearfully, and then looked at her. His lips moved and she put her finger to hers, to silence him.

She bent closer and said, "If you can hear me squeeze my hand." She felt a weak movement and continued, speaking slowly and deliberately. "You've been wounded, Roly. Your jaw was injured. Don't try to speak. You must rest and try to drink. Here..." She held a tin cup and he sipped a little, watching her face. He grimaced with pain as he swallowed.

"We're going back to Blantyre," she said. "You'll be well cared-for there."

He closed his eyes.

Two hours later he opened them again; a passing soldier called her, and she sat beside him, noticing that he lifted his hand a little. The gesture seemed to indicate that he wished to write, so she fetched a sheet of paper and a large chart pencil. His efforts were pitiful, and he soon stopped.

"Squeeze once for 'yes'," she suggested, "and twice for no. Do you need something?"

He squeezed once.

"Water?"

He squeezed again, and she fetched him some, holding the tin cup for him to drink.

"Do you feel pain?"

He squeezed once.

Patiently she continued the one-sided conversation, while an NVR volunteer changed Roly's clothes and swabbed him with a wet cloth. At times when he was conscious she explained the nature of his injuries, reassuring him that his jaw could be repaired, though he would probably have to be taken to South Africa or England.

Sitting with him that night she mused about the events of the last two days. How ghastly it had been. The little lake-side settlement erupting into battle, broken men brought in to her hospital, burials under the great baobab tree, and mournful bugle calls echoing into the forest.

Only three months ago I was in Rhodesia, she thought. It was so peaceful then. Of course there was talk of war, but the bickering countries were so far away. She and Kirsty, and their friends, virtually ignored the news, and carried on partying and enjoying themselves.

She walked up to the prow of the *Chauncy Maples*, an area reserved for Europeans. There was no one there. All the other Europeans were wounded patients, except for the skipper, a cheerful bearded Scot, who seemed to spend most of his time with the engine. The breeze from their passage swept her hair back and made her skin tingle. She had always found the lake mysterious, almost sinister in its depth and unpredictability.

Strange, she thought, that Roly had been wounded just as she was getting to know him, although her feelings for him were confused. She had always rather liked him, from the time they met on the journey from Beira. He was sometimes brash and over-confident, but also naïve about Africa. Yet, he was worldly and easy-going, friendly and good-natured.

Did she love him? She doubted it.

—•—

15

Nyasaland – November 1914 – January, 1915

"Let us begin with a prayer," announced John Chilembwe. A young African of less than medium height, slim and smartly dressed, he wore a suit with buttoned waistcoat and a bow tie, his black shoes shining. The local white settlers hated the way he dressed – 'apeing us Europeans', they said.

"Now, to business. I have a plan. It is of the utmost secrecy – Jacob, you must put nothing on paper."

Jacob Mbalo, sitting at a desk to the side of the meeting table in the church office, put down his pen and regarded his mentor with open admiration.

"My plan is to show the Europeans that it is time for us to take over our own country." Chilembwe looked around the eleven Africans sitting at the table; the only woman present was his wife Ida, sitting primly, her hands in her lap. His other disciples included his deputy, John Gray Kufa, wearing a serious expression.

They were meeting at the church of the Providence Industrial Mission at Mbombwe, near the Bruce estates. An imposing brick structure, its walls were three bricks thick and two solid towers stood at either end. The minister designed it himself, and it was built under his instructions by his parishioners.

"We must start with a grand gesture of defiance that will bring our fellow men flocking to join us." said Chilembwe gravely. "My plan is to kill the European managers on the Bruce Estates."

There was a gasp of surprise from the disciples. “Kill them?”

“Yes. It will show that we have the power to destroy them.” Chilembwe looked at his followers, each in turn, to assess their reaction. He saw mostly astonishment, but glowing admiration from Ida.

“Why have you chosen those people?” asked Kufa, one of the calmest and most respected men at the meeting.

“Because they are well known throughout the country – better known than minor government officials. One is a relative of the great David Livingstone.” Chilembwe smiled. “It is not important that they are hated by us – especially William Livingstone, who burned down our churches and has no respect for us...”

“He will learn respect,” said Ida. It was the first time she had spoken. She wore a long cotton dress with frills down her bosom. On her head perched a small hat with ribbons trailing down her back.

“Yes. We will kill Livingstone, Robertson, Ferguson and MacCormick...”

“What about the women and children?” asked Jacob Mbalo, surprised at his bold interruption.

Chilembwe turned to him and smiled. “They will not be harmed. I want to show the *azungu* that we are not savages – by protecting the safety of the women and their children.”

“Is that all you plan to do?” asked John Gray Kufa. His faint smile gave the impression of mild scepticism.

“No, John. That is not all. We need to arm ourselves. So I want you to lead a raid on the Mandala armoury at Blantyre – you know the area well. We should be able to take several dozen rifles and hundreds of rounds of ammunition. It must be done at night, of course.”

“We will be attacked,” said Kufa. “The Governor will send the KAR to kill us.”

“Of course,” replied Chilembwe, smiling patiently as he wiped his forehead with a white handkerchief. “I have no doubt that the

Government will try to punish us, but..." He paused. "They have limited resources here in the south. As you know, most of the planters and *askaris* are in the north, fighting the Germans. Also, it is my belief that the *askaris* will not fight us – we are their own people. The *azungu* will be powerless without their support."

Kufa said, "I hope you are right, John. Do you have a plan in case you are wrong?"

This time Chilembwe frowned, and his eyebrows twitched. "If we fail, and, God help us, I hope we don't, we must escape over the border to Portuguese territory."

—•—

A few days after Chilembwe's meeting, and knowing nothing about it, the Governor of Nyasaland, recently knighted Sir George Smith, came out to *Khundalila* to shoot guinea-fowl, and to talk to Alan Spaight. He drove out in the official car, arriving at four on a grey thundery afternoon. After a quick cup of tea on the verandah, during which he chatted to Jess, he set off on foot with Alan. They had not gone far from the house when the Governor broached his subject.

"Alan, I want to talk to you about Chilembwe – the Baptist minister at Magomero. His activities are concerning me greatly, and I want your opinion – in confidence, obviously. What do you know of the man?"

Alan shifted his shotgun from his right shoulder to his left. He still felt twinges from the wound he suffered in the anti-slavery fight near Karonga in 1888. Because the Governor asked to be taken shooting on his own, without either Mac or Drew, he expected some private discussion, but the subject surprised him.

"Chilembwe? I've known him slightly, off and on since the '90s. I first met him with his mentor Joseph Booth, before they went to America – you know that Chilembwe had some training in the United States? How much detail to you want?"

"Tell me all you know."

"Hm – he's an unusual man – a Yao – a disciple of John Booth – you know, the British missionary. Booth wanted to create an African Christian Union in Southern Africa, and he was thinking of buying some of the B&EA land – near here. Booth sought me out – to talk about the potential for a mission farm. I asked him how he expected to find the money to buy the land; he told me that thousands of Africans would subscribe – in pennies. Chilembwe was with him when he visited..."

"What did you think of him?"

"Chilembwe?"

"Yes."

"He seemed very bright – quiet, spoke good English, smartly dressed. I presumed that most of what he'd learned came from association with Booth."

"Did he show any indications of being anti-white?"

Alan pondered. "No, George."

When they were alone like this, they used their first names, at the Governor's insistence, whereas in public Alan addressed him as 'sir'.

"I would not say anti-white. He struck me more as wanting Africans to be on equal terms with the Europeans – not subservient. He said that local Africans had more potential than they were allowed to use. My conversations were mostly with Booth, but I think Chilembwe was present at most of them – Booth encouraged him to express his opinions, and he did."

The two men, walking slowly, crossed a *dambo* – a wide expanse of grassland – where Alan's small herd of beef cattle were grazing, attended by two African herdsmen. Alan called to them to take the herd into their night paddock near the homestead.

"Too many hyenas around to leave them out at night," he said to Smith.

"Was Chilembwe influenced by what was happening in South Africa?" asked the Governor.

"Probably. As I recall, he did not go there – although Booth did – but he must have heard all about it when Booth returned..."

"About what?"

"The African disillusionment. I'm talking of the African Christians that Booth associated with. He told me that they all distrusted the whites – with good reason, I have no doubt."

Alan paused to listen for the characteristic chirruping of guinea-fowls. It had rained the previous night and the bush was full of fresh scents and sounds. He relished afternoons like this, early in the rainy season, spring, when the trees were bursting with new foliage.

"What about Chilembwe's visit to the United States? What do you know about that?"

Alan sensed the Governor's impatience and realised they were unlikely to do much bird shooting on this visit. He guided his guest along a track on the fringe of the dambo, where it was easier for the two men to walk side by side.

"I remember him saying critical things about the situation in the United States – like segregation and lynching. He told me that he and Booth had stones thrown at them for walking together – a black man and a white man, in Virginia. He said it was disappointing that, after slavery had been abolished in America, there was still segregation, and the negroes did not have the vote."

"What did you think of Chilembwe then?"

Alan laughed. "Fifteen years ago? I was intrigued – he was a young man with a rural background who had studied in America. He was interested in education – that's why I met him again. He wanted to see the farm school. I arranged for my manager to show him round. Goodwill talked to the man for longer than I did. Chilembwe came with Jacob Mbalo – I've known Jacob since he was a child – recently returned from slavery."

"Did you entertain Chilembwe?" Smith glanced sideways at his companion.

"Jess and I gave him tea on the verandah."

Smith laughed shortly. "You're certainly different to the typical planter – I mean in your attitude towards the Africans."

Alan shrugged. "Perhaps. I've been fortunate to see the natives in a wide variety of situations, from rural villagers, with negligible exposure to our culture, to educated men like Goodwill – and John Chilembwe. I see no reason to treat them as inferiors. They have different cultures and languages, but their colour does not define them as baser than us."

The Governor grunted, then said, "Did you have any contact with Joseph Booth at that time?"

"Booth and Chilembwe had split up by then. I saw Booth only once, before he joined the Watch Tower movement – you know he was a Seventh Day Adventist?" Alan laughed. "He certainly had a knack for raising money from supporters overseas."

"And Chilembwe?"

"I had the impression that he was not really interested in doctrinal matters – such as the day of the Advent. He struck me as being committed to his 'industrial mission' concept. He invited me and Goodwill to his church at Mbombwe – about four or five years ago. I think he wanted to show us that Africans could build a church and a school, and develop a farm, without European assistance..."

"But not without European funding?"

"Actually, George, I think he got his funding from negro supporters in the United States."

"Very well. Now what about the rebellions in Natal and German East? Did you discuss them with Chilembwe?"

It was growing dark quickly. The prospects of finding guinea fowl had gone, as they would now be seeking their roosts. Alan decided, reluctantly, that they had to head back to the farmhouse.

"The Natal Rebellion was in '06, and the Maji-Maji Rebellion in German East about the same time?"

"Correct."

"Hmm, I've no doubt Chilembwe would know about them, but 'influence'? Do you suspect him of fomenting rebellion?"

"I don't know, Alan, but my nightmare is a native rebellion – especially at a time like this, when our forces are tied up fighting the Germans..."

"Do you suspect Chilembwe of...?"

"I'm hearing that his preaching is seditious. What I have to determine is the degree of risk that he poses – and whether he should be deported."

Alan pondered; they were approaching the homestead, along a farm track, the light failing. "You should speak to Goodwill. His ear is closer to the ground than mine. Besides he talks regularly with Jacob Mbalo – you know, the man I mentioned to you earlier, who escaped from slavery with Goodwill."

The Governor nodded. "I would welcome a meeting."

"Will you stay for a beer – or a whisky? I know you have to get back to Zomba."

"It's six now. If I leave in half an hour that should give me time. We have people coming for dinner at eight."

Alan seated the Governor on the verandah, while Jess brought him a cold beer. One of the servants was sent to fetch Goodwill, who arrived five minutes later, dressed in white shirt and khaki trousers. He was accustomed to discussions with Alan's visitors, and was relaxed greeting the Governor in formal manner, his right arm extended for the handshake, while his left hand held the right forearm. The men remained standing.

"Good evening, sir," said Goodwill.

"Good evening, Goodwill. Thank you for coming to talk to me."

Alan said, "His Excellency is interested in the preaching of John Chilembwe. What have you heard?"

The African did not answer at once. He had expected this enquiry and knew he should tell the *azungu* what he knew, but he was always conscious of being regarded as the white man's poodle. "I have not heard Chilembwe preach myself. I only know what Jacob tells me." Goodwill looked carefully at the Governor. "Jacob is a disciple of Chilembwe, and has been for about ten years. I see him every month – have known him since he was a boy of ten..."

"What does Jacob tell you?" Smith glanced at his watch, frustrated that he was short of time to extract information.

"He is careful not to say too much," replied Goodwill, "even to me. He knows that I speak to Mr Spaight. But he has told me that Chilembwe preaches about the inferior position of Africans compared with Europeans. The minister says Africans should not be treated as inferior; they ought to be allowed to purchase land. He is opposed to the increase in the hut tax – he says that many native people cannot afford to pay it. He is oppósed to *tangata* – you know?"

"The system of tenants working for Europeans to pay their rent."

"Yes, sir."

"Who are his disciples?"

Goodwill shrugged. "I think they are mostly educated men who agree with Chilembwe's views."

"Are they from any particular tribe?"

Goodwill paused and stroked his chin. "Chilembwe is a Yao. Because of that he attracts the *anguru* – the Yao people who have come into this country from Portuguese territory. During the famine – two years ago – they came to him because they were starving. His mission grows food crops, and he has money to buy food, so he was able to feed them."

"Where does he find the money?"

"From his supporters in America."

"Have you heard Jacob speak of Chilembwe's views about... what he would like to change in this country?"

"Hm." Goodwill shifted his weight. "Apart from the hut tax and *tangata*? Hm. Jacob said the minister wants the country to belong to the Africans. The *azumgu* – the Europeans – can stay here if they wish, and to help."

The Governor again looked at his watch. "I had better leave. Thank you, Goodwill. We would like to hear more from you. Don't tell anyone about our meeting."

He shook hands with the African, who then left. "Thanks, Alan. I would like my CID man to come out here to speak with you and Goodwill."

"Malloch?"

"Yes. He'll be in touch with you."

—•—

Three days later, Jock Malloch, the police inspector in charge of the CID branch, came out to the farm. He spoke to Alan first, and then they were joined by Goodwill. They sat at a trestle table in the shade of a *Eucalyptus* tree. The conversation covered much the same topics as with the Governor. Malloch was burly and ginger-haired, with a hearty demeanour. Alan could imagine him propping up the bar after a rugby match.

"Based on what you've heard, Goodwill, what does Chilembwe have to say about the war?"

Goodwill studied the policeman impassively, trying to gauge him, uneasy about all the questioning. He respected Alan's judgement, but he did not want other people, like this visitor, to spread the word that he was an informer.

"Jacob says the minister is opposed to the use of African soldiers in the war. Chilembwe says the war was made by the *azungu*, and they should not recruit Africans to do their fighting – and to carry their weapons."

"Has he said whether he will try to stop the recruiting?"

Goodwill shook his head. "From what Jacob says, I think the minister is critical, but not wanting to take an active role."

"I hope you're right." Malloch turned to Alan. "Have you seen that church of his?"

Alan nodded. "He invited me and Goodwill to see it. I was impressed – not so much because of the architecture, but thinking of how much it must have cost. It's said that Chilembwe built a brick church because Bill Livingstone burned down his other churches..."

Malloch coughed. "Because they were built on the Bruce Estates. He did not want Chilembwe preaching anti-white rubbish on his own property."

"On property that he managed," Alan corrected mildly. "But one of the burned down churches was on Government land, outside the Bruce Estates."

Malloch did not reply, but said to Goodwill. "I want you to find out anything you can through your friend Jacob Mbalo. We think the minister, Chilembwe, might be preaching against the Government. Anyone who hears this, and does not tell us, is in serious trouble. If you hear anything, you must inform Mr Spaight, and he will contact me."

As an afterthought, Malloch interrupted his departure.

"You're an educated man, Goodwill. What do you think about Chilembwe's view?"

"About what, sir?"

"About the African position in this country?"

Goodwill coughed, feeling uneasy about the line of questioning. "We Africans do not have the education and experience to manage a country." He paused, watching Malloch nod. "But in years ahead there may be sufficient of us. The *azungu* can show us how to do it – how to run the government departments, the Treasury, the laws and courts. Then it will be right for us to be in charge – for it is our country."

—•—

Goodwill came to speak to Alan one morning after the farm labour had been allocated their tasks. They walked side by side to a place where they could not be overheard.

"Sir," Goodwill said, "I am concerned about Jacob Mbalo. He would like to marry one of my daughters, but I have not encouraged it."

"What does he tell you?"

"About Chilembwe? He says Chilembwe does not like the *azungu*. He preaches that they have taken all the land, leaving nothing for the local people. He says the *anguru* are badly treated..."

"But they are not local people."

"No, sir, but there are many of them working on the Bruce Estates."

"And what does Chilembwe plan? Is he trying to... to get his followers to take up violence?"

"I don't know, sir. But he preaches sermons that make his followers very angry about their situation."

"Hmm. Look, Goodwill, see if you can find out more from Jacob. Question him carefully, but don't let him know that you are digging for information. In the meantime, I will report what you have said to the authorities."

—•—

After discussing the matter with Jess, Alan went to see Jock Malloch, who then took him to the Chief Secretary, Hector Duff. They sat in Duff's office drinking tea.

"Thanks for bringing me this information, Alan," said Duff. "We've been keeping an eye on Chilembwe. I've had discussions with Bill Livingstone about the man's activities on the Bruce Estates. Between ourselves, Chilembwe wrote a letter to the Nyasaland Times about his countrymen 'shedding their blood in a cause that was not theirs'. Needless to say, the letter was not published, and H.E. has almost decided to deport Chilembwe and some of his henchmen. Don't mention this to anyone, but we're trying to find a suitable spot to send him to."

Alan asked, "Do you have any evidence that he's plotting anything – like a rebellion."

Duff laughed. "We have plenty of hearsay evidence, and we don't need any more, because we're under the equivalent of martial law. We can't take any chances."

—•—

16

Cape Town, South Africa – November 1914

Roly watched the surgeon approaching, with his retinue of junior doctors. He had met Mr Louis Viljoen several times and liked him. The surgeon was jovial and confident, much preferable, Roly thought, to an ascetic uncommunicative type. He had heard that Viljoen was hugely experienced in facio-maxilliary surgery, after treating soldiers wounded in the Boer War. He now had an international reputation.

"Good morning, Roly," said Viljoen heartily. "Thumbs up if you're feeling good."

Roly turned his right thumb up, but made it waver a little.

"That's good." The surgeon turned to the junior doctors. "Now, gentlemen. We have here Captain Roland Benting-Smith, who was wounded by the Germans in Nyasaland, in September. Dr Roberts, please tell us the nature of his wound."

A short, thin young man, wearing spectacles, cleared his throat nervously, glancing at notes on a clip board. "Sir, a bullet struck the patient's mandible a glancing blow, and then ruptured the maxillary artery before exiting at the angle. The mandible was broken and some of the teeth dislodged. The temporamanibular joints appear to be damaged."

"What was the immediate effect on the patient – Dr van Heerden?"

A tall man standing at the back of the group shuffled forward. His English was spoken with a strong guttural accent. "He was rendered unconscious for over twenty-four hours. He was in considerable pain and was administered sedatives. He has been receiving water and food through a feeding tube. He has lost weight, but otherwise seems to be in good health."

"Hm." Mr Viljoen looked at Roly. "Is there anything you would like to add? Two fingers for 'no'; one for 'yes'."

Roly held up two fingers. He knew that the surgeon would now propose his course of treatment.

"What Roberts and van Heerden did not mention is that the captain's jaw has become mis-aligned. This was a result of it becoming unhinged. We need to re-align the jaw, but we may not be able to repair the damage to the joints." He looked sharply at the group of young doctors. "What about the missing teeth?"

A burly red-faced young man blurted. "Surely they aren't important at this stage, sir?"

"Quite right, Massey. I'm glad you can think clearer here than on the rugby field."

A ripple of laughter followed, and Dr Massey flushed.

"Yes," added Viljoen. "We can deal with his teeth when the mandible and joints have been repaired. However, I have asked Mr Williamson, our dental surgeon, to attend the operations." He glanced down at Roly. "I expect Roly would like to know how long this will take." Looking back at the doctors he asked, "Any suggestions?"

Roberts held up his hand and the surgeon nodded. "A week or so of preparation. Three weeks for the hinges and re-alignment breaks to heal – say four to six weeks."

"Good, Roberts. You mentioned re-alignment breaks. What did you mean?"

"Sir, the mandible has started knitting in the wrong alignment. It may have to be deliberately fractured to... er, straighten it."

"That's correct. Now, gentlemen, we haven't discussed the outer wound along the jaw. I think there is sufficient skin to draw across and seal it."

He turned abruptly. "Let us move on, but before we do, remember that we need to discuss the anaesthetics – I do not want to bore the patient with those details."

—•—

Roly was tempted to write to Mandy, but decided to address the letter to the Spaight family.

Dear Mr and Mrs Spaight, and Mandy, Kirsty, Mac and Drew,

I wanted to thank you for looking after me when I was in transit, on my way down here. Special thanks to Mandy, for caring for me in Karonga, and on the voyage down to Fort Johnston. I regret that I cannot remember any of it, Mandy, but I've been told that you were the perfect nurse. I do remember a little about Fort Johnston hospital and seeing both Mandy and Kirsty there. The ambulance journey to Limbe was very uncomfortable, and I remember thinking I would have been better off in a machila! I do remember you, Mr and Mrs Spaight, visiting me in Limbe, before I was put on the train – so good of you to take the trouble.

The journey to Cape Town seemed to take forever, although it was only four days. I was starting to be more aware of what was happening, but it also meant the headaches were worse. I must not complain. I know I was extremely lucky not to be killed at Karonga.

The Somerset Hospital where I am now a patient is at Green Point, but I have been confined to my bed, so I might be anywhere. My surgeon is Louis Viljoen, who has a great reputation – according to the nurses. His wife is Pauline (née Venter), who you have met (I think). The family are friends of the Russell family, with whom you stayed, Mandy and Kirsty.

Mr Viljoen will do some operations to repair my jaw. He says it will be several months before I can go back to normal life, which I hope means I can continue my Army career.

My mother has threatened to come here – she would have come earlier but my father was not well. We know some people – the Fountaines – who are in Cape Town, and she will stay with them.

This letter has been all about me. I trust that you are all well. I follow the news, but it is mostly about Europe and South-West Africa, so it is not easy to find out what is happening in Nyasaland. In fact, most people here have not heard of the military events in your country!

This letter has been written for me by a very kind lady, who volunteers to visit the ward.

My best wishes to you all,

Roly Benting-Smith

—•—

On the following day Roly saw his mother advancing down the ward with a young nurse scurrying behind her. He was both pleased and apprehensive to see her. She had written to say that she would come to Cape Town on the next available liner, and would stay with her old friends the Fountaines, who lived in Claremont. General Fountaine was on the British High Commissioner's staff, and moved between Pretoria and Cape Town. Their daughter, Emily, lived with them, while their son was on active duty in France.

"Roland, darling!" she brayed. "You look like an Egyptian mummy. You poor thing. Can you speak? No? Then how can we communicate? You can write on the slate? Wonderful. I dare not kiss you..."

"No, please, Mrs Benting-Smith!" said the nurse. "We have to be very careful not to bump his head."

"Of course." She settled her ample self on the small chair beside the bed. "What a terrible thing to happen, you poor boy; and at the very beginning of this awful war. They tell me that they will perform an operation to repair your jaw..."

Roly started to write on his slate and his mother watched him. The nurse moved away to attend to other patients. Mrs Benting-Smith waited and then read from the slate when Roly handed it to her. *"I am very lucky. The bullet might have killed me. Tell me about the family."*

She gave him news about his father and his siblings in England. Then she told him about the Fountaines and their friends, until he became tired, when the nurse came to escort her away.

—•—

Two weeks later Mrs Benting-Smith returned to England, and a few days after her departure Roly opened his eyes to see a woman of about fifty sitting on the chair beside his bed, and behind her a young woman.

"I'm Betty Fountaine," said the woman. "Do you remember me? I'm a friend of your mother. And this is my daughter, Emily; I think you knew each other several years ago."

He did recognise Mrs Fountaine. She was quite tall, with a matronly build. Her pale English complexion showed signs of recent sunburn. Her accent was upper-class English, and she seemed to be in good humour.

By contrast, Emily looked bored, casting glances around the ward. She was undoubtedly pretty, her small slim figure enhanced by proximity to her large mother. Recognition grew quickly as he remembered talking to her at parties when he was at Sandhurst; he supposed she was a schoolgirl then. He danced with her a couple of times, and their height difference was awkward.

"Your mother told me you don't like visitors?"

He pointed to his jaw, then wrote on his slate, *"Please stay."*

"Alright, we will. I understand you were wounded in Nyasaland. We visited there before the war – stayed with the Governor – his wife is an old friend of mine. We know a family that farms there, don't we Emily? Their name is Spaight. I don't suppose you know them?"

Roly tried to exclaim but made an embarrassing mewing sound. He scribbled, *"I was H.E.'s ADC, Know the Spaights well."*

"Fancy that. Emily went out shooting at their farm. She got to know Drew Spaight quite well."

Roly looked at Emily, who appeared to be paying no attention to the conversation, and was watching a new patient entering the ward.

"We hope you will come to stay with us, young man – when you are discharged from this hospital."

—•—

He came round after the operation with a fearsome headache. His head was encased in a metal cage with rods extending to his skull and jaws, which could be screwed to hold it tight. He knew that the contraption was to ensure that the re-alignment of his jaw and skull were not disturbed. The pain was excruciating.

When Mr Viljoen and his retinue came round they pronounced themselves pleased with the operation and the aftermath. "We'll prescribe some painkiller for the meantime," said the surgeon, and moved to the next patient.

Roly's neighbour was a newcomer – the nurses told him that he was a soldier who was wounded in British East Africa. Further details emerged gradually; he was a corporal in the South African Artillery, and his lower jaw had been mangled when the limber of a field gun broke and bashed into him. The mess of flesh, bones and teeth had become septic, and the field doctor, in desperation, cut the whole thing away. Now, all that was left was a gaping hole, exposing the unfortunate man's throat.

Roly could hear Mr Viljoen explain at length how he planned to take lengths of cartilage from the ribs of the patient and use them to reconstruct the jaw. He would then graft skin over the cartilage, to restore some of the shape of the man's face, even though the jaws might not articulate well.

"Because we have no local skin, we will take a tube of living skin from the patient's shoulder; when the graft has taken it will be separated."

Roly dozed off while the doctors droned on about mucous skin for the unfortunate man's mouth lining. He realised that despite his own tribulations he was much luckier than the soldier in the bed next to him.

—•—

Betty Fountaine and Emily visited Roly at least once a week, watching the slow healing process, and listened to his attempts to speak. Eventually, the metal cage was removed, and he was able to start making noises, at first incomprehensible, but with the help of his therapist developing into speech. Emily took growing interest in his recovery and became particularly adept at interpreting his noises.

After two months he was walking in the ward and then in the grounds of the hospital. One day he saw Mrs Fountaine and Emily approaching, with a grey-haired army officer, who introduced himself as General Fountaine.

The General shook hands with Roly, eyeing him judiciously. "I hear you have made a good recovery, Captain – Roly? Will you be able to return to the army?"

"Oh yes, sir. I hope so. They say in two or three months." Roly's voice was still rasping and fitful. "I might have to do only light duties."

"It's commendable that you should wish to return to active service, my boy. I'm sure your military experience will be valuable somewhere."

The general indicated that they should walk side by side along the path. In front of them rose the massive Table Mountain, on which rain clouds were shredding like tearing cloth, sending curtains of rain across the steep escarpments.

"I'm so sorry about your wounding," said the General. "I hope you will regard it as a badge of honour. You will be able to tell your children and your grandchildren about the battle." He paused.

"You know, Roly, there was a certain nobility in past great wars – the storming of the castles in the Peninsular, the stoic defences at Borodino, the enduring squares at Waterloo, Pickett's Charge at Gettysburg – even the great battles of the South African War. But from what I've seen and heard there's precious little nobility in this war. What about your particular battle?"

"It was a scrappy affair, sir," Roly croaked. "However, I believe the defence in the town was noble. Just a few volunteers and civilians, some of them women, supported by KAR *askaris* – heavily outnumbered."

"Indeed? I look forward to hearing more – when it is more comfortable for you to talk." He shook Roly by the hand. "I will tell General Smuts and General Northey about you. I'm confident they will find a role for you."

—•—

17

Shire Highlands, Nyasaland – January 1915

Shortly before dusk Mac Spaight rode out to Duncan MacCormick's house on his motor-cycle. The young section manager on the Bruce Estates had asked for help with his own bike, which was giving trouble starting. Although they were not friends, meeting only at NVR training sessions, MacCormick suggested that Mac spend the night.

It was warm and humid; clouds heavy with rain drifted gloomily above, threatening a downpour. Mac listened to the pulse of his bike's engine, peering ahead as the light faded. He switched on the headlight and the beam juddered as the bike bumped along the corrugations on the dirt farm road to the manager's house.

It was a Triumph Type H, with a 499 cc air-cooled four-stroke engine, a belt drive and Sturmey-Archer three-speed gearbox. Mac's father had an earlier model, the Type A, and taught him how to take the bike apart and re-assemble it, and how to de-carbonise the engine and grind in the valves. The bikes were much modified, including the front fork springs, strengthened for the rough roads on the farms.

—•—

"What's the problem?" asked Mac, after they shook hands.

"She's a beast to start in the early morning."

Mac frowned. "Mm. Could be condensation on the spark plugs. Try wiping the connection with a warm dry cloth. Could be the carburettor. Let's look at the petrol."

He turned off the tap and disconnected the fuel lead, then drew off some petrol into a glass tumbler brought from the house by MacCormick. He held up the glass to a paraffin light on the verandah.

"Looks as if you've got water in the petrol. Better strain it all."

MacCormick nodded. "Thanks, Mac. Come and have some grub."

"I will, but I won't stay after."

—•—

Kate Livingstone called from the bathroom, "Bill, I forgot to put the cat out; please do it for me."

She stepped into an oval zinc tub, earlier filled by their servant with a couple of four-gallon tins of hot water. It was one of her luxuries, immersing herself in the hot water, scented with the smoke of blue-gums. Habitually she would mull over the happenings of the day, and make plans for the next

Her husband, William (Bill) Jervis Livingstone, was a distant relative of the famous missionary explorer. They lived in a modest house on the Magomero section of the Bruce Estates, where Bill was the General Manager of the vast farming enterprise owned by Alan Spaight's friend Alexander Bruce, himself a grandson of David Livingstone.

Bill Livingstone had a reputation for arrogance and bad temper, and for mistreating his labourers, many of whom were *anguru*, immigrants from Portuguese East Africa. That evening the Livingstones had a house guest, Agnes MacDonald, a friend of Kate's, who had gone to bed after supper. Now Bill was on the bed in his pyjamas, playing with his little daughter Mary; the baby was in its crib.

No sooner had she entered the tub than Kate heard her husband shout; five year old Mary started to wail. Seconds later she heard a series of thumps. Alarmed, she climbed out of the bath and pulled on a thin cotton dressing gown.

When Bill Livingstone opened the front door he was confronted by a gang of Africans. Their eyes were wide and frenzied, their sweat-soaked skin glistening in the light from the room. Forcing their way in they lunged at him with spears. He shouted at them, retreating into the bedroom, where his rifle was kept. Blood from his wounds streamed over his face and chest.

"Kate, take the children and run!" he shouted hoarsely as he grabbed his rifle. It was not loaded, so he wielded it as club to defend himself.

Some of the assailants rushed past him and caught hold of Kate, forcing her to sit in a chair, where they held her down. She watched in horror as her husband was beaten to his knees. He was held strongly by his assailants, one of whom chopped savagely at his neck with a small axe until he was decapitated. This man picked up the bloody head and threw it onto Kate's lap. Standing beside her, little Mary watched, stupefied, her clothes spattered with her father's blood.

From the guest bedroom Agnes heard the sounds of the assault and guessed that something awful was happening. Opening her window she saw about a dozen Africans gathered round the front of the house, shouting and brandishing spears. She called to her servant, who was in the quarters at the rear of the house; he came in through the back door.

"Help me," she whispered, indicating that she wished to clamber through the window.

He supported her as she struggled up to the sill, then swung her legs out and dropped to the ground. She took a moment for her eyes to adjust to the dark, and then tried to see whether she had been spotted, but the group of Africans at the front of the house did not notice her. She slipped away into the night.

—•—

While Mac was having supper with MacCormick the houseboy and cook both came into the dining room in a state of agitation. They looked at each other, waiting for one to speak, shifting their feet.

"What's the matter?" MacCormick asked, irritated at the intrusion.

"*Bwana*, there is trouble at *Bwana* Liston's house," stuttered the houseboy, his eyes wide.

MacCormick sighed wearily. "What trouble?"

"Some men are attacking his house..."

"What men?" He stood up, alarm growing.

"Chilembwe's men."

Both MacCormick and his visitor knew that Chilembwe was the upstart minister with the big brick church, but they still thought this was more likely to be a labour dispute, a not infrequent occurrence on the estate.

"I'll go and see what's the matter," said MacCormick.

"Well, I'll head home. Thanks for supper."

"Thanks for coming, Mac. I'll clean up the petrol."

MacCormick set off, not bothering to take any weapon. It was a short walk to the Livingstone's house. He could hear a clamouring noise and thought the labour must be excited about some issue – probably wages. Meanwhile, Mac Spaight started his motor-cycle, the sound drowning the noise of the crowd at Livingtone's house; he rode off in the opposite direction.

One of the group of Africans attacking the Livingstone house noticed MacCormick's approach and warned the others, even though the white man was unarmed. They hid behind the house until he reached the front porch. Then they rushed out, shouting, and stabbed him to death.

—•—

Chilembwe's men pulled Kate and her children out of the house, allowing her to carry her infant son, while Mary trotted beside her mother, holding the sleeve of her dressing gown. One of the men brought Bill's head from the house and stuck it on a pole. They all headed for the nearby house of the estate engineer, John Roach.

"Why have you people attacked us?" asked the distraught woman, trying to stay calm for the sake of her children.

"We are killing all the *azungu*," was the reply in English, from a man who held her.

"Only the men," corrected another. "You women and children will not be harmed."

In a loud voice she said, in ChiNyanja, "We sent one of our men to call the soldiers. They will bring their big guns."

On hearing this her captors stopped to parley, arguing excitedly. Some of them went off, while the main group continued towards the Roach house. Kate knew that John Roach was away in Blantyre, but his wife Alice was at home, with her sister-in-law, Emily Stanton, visiting from Zomba.

When they reached the house Kate watched anxiously as the rebels broke in and roughly pulled out Alice and Emily, with the three Roach children, who were wailing in terror.

"What's happening?" shouted Alice above the hubbub.

"They've killed Bill," answered Kate, breaking down and sobbing for the first time. Her strong Scottish temperament had finally given way. Alice and Emily hugged her and brought the children into a collective embrace, terrified for their lives, though Katherine assured them the assailants were killing only men.

When the rebels came out of the house, having searched in vain for John Roach, they brought with them two rifles and several boxes of ammunition. They also gathered up the house servants, placing them in a group with the white women and children.

—•—

About five miles away, on a further section of the Bruce estates, another manager and Scot named John Robertson, was locking his house before going to bed. His wife tidied the dining room after supper; the servants had already left the house. The couple heard a loud banging on the front door.

"Who is it?" called Robertson.

"Come to the door, *bwana*," was the reply from outside. "We have something to tell you."

"What is it, dear?" asked Mrs Robertson from behind him.

"It's probably the *alonda* – the night watchman – again," replied Robertson.

He lifted the latch on the front door of the house and started to open it. Suddenly a spear was thrust in, cutting his arm and plunging into his chest. He staggered back, pushing the door shut in the process. His wife ran to his side.

"Oh, Lord, John!" She gently pulled the spear out and pressed his shirt against the wound to stem the flow of blood.

Pulling his wife back to the bedroom, Robertson gasped, "There must be a whole gang of them out there. Listen to the commotion." He waved towards the cupboard. "Get me my rifles, and a box of cartridges. You have to load for me...my arm." He indicated that his wounded arm was useless.

—•—

Another estate house stood a hundred yards from the Robertsons, where the livestock manager, another Scot, named Robert Ferguson, was reading his mail in his bedroom. Suddenly, his door burst open and a group of African men attacked him with spears; one was thrust into his chest. He managed to struggle away and flee through the back door. His first thought was to hurry to his neighbours, the Robertsons. Staggering the short distance, he almost instinctively used the back door, thus avoiding the main mob of assailants who had retreated from Robertson's front door into the bush at the perimeter of the garden.

Meanwhile, John Robertson was firing at the rebels from the windows of his house using two rifles, while his wife crouched behind him, re-loading. The thatch on the roof had been set alight by Chilembwe's men and smoke started to seep into the house.

"We have to get out," muttered Robertson to his wife.

She nodded, then turned in alarm as she heard groaning at the back door. Ferguson stumbled into the house, a spear protruding from his chest. Stifling a scream she hurried to help him, pulling out the spear and supporting him onto the sofa in the living room. She could tell that he was in his last throes, but did not want to draw her husband away from his firing position at the window. She held Ferguson's limp wrist and searched for a pulse.

"Is he alright?" asked Robertson.

"I'm afraid not. The poor man has died."

"We must get out – the back way!"

The Robertsons hurried out through their back door, John carrying the two rifles, and his wife the ammunition. They headed for the outside kitchen, a grass hut, detached from the main house. They found, cowering inside, Joseph, their house servant.

"If this roof catches fire were done for," said Robertson. "Go and see what's happening, Joseph. Come back and tell me how many there are."

Joseph was terrified and did not move.

"Come on, man. They won't harm you, because you're an African."

He half pushed the reluctant Joseph out of the door, and watched as his servant crept round the side of the house. Suddenly, a group of Africans came out of the darkness and attacked Joseph, stabbing him with their spears.

"Oh Lord! We must make a run for it," said Robertson. "Come on!"

They ran out, taking the opposite direction from the unfortunate Joseph. Soon they were away from the light from the burning house and in semi-darkness, stumbling through a field of waist high cotton and into the bush beyond. Looking back they could see their assailants watching the house go up in flames.

"Aren't you going to shoot at the devils?"

"No," said Robertson. "It will give our position away. They think we've perished in the house. We must wait here, then go to seek help at Magomero."

—•—

The Robertsons waited, shivering in their night clothes, and two hours later were confident that their attackers had dispersed. They set off along a path leading to the main estate compound at Magomero. There were several small groups of huts along the route, which they passed through cautiously; the inhabitants were all asleep. The path eventually brought them out to the main Blantyre-Zomba road. In the first light of dawn they could see three Africans coming along the road.

"*Peta kuti?*" asked Robertson. "Where are you going?"

They did not reply, but looked sullenly at the dishevelled white couple. Robertson repeated his question, and when they did not reply he raised his rifle. The three men regarded him truculently, so he shot one of them and killed him. The other two fled.

"I think we should go to Zomba," said Mrs Robertson. "There's no sense in going to Magomero."

Robertson nodded. "Are you alright? Can you keep going?"

"I'll do."

They set off, and half an hour later saw a European man on a horse coming towards them, a planter named Kemper, whose *Namiwawa* estate was alongside the main road. He was shocked at the appearance of the Scottish couple, who wore tattered nightclothes spattered with blood, and were plainly exhausted.

"What in heaven has happened to you?" asked Kemper.

"We were attacked by a mob of Africans. They killed Ferguson."

"My God! That's terrible. My servants told me that something was happening. That's why I came out. They said that the Livingstones were attacked. Did you hear that?"

"Yes," replied Robertson. "Look, Kemper, why don't you ride to Zomba and tell them what has happened..."

"And leave you?"

"Of course. We can look after ourselves. I have two rifles. You go ahead."

"Very well." Kemper wheeled his horse round and cantered down the dirt verge of the road towards Zomba.

—•—

That same night a group of John Chilembwe's followers, led by John Kufa, headed towards Blantyre. Their objective was to plunder the African Lakes Corporation's weapons store. Unlike the rebels who attacked the isolated houses at the Bruce estates, this contingent headed into the heart of the country's main town. This fact was brought home to them when they heard raucous noises coming from the Blantyre Sports Club, where a large group of Europeans had congregated, many of them drinking in the bar. They knew nothing of the evening's attacks at the Bruce estates, because the rebels had cut the telephone wires between Blantyre and Zomba.

Kufa's gang were seen by two *alondas*, one of whom they shot and killed. The gunshots alerted the Europeans at the club, who came out of the building. One of them started up a large single-cylinder motor-cycle, and the rebels thought the sound came from a machine gun. Many of them bolted into the night, while the remainder broke into the Mandala store, escaping with three Martini-Enfield rifles and two Snider rifles, as well as some ammunition.

—•—

During the night John Chilembwe stayed at his Providence Industrial Mission church with a few of his senior lieutenants, including Jacob Mbalo. Also with Chilembwe was his wife Ida.

"I wish we knew what is happening," Chilembwe muttered to his wife as he paced up and down; they usually conversed in English. "This waiting is trying me."

"We will hear soon," said Ida. Although she supported her husband, she now had grave doubts about the actions that were being taken that night.

Chilembwe turned to Jacob. "Go outside and see if any messengers are coming."

He continued his pacing, while his wife watched with growing apprehension. She feared that the edifice of their large brick church would be destroyed. Chilembwe, too, was concerned. He had no doubts about the cause: to bring down the Europeans who, he thought, were exploiting the local Africans. His concern was whether sufficient Africans would support the rebellion.

Jacob returned, shaking his head. "There is no sign of any messenger." He watched Chilembwe's expression, admiring the minister's apparent calm demeanour.

An hour later John Kufa came into the church, blinking in the light of the lamps, his face glistening with sweat.

"What happened?" asked Chilembwe, trying to contain his anxiety.

"We attacked the Mandala store. We stole some rifles..."

"Have all of you returned?"

Kufa shook his head. "We left five behind. One of them was cut by glass when we broke the window of the store."

"Then the Europeans know about our rebellion." He now knew that retribution would soon follow. "What about the others? Did they kill the estate managers?"

"I heard that Mr and Mrs Robertson escaped and have gone to Zomba," replied Kufa.

Chilembwe frowned. "Did no one try to stop them?"

"Robertson had two rifles." Kufa was uncharacteristically ruffled. "What shall we do? It will not be long before the *askaris* come from Zomba. Do you think they will attack us?"

Their conversation was interrupted by a commotion outside. One of the rebel leaders, Abraham Chimba, entered the church, followed by several of his group. He carried a wooden stake, at the end of which was Bill Livingstone's head. He held the pole towards Chilembwe, as an offering.

The minister looked in disgust at the bloody head, with its tangled hair and beard. The dull dead eyes gazed at him, as if rebuking.

"Were others killed?" he asked.

"Ferguson and MacCormick."

"Is that all?"

Chimba nodded. "We took the women and children with us. They are at Maniwa's house."

"They must be brought here. I want them to be here when the authorities come. I want to show them that we killed only the men."

"They will punish us," said Kufa gloomily. "Even if we killed one man our fate is sealed. Only if our brothers come out to fight with us will we be saved."

—•—

18

Shire Highlands, Nyasaland – January 1915

On the morning after the attacks the Spaights were having tea on the verandah at *Khundalila,* discussing the progress of the war, and the probable whereabouts of Drew and the girls.

The dogs started barking, their hackles raised, and Mac went down the front steps. An African messenger, wearing a government khaki uniform approached cautiously on a bicycle, clearly nervous of the intentions of the Ridgeback hounds, who reluctantly drew away when Mac called them. The messenger, sweating heavily, handed over an envelope bearing the Governor's crest. Inside was a letter requesting Alan's presence at Government House – 'Serious native uprising in Magomero District. Come with the utmost urgency and bring rifle.'

"Very enigmatic," he said to Jess as they went out to the garage where he kept his motor-cycle.

"I was at Magomero yesterday evening," said Mac. "There was some trouble at the Livingstone's house. MacCormick thought it was a labour dispute."

Alan nodded. "It may be nothing more than that." He turned to Jess. "I hate to leave you alone, if there's trouble brewing among the Africans. Will you come in to Zomba and stay there?"

"Where would I stay?" She smiled. "Would I be any safer there? Mac's here and I'll keep the dogs near me – and a rifle." She patted him on the shoulder as he mounted the bike. "For heaven's sake be careful, darling."

Mac had mixed emotions, watching his father ride off. A local uprising might be an opportunity to prove that he could be a worthwhile fighter, and he relished the prospect of punishing rebels. At the same time he was deeply concerned about his mother's safety. Although she was not his biological mother he had known her all his life; she was integrated in all his earliest memories. Any feelings of love that he could muster were for her.

He respected his father, as the man who adopted him, recognising that Alan did not favour his biological son, Drew. Even so, Mac was intensely jealous of Drew, for his stature and good looks, and his natural ability to attract women. The older brother was frustrated because he had never had a girl friend. He knew his physical disabilities were a perpetual obstacle, despite all the reassurances of his family.

He was consumed with lustful desires, some of which were directed to his sisters. Before they went to Rhodesia he would spy on them whenever he had an opportunity. He enlarged a knothole in the outer door of their bathroom, through which he watched them. He could do this only after dark, and the girls usually bathed in the late afternoon when they came back from riding on the farm. Perhaps once a week they would take a bath after dark and he would stand outside the door in a fever of excitement. Sometimes they would undress and bathe alone; on other occasions they would be together, talking to each other.

After these occasions he would return to his room, enveloped in guilt that he tried to mitigate by telling himself that the girls were not really his sisters, since both his dead parents were not theirs.

—•—

Alan rode as quickly as he could into Zomba, covering the five miles in just over seven minutes. After signing the guest book at the gate he parked the Triumph near the *port cochere* at Government House. He was soon seated at the large table in the meeting room, with the Governor at the head. Captain Triscott of the KAR shook his hand as he sat down. They knew each other slightly; Alan had always thought him rather pompous, but now he seemed subdued. Also present were the Chief Secretary, the Chiradzulu District Officer and the Superintendent of Police.

The meeting had already been in progress intermittently for several hours, with participants coming and going. They were now discussing retaliatory action. The Governor had an ashtray beside him, on which a cigarette burned. He also had a cup of coffee, and Alan noticed that others had cups or mugs. As if he had read his mind, the Governor said, "Help yourself to some coffee." He nodded to the jug on the sideboard. "We won't allow any servants in."

Then he added, "Alan, I thank you for coming. News is trickling through to us about an uprising that occurred last night. It seems that dozens of natives attacked the Bruce Estate compounds, and another large group went to attack the Mandala arsenal in Blantyre. Three Europeans were killed in the Bruce compounds, and some women and children were taken captive. The attack at Blantyre failed. Hector will give you more details." The Governor slumped back in his seat wearily.

The Chief Secretary, Hector Duff, went to a map on the wall and turned to face Alan. His sallow face was shining with perspiration, and Alan wondered whether he was feeling any guilt for not having foreseen this uprising.

"I'm getting information all the time from my district officials," said Duff. "Chilembwe's church, as you probably know, is here at Mbombwe, south of the Bruce Estates. As far as we know, three groups of natives left the church compound. The first went to the European managers' houses at Magomero, where ten Europeans were in residence – this was at about nine o'clock last night. One gang broke into Bill Livingstone's house, killed him, but spared his wife and two children. They had a friend, a Mrs Macdonald staying with them, and she escaped through a window with a servant and fled. Mrs Livingstone and her children were taken away on foot – we don't know where they are. Livingstone was decapitated and his head was carried to Chilembwe's church on the end of a pole."

A murmur of horror rose from the men circled round the table, but they did not interrupt. The Chief Secretary went on: "A Mr MacCormick, who was one of the farm assistants, was killed by the gang. Another gang went to Mwanje, here." He pointed out the compound within the Bruce Estates. "There were two European men there; one was killed – Ferguson – the other – Robertson – escaped with his wife."

"A third, larger, group of natives left Chilembwe's church, apparently with the intention of capturing the armoury in the Mandala compound at Blantyre. They were only able to steal a few rifles and a few hundred rounds of ammunition before they were disturbed and fled."

"Excuse me," said Alan. "What is being done to deal with these people?"

The Governor cleared his throat. "We're coming to that. As you know, we have a skeleton garrison of KAR here in Zomba – mostly recruits – and they must remain here, to guard the Secretariat and the power station. I sent a telegram to Karonga asking for a company of 1/KAR to be sent here as soon as possible. Alan, I would be grateful if you would round up as many of your NVR men as you can find, and send them with Captain Triscott to Chiradzulu. He will take some of his KAR *askaris*. They must capture or kill these rebels. I want you to come back here."

Alan asked. "Have there been any incidents on other estates? I presume they attacked the managers of the Bruce Estates because they are nearby, but is there any evidence of intention to attack others?"

Hector Duff cleared his throat. "Actually, we haven't heard of other incidents."

After a few more exchanges the meeting dispersed.

Alan went outside with Triscott. "There are hardly any of us left, Lionel," he said. "As you know, virtually all the NVR members are up north at Karonga and Fife. I might be able to find a dozen or so old lags. Where do you want them to meet you?"

"What about the *boma* at Chiradzulu – at noon. Can they make it by then?"

"They'll be there. I'll send my son Mac, and as many more as I can find."

"Whatever." Triscott, as a regular army officer seconded to the KAR had little regard for the NVR. In his opinion they were a ragtag of under-trained and overweight settlers.

They shook hands and parted. Alan and Mac spent the several hours riding their motor-cycles to houses in and near Zomba, and sending messages to estates between Zomba and Chiradzulu.

—•—

John Chilembwe held a celebratory service in his big brick church at Mbombwe. On a table beside the altar, resting on a metal dish, was the dishevelled, bloodstained head of Bill Livingstone. After its journey from Magomero, spiked on a pole, it looked distinctly the worse for wear. The congregation of Chilembwe's followers could not take their eyes off it, even as they listened to their leader preach about their need to be brave and resolute.

Meanwhile, Kate Livingstone and her children, who had spent a night of exhaustion at Maniwa's house, were on the move again, walking hurriedly towards Mbombwe. They had been treated with courtesy, and had received *nsima* to eat and water to drink, but they feared an uncertain fate.

—•—

Mac was exhilarated as he limped along beside Triscott towards Mbombwe, but self-conscious about his disability. The dirt track was wide enough for carts and they could have ridden their motor-cycles along it, but they were afraid that the noise would alert the rebels.

He was apprehensive about the platoon of KAR recruits strung out behind them. Would they turn on the Europeans and support the rebels? Would they wilt and flee under fire?

The column came to a stream; the road crossing was a crude bridge of logs. Triscott halted them, afraid that they would be too exposed if they crossed.

"There they are!" came a barely muted whisper from an NVR man. "Bastards!"

Mac saw them a moment later, dark figures lurking among the trees on the far side. Between them and the stream was a maize field, the plants growing from little hills of soil – the customary system of cultivation used by Africans. As he watched the rebels started to move forward. Evidently they had seen the posse, because they started to fire; the dull reports were distinctive of their muzzle loading guns.

"Fire!" shouted Triscott.

Bullets crashed through the foliage of the trees along the bank of the stream, their only cover. Mac stooped and moved sideways, trying to find a tree that was large enough to stand behind. He found an *mbawa* with a trunk at least five feet in diameter and clipped the harness along his arm and around his wrist, feeling the tension and strength from the metal rods. Holding his rifle against the tree he peered ahead.

The rebels were not easy to see, strung out about a hundred yards away, and offering only glimpses as they shuffled forward. Be patient, he said to himself, and waited for several minutes. Then he saw a man in a stained khaki jacket creeping on hands and knees through the maize plants towards an anthill. He brought the foresight onto the man and squeezed the trigger. The man fell over and lay still.

"Got you!" Mac muttered. He glanced sideways and saw Triscott beckoning to him. Mac shook his head, thinking that he was in a good position and did not want to be moved.

The KAR officer crawled towards him and said. "I'm going to call it off." Triscott was panting, wiping sweat from his face as he sat with his back to the tree. "We're running short of ammo..."

"How can that be? We've barely started."

"I issued six rounds to each man."

Mac frowned as he groaned. "Didn't you trust them?"

"That's right. I didn't." Triscott peered round the tree, then signalled to the KAR bugler, who sounded the retreat.

"We'll go back to Chiradzulu," said Triscott. "We'll come back tomorrow morning."

"They'll be gone by then." Mac could not conceal the irritation in his voice.

"Perhaps. Will you come with us?"

"I'm going back to the farm tonight."

—•—

On the following morning Mac set off with the intention of re-joining Triscott's posse of KAR *askaris* and NVR men, at Chiradzulu. As he approached Zomba he was waved down by an African messenger who gave him a note. It was from Major Stevens, commanding the NVR while Alan Spaight was attached to the Governor. The message asked Mac to proceed at once to Mikalongwe, where he was to help an NVR section heading south-east towards Fort Lister.

It took him over an hour to reach Mikalongwe, where he heard that two motor cycles were broken down on the rough road ahead. They were not far from each other, one with a broken wheel, and the other with a twisted front shock absorber. He told the men there was nothing he could do to repair the bikes in the bush, so they were loaded onto a bullock cart and sent back to Blantyre.

One of the motor-cyclists was a NVR corporal named Hayter, who Mac knew slightly – a farm assistant from Cholo – who said, "Let's go on to Fort Lister. We've heard that Chilembwe is heading for Portuguese territory. Maybe we can catch him before he gets there?"

Mac nodded and pointed to his pillion. The other NVR man looked dismayed. "What about me?"

Mac twiddled his fingers to indicate that he should walk, then mounted his Triumph and kick-started it.

—•—

On reaching the *boma* at Fort Lister they found three uniformed NVR volunteers with the District Officer. These men had strengthened the fortifications, and piled sandbags around the office buildings. Patrols of African policemen were being sent out to investigate alleged sightings of rebels in the district. It was rumoured that two natives in European clothes had been seen.

That night the European men congregated in the DO's house; he was a bachelor, a nervous Englishman, younger than Mac, and only too happy to have company. They grilled chickens on the barbecue in the garden – a half oil drum with a metal mesh, fuelled with locally-made charcoal. A liberal supply of beer was found and after supper they sat round the fire swapping yarns.

"Jimmy," said Hayter to his friend the DO. "Tell them the story about the lion you tracked..."

The young man nodded and the others fell silent. The only sound came from the crackling of the fire, and the darkness seemed to draw in on them. At the same time, night sounds started: birds squawking in their roots, a querulous call from a young hyena, a jackal's yelp.

"I was called out a couple of months ago, because a lion was killing villagers' cattle. They said it was an evil spirit – of an ancestor who was unhappy. I organised a beat through the place where it had its last kill, and we flushed it out. I had a good shot, and couldn't understand how I missed. The natives said it was a 'spirit' lion."

He took a long draught from his bottle of beer. "Anyway, we followed it next day and came across fresh tracks. The villagers were very excited and nervous, because they said it might jump out of the bush at any moment. I had my best tracker in front and I was just behind him. The lion spoor was quite distinct – it hadn't rained for several days and the paths were dusty."

"Suddenly, my tracker stopped.'Look at this, *bwana*,' he said – he was shaking like a leaf. I looked down to where he was pointing, and I could see the lion spoor. 'What's the matter?' I said. 'Look here,' he pointed further up the path, and then I saw that the lion's spoor faded out and were replaced by a man's footprints!"

"Go on, Jimmy; you don't expect us to believe that!" Several men guffawed.

The DO went on. "I'm only telling you what I saw. The tracker said the lion had turned into a man. I couldn't see any more lion prints, only the large footprints of a man. 'We must find him,' I said. But my tracker did not want to go on – I had to bribe him, and eventually he moved forward again. I looked ahead as I followed him, and about ten minutes later I saw the figure of a man; he was tall and skinny. 'We must catch him,' I said, and we hurried along the path."

"The man was about a hundred yards ahead and he went around a bend. When I got there he had disappeared. We pushed on and came to a *dambo*, and there was a lion ahead of us. It looked round at us and then slipped into the long grass. I looked down at the man's footprints and they had disappeared; only the lion spoor was there."

—•—

Early next morning Mac was working on the motor-cycle of another NVR man, tuning the engine, when an African policeman rode into the compound on a bicycle and announced that a patrol had found some rebels and killed them. There was immediate speculation that one of the rebels was John Chilembwe.

Hayter said, "We'd better get there as soon as we can. You can ride along the paths, Mac; take me on the pillion – my bike's useless."

Mac nodded, wiping his hands. "This policeman will have to show us the way, we'll follow him."

He instructed the constable to cycle only on paths that were wide enough to take the motor-cycle, and they set off. The motor-cycle was much faster than the pedal bicycle, but Mac had to slow down frequently to negotiate rough places, where there were stones and rocks on the path. At *dongas* they had to dismount and manhandle the motor-cycle, while the policeman waited for them.

It was near noon when they came to a group of Africans standing in the shade of a grove of trees near the path. They propped the motor-cycle and walked cautiously forward, Mac with his revolver in hand.

"You talk to them," said Hayter. "Your ChiNyanja is much better than mine. Ask them to show us the man they think is Chilembwe, because I know him."

Mac greeted the Africans and a police lance-corporal came forward. "I am Mandanda. We have shot two rebel men." He pointed to a tree, under which were the two bodies.

Mac and Hayter walked to the corpses, lying on their backs, flies buzzing round them, sipping moisture from the dead men's eyes. They were dressed in European clothes: long trousers, white long-sleeved shirts, and black shoes. One of them had a bullet wound in the head. The other had a large patch of congealed blood on his chest, suggesting that it had been his fatal wound.

"That's him alright," announced Hayter, pointing to the smaller of the two bodies. "Ask them what happened."

The policemen, three of them, came forward. Mac questioned them and translated for Hayter. "They were following footprints – shoes – which struck them as strange, because the local natives don't wear shoes.

Then they saw these men ahead and called for them to stop, but they fired back with a rifle – that one." The weapon was lying beside the bodies. "The policemen fired back and killed – this fellow – not Chilembwe, who continued running. They chased him for another mile and then they exchanged shots, killing him. They brought the bodies back here."

"We had better bury them now," said Hayter. "Their bodies may be needed for enquiries. Get them to dig a grave – large enough for both bodies."

Mac instructed the policemen, who called to some villagers; they brought *badzas* to dig the grave under a large tree that would serve as a landmark. Hayter cut a cross in the bark. The villagers laid the bodies in the grave and re-filled it with earth, then piled rocks on top, to prevent hyenas from digging up the corpses.

—•—

Goodwill was woken by furtive knocking on his front door. Always a light sleeper he sat up to listen again, thinking it might be one of the labourers in trouble.

"Who is it?" His voice was rasping.

"Jacob," came the faint reply.

Goodwill opened the door and let him in, looking carefully behind in the moonlight to see if there were others. "Are you alone?"

"Yes." They always spoke in English, because they both spoke the language fluently, and found it easier to express themselves."

"Come." Goodwill lit a hurricane lamp and saw that his friend was in a dishevelled state, his clothes covered in dust, his sandals caked with mud. "Do you want food? I could heat some *nsima*."

Jacob shook his head. "I am in great trouble, *bambo*." He had always called Goodwill by the ChiNyanja word for 'father'. He started to weep.

Goodwill put his hand round Jacob's shoulder. "Sit down; tell me about it."

Goodwill's wife, Sheila, came out of the small bedroom, rubbing her eyes, and he said, "It is Jacob. Go back to sleep..." She turned and left without a word.

The older man said, "We're you involved in the murder of those Europeans – the *azungu*?"

"No!" It came from Jacob as a quiet wail. "As soon as I heard John Chilembwe speak of it I ran away."

"Where did you go? Can you prove it?"

"I wanted to come here, but there were *azungu* using the roads, searching for disciples of John. I went to stay with a friend in Domasi..."

"One of Chilembwe's people?"

"No. But he was afraid to be associated with me – so I had to leave..."

"Where is Chilembwe?"

"He ran away. I heard he was killed."

"How did you hear that?"

"I heard two *azungu* talking in Zomba – I was hiding by the side of the road. One of them said, 'We've got the bastard.'" Jacob started to weep again.

"That could mean that he was captured."

"No. They then said that he had been killed by a police constable, near Fort Lister." Jacob started shaking uncontrollably. "These men said that they would find any man who was a disciple of John Chilembwe and put them in front of a firing squad – or 'string them up'. I know that means they will hang me."

"Jacob, Jacob," said Goodwill soothingly. "Not if you could prove that you left Chilembwe when he advocated killing the *azungu*."

Jacob started to rock back and forth, wailing pitifully. "*Eee, bambo*. They will hang me. They do not have a trial; they ask a few questions, and then..."

"I will try to help you..."

"No." Jacob stood up. "I must leave. I do not want them to see you associating with me."

"Sit down! They know I am not Chilembwe's man. Bwana Spaight would protect me..."

"He is not here, is he? I heard he had gone to Fort Johnston."

"Yes, but *Dona* Spaight is here." Goodwill pondered. Better to wait till morning. "I will speak to her in the morning. Drink some water and sleep." He gave Jacob a blanket.

—•—

Goodwill went to the big house in the early morning, when he knew Jess would be having tea on the verandah. She saw him approach and her heart started to beat rapidly for a moment, until she reminded herself that she could trust this man. She had known him for so many years. He was not one of Chilembwe's men.

They greeted each other, the African standing at the foot of the steps leading up to the verandah. Then Goodwill told her Jacob's story.

"If the *azungu* find Jacob they will hang him," he said.

"Not without a trial, and he can prove that he ran away."

Goodwill shook his head. "No, *dona*. They do not have a proper trial – just a few questions."

Jess thought about who could help her. With Alan away, she knew she could approach the Governor, or Major Stevens, but she did not want to bother them, knowing of their heavy work load. David Casson, the Superintendent of Native Affairs was an acquaintance, and she decided to go to see him.

"Keep Jacob out of sight," she instructed. "Don't let anyone know he's here. I will go to Zomba and speak to a friend."

—•—

"Jess! How nice to see you," said Casson, beaming. "Do sit down." He waved her to a chair. "To what do I owe the pleasure of your visit? No, first tell me about Alan. I hear he went to Fort Johnston?"

Jess sat down, thinking that, in this small town, everyone knew what was going on. She faced the Superintendent across his desk, which was littered with papers and files. He was an imposing man, with large intelligent eyes, and a deep voice.

"It must be worrying for you. By the way, Jess, why didn't you Spaights come into our *laager*? We worried about you. I think it's all fizzled out, though. Did you hear – Chilembwe was killed."

"Really? It would have been better to have tried him?"

"Perhaps not. Better he's not seen as a martyr." Casson looked at his loaded desk and then up at Jess. "How can I help you?"

She told him about Jacob and his expression grew serious. "David," she said, "there's no doubt that he was a disciple of Chilembwe, but he needs a chance to prove that he left when there was talk of killing Europeans."

Casson nodded. "I'm trying to put a stop to these kangaroo courts. It's almost as bad as American lynching. But we have to take this man Jacob into custody. And you can't be seen harbouring a rebel on the farm – or at least, that's how it might be seen."

"Can you promise me that he'll be given a fair trial?"

"No promises, Jess, but I'll do my best."

—•—

On the verandah of the KAR mess, uniformed soldiers, some of them South Africans, were drinking beer. On the far side of the parade ground they could see the scaffold where the rebels were hanged. They knew the authorities had had difficulty finding a hangman, and the current incumbent was evidently not very efficient. His victims took a long time to die, and this became the subject for some macabre gambling.

"There's three of them still kicking," said a large sweating sergeant. "I'm putting my money on the one at the end. What about you fellows."

"He's too big, Sarge," said the corporal beside him. "I'll go with that small one in the middle, with the red socks."

"All right. Anyone for the begger next to mine?" rasped the sergeant. "You, Jepson. Very good. Shillings in the pot. Where's the man with the binoculars?"

Another soldier stood behind them. He studied the line of six Africans dangling from the scaffold, to see any movement. "The one with the socks has stopped. That leaves yours, Sarge, and...Oo, the little man did a jig for us, but now he's stopped. Looks like the money's yours, Sarge. No, wait a minute. The little man is still jiggling."

"Someone should put an end to it," said another NCO. "They should be pulled after the drop."

"What now?" asked the corporal. "Is my man still moving?"

The man with the binoculars shook his head. "Sarge wins."

They cheered ironically, and the sergeant pocketed his shillings, saying, "It won't be long before we have another wager. They're rounding them up fast."

—•—

The young District Officer sat facing three Africans across a wooden table. His height, and his pressed white shirt and khaki shorts, contrasted with the small figures of the three African men, standing with their hands manacled behind their backs, wearing ragged dirty clothes, their faces shaded with dust, so that the whites of their eyes were emphasised. Beside the white man was an African interpreter, short and officious, and standing behind the three plaintiffs was a taciturn black corporal of the KAR, in splendid starched khaki uniform.

Casson ambled up to the table. "Williams? I didn't know you had been assigned to these trials. When did you get back from the front?"

"Two weeks ago, sir. I'm better now." He was somewhat irritated by the senior man's appearance. He wanted to get the trial over and go away for the weekend with friends. The three men in front of him were plainly guilty and destined for the rope.

"So you'll be going back to the front?"

"Yes, sir. I expect so – when the doctor gives me the nod."

"Well don't let me interrupt you."

Williams turned to the Africans and addressed them together in halting ChiNyanja. "Did you know John Chilembwe?"

They nodded hesitantly.

He asked in English, "Did you follow Chilembwe?"

The interpreter repeated the question in ChiNyanja. This time none of the men moved. They gaped at the interpreter as if he had spoken a foreign language."

"*Kudziwa?* Understand?" asked the DO impatiently.

The men nodded slowly.

"Which one of you is Jacob Mbala?" asked Casson in English.

Jacob raised his hand.

"You speak English?"

"Yes, *bwana*." Jacob smiled timidly.

"Do you know the other two men?

"I have seen them before, but I cannot remember where."

"Their names were on a list in the church office at Mbombwe – as was yours. That means you were followers of John Chilembwe."

"I know nothing about these men," repeated Jacob. "I worked for John..."

"For how long?" Casson was now the sole questioner, and the interpreter was not needed.

"Three years, *bwana*."

"Did you hear him order his followers to kill the white men?"

"Yes, *bwana*, but..."

"Ask the others," instructed Casson to the interpreter, who repeated the question in ChiNyanja.

The other two men shook their heads.

"Send them back to the remand prison for further questioning," said Casson to the DO.

The young man stood up. "Sir, I have orders to convict any African who is on the list found in Chilembwe's church. I have a copy of the list here." He held up a sheet of paper. "The names of these three men are on the list."

Casson beckoned to the DO and led him round to the far side of the verandah. The two men faced each other, Casson calm and commanding, the DO red in the face, perspiring.

"The fact that they attended Chilembwe's services does not mean that they are guilty of insurrection," said Casson. "We need to find out how closely they were associated with the man. I don't think this is the right forum for such investigation. I will instruct the CID to question them."

"What about the other man – Jacob what's-his-name?" The DO's tone was belligerent.

"He's different," replied Casson calmly. "He's known to me. I intend to question him myself."

—•—

"Look at this." Alan handed a letter to Jess. They were sitting on the verandah, after breakfast, reading the newspaper and mail.

"It's from Casson – about Jacob."

Jess read the letter:

Dear Alan and Jess,

I hope this finds you well. I felt I should tell you that I've failed to get the Chief Justice to commute the

sentence of Jacob Mbalo. I know you both felt he was not implicated in the rebellion, but the evidence of his association with Chilembwe was too compelling. He will be executed next Friday.
Yours aye,
Donald Casson
Senior Native Superintendent

Tears welled in Jess's eyes as she handed the letter back to her husband. "Is there anything we can do?"

He shook his head slowly and called to a house servant to fetch Goodwill. "We can't challenge a ruling of the Chief Justice. They obviously have a lot of evidence."

He stood up and poured a cup of tea for Jess and handed it to her. Looking out at the driveway he saw Goodwill approaching. What would he think? The old fellow was always rather inscrutable.

"Come up," he invited Goodwill to the verandah and waved him to a chair. Goodwill bowed to Jess and sat down.

"I've had a letter saying that Jacob is to be executed – hanged – because of his association with Chilembwe."

Goodwill looked at Jess and she shook her head. "I am sorry to hear that, sir. I truly believe that Jacob would not be involved in killing people. He told me so, and I believe him."

"Yes, but I'm afraid there's too much evidence that he was with Chilembwe when plans were being made. He did not warn the authorities, so they assume that he was a participant."

"Can you do anything, sir?"

"I'm afraid not. Mrs Spaight tried, and I cannot argue against the judgement."

Goodwill bowed his head, and when he looked up there were tears in his eyes. Alan was shocked, because he had never seen the African display much emotion.

"He was a little boy," said Goodwill, "about ten years old. The slavers left him by the path, because he was too sick to walk. Kawa and I tried to give him shelter and food, but we were captured by villagers. Luckily, they were friendly, and the women nursed Jacob to health. I watched him grow up and receive a good education, become a Christian. It is sad that he joined Chilembwe's church, but we did not know there was anything wrong until about two years ago. Jacob was unhappy about the way the minister was preaching, but he admired him."

He stood up. "It is sad. I would like to see him before he is hanged."

"Be careful," said Jess. "They may think you have some link to the rebels."

"I cannot let him die without words from a friend."

"Will you let me come with you?" said Alan. "I can try to arrange it. I know the authorities – the Chief Justice and the Superintendent of Native Affairs."

Goodwill nodded. "Thank you, sir."

—•—

Goodwill was permitted to say goodbye to Jacob for ten minutes, on condition that he was accompanied by Alan Spaight, who was required to ensure that there was no political discussion. The severity of the punishments for the rebellion were such that this concession was wrung from the government by Alan with difficulty.

They were shown into the cell in the Zomba jail, where Jacob sat on a low cot, his head in his hands, a diminished man, in a grey prison uniform. He stood up and hugged Goodwill, then thanked Alan for coming.

"Your faith in God will give you strength," said Alan.

Goodwill spoke to his friend in low tones. Jacob had lost his family when taken by the slavers, and he regarded Goodwill and Kawa as his elder brothers.

"Do not be afraid, Jacob. You know you have not done wrong, and God knows it. You will find peace in heaven, and you will meet your father and your mother, and your brothers and sisters. In time, Kawa and I will come to join you, with our families and we will be happy together."

Jacob nodded as tears streamed down his cheeks. Then the guard signalled that it was time for the visit to end. Alan patted Jacob on the shoulder and turned to leave. When Goodwill joined him in the passage they walked out together in silence to the car.

"Will they be cruel?" asked Goodwill when they were driving back to the farm.

"No. A minister will say a prayer with him, because he's a Christian. Then it's quick and efficient. It will be over before he has time to wonder what's happening."

Goodwill nodded, as if satisfied.

—•—

19

Lake Nyasa – May 1915

Gavin Henderson swam slowly down into the translucent depths. Around him darted golden-bronze and peacock-blue fishes – hundreds of chiclids, glinting in the beams of sunlight that penetrated the water. But he was not watching the fishes. Above him was Kirsty, drifting around the pillar of rock. Her long black hair swirled as she languidly moved. Her limbs were whiter that her swimming costume, and swept the inquisitive fishes away. She turned to look down towards him, smiled and beckoned, then faced the surface, drifting up.

He waited, knowing he had another half minute of air in his lungs, watching her reach the rock, her white legs dangling. She pulled herself out. He was alone with the fishes, the water warm and caressing, heavy as it slid around his limbs. Then the light faded as the sun went behind a cloud and the fishes darted away as he swept up to the surface.

The rock was ten yards away, Kirsty standing on it, her wet costume clinging to her body. She was looking beyond him and waved to him, beckoning. He wanted one more dive and flipped over to head down.

Kirsty had seen a hippo blow about two hundred yards away. She knew that this lumbering creature could be dangerous for swimmers, especially if there was a calf with it. Gavin had not understood her signal, so she dove in towards him. At first she could not see him; then his elongated shape appeared below her; he was about ten feet from the surface. The floor of the lake was ten feet further down, a plain beige surface with a few scattered stones. She swam down to him, caught his arm and pointed upwards. At first he tried to hold her in an amorous embrace, then he saw the alarm in her expression and released her. They struggled to the surface together.

Gavin scrambled onto the rock, grazing his shin; he bent to pull her up, effortlessly, noticing blood in the water. The rough granite surface was quite flat and about the size of a billiard table. The painter of their sailing boat was wedged in a crevice, and the boat bobbed about ten feet away; its sails lowered and lying unfurled in the hull.

"There it is!" Kirsty pointed to the puff of spray where the hippo had exhaled. It was only fifty yards away. "It's coming straight towards us."

"Surely it can't harm us." Gavin was slightly amused at her agitation.

"If it has a calf with it…" She gazed intently at the calm surface of the lake. She wore a white camisole bathing dress that left most of her legs bare. Her skin was white, because she had been taught by her parents to minimize exposure to the harsh African sun.

"Oh!" she squealed, and drew back as the hippo surfaced just feet away from the rock.

Its small glinting eyes regarded them, seemingly without malice. Gavin thought the creature's huge eyelashes were extraordinary. It snorted and rose out of the water. For a moment he thought it would try to clamber onto the rock, but it turned and rammed into the dinghy. The painter stretched and snapped; the boat scudded a few yards. This seemed to enrage the hippo. It opened its huge mouth and lunged at the dinghy, clamping onto the gunwale, which snapped with a loud report. The hippo snorted again and disappeared.

Gavin and Kirsty watched in silence, side by side. He could feel the girl shivering and hugged her closer. After a few minutes he said, "I think it's gone."

"I was so scared." She started to cry with the release of tension, but soon stopped. "The boat's drifting away."

"I'll get it." He prepared to dive in, but she restrained him.

"Wait until we're sure it's gone."

They scanned the surface of the lake, but it was nearly ten minutes before they saw the tell-tale puff of spray in the distance.

He swam to the dinghy and saw, to his dismay that it was filling with water. The hippo's huge teeth had crushed the gunwale and penetrated the hull in several places. He grabbed the painter and started towing the boat towards the rock. As it sank lower in the water it became heavier to pull. By the time he reached the rock he was exhausted and the dinghy was sinking.

"Catch the painter in the crevice," he shouted to Kirsty as he threw it to her, but she was too late. It slipped from her grasp and the little boat disappeared under the water.

Gavin lay on the warm rock trying to get his breath back. He knew the water was about twenty feet deep, and the painter was much shorter than that. There was a spare halyard in a locker near the stern. If he could tie that to the painter the combined length would reach the surface. Would they be strong enough to pull the dinghy up? Even if they could, how could they prevent it from sinking?

"Pa and Mandy will start worrying soon," said Kirsty. "We said we'd be back by four." She looked at the sun and said, "It must be about that now."

"There's no way they can come to find us, is there?"

"There's the old dugout that Pa uses for fishing, but it would take an hour or longer to get here."

Gavin looked towards the shore; it was about five hundred yards away. "We could swim to the shore, but then what would we do?"

"It's all reeds and thick bush. It would take ages to get back to the house."

He turned to her and looked into her troubled eyes. "Don't worry, sweetheart. We'll be alright. Even if we have to spend the night here, we'll be safe."

She smiled, but said nothing. He announced, "I'm going to pull the boat up. Actually, we're going to pull it up together." He explained how he would join the spare halyard to the painter.

"But it'll just sink again."

"I have a plan to plug the leaks." He stood up. "Wish me luck."

She watched as he dove in. She could see him clearly as he reached the dinghy and started to open the locker. He pulled out the halyard and brought it to the end of the painter before he ran out of oxygen and had to come up to the surface. He grinned at her, took a deep breath and went down again. She watched him tie the rope ends together, then he brought the end to the surface.

"We have to lift her gently, because she's a dead weight, and we don't want the line to break. When we get her to the surface we must pull the bows up onto the rock here. That'll hold her from sinking until I can make her watertight."

They stood together and pulled carefully. It was exhausting work, but Gavin was immensely strong. It took them nearly twenty minutes, but finally the bow of the dinghy emerged and they dragged the forward half of it onto the surface of the rock. There were several holes made by the hippo's teeth, and the fractured gunwale left a fissure stretching half way to the keel.

Gavin unfastened the mainsail and wrapped it around the outside of the hull, tying it into position with the halyard. He tore up his shirt and used the pieces to plug the holes. "The water pressure will hold the material against the hull."

"Won't the water leak through the sail?" asked Kirsty.

"It will, but slowly. I hope we can bale faster than it leaks in."

"And what are you going to bale with?"

He laughed. "My hat."

It was not the ideal receptacle, but he had plenty of energy. As he baled out the water in the hull it started to float. He climbed in and watched the water seep slowly through the material of the sail, gratified to see that the rate was within their control. He rigged the jib, and helped Kirsty aboard.

The slight breeze was from the east, on their beam, but they made slow progress because of the dragging effect of the material round the hull. Kirsty took the helm, while Gavin knelt to bale out water with his hat. She watched the muscles working in his broad shining back and wanted to touch them.

Half an hour later they rounded a rocky headland and saw the house. As they drew closer they saw Alan standing near the shore. Gavin beached the dinghy and went forward with Kirsty, who hugged her father. In a rush of words she told him what had happened, while he listened gravely, his expression full of concern.

"You were both fortunate that the hippo did not harm you," said Alan. "Someone was watching over you."

"And very resourceful of Gavin, wasn't it" said Kirsty, "to get the dinghy afloat?"

Goodwill came to join them. He greeted them and Alan told him what had happened. He said nothing, but his large eyes seemed to absorb everything as he examined the damage, while Gavin unwrapped the sail from the hull.

Goodwill clucked his tongue. "*Mvu* can be very savage," he said quietly.

Gavin and Goodwill pulled the dinghy further up the beach, Gavin remembering that one had to be careful of the seiches on the Lake, when wind from a certain direction piled the water up, like a tide. There were no recordings on Lake Nyasa, but he knew that they could reach several feet on the Great Lakes in America.

"We'll have it carried up to the shed tomorrow," said Alan. "Come along you two. You must be exhausted after your adventure."

—•—

20

Nyasaland, the Northern Front – June/July 1915

A War Council meeting was held at Government House in Zomba, with members of Legco and Captain Barton, KAR, who had been awarded a DSO for his leadership at the Battle of Karonga. Sir George Smith, the Governor, chaired the meeting, sitting at the head of the large meeting table, a cigarette ever present. Alan smoked his pipe; a fan pushed all the smoke through an open window.

"Our communications with the forces on the northern front are at risk," he said. "The telegraph line from Abercorn to Karonga, along the Stevenson Road, is extremely vulnerable. What can we do?" He looked expectantly at Captain Barton.

The young officer cleared his throat. "Sir, we don't have enough men to defend the telegraph line – we can barely patrol it. We can't use radios because the signals are not strong enough – the terrain is too mountainous."

"What about heliographs?"

"They need the sun, and there's risk of interception."

"We could use runners if the line is cut," suggested Alan.

"Hm – terribly slow," said the Governor. "It's about two hundred miles from Abercorn to Karonga, isn't it? That means it would take at least four or five days to get messages through. And how would they carry the messages?"

Barton replied. "In coded letters."

"In a forked stick?"

Alan waited for the laughter to subside, and then said, "If we could make the road passable to motor-cycles we could use dispatch riders. But that wouldn't work if the Germans occupied any section of the road..."

"Wouldn't a bike make too much noise?" asked Barton. "The Huns would hear the exhaust from far away."

"True, but my son Mac has done a lot of work to modify the silencers – with success. If we can't use bikes, then runners would have to be used, because they could circle round any German-occupied sections of the road."

The Governor looked at him hard. "Alan, I want you to send a couple of NVR men to work this out. I wish I could send you, but you're too valuable to me here. I think your son Drew would be ideal. He rides all over the place on his bike and he knows how to look after himself in the bush."

As Alan left the meeting the Governor put his hand on his shoulder. "These are difficult times."

Alan nodded, distracted at the thought of Drew going to the front; he felt his guts sinking. The task would be very dangerous, with German patrols likely to intercept any traffic on the border road. But he had to agree with the Governor that Drew would be a good choice.

—•—

Alan gave Drew his orders at the farm. "Son, you have to take your bike and go, with Goodwill, by lake steamer to Karonga; then make your way to Abercorn, where you will report to Colonel Hodson. You can discuss with him the options for communications and proceed from there. I presume you'll be attached to the Northern Rhodesia Regiment or the Northern Rhodesia Police, but the Governor will ensure that you'll retain your rank of Lieutenant."

"What about Goodwill? Will he be seconded to the army?"

"Yes. If he agrees to go – and I won't force him – he will be made a sergeant in the KAR."

Drew laughed. "I wonder what he'll think of that – Sergeant Goodwill." Then his expression clouded. "Pa," he started, then stopped.

Alan put his hand on his son's shoulder. "I wish you didn't have to go to war. Your mother and I will worry about you until you come home safe?"

"Pa, I want to tell you something. I'm not afraid now. But I'm afraid of being afraid. Do you know what I mean? I don't want to be a coward – I don't want others to see that I'm terrified."

"It's normal to be afraid. I was, when I was in the fights against the slavers. And before that I was almost paralysed with fear when the dervishes broke into our square at the Battle of Tofrek."

Drew nodded and swallowed. "Let's see what Mac can do to make the bike run even quieter.

The two men went out to the garage and discussed their options with Mac, who was plainly annoyed that his brother had been chosen to go north. With a shrug he suggested splitting the single exhaust pipe into two, each with a longer muffler casing.

"It will reduce the efficiency of the engine," he said. "I would think the power would be reduced by about a third. Could be a problem?"

Drew laughed. "Making too much noise would be a greater problem."

—•—

The modified exhaust was a great success. The bike's customary roar was reduced to a masculine mutter. When Drew rode it round the farm he sensed the reduced power from the 500 cc engine, but he was able to take Goodwill on the pillion as well as saddle bags filled with provisions. Mac strengthened the front forks and the back struts, and collected spare parts in a wooden box that could be shipped with the bike to Karonga.

"Wish I could go with Drew," said Mac, when he was alone with his father, "even as his mechanic."

"You're much too useful here," Alan replied. "The Governor says it's essential that we keep producing food, and export crops – and employing labour."

"But I'll feel rather useless."

Alan turned serious. "Look, Mac, one of us has to stay behind. We can't leave your mother on her own, even if one of the girls came back – and there doesn't seem much prospect of that."

—•—

The *Domira* steamed up the lake with Drew and Goodwill on board. Their voyage was uneventful, but made more interesting for Drew when Goodwill told him the details about his involvement in the fights against the slavers, culminating in the capture and execution of the most notorious slaver, Mlozi.

At Karonga they were greeted by Mr Webb, who provided them with accommodation, Drew in the new government rest house, and Goodwill in the African messenger's lines. They spent the day after their arrival preparing the motor-cycle and testing it, much to the interest of the inhabitants of the town, none of whom had seen a motor-cycle as quiet as this.

They set off on the following morning along the Stevenson road, first across the narrow littoral plain, and then winding up through the hills to Chirenje Mission. Each man had a .303 Lee-Enfield rifle slung across the shoulder, and Drew a Webley revolver in a holster at his side.

Goodwill enjoyed riding on the back of the bike, where he was quite comfortable, though a bit cold, because it was mid-winter and the sun was barely up. He was apprehensive about the prospect of encountering a German patrol, because Mr Webb had said that it was possible that German-trained *askaris,* or *ruga rugas* – armed levies, or mercenaries – might be patrolling across the road.

At Chirenje they were given a simple meal at the mission station, and filled the tank of the bike with petrol, from a store kept by one of the missionaries who used a similar machine and was intrigued by their modifications.

Drew's bike stood up well to the rough road. He rode very carefully, averaging only fifteen miles an hour. Their next stop was Fife, a government *boma* about half way between Karonga and Abercorn. The road in this section wound through mountainous countryside; in many places it had been washed away in the rainy season. The looming war and manpower shortages prevented maintenance being completed. In many places temporary 'corduroy' crossings were built with tree trunks and branches across depressions and stream beds.

Reaching Fife by early afternoon they were greeted by the District Officer, wearing a moth-eaten sweater over his khaki suit. Drew accepted his invitation to spend the night, rather than embark on the uninhabited eighty miles stretch of road to Saisi, the next *boma*.

"Have you seen or heard anything of the Germans?" asked Drew.

"Not yet," replied their host, a very young man, just out from England. Drew thought him too inexperienced and uncertain to be in command of this important outpost.

"I suppose they're not far away," he continued. "We hope to have some *askaris* sent here. I've pulled in my four policemen – from their posts in the bush – and we have two more here. That gives us seven rifles, and I have another hunting rifle. Not much, is it?"

"I see you've started to fortify the place."

The young man shrugged. "I'm trying. We've made some sandbags. I don't know much about how to do it. Can you give me any suggestions?" He seemed almost in a daze, overwhelmed by the work that was needed.

They walked around the compound, which consisted of a group of office buildings and storerooms, built with kiln-fired bricks and roofed with corrugated iron, covered with thatching grass to keep it cooler. The DO house and the guest house were to one side, and on the other were small houses for the African staff. The bush had been cleared for about a hundred yards around, and beyond that the open forest stretched away on all sides.

"I suggest you extend the clearing," said Drew, "to five hundred yards at least..."

"There's not much labour here," replied the DO. "It will take weeks to do what you suggest."

"You can make a start. You could cut and burn the trees. The main thing is to be able to see the enemy at the furthest limit of your firing."

Drew ate supper with him, then retired to the guest house, where he found Goodwill standing outside, with his rifle and belongings, a blanket round his shoulders.

"Haven't they given you a room to sleep in?" Drew asked.

"It is very dirty, *bwana*. I will sleep on the ground out here." Goodwill indicated the beaten earth of the lean-to porch outside the guest house."

"It's too cold, Goodwill. Come inside."

A servant had laid a fire in the living room of the guest house. They lit it, and Drew helped Goodwill to fold the reed mat that served as the room's carpet into a makeshift mattress, on which the African placed his blanket. Drew then went to his own room; feeling reassured that he would have a companion if they were attacked during the night.

They breakfasted next morning, Drew with the DO, and Goodwill with the African policemen, before setting off for Saisi. The countryside was much flatter here, on the high plateau between the two great lakes, at an altitude of around five thousand feet. The *miombo* forest was open, with visibility of a hundred yards or more, except where a *dambo* opened even wider vistas. It was only in these stretches of grassland that they saw game animals – waterbuck, reedbuck, and wild pigs rooting.

Drew was able to coax the bike along at low revs, to conserve fuel and reduce the noise. They had a routine for slowing the bike as they approached low spots, and then walking it across the corduroys of logs and branches.

It was after one of these crossings that Goodwill tapped Drew on the shoulder and pointed ahead. A group of Africans stood beside the road in the shade of a large tree. Drew could see that they carried spears, but he was not sure if they had guns. His heart started pounding as he took in their dishevelled and menacing appearance.

"I'll go and talk to them," said Goodwill. "Wait here."

Drew propped the bike on its stand and squatted behind it. He placed his rifle on the saddle of the bike and aimed to cover Goodwill as he strolled towards the men, who were about a hundred yards away.

To Drew's disgust he realised that he was shaking. Although a good shot, he knew his aim would be thrown out by his uncontrollable movements. I'm shit scared, he thought to himself, and it's probably just a bunch of local villagers. What's the matter with me?

After about five minutes talking to the men Goodwill returned. He seemed very calm. "They are hunters. They say they have not seen or heard the Germans."

"How did you talk to them – what language?"

"They are *WaTumbuku*, but I spoke to them in *ChiSwahili*."

They set off again, waving to the hunters as they passed, Drew hugely relieved that he had not encountered a German patrol.

It took another four hours to reach the *boma* at Saisi, a group of farm buildings and offices similar to the one at Fife. The DO here turned out to be a former schoolmate of Drew's; they had been pupils together at Prince Edward School in Salisbury. He was a rather lugubrious young man, dark and lanky, who introduced his assistant, a young trainee, whose face was beaded with perspiration. It was obvious that they were both very nervous about the possibility of an attack.

Before having lunch Drew walked with them round the compound. The buildings were on the south side of the Karonga-Abercorn road, and the telegraph line, which followed the general route of the road, passed through the complex. The DO was thus able to send and receive telegrams to and from Abercorn, twenty-five miles away, as well as to Karonga.

"The Germans have a base at Bismarcksburg," he said gloomily. "That's on the shore of Lake Tanganyika, only twenty miles north of Abercorn. Just a matter of time before they attack in strength. They have lots of Europeans, and hundreds of well-trained *askaris*, as well as mercenaries – and they have artillery pieces. We don't stand a chance."

Drew shared his concern, but patted him on the shoulder encouragingly. "We'll get reinforcements from Kasama, and the Rhodesians will send men here. We may even get some South Africans."

"They had better hurry." The DO was not reassured.

—•—

Drew and Goodwill rode on to Abercorn, where they were greeted by the Provincial Commissioner and Col Hodson, who were both impressed with Goodwill's credentials to recruit and train messengers.

"I think it's an excellent idea to have a team of runners to go between here and Karonga," said Hodson. "It'll be difficult for them, because they'll have to stay off the track to avoid being ambushed. I doubt your motor-cycle would be safe to use, Spaight, except perhaps between here and Saisi."

Hodson and the PC had already organised a defensive *laager* of breast-high sandbag walls around the main buildings in the little town. Half a dozen European farmers and their families lived in the *laager*, now being stocked with food and water. All the native policemen had been ordered in from their outlying stations.

"We had sixteen rifles before you arrived," said the PC. "Now we have eighteen. Not enough. Those reinforcements had better hurry."

—•—

Drew returned to Saisi two weeks later, on his way back to Karonga. He found the *boma* had been transformed by a detachment of Northern Rhodesia Police under Major O'Sullevan. A network of trenches and earth barricades now made the place quite defensible. The Major sent patrols into German territory, where they encountered so many of the enemy they thought it just a matter of time before the Germans attacked Saisi.

"Tell me about yourself," said O'Sullevan, an affable Irishman in his mid-thirties with sleek black hair and long moustaches. He proffered a mug of tea to Drew as they sat at a trestle table in the mess dining hall.

Drew told him how his father had appointed him to investigate the use of runners on the Stevenson Road. "Colonel Hodson thought it was a good idea, too."

"Did he?" O'Sullevan smiled and glanced at his adjutant, Patrick Brien, who sat with them, a file of papers in front of him. "So, how many runners have you recruited?"

"Two, sir – so far."

"And where are they now?"

"Here, sir. In the compound. My sergeant is training them."

"Is he, by God? Well we may have to use them. The Huns have cut the telegraph lines. I need to get a message to Abercorn and this damned rain makes the heliographs useless."

O'Sullevan looked at Drew hard, making him feel quite uncomfortable.

"Do you speak any African language? And I don't mean 'Boy, bring me some tea'."

"I speak ChiNyanja, sir."

O'Sullevan turned to his adjutant. "The Bemba lads would understand ChiNyanja, wouldn't they, Patrick?"

"I suppose so, sir. We could find out." Brien shouted to his orderly sergeant, a huge African with a tasselled fez the size of a flower pot on his head. "Ezekiel, *Bwana* Spaight will give you an order in ChiNyanja. I want you to translate it to me, to see if you can understand him."

The sergeant nodded and said. "We can understand ChiNyanja, sir."

"Even so, I would like to test it."

The adjutant scribbled on a piece of paper the words: "Go to the large tree over there and dig a trench. When you have finished come back and report to me."

He handed the paper to Drew who read it, then gave the instruction to the sergeant, who was smiling, as if this was some game that the *bwanas* were playing.

"So, Ezekiel, what did I write."

Ezekiel smirked. "I am to go to the big tree to dig a trench, and then come back to *Bwana* Spaight – when I finish." The sergeant giggled. "I am from Chipata, sir. My people speak ChiNyanja."

"Does *Bwana* Spaight speak it well?"

"*Eee, bwana.* He speaks like one of us."

"Have you commanded men, Spaight?" asked O'Sullevan.

Drew coughed in embarrassment. "Actually, no, sir."

"Well, you will now. I'm making you a platoon commander. Ezekiel is the company sergeant, but he has a good platoon sergeant to work under you."

"Thank you, sir. What about my own sergeant, Goodwill?"

"I was coming to that. Do you know the man, Ezekiel?"

"I have spoken to him, sir. He is not from one of our regiments; he is KAR."

"Please find him and bring him here." The sergeant saluted smartly and hurried out. O'Sullevan said to Drew. "Tell me about this man Goodwill?"

Drew told the Major about Goodwill, and he listened attentively, while sipping his tea. The subject arrived within five minutes, shown in by a grinning Ezekiel; both men saluted.

O'Sullevan leaned back in his chair. "Good afternoon, Sergeant Goodwill. How is it that you are a sergeant?"

"I am not a soldier, sir, but I was given the title 'Sergeant' by Major Spaight."

"Indeed." A small smile played on the Major's face; he was intrigued with this tall upright African who spoke such good English. "I understand that you have trained two runners to carry messages."

"Yes, sir."

"What training did you give them?"

"Sir, most of the time I wanted to make sure that they could run or walk for several days through the bush, because using the road might be too dangerous."

"Did you tell them what to do if they are captured?"

"Sir, I told them to drop the message – so that it could not be found. Also, to say that they are going on leave."

"Did you tell them the Germans might kill them?"

"No, sir, but I said they might be made prisoners."

"How long would it take them to get to Abercorn?"

"They would reach that place at the end of the second day."

"Very well, Sergeant. I want your messengers to go to Abercorn. One to leave this afternoon, the other tomorrow morning. Bring them here to be given the messages. After that, you will remain with Lt Spaight, as his assistant."

Goodwill saluted and left. Then the Major said, "Sergeant Ezekiel, please introduce Lt Spaight to the men of his platoon."

—•—

The Germans made their move a week later, starting with a field gun bombardment. Then they advanced with seven hundred Europeans and *askaris*. Drew was now in command of a platoon of ChiBemba-speaking African policemen from the Lusaka area of Northern Rhodesia. It was their first action and they were plainly terrified as they cowered in the trenches.

"Keep firing!" urged Drew, and his orders were further relayed by Goodwill, who never left his side.

The noise was astounding. Although the field guns were now silent, the Germans were using mortars to augment their rifle fire. However, they were at a severe disadvantage, having to advance over the wide cleared perimeter, while the defenders were deep in their trenches.

It started to rain. Drew crouched in his wet dugout, drenched in sweat and shivering with fear. On either side lined a dozen of his men, standing at the bank of the trench, rain capes glistening wet on their shoulders. The water was now ankle deep and carried the urine, excrement and vomit of the men in the platoon. The stench was overwhelming.

"Can you see the Germans?" Drew asked fearfully.

"They have not moved for a long time, *Bwana* Drew. There is no cover for them..." Goodwill was interrupted by a shower of mud clods that rained down from a mortar explosion.

"Do you think they will charge?" asked Drew.

"*Eee*, I don't think so, *bwana*. The distance over open ground is too far."

"Perhaps they will come at night – when we can't see them?" Drew's voice quavered and he was ashamed.

Goodwill muttered. "We can use the big lights, and the flares. It would not be much better for them than the day time."

"What's the matter with me, Goodwill? I feel like a puddle of … I'm useless."

"All men are afraid, *Bwana* Drew. I have known fear all my life. There are few men who do not feel it. Perhaps they are not what we call 'brave'. The brave men are those who know fear but put it aside."

"I can't do that. I feel paralysed."

"You must not let the men know, *Bwana* Drew. They will say, 'If the *mzungu* is too scared to move, then why should we'. Do you know what I mean?"

"Yes. Could you tell them that I'm not well – that I have fever?"

"I will tell them, if I have to."

—•—

The Germans fired sporadically through the night, but did not make a concerted charge. Next morning they were gone. Cautious probes into the bush north of Saisi found only empty cartridge cases and mounds of graves.

Goodwill was suspicious about the graves. "If they are for *azungu* there are too many. The Germans would take their own dead people with them. The *askaris* would put rocks and stones on the graves."

"We could dig one up?" suggested Drew. He went to find Major O'Sullevan and asked him for permission. Then he returned to his platoon and ordered them to dig up a grave.

"Ye Gods! You're right, Goodwill."

The grave was filled with ammunition boxes. Rather than carry the heavy boxes away, the German has buried them.

O'Sullevan came over and looked at them balefully. "You know what that means, Spaight? They're coming back to attack us again. Better get prepared."

—•—

The defenders at Saisi were augmented by Belgian troops from the Congo, so that their number approached five hundred. But the Germans were thought to have twice as many.

"This is no skirmish," said O'Sullevan, when they were eating supper in the mess shed. "This is a big set piece. Nothing like the battles in Europe, of course."

The Germans attacked again on 25 July, 1915. For four days Drew stayed with his platoon of Bemba policemen, constantly under fire from field guns, mortars and rifles. It rained much of the time, and the trench water deepened to the level of their knees. The askaris went barefoot and their feet swelled. The officers said that the men had to apply grease or oil, otherwise they would suffer the dreaded 'trench-foot', with necrosis and fungal growth.

Their earlier fear had changed to confidence; they knew they were more than a match for the German *askaris*. They sang during the day when they were not firing, and snored during the night. They were constantly short of drinking water and had to send night patrols to the little Saisi River, which was between them and the German lines.

Drew stayed with his men in the trenches, but he was almost paralysed with fear. He heard Goodwill tell the men that their officer had very bad fever, and they made clucking noises in sympathy. He was buoyed by their singing; a soldier would take his turn with the refrain, then the others would sing a rousing chorus, with harmonies that came naturally to them. The words were simple, about life and happenings in the village.

A rumour came to the trenches that the Germans had asked O'Sullevan to surrender; an offer he refused. One day they heard intense firing to the west, and were later told that more Belgians were trying to come to their assistance, but had been driven off.

The sixth day dawned bright and sunny, with rumours that the Germans had gone. An hour later the news was official, and the men climbed out of their trenches, joked and laughed, and stripped off their wet uniforms. The siege of Saisi was over.

—•—

21

Rhodesia-Nyasaland – August-November 1915

Martin Russell had waited for a year in frustration since war was declared. He was no closer to his ambition of joining the fighting in German East Africa, although Southern Rhodesia raised two regiments. The first went to South Africa to help suppress the Maritz Rebellion; when not needed they moved on to German South-West Africa, where they fought with General Louis Botha's men in the successful campaign. The second regiment went to British East Africa (now Kenya), where they fought with distinction against Colonel von Lettow-Vorbeck's Germans.

As a Major in the BSAP Reserve Martin commanded training and military exercises. He often conferred with Colonel Edwards, the Commandant of the armed forces in Rhodesia, an old friend, formerly Commissioner of the Metropolitan Police in London. It was he who invited Martin to a meeting at BSAP Headquarters on a crisply cold morning.

It was an informal but confidential affair, with no minutes taken. Present, besides Colonel Edwards and Martin, were three BSAP officers: Captain John Ingham, a former civil servant, Major Ron Murray and Major Baxendale. Murray had risen through the ranks through courage and efficiency during and after the Boer War. He was a tall, broad-shouldered South African with a swarthy complexion –

his nickname was 'Kaffir' Murray. He had a reputation for driving his men hard.

Baxendale was a well-known citizen of Bulawayo, where he had been mayor three times. He had fought in the Matabele Rebellion and the Boer War, becoming a Colonel, but renounced this rank to volunteer, knowing that it would be awkward for Edwards to fit him into the command structure. An affable, portly man, he leaned back in his chair with a smile, watching the others.

"Gentlemen," said Edwards, "I want to tell you about our plans – you may be aware of some of what I'm going to say. Even so, I would be grateful if you would keep it to yourselves for the time being."

Pausing to light a cigarette he watched the blue smoke curl up towards the ceiling. "We've decided to form a Southern Rhodesia Column to fight on the northern-eastern border. The officials higher up have agreed that our prime responsibility is to preserve our border against German invasion. We don't want all our fighting men to head for the Western Front!"

He leaned back and looked around the other four men. "We'll have two companies in the Column. Ingham, you'll command 'A' Company, which will go to the Northern Rhodesia border via Ndola. The other company – 'B' Company – will be commanded by you, Baxendale; you will travel via Beira and Nyasaland. Ron, you will be Chief Staff Officer, with the rank of Lt Colonel, in charge of whole Column, reporting to me. Martin, you will be Chief Intelligence Officer under Ron Murray, serving both companies. Ron, I want you and Martin to travel with 'B' Company, via Nyasaland. Any questions?"

There was a long pause before Murray spoke. "Colonel Hodson is already in command of the Northern Rhodesia Rifles and the Northern Rhodesia Police – I believe he's now in Abercorn. Where will he fit into the command structure?"

Edwards nodded in acknowledgement. “At present Hodson reports to me, but I want him to work closely with your Column. As you say, he commands the NRR and the NRP, and you command the Rhodesian Column, so you’ll have parallel commands. He is the senior officer, but... Look, Ron, we’ll have to see how things develop. Frankly, I think it’s just a matter of time before Whitehall appoints a Brigadier or a Major-General to the front.”

Martin asked, “We’ve heard rumours that the South Africans will send troops to our front. When is that going to happen?”

“Yes. From now on you’ll be fully briefed about all this. We expect a couple of regiments to be sent soon. They may reach Nyasaland at about the same time as your ‘B’ Company...”

“How will they fit into the command structure?”

“They’ll have their own commander – Colonel Hawthorn – at least to begin with. So many colonels! That’s why I think we’ll have a General in command quite soon – to unify the command.” Edwards stood up. “Now, you have to move quickly. I want you to be out of here by the middle of August.

—•—

Martin broke the news to his children at supper that night, having already discussed matters with Helen. “Children, I’m sorry I have to leave you. Your mother and I have asked Betty Carter to come and stay here with you – and you can always call on Tom Ellsworth.”

“How long will you be away,” asked Ben, holding back tears.

“I don’t know, son. It may be a few months.”

Clare asked, “Is Betty willing to stay here as long as that?”

“She said so. As you know, she’s your mother’s best friend. She loves you all.”

“We love her,” said Clare, “but it’s not the same as having a man here.”

“What will you be doing?” asked Richard, always the serious one.

"I'm not allowed to tell you much – I'm sorry. But I can tell you that I will be the Chief Intelligence Officer – a rather unwieldy title."

"Does that mean you have to gather information?"

"Have they chosen you because you're intelligent?" interjected Richard.

Martin laughed. "No, I think they chose me because I've had a lot of experience in the bush. Also because I can speak Afrikaans and ChiShona..."

"But they don't speak either of those languages up north," said Ben. He was very unhappy about his father leaving, and realised he would be the man of the family.

"True," Martin answered, "but we expect that some South Africans will join us, so the Afrikaans will be useful. As for the Shona, well, it is related to the other Bantu languages, and I've been learning some Swahili from Moses. It's commonly spoken in northern Nyasaland and the southern part of German East Africa. By the way, I'm thinking of taking Moses with me..."

"Can you do that?" asked Helen. "Can you just add him to the retinue – like a piece of baggage?"

He smiled in a placatory way at the acidity in her tone. "I'm allowed to have a batman, and as you know he's been out camping with me many times. But more important, he speaks Swahili, so he can teach me, and act as my interpreter to begin with. He's very keen to go."

"I hope you'll make him aware of the dangers," said Clare sadly.

That evening, when the children had gone to bed, Helen expressed her anxiety. "It's not that we can't cope without you. We're well able to look after the farm. I'm concerned about you. You're not a young man, darling. From what I've heard the conditions will be very harsh..."

"They may be. But I've had experience of hard conditions before – in the trek up here in '90, and in the War in '93."

"Yes," she sounded exasperated, "but you were much younger then – more resilient. You've been living a rather comfortable life for the last ten or so years – a softer life..."

"I've been on camping trips."

"Rather luxurious ones, you must admit. You had all the food you wanted, Moses to look after you. If the weather turned foul you could retreat to the truck." She smiled at him wryly. "You must have your wish – to be a soldier again. I don't understand it – why you can't leave it to younger men."

"They will do the fighting, my love. We senior officers will not be in the front line. We're the planners – the organisers."

"The Germans may penetrate the front line and reach the command centre..."

"It's possible, but not very likely."

"Make sure you come back, darling."

He hugged her. "I'm sorry to leave you with all the responsibility – looking after the farm and the children."

She shrugged. "If they don't behave I can always tell them how cross you will be when you return."

—•—

Next day Clare came home from nursing school with news that startled the whole family. She made her announcement as they sat round the table at supper.

"I've asked to be sent to Nyasaland," she said, grinning, but nervous as she looked at her parents. "Three of us have been accepted as civilian nurses to work in the hospitals there..."

Martin exploded. "I've heard nothing about this, Clare."

"Why didn't you ask us?" Her mother was plaintive.

"I want to go..."

"Where would you live?" asked Martin.

"The three of us will live in a house near the hospital, in Zomba," replied Clare. "I'm sure Uncle Alan and Aunt Jess will help me. I can always go to them if I have any trouble."

Helen was silent; she had stopped eating, dismayed at the thought of her daughter leaving home. "It's different there..."

"I know, Mother. I've heard a lot about it from the Spaights over the years. It's almost as if I know it – far fewer Europeans, of course. But I won't be alone. I'll have Dora and Meriel with me... They say they may send a Sister."

"Surely they have to ask your parents for their permission?"

"Yes, they do, because I'm under twenty-one. I said you wouldn't refuse."

"I don't want you going anywhere near the fighting." Martin helped himself to more roast guinea fowl, thinking his girl was admirable.

Clare smiled in a conciliatory way. "Zomba will be the first hospital for the men coming back from the front. There will be lots of Europeans there – they say the numbers have doubled already."

"Why?" asked Richard. "There hasn't been much fighting."

"Malaria," replied Clare. "There's lots of it – and dysentery, and sleeping sickness."

—•—

Two weeks passed at a pace that astonished Martin. He had to make arrangements for all the farming activities, not knowing when he would return. His manager was competent enough, and Helen was very capable of looking after the livestock. He spoke with Tom Ellsworth, who promised to come out to the farm at least once a week.

He had to consider what might happen if he did not return, so he paid a visit to his attorney in Salisbury, to make sure his will was current and his financial affairs in good order. Betty, a widow, settled in; she had known all the children since they were born and was godmother to both girls.

Martin spoke at length to Moses about the campaign ahead. "There will be fighting, Moses, and men will be killed. War is different now; the guns are more powerful and they cause greater damage, to men and horses – and buildings. I expect there will be many hardships. You will be leaving your wife and children."

"Sometimes men have to do these things, *bwana,*" replied Moses. "You and I have been on *ulendo* in the bush many times. We know how to live in the bush. And the fighting? In the former times my people were attacked many times by the Angoni tribe. Many people were killed."

"This war will be much bigger. It will cover several countries and many tribes. Besides, you won't have a young wife to bring you hot *nsima* and fresh *pombe* – and keep you warm at night."

Moses laughed. "That is true, but a man who enjoys comforts all his life does not enjoy them as much as a man who has known hardship."

—•—

Every day Martin met with Colonel Murray, usually with the two company commanders. They had to ensure that all the men and supplies were ready for the long journey. The men were told not to give information about their final destination, although it became common knowledge and was eventually divulged.

A meeting of all the men was arranged on one evening at Murray's request. He had chosen Martin Russell to advise the men about how to look after themselves in the bush. They met in the Police Hall, two hundred of them, excited, and a little apprehensive, at the prospect of going to war.

"How many of you have been to Nyasaland?" asked Martin. Not a single hand was raised.

"I haven't been there either, but my cousin, who lives there, has told me a lot about it. Most of you are from the towns, and may not have much experience of the *bundu*, so I'll give you an idea of what to expect. And don't be alarmed!"

"First the diseases. Malaria is the most dangerous, so try not to be bitten by mosquitoes. Easier said than done, but I recommend you wear long trousers in the evening, and tuck them into your boots, and wear long sleeves. That leaves your hands, neck and head – and I suggest you rub on repellent, like citronella. Living here on the highveld you've been spoiled. There will be many more mosquitoes where you're going."

"Next, water. You must drink a lot, but it must be clean water, preferably boiled. Don't go to a stream and assume that you can drink the water. Dirty water carries germs of dysentery and typhoid. We'll give you tablets to put in the water if you can't boil it."

"Wild animals? Really, there's none to worry about. Just be careful of snakes and scorpions, under wood and stones, or if you dig holes or trenches. At night, if there are lions or hyenas around, stay by a fire..."

A voice from the back called, "What if we're not allowed a fire?"

"Good question," replied Martin. "Use thorn branches, or any branches you can find, to make a protective barrier – then one person should stay awake in case an animal tries to break in. You'll probably have a sentry. Remember that most wild animals will try to get out of your way. One exception is the crocodile; be very cautious approaching any water, and when crossing streams and rivers. Some people say that there's safety in numbers – don't believe it. Crocs have been known to pick out humans or cattle from groups making lots of noise."

Another voice called out, "With dangers like these, who needs an enemy!"

—•—

Martin had lunch with Colonel Edwards one day at the Salisbury Club, where they were both members; Edwards arranged that they sit in a private room. Martin thought the Colonel had aged in the two weeks since they last met. His long face was pasty and his moustaches drooped.

"Frankly, Martin, I'm concerned about the command structure. Even if a General is appointed, there's bound to be friction. I'm glad I've got you in the system – to apply some soothing oil where it's needed. You must let me know how it goes."

"I can't send you messages behind Murray's back."

"You may have to." Edwards sipped his beer. "You have a cousin in Nyasaland, I hear; perhaps you can use him."

"Yes. Alan Spaight. He's a sort of Military Attaché to the Governor. I gather from a recent letter that he finds it rather irksome. He wants to get to the front."

"Probably too useful to Sir George Smith. I've met him you know; at a conference in London – decent fellow. You'll like him."

"By the way, sir, I would like Alan to work with me. He knows the northern part of the country. He speaks ChiNyanja fluently, and Swahili quite well. He has a military background – went to Sandhurst, and had a commission in the British army."

Edwards laughed. "I presume that's why the Governor wants to keep him in Zomba."

—•—

'B' Company followed the same route that Alan and his daughters used the previous year, by train from Salisbury to Beira, by steamer to Chinde and Chindio, and by train again to Limbe. The journey took five days, and the senior officers spent most of their time planning the logistics and ensuring that the men and their supplies were in good order.

The troops were eager to get to the front. They were mostly young men from farms and offices, all volunteers. Colonel Murray pushed their training hard, and appointed Martin as their weapons instructor. He spent many hours showing them how to use their .303 Lee-Enfield rifles, how to take them apart and clean them, and how to shoot accurately. He made them strip and re-assemble the bolts and magazines of their rifles blind-folded, explaining that they might have to do it in the dark. The troops were given many hours of bayonet drill.

"You must be able to defend yourselves in a bayonet attack," said Martin. "Imagine a dozen German-trained *askaris* charging towards you, bayonets at the front. You might be able to get off one shot. Then what?"

He and the senior NCOs showed the men how to deflect a charge and parry thrusts, until it became second nature for them. The gun crews had special training with their Maxim/Vickers machine guns.

At Chindio the Company was met a young KAR subaltern. He had been sent by Sir George Smith to assist them in their rail journey to Limbe. After the introductions he handed Martin a letter from Alan Spaight.

Dear Martin,

I hope your journey has gone well and that you enjoy the last lap. Hutchins will look after you.

I'm very glad you're coming because I want you to get me to the front. I don't want to spend the war in Zomba – though Jess would not mind! I would like to join your outfit, and would be grateful if you could put in a good word for me with your commander – Murray?

Tell him that I know the north end of the Lake, and that I speak Swahili quite well. I can look after myself in the bush. I would really like to do intelligence work with you.

We hope you will come to stay with us at the farm. Looking forward to seeing you again.

Yours aye,

Alan

—•—

During one of their many meetings on the train Martin broached the subject with Murray. "I would like to recruit one or two officers in Nyasaland – men who know the north and can speak the languages. Ideally, they should bring African scouts with them."

Murray frowned, and Martin expected a negative reply, but the commander then nodded. "Yes, see who you can find. But make sure the Africans they bring are thoroughly reliable."

Most of the young officers were intimidated by Col Murray. They saw a man who was likely to explode into incandescent rage at any moment, and who had no patience for officers who did not measure up to his exacting standards. His habitual expressions were a frown or a scowl.

However, he did relax sometimes, usually only after supper in the evenings, when he liked to sit with Martin and Baxendale and reminisce about the Boer War. He would sip his favourite Cape brandy and start to smile, and even laugh. Those who saw him were surprised; they were occasional visitors, or message bearers, and it was made plain to them that they were disturbing his evening.

Martin grew to like his commander, and encouraged him to delegate more, to relieve the stress of his command. In turn, Murray cautiously gave Martin more to do as he realised that he was competent and well-liked by the men.

—•—

When 'B' Company arrived at the terminus in Limbe they were fêted by the local population. The Mayor of Blantyre came to deliver a speech of welcome, and the soldiers were given sweets and cigarettes. Murray hated these festivities and delegated the affable Major Baxendale to represent the Company.

Alan Spaight came to greet the Company on behalf of the Governor and was invited to a meeting with Murray's staff officers at Ryall's Hotel in Blantyre, held in a private dining room. A large map of the region was spread out on the table and Murray invited Alan to describe the current situation.

"At Government House in Zomba we receive regular encrypted telegrams from Colonel Edwards in Salisbury and from Colonel Hodson in Abercorn. Also, our outpost in Karonga – here, at the north end of the lake – sends us information about action along the front, which stretches from Karonga to Abercorn – here." He pointed to their positions on the map. "We share our information with Colonel Hawthorn, commanding the South African contingent. They've just arrived at Fort Johnston – here."

Alan paused and looked at the other officers before continuing. "We have only limited information about the disposition and strength of the Germans. As you know, they invaded about a year ago and fought us at Karonga. This July they attacked in strength at Saisi – here – but were beaten off. Since then they have restricted themselves to isolated skirmishes, and it seems they want to avoid fights involving more than a few dozen troops..."

"They were soundly beaten at Karonga?" said Murray, and then waved his hand to apologise for interrupting.

"Yes," continued Alan, "and that may have influenced their strategy. However, we should not assume that they won't invade again."

"How do you gather your intelligence?" asked Murray.

"With difficulty. Most of it comes from Africans, either captured German *askaris*, or disaffected ones who come over to our side, or from headmen and villagers in the area. We have teams of interrogators who pass the information to the Intelligence Officers at Karonga, Fife and Abercorn. It all comes to me for the final analysis."

"Do you send scouts into German territory?" asked Martin.

Alan nodded. "Yes, we do. It's very difficult country for them to work in. There are many small local tribes. An African stranger is very obvious, especially if he doesn't speak the local dialects."

"Isn't there a big risk from defecting German *askaris* – they might become double agents?"

"Yes, there is, sir. We have to be very cautious, and balance the risks against the information they give us."

"You had a rebellion in January. Could that happen again?"

Alan shook his head thoughtfully. "I doubt it, sir. Chilembwe was a charismatic minister with a few dozen disciples. He never achieved widespread support. The rebels were rounded up and most of them were executed. It was a harsh lesson – well publicised."

Murray nodded and said, "How do you see the longer-term development?"

Alan stroked his short beard as he considered his answer. "All evidence points to von Lettow-Vorbeck continuing to fight a hit and run campaign. He has been successful so far – I expect he will build on that experience. I would hazard he will eventually go round us..."

"Into Portuguese territory?" Murray's interest was aroused.

"Yes."

"Why?"

"He would then be threatening our eastern flank, sir, while being supplied from the coast. If he goes far enough south he could threaten Beira."

"Are you suggesting his strategy is to threaten and not attack?"

"Yes. That's the way he seems to like operating. He's keeping thousands of allied troops away from the European theatre of war. Of course he'll attack locally if he thinks he can succeed, but generally he has been fighting defensively. It's very frustrating, because his forces keep withdrawing – he's like a boxer that you cannot punch."

"Could we put him into a corner?" Murray's questioning was relentless.

"The ring is too vast. Essentially there are no corners. There's the Indian Ocean to the east, Lake Nyasa to the west, with over three hundred miles of bush in between."

—•—

22

Zomba, Nyasaland – November 1915

Next day they set off for Zomba in Alan's private car. Murray was impressed by the smooth tarmac surface as Alan gave them a sporadic commentary, pointing out Mount Chiradzulu, site of the Chilembwe uprising, Mount Mlanje, mysterious and purple in the distance to their right, and Mount Zomba looming ahead, its rock faces glistening after recent rain.

Alan wanted his cousin to stay at the farm, but Martin explained that he had to remain near his commander, who was inclined to demand discussions at any time of day or night. The two Rhodesians were put in temporary quarters at the KAR cantonment on the outskirts of Zomba; the place was half empty, since most of the KAR officers were at the front.

A courtesy visit to Government House was arranged for that afternoon. They were greeted by Sir George and Lady Smith, and after tea on the lawn the men adjourned to the meeting room to discuss strategy with the Chief Secretary, Hector Duff. After a couple of hours they had dinner, a semi-formal affair, to which the Governor had invited Mrs Duff and Jess Spaight.

Martin had not seen his cousin's wife for several years and was delighted to be seated next to her. By general agreement the war was a topic to be avoided, if possible, but there seemed little else to talk about. Martin asked Jess about her children.

"Drew is in Fife – that's on the Stevenson Road between Karonga and Abercorn. I know we're not supposed to talk about the war, but I can tell you that he's seen very little action since the attack on Saisi. The waiting is getting the men down..."

"And I hear Mandy and Kirsty are up north too."

"Yes, Mandy was at Karonga when it was attacked, but she came south with a bunch of wounded soldiers. Now she's with Kirsty in Fort Johnston. They're looking forward to seeing you; they're coming home this weekend."

"What do they do in Fort Johnston? Ward nursing, I presume."

"They work at the hospital. It's a staging place, caring for wounded and sick soldiers on their way south to the main hospitals, here and in Salisbury. The wounded South Africans are eventually sent on to Durban. Of course not all patients are wounded; there's a great deal of sickness, from tropical diseases – malaria mostly, but also dysentery and a few cases of cholera."

"How do you get news from the girls?"

"Letters. The mail service is quite good. It takes only one or two days from Fort Johnston. It's close enough for them to come home one weekend a month."

"I hear that Kirsty has a young man?"

Jess smiled. "She has an understanding with a young naval reserve officer. He's been serving on the *Guendolen* – has seen action on the lake. We're not supposed to know what he's doing now. Mandy had a young man too? He's a young Captain – Roly Benting-Smith. He was wounded at Karonga, poor man. Shot in the jaw, but he's made an amazing recovery, or so we hear. He was treated in Cape Town by a surgeon we know – oh, of course you know him – Louis Viljoen."

Jess laughed lightly. "Young people are different now. When I was their age one decided on a young man and stuck with him. Now, they seem to drift in and out of friendships and relationships. Kirsty, as you know, is the more serious of the two girls. As for Mandy? I think she's not ready to settle down. And there's another thing. This war is so disturbing for them. They're moving all over the place. Most of the time they can only write to each other." She turned to him with a smile. "I expect you'll see them soon. You can ask them yourself."

As they left Government House, Alan and Jess invited Martin and Ron Murray to *Khundalila* for the weekend. There was an awkward pause, when Martin was convinced that the Colonel would refuse. Then, to his surprise, Murray, accepted.

"That's very good of you," he said. "It will be a great pleasure to visit a Nyasaland farm. I think Martin and I deserve a short break."

—•—

The two officers were to have driven out to *Khundalila* on a Saturday afternoon, in a staff car allocated for Murray's use; but it needed repair, so Alan came to fetch them in his Wolseley. As he drove the five miles from Zomba he pointed out Lake Chilwa ahead, a shining silver disk, about fifty miles in diameter, Chisi Island rising incongruously from its surface like some wallowing primeval monster.

"Great duck shooting," said Alan, "and geese – spurwing and Egyptian – and teal."

Further on, they passed the airfield, an expanse of grassland where the local planters sometimes played polo.

Alan said, "We're hoping that one day we'll get an aeroplane here."

At *Khundalila* they were met by Jess, and the girls, who had arrived that morning from Fort Johnston. Martin thought they looked thin and wan, though they greeted him cheerfully. The two visitors were taken to the guest cottage, and met the family for tea on the verandah, looking across the Likengala River towards Lake Chilwa. Jess and a house servant brought tea and cake, which were served by Mandy and Kirsty.

"How are you coping, Mrs Spaight?" asked Murray. "Alan is away a great deal. Do you have help with the farm?"

"I can manage," she replied. "I'm quite used to him being away, at least for shorter periods. I have my elder son, Mac, here – you'll meet him at supper – and a very capable African farm assistant."

"Tell me about your nursing," said the Colonel to the girls.

They looked at each other, and then Kirsty spoke. "We're very fortunate to have had formal training in Rhodesia, but it didn't really prepare us for the things we have to deal with here. The forward hospitals, like Fort Johnston and Karonga, are quite primitive compared with Zomba or Salisbury. That means we mostly just patch up the patients before sending them on to a better hospital – or cure them of their fever."

"What sorts of things are lacking?"

"Phew." She blew out her cheeks. "So much. Trained staff. There aren't enough doctors and nurses, or orderlies. Actually, sir, since you ask, what we need are proper forward first aid units – field hospitals. You see, most injuries need rapid treatment as soon as possible after they occur."

"Give me some examples."

"Well, many wounds need staunching of the blood that's escaping, and replacement with saline solution. Ideally it should be done by a doctor, but a field hospital orderly can do a lot..."

"Hm." Murray was evidently impressed with this forthright exposition. He turned to Martin. "We must see what we can do."

After tea Alan showed the visitors round the farm, and brought them back before dark. Before supper they had drinks in the drawing room and were introduced to Mac. He frowned and frequently pushed his hair back from his forehead as he watched the visitors with suspicion.

"I understand that you have modified motor-cycles, to make them stronger," said Murray, to start a conversation.

Mac nodded. "And quieter. It depends what the bike is used for. They can be noisy."

"I heard you were involved in suppressing the rebellion," prompted Martin.

Mac scowled and looked sideways, as if there was a rebel lurking in the room. "We went into action as quickly as we could. Most of the regular troops were up north, so there were only a few of us NVR men here – and some *askaris*."

"Did you come under fire?"

"We did; but the stupid KAR officer had issued only seven rounds to his *askaris*. He doubted their loyalty, but I don't understand his logic. One round would have been enough to shoot us in the back."

"I heard you were visiting one of the homesteads when the attacks started," said Martin.

Mac scowled at him. "I had supper with one of the men who was killed – I left before it happened."

"You were lucky!"

—•—

They ate supper in the dining room, sitting round the big *mukwa* table. Martin had Mac on one side, who never uttered, and Kirsty on the other. It was the sort of fare he liked, simple farm food: pumpkin soup, roast guinea fowl with potatoes and green beans, and mango fool with fresh cream. Looking across at Ron Murray he could see that his Colonel liked it too, his usually stern expression had mellowed, and he even laughed now and then. Jess had her servants well trained, and the meal went forward without any fuss.

They had no wine, but at the end of the meal Alan offered brandy and liqueurs. He suggested that the men adjourn to the verandah to smoke, but Murray asked if Jess and the girls could come out with them. This time Mandy sat beside Martin and he found an opportunity to talk to her.

"When do you have to return to Fort Johnston?" he asked.

She glanced up at him with slight smile. "On Sunday afternoon. There's a lorry going there. We have to be at work on Monday morning."

"We're going there too," he said. "Not sure when..."

"Will you stay there?"

"Not for long. We're heading north to Karonga and then Abercorn."

—•—

Murray's Rhodesian Column wended its way north, by car and lorry to Fort Johnston, by steamer to Karonga, and by road again to Abercorn. After reluctant agreement by the Governor, Murray was permitted to take Alan Spaight, on condition that he returned to his post as military attaché as soon as the Column reached Abercorn. Alan's role was essentially to brief the Rhodesians about conditions in Nyasaland and the threat of another invasion.

They spent one night at Fort Johnston and had supper with the Spaight girls. At nine o'clock there was mutual agreement that they should retire for the night. Mandy and Kirsty went off to the nurse's house, while Alan, Martin and Murray went to the hostel for visiting staff officers.

Before going to bed Martin went out onto the small verandah of the hostel to smoke his pipe. The summer night air was dense and balmy. An electric storm flickered over the Kirk Range, its larger flashes illuminating the lake with an eerie glow. A night watchman passed, lifting his hand in salute.

—•—

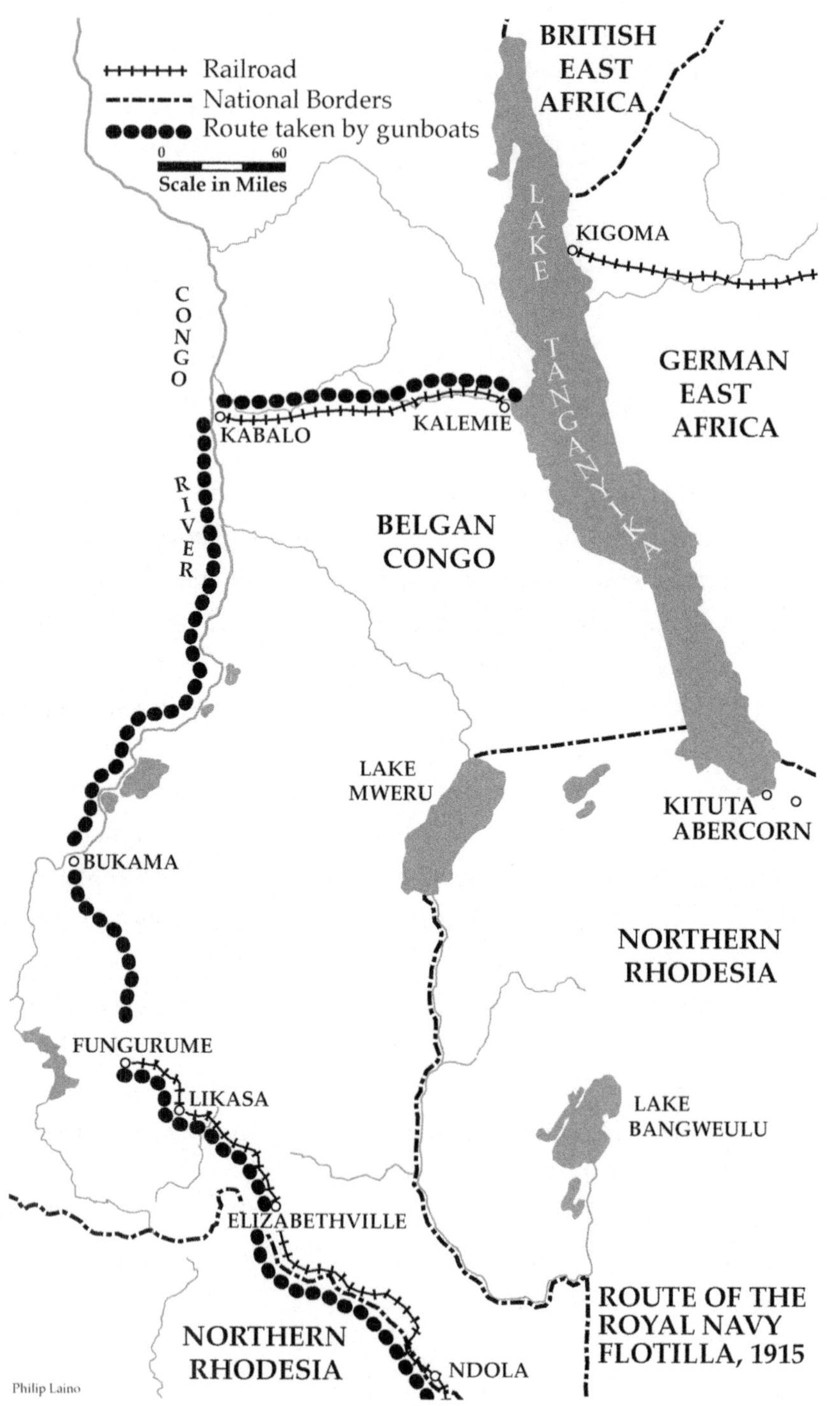
Railroad
National Borders
Route taken by gunboats
0
60
Scale in Miles
BRITISH
EAST
AFRICA
LAKE
TANGANYIKA
KIGOMA
CONGO
RIVER
GERMAN
EAST
AFRICA
KABALO
KALEMIE
BELGAN
CONGO
LAKE
MWERU
KITUTA
ABERCORN
BUKAMA
NORTHERN
RHODESIA
FUNGURUME
LIKASA
LAKE
BANGWEULU
ELIZABETHVILLE
ROUTE OF THE
ROYAL NAVY
FLOTILLA, 1915
NORTHERN
RHODESIA
NDOLA
Philip Laino

23

Belgian Congo– August-December 1915

Gavin Henderson sat at the large table in the meeting room at Government House, waiting nervously. Taking a cup of tea brought on a small tray by a uniformed servant, he walked around the room looking at the portraits hanging on the walls. The most prominent was of the King and Queen, and there was a large one of Queen Victoria, looking, he thought, rather supercilious. Former commissioners of British Central Africa were represented, and Gavin remembered Alan Spaight saying that he had known them well.

A few minutes later the door opened and the Governor, Sir George Smith entered, followed by Alan, recently returned from Abercorn. Gavin stood up rigidly and wondered if he should salute – no, not indoors. He felt distinctly uncomfortable, his best white uniform too tight.

"Ah, Henderson," said the Governor. "Thank you for coming here. Do sit down."

They shook hands and sat down. Alan spread a large map of Central Africa on the table.

The Governor cleared his throat. "You are to go on a special assignment, Henderson. I must say, I'm sorry to lose you, but I hope you'll come back to us." He lowered his voice. "This is top secret, and between the three of us. You will be asked to sign an undertaking that you will not tell anyone about the mission."

He paused and pointed to the map. "You are to go as soon as possible to Elizabethville, in the Belgian Congo. Two gunboats are being sent out from Britain for use on Lake Tanganyika. They have already been off-loaded in Cape Town, and are on their way to É'ville – as the locals call it. You are to proceed, via Beira, Salisbury and Bulawayo, to É'ville. Alan and I reckon it will take you four or five days, and by that time the gunboats should be there, preparing for the final stage of their journey. You will report to Lt Commander Spicer-Simson, the leader of the flotilla."

"You have been chosen for your naval experience, for your knowledge of the German language, and of Africa, and because you have proved your mettle here. I have to say that I endorse the Admiralty's choice." He paused. "Alan, why don't you give him the background."

Alan sat down, and accepted a cigarette from the Governor, who then passed the box to Gavin, who lifted his hand to indicate that he would not smoke. Alan spoke in his usual precise and thoughtful way, commanding respect.

"We were somewhat surprised when we read the despatch. My first thought was – why not send the gunboats through Lake Nyasa, and up the Stevenson Road to Lake Tanganyika? He smiled. "Ours not to reason why."

"Quite so," added the Governor.

"What size are they, sir?" asked Gavin.

Alan looked at the file. "Forty foot, eight foot beam, 100 horse-power petrol engines, twin-screw – made by Thorneycroft – they can do nineteen knots; that's impressive!"

"Phew, I'll say," said Gavin. "Are they wooden?"

"Yes," Alan glanced at the file again. "Mahogany 3/8 inch."

"May I ask, sir...?" Gavin said hesitantly. "Is the plan for the gunboats to destroy the German shipping on Lake Tanganyika?"

"Precisely," said the Governor. "We want to have control over that lake, as we have with Lake Nyasa. The strategic implications are huge."

Gavin said, musing. "The Germans have some pretty big ships on the lake. It will be an interesting contest – fast small gunboats against slower ships with more gun-power."

"We'll give you a pass," said the Governor, "which will cover your expenses for the journey to É'ville. After that you'll be under Spicer-Simson." He stood up and shook Gavin's hand. "Remember, not a word to anyone. Good luck."

—•—

"When will I see you again?" Kirsty was tearful. They walked within the hospital compound at Fort Johnston, where Gavin had gone to collect his belongings. She wore a stained uniform, but had removed her nurse's cap, letting her dark hair down. He thought she looked tired, as she often did nowadays.

"They can't say, sweetheart. I wish I could tell you more, but I've been sworn to secrecy."

"I understand that, but can you tell me if you'll be in Africa, or are they sending you to Europe?"

Gavin frowned in concentration. "I'll be in Africa, and I'll write to you. Of course my letters will be censored, but we're used to that, aren't we. As for how long? If we could defeat von Lettow – well, then we might all have to go to Europe."

She started to weep. He had never seen her like this before, and he was gratified that she was so upset, until she said, "I can't bear all this suffering. It's all so unnecessary – to further men's ambitions – and politicians striving for popularity..."

He listened to her glumly, and then interjected. "I have to go, darling. Please stay faithful to me..."

"And you to me."

"There are no women where I'm going."

"There are women everywhere, Gavin, and that's not the point."

He hung his head. "I know what you mean."

—•—

Five days later, his train steamed into the station at Elizabethville, in the copper-rich southern corner of the Belgian Congo. Although weary, he had enjoyed the journey, at least after boarding the train at Beira. He changed trains at Salisbury and Bulawayo, crossed the Zambesi River at the Victoria Falls to the Northern Rhodesia town Livingstone, and Ndola, on the Copperbelt. The formalities of entering the Belgian Congo were minimal. His instructions were to take a room at the Hotel Neuve Bruxelles.

A taxi car took him from the station to the comfortable single story building, festooned with bougainvilleas, not far from the huge copper mining complex. He was told that Commander Spicer-Simson was at the Mine Club, and on the advice of the hotel manager he went there in a bicycle rickshaw. He walked into the crowded smoke-filled saloon, where most of the members and guests seemed to have gathered.

Sitting hunched over the bar counter was a tall man in a British naval officer's uniform: short-sleeved white shirt and long white trousers; his bare arms were covered in tattoos. He was talking in French to three men in civilian clothing. Gavin's French was quite good, and he could tell that the British officer was telling a story about hunting tigers in China. Guessing he must be the Commander, Gavin approached.

Spicer-Simson looked up and saw him, then turned away and completed his story before extending a hand. "You must be Henderson? Welcome aboard!"

He offered Gavin a drink and asked him about his journey before saying, "We arrived here a couple of days ago. I've let Lee go, so it's just as well that you've joined us." Gavin knew that Lee was the enigmatic man who had conceived the plan to bring the gunboats the Lake Tanganyika.

The Commander called to two other men further down the bar and introduced them as Magee and Wainwright. He then reverted to French and started another story, this one about entangling with crooks in Hong Kong.

Lt Wainwright, a large florid man, in a white shirt and khaki trousers, looked bored. After a few minutes he excused himself, saying that he was going to check on the boats. He invited Gavin to join him and they took a rickshaw to a fenced compound with a railway siding, about a mile from the club. Wainwright explained that the place had been rented for the boats while they prepared for the next stage of the journey.

"The Commander leaves the logistical work to me," he said, in an uncomplaining tone.

"He seems to be a character..."

"You can say that again... those stories at the bar?" He paused to laugh. "It's one of his favourite occupations – telling fantastic stories; you heard him. He's like Baron Münchhausen."

Wainwright showed Gavin to the siding. "Here they are. My babies – *Mimi* and *Toutou*."

There must have been raised eyebrows about those names in the Admiralty, mused Gavin, as he looked at the two gunboats, on flat-bed carriages, covered with tarpaulins that effectively covered them. The concealed shapes seemed to epitomise the clandestine nature of the expedition, as well as its potential menace.

Around the perimeter of the siding were tents for the staff, some of whom were on guard duty.

"We're leaving tomorrow," said affable Wainwright, as he showed Gavin the tent allocated for him. "I'll introduce you to the others at breakfast. Reveillé at six."

"But I've booked into the hotel," said Gavin.

Wainwright guffawed. "Stay there. Just make sure you're here before six."

—•—

Gavin was introduced to the other men by Lt Wainwright at the morning parade, an informal affair, because the Commander was still at the hotel. Gavin soon discovered that the mission doctor was an old friend of the Commander. Other officers were Lt Eastwood, the Paymaster, and Lt Cross, an engineer. There were also two experienced NCO mechanics. Gavin was told that another young officer, Lt Douglas Hope, had gone north to reconnoitre the route.

The boats, on their railway flat trucks, were rolled out of the siding, and the expedition set off for Fungurume, 140 miles to the north. During the journey Wainwright sat in the same compartment as Gavin, and told him more about the prospect that awaited them on Lake Tanganyika.

"The Huns have two gunboats on the lake: the *Hedwig von Wissmann*, which is 100 tons – not to be confused with the *Herman von Wissmann* which they had on Lake Nyasa – and the *Kingani*, which is about 45 tons. So we'll have our hands full if we have a fight with them! We've recently received reports that the Huns are building a much larger ship – indeed it might have been launched. They've destroyed what Belgian ships were of any consequence. They even towed away and scrapped the *Cecil Rhodes*, one of our old ships, at the south end of the lake – though she was virtually derelict."

"So they're now unchallenged on the lake?"

"Exactly, and that dominance is what we plan to end. But it's a long haul from here. The end of this railway is at Fungurume. We then have to take the boats overland on trailers – through the bush – to another stretch of railway at Sankisia that takes us to the Upper Congo River – then onto a steamer that will take us down river to

Kabalo. There, we take them on another railway line to Lukuga on the lake."

"Quite a journey!"

Wainwright laughed. "Lee thought it out, and the Commander says we'll do it."

"What's he like?" Gavin asked tentatively.

"The Commander?" The older man looked at him carefully, assessing how much he should confide. He judged Gavin to have integrity. "He's a strange man. Sometimes he's the extrovert – as you saw him last night at the club. At other times he keeps to himself and says little. He can be over-critical and demanding, but he can also be relaxed and full of praise. The problem is that you never know which mood he's in."

"What happened to Lee? I thought he was the man who conceived this expedition and did all the groundwork."

"He was, and he did. At first we used to call it 'Lee's expedition', but the Commander soon stopped that. I think he decided that as long as Lee was around he would get most of the kudos. So he and Hope concocted some story to denigrate Lee, who was sent to the Cape; he had no chance to defend himself."

"So how do we get the boats overland?"

Wainwright heaved a sigh. "We've brought specially built boat-trailers, pulled by wheeled traction engines – they'll meet us at Fungurume. I'm really looking forward to seeing them – I used to be a loco driver in England. They're huge steam-powered locos, the furnaces fuelled with firewood; they have their own trailers to carry the fuel wood. Their metal wheels have strakes that will grip the dirt tracks and roads."

"And over the mountains?"

"If necessary the two locos can join forces, to pull one boat at a time."

—•—

When they reached Fungurume the two gunboats were taken off the rail-cars and winched onto their respective trailers. The expedition then set off with the locomotive engines hauling the boat trailers, belching smoke and steam. They had not gone thirty miles when both boat-trailers fell apart and had to be repaired and strengthened. The very first bridge they tried to cross collapsed and the ever resourceful Wainwright has to design a replacement, essentially filling the gap with logs.

"There are a hundred and fifty more bridges to cross!" he said cheerfully.

Water for the traction engines boilers was sometimes scarce – it was the dry season – and they sometimes had to recruit teams of women to carry the precious liquid in pots. For transport they also used three teams of oxen with their own Afrikaner overseer, who had problems feeding and watering the animals. In areas where there was human habitation they recruited local people to cut firewood and to haul and manoeuvre the boat trailers.

Most of the work was organised by Wainwright, who had been a locomotive engineer in Britain, and then a farmer in Rhodesia. He was immensely capable, and was assisted by Arthur Dudley, who joined them in Fungurume; a former officer in the Rhodesia Rifles, he had served in the Boer War.

Gavin worked closely with them, trying to learn from their considerable combined practical experience. Meanwhile, the Commander, preferring to delegate, was absent for long periods. He said he was negotiating with the Belgians and writing despatches to the Admiralty.

Gavin soon made friends with Dr Hanschell, an earnest man with much practical knowledge of tropical medicine. Although he had known the Commander before, and their wives were reputed to be friends, Gavin noticed that Spicer-Simson was not really friendly with Hanschell, and often scorned him. When the doctor started to confide in Gavin it was clear that he was baffled by the Commander's eccentric behaviour. For example, Spicer-Simson was boastful about his shooting prowess, but when an ox was brought to the camp for slaughter, he took three shots to despatch it at point blank range.

—•—

The expedition made slow progress, sometimes moving a few miles, sometimes only a few hundred yards. Over camp fires the Europeans coalesced in groups with common interests, drinking tea, and occasionally brandy, and smoking pipes. Gavin usually sat with Wainwright, Hanschell and Dudley. The doctor was assiduous in his efforts to keep the men healthy, insisting that they sleep under mosquito nets and drink only boiled water. The other two often spoke about Rhodesia, extolling the virtues of their adopted country.

"Tell us about your farming experiences, Gavin," said Wainwright one evening.

Gavin explained how he had gone to the Moshi area at the invitation of a relative of a German friend. "They had a large coffee plantation on the lower slopes of Mount Kilimanjaro. It was a lovely place, a healthy climate. The family were good to me – they taught me all they knew about growing coffee and about Africa."

"But you moved on," said the doctor.

Gavin sighed. "Yes, it was partly because I wanted to see other countries in Africa, but also I thought I might start my own farm. I saw an advertisement for a farm manager, to work in Nyasaland, so I applied and was offered the job."

"Do you speak German well?" asked Dudley.

"I could speak it before I went to Moshi, because my family had holidayed in Germany for many years. I also studied it at school. Living with the family at Moshi just improved my fluency."

"Hm. I would have thought the Navy could make better use of you. Do you speak Swahili?"

Gavin nodded. “My Swahili is quite good, because I worked a lot with the labourers on the coffee plantation. It’s become a bit rusty recently because I’ve been learning ChiNyanja – on the coffee estate in Nyasaland.”

“The languages must be quite similar?” asked Wainwright.

“They have similarities. I suppose something like Italian and Spanish – perhaps closer, but not as close as Spanish and Portuguese.”

—•—

Mountains loomed ahead. As they plodded forward the forest became tinder dry and they barely escaped a huge fire that swept down on them. Wainwright instructed the men to burn downwind of the track, and they moved onto this area before the fire reached them. Negotiating the lower slopes they developed techniques for pulling the boats up the track, which had been cleared by gangs of labourers ahead of them. Large trees beside the track were used with windlasses to assist the traction engines. The experience of Wainwright and the naval officers was invaluable.

In a near disaster, *Mimi* and her trailer broke their cable and started to run downhill. Only the intervention of a large tree prevented the boat from hurtling to destruction down the mountainside. The cables were doubled to prevent this from happening again.

At last they reached the summit and a narrow plateau, but were soon on the steep down-slopes to the Upper Congo River. Now their haulage problems were reversed, with the traction engines, the oxen-drawn wagons, and the labourers struggling to keep the boats from hurtling down the track.

At the railhead village of Sankisia they waved farewell to the Afrikaner teamster and the contract labourers and transferred the boats onto a narrow-gauge railway that ran for fifteen miles to Bukama on the Upper Congo River. In contrast to their earlier slow progress, this stretch took only two hours.

At Bukama they found the river at its lowest level for six years, and the expected steamer had not been able to come upstream to meet them. However, Captain Mauritzen, a Danish seaman, assigned to the expedition as a river pilot, proposed that they float the gunboats down the river, using empty petrol drums to increase their buoyancy.

Flying the White Ensign, the first British naval vessels in the Congo meandered downstream, negotiating numerous sandbanks. At a riverside village they met their assigned steamer, the *Constantin de Burlay*, whose captain warned about the dangers of hidden rocks and trees in the river ahead. Spicer-Simson decided it would be safer to load the precious gunboats onto a barge. Again, Wainwright's ingenuity enabled them to raise the boats from the water, using bank-side trees, and gently lower them onto the barge. They set off again with a cargo of African passengers surrounded by all their paraphernalia of clothing bundles, live chickens, and baskets of fruit. But the skipper of the steamer seemed incapable of avoiding sandbanks and eventually stuck fast.

Luckily they were rescued by another steamer, the *Baron Jansenn*, which took them to Kabalo, from where a railway ran east to Lake Tanganyika. The town was an uninviting collection of mud-brick buildings with corrugated iron roofs, surrounded by villages of grass huts. Oppressive heat sapped everyone's energy; it was the beginning of the rainy season, and thunder echoed through the surrounding hills.

In Kabalo they were met by Lt Hope, pale and nervous; he was soon dismissed by the Commander, ostensibly for drinking, and quarrelling with the Belgian officials. Meanwhile, the gunboats were taken off the barge and transferred onto railway trucks for the journey to Lake Tanganyika.

At first they made good time across a flat plain, but when entering hilly country the locomotive was exchanged for a smaller one, because the relatively new railway line had many temporary bridges. At each one the train stopped while the locomotive driver and engineer examined the structure, and discussed whether it was safe to cross. Sometimes they would uncouple the gunboats and take them across one at a time.

The railway ended a few miles short of the lake, so Gavin walked ahead to look for their camp site. The water was steel-grey with patches of indigo and blue where the sun shone through lowering rain clouds. He scanned the lake for signs of the German boats, thinking they might have got wind of the expedition's arrival. The expanse of water was enormous; fifty miles longer than Lake Nyasa, and just as wide. The far shore was beyond the horizon, but the mountains behind rose majestic and menacing. He recalled a brief visit to the lake when he was working at Moshi; they had fished for Nile perch from native *dhows*.

Gavin and Eastwood walked down to the camp, being constructed by their Belgian allies. They found the Commander already in his hut – the largest – sewing a flag from material brought from England. When raised on the flagpole they all recognised it as a Vice-Admiral's flag; it became an object of both admiration and scorn among the naval personnel.

That evening the expedition officers sat on the verandah of their mess and watched with binoculars as a German ship passed along the lake, evidently patrolling. She would have been able to see the smoke from the locomotive bringing *Toutou* to the coast. The Belgians tried to go out in their armed barge, but by the time they were on the lake the Germans had vanished.

Most of the British officers wanted to move the camp to Kalemie, two miles to the south, where there was a better harbour site, but the Belgians objected strongly, having gone to much trouble to build the camp at Kaluga. During the debate Gavin had his first argument with the Commander, who asked him for an opinion.

"It seems to me, sir," he replied earnestly, "that Kalemie is the better site, because the access from the lake is likely to be more reliable. The Kaluga River mouth is like the Shire on Lake Nyasa, subject to fluctuating flows and blockages. I've been reading..."

"Yes, Henderson. I think the situation here is completely different to Lake Nyasa."

"With respect, sir, both have only one outlet, with a bar that affects the lake level."

"I'm not interested."

"I'm sorry, sir, I thought you asked for my opinion."

Spicer-Simson turned aside irritably. Later he supported the majority of the officers favouring a move to Kalemie. The Belgians eventually capitulated, and their engineers confirmed that Kalemie was a better site, less fickle than the Kaluga River.

They quickly built a new camp on a hillside overlooking the new harbour. Rocks were trucked in to build breakwaters that enhanced the natural protections, and the expedition members settled in, bringing out their precious personal possessions from packing cases.

Gavin was the only officer who seemed to have only the most basic items, his uniforms and camping gear. He spent most of his spare time writing long letters to Kirsty, guessing they would take at least two weeks to reach her, and possibly much longer. He could not give her any real news or personal observations about his colleagues, because all outgoing letters, except for those of the Commander, were censored by Dr Hanschell.

—•—

The British expedition discovered, through their Belgian allies, that there was a third ship on the lake – the *Graf von Gotzen*. She was large enough to carry eight hundred troops, and had two 4.1 inch guns, thought to have come from the German cruiser *Konigsberg*, which had been trapped by British warships in the delta of the Rufiji River, where the Germans scuttled her and stripped out all her armaments.

In the officer's mess, a large grass hut overlooking the lake, arguments developed about the relative strengths of the two flotillas. Lt Dudley and Gavin thought that *Mimi* and *Toutou* would have enough superiority in speed to out-manoeuvre the German ships. The Commander argued that fire-power was more important than speed.

"The only reason our gunboats are fast is because they are lightly built and armed. One shell from the *Wissmann* or the *Gotzen* will blow them into matchwood."

"But they'll be difficult to hit, because they'll be moving so fast," argued Gavin.

The Commander frowned. "You have absolutely no experience of these things, Henderson. I have, and I can assure you that we are seriously disadvantaged."

"But, sir, we have to attack them, surely," said Dudley.

"Of course, but I'm thinking of a way to capture one of them – to increase our fire-power."

—•—

One morning, while Gavin and Wainwright were drinking mugs of tea, they saw the Commander emerge from his large hut, wearing a white shirt with epaulettes and a khaki 'skirt'. Seeing them gaping, he ambled over.

"My wife makes them for me," he said, indicating the skirt.

"Is it a kilt?" asked Wainwright.

The Commander chortled. "Are you wondering whether I'm wearing anything under it? Wonder away, Wainwright." He rolled up his sleeves, showing his arms covered with tattoos, mostly depicting snakes.

Spicer-Simson seemed immune to the attention and derision caused by his new attire. The British men thought it bizarre, and were embarrassed for their commanding officer. The Belgians sniggered and referred to him as *le Commandant á la jupe*. The Africans were more interested in his lavish writhing tattoos.

Commandant Steinman, the senior Belgian officer walked up to them. He nodded a greeting to the junior officers and said to Spicer-Simson. "There is a big storm approaching. I recommend that you keep the boats on shore."

The Commander said nothing.

"Another thing, *mon Commandant*, the Germans know about the boats. We can expect a visit from them."

"I trust you have taken all the necessary precautions." The Commander turned to Wainwright and added, "Make sure all the ratings are prepared for defensive action."

—•—

On the first morning of December Gavin was woken by the sound of guns firing from the Belgian shore battery. He scrambled into his clothes and ran up to the bluff to join the other men. The *Kingani* had approached the shore, but as soon as the firing started she hastened away. Although shells fell all around her she escaped. The British men were scornful of the Belgian gunners, but Spicer-Simson's offer of his own men was refused. Two days later, and the day after that, the *Kingani* reappeared, but stayed out of range of the shore battery.

On the third morning there was great excitement when some Belgian *askaris* discovered a European man near the shore and captured him at bayonet point. He was no less than the skipper of the *Kingani*, a former officer from the *Konigsberg*. He had come ashore to spy on the British and Belgian activities.

"Come with me, Henderson," said the Commander. "We'll see what we can winkle out of the Hun."

They went to the office of Commandant Steinman, but he refused to allow them access to the German skipper.

Shrugging eloquently, the Belgian said, “I regret, *mon commandant*. It is the orders of my superiors.”

Spicer-Simson was extremely annoyed. “It’s a disgrace, Henderson. You see, in war you can be killed in a second, but there are factors behind the story – the petty desires and envies of the men who control events.”

He marched briskly back to the British camp without another word to Gavin, who ambled along beside him. It was undoubtedly a missed opportunity, although the German might have refused to say anything.

—•—

Gavin was invited to dinner with Commandant Steinman’s family, who all spoke fluent German. Mrs Steinman was round and jolly, laughing as she produced a multitude of wonderful things to eat, mostly in the sweet category. Visiting from Belgium was their daughter, Lisa, studying at the University of Liege. She was pretty and vivacious, with dark hair, a perfect pink mouth and a smile that hinted of sexual interest.

She professed to be bored with life in Kalemie. “There are no young people of my age – Europeans, that is. What can I do except read – and help Mama in the kitchen. Will you take me on the lake in one of your boats?”

He looked at her with sympathy. “Alas, Lisa, they are naval vessels, so I would not be permitted to take you. We could take a walk along the shore.”

She smiled brightly. “Yes, please, Gavin. I would like that.”

He felt guilty as soon as they set off, imagining Kirsty in a situation where the roles were reversed. Would she accept an invitation from a young man? He would not be able to mention Lisa in his letters, because it might make Kirsty jealous; she might think he was doing more than take a lonely young girl for a walk. It was as if writing about it was the test of propriety.

They walked along a cliff path above the lake, cooled by a breeze from the water, admiring the ever-changing skeins of light and movement on its surface. A small promontory that jutted into the lake would have made an ideal lookout.

Lisa turned to him. "You are so kind to take me out like this."

Her smile was bewitching. She reached out and took his hand. "Are you shy?" Her eyebrows rose with the question. "Perhaps you have a wife or a sweetheart that you have not mentioned to us?"

He looked down, crestfallen. "It's true, Lisa. I have a girl-friend in Nyasaland. We hope to be married when the war is over."

Her smile faded. "I guessed as much. And you don't want to be unfaithful to her. I admire the sentiment. But, surely we can enjoy each other's company. I have a young man in Brussels, who is waiting for me to return. My parents don't know about him." She led him back along the path. "As a matter of fact, he might be conscripted into the army. He did not pass his medical examination, but now they do not care about those things – they take anyone who can walk."

—•—

The rains were approaching, and every evening Gavin watched with awe the pyrotechnic display in the clouds above the lake and the surrounding mountains. Huge cumulus clouds flickered with internal lightning like giant lanterns. Thunder rolled and echoed round the vast rift valley, as if heralding the storms to come. The first strong blow came on December 12, when some of the breakwaters were washed away – the rocks they used to build them were too small. Wainwright set out to find more suitable materials and located a site much closer to the harbour than the quarry they had been using.

Within a week the Belgians decided that the new harbour was ready to be occupied. They brought in their flotilla, consisting of the *Ten Ton*, the *Netta* – a small but fast motor-boat with a machine gun, and a *vedette* – a scouting boat. Meanwhile, Wainwright planned the launch of the British gunboats, hidden in the forest.

"I'm thinking," he said to Gavin, "of extending the railway line to the harbour. The Belgians don't like the idea, but I'll work on them. Perhaps you can help me. My French is non-existent."

Gavin was now Wainwright's unofficial assistant. The older man's experience made him the only officer that Spicer-Simson acknowledged as worth listening to. He looked like a huge schoolboy, in vast shorts and a wide-brimmed felt hat. He shouted at the labourers in *Fanagolo*, the South African *lingua franca,* sometimes called 'kitchen kaffir'. None of them understood him, but his gestures were sufficient.

The Belgians were finally persuaded to adopt the plan. The naval ratings and labourers built a slipway, while the Belgians and their workers laid the tracks. Wainwright extended the lines so that the rail trucks carrying the gunboats could enter the water. Three days before Christmas 1915 *Toutou* was brought from her hiding place to the harbour and within twenty minutes she was afloat; *Mimi* was launched the following day.

On Christmas Day both gunboats were taken out for a trial on the lake and fired a few shots. That evening the officers sat in their mess, feeling rather disconsolate because they were so far from home. Spicer-Simson, who had been sitting silently sipping Vermouth, suddenly erupted in anger.

"I was supposed to command this base, and Lee and Hope were supposed to take out the gunboats. Now I have to do it myself because there's not a seaman among you." He glared around the silent officers, then laughed scornfully and left the mess.

—•—

24

Zomba, Nyasaland – December/January 1916

Jess walked back to the house after checking the morning milking and saw a horse and rider approaching. For an instant she thought it was Drew, who rode upright with a ramrod-straight back. However, she soon realised it was not her son. The man was about thirty, his face gaunt and eyes sunken. As he came closer she saw the scar on his jaw and at the same time recognised Roly Benting-Smith.

He dismounted slowly as she called a groom to take care of the horse. She took his hand, and then looked closer at his face while he smiled sheepishly. Mandy had told her about the wound, and she was surprised to see so little evidence, other than a long thin scar running from chin to ear. More obvious was a change was in the shape of the jaw; the slightly receding chin replaced by a much firmer line, giving him a resolute demeanour.

"Well, Roly, you're looking well, albeit a trifle thin. I see little evidence of the wound that took you away."

He stroked the scar on his chin shyly. "I had a marvellous surgeon in Cape Town – actually, someone you know: Louis Viljoen, at the Somerset Hospital."

"Oh yes, Pauline's husband. Did you meet her and the family?"

"I did, indeed." He gave his characteristic braying laugh. "I was fortunate, too, to stay with the Fountaines in Cape Town. Mrs F and

Emily told me they met you here before the war started. They send you and Alan their best wishes."

They walked to the house and Jess ordered lemon squashes brought to the verandah.

"Alan told me you had been appointed to General Northey's staff – when he arrives. I'm so glad that you were able to come back here. Mandy and Kirsty are looking forward to seeing you again." Anticipating his question, she added, "They are both at Fort Johnston, but Mandy is due for some leave, and may come down here this weekend."

"How are they?"

"As well as can be expected. I've been up there once to visit them. It's a hard life – long hours and emotionally draining for them – constantly dealing with men who are in pain and dying. Whenever they have an opportunity they come down here – and spend a lot of the time sleeping."

—•—

Jess invited Roly to *Khundalila* for Sunday lunch. Looking forward to meeting Mandy again, he borrowed a car and drove out to the farm. Fending off enthusiastic greetings from the dogs he climbed the steps to the verandah, where she was standing alone. He guessed that Jess and Kirsty had retired discretely to the kitchen.

He thought he detected a reserve when she greeted him, embracing him, but not warmly. She moved away, and he saw her examining his scar, though surreptitiously, as she enquired about his months in South Africa. When Jess and Kirsty came out onto the verandah he was plied with a beer and snacks, and was asked to talk about the families in South Africa.

"The Viljeons – Louis and Pookie – wanted me to help their children with their English," he explained. "So I had a very pleasant few days with them in Cape Town. They passed me on to the Davenports in

Johannesburg, where I stayed for a couple of days before taking the train to Durban."

"And you stayed with the Fountaines in Cape Town," prompted Jess.

"Yes. Of course, you girls did not meet them when they came here – you were in Rhodesia. Philip Fountaine is a major-general; he was sent out to South Africa – something to do with the High Commissioner's office in Cape Town. Mrs Fountaine is an old friend of my mother, and also of Lady Smith, H.E.'s wife."

Jess said, "We remember when they were here – before the war started. Sir George brought Emily out here, and Drew took them shooting."

"Yes," Roly drawled enigmatically. "She evidently enjoyed her time here."

Mandy asked, "What do you know about General Northey? We're all wondering what changes he'll make."

"I have not yet met him," replied Roly. "He's supposed to be ultra-efficient..."

Jess laughed. "We need someone like that in command."

—•—

While they were sitting on the verandah at tea time a motor car drove up and out stepped Martin Russell. Jess saw at once that he'd lost weight, which she supposed was due to the privations of living at the front. His usually tanned face looked pale and drawn.

"I came back to Zomba at the behest of Colonel Murray," he said.

Jess introduced him to Roly, and the two men shook hands; during some conversation they appraised each other. Martin saw in Roly a typical upper class army officer, of a type he'd met frequently in India and during the Boer War. He was obviously intelligent, but had the drawling voice and arrogant demeanour that

Martin disliked. He could not understand how Mandy liked him. He thought she would have recognised the man as something of a caricature.

Roly saw in Martin an ageing colonial type; the British army man turned settler, stolid, pompous, opinionated. He knew that Mandy was fond of the man, but had no inkling that there was anything more, nor would he have suspected it, since Martin was so much older.

"I'm sorry you got that wound, Roly," said Martin. "I've heard about the scrap at Karonga. You fellows put up a good show."

"It was bad luck," replied Roly, stroking the scar. "Actually, sir, I was lucky not to be killed."

"It's surprising that you two haven't met before," Mandy said. "Roly was with us on the journey from Rhodesia in 1914. He must have been invalided out just before you came here."

—•—

It was considered safe enough for Jess and Mandy to travel the short distance to Zomba by car. They were greeted at the club by Martin and Roly, who had waited together in uncomfortable silence on the verandah. The interior was for dancing, with a small band on the dais. Tables on the deep verandah allowed guests to sit in the cool evening air between dances, while white-uniformed servants plied to and from the bar with drinks.

There was some formality, since the women had programmes. Mandy had requests from Martin and Roly before she could sit down. Soon other men clustered round. Jess was not ignored and her programme soon filled. They were joined at their table by Andrew and Flora Bruce and the Duffs.

Mandy's first dance was with Roly, who held her strongly; he was an accomplished dancer, holding her close, so that they could talk despite the sounds from the band.

"Have you found another man – while I've been away?" Roly tried not to sound plaintive.

She laughed shortly. "I haven't been looking for anyone – I've been too busy. You probably don't know how hard it is to be a nurse in Fort Johnston..."

"I'm sorry. It was inconsiderate of me..."

"A lot has changed, Roly. I'm much more involved in my nursing than I was when... when we... when we were in Karonga. I've decided to give the work my full attention until the war is over."

"That could be a long time."

"Do you think so?"

"We haven't had much success so far. But it could all change quickly – if von Lettow is defeated. You know, he might be caught in an ambush and killed."

"But the war would continue."

"In Europe – yes. But you wouldn't go there, would you?"

"I don't know."

The music stopped and they returned to their table.

Mandy's next dance was with a young soldier. Evidently recuperating from wounds he could barely walk, and stayed with the girl in the centre of the hall. He said nothing and was content to shuffle a few steps to each side. He thanked Mandy politely when he returned her to her table.

"What was the matter with him?" asked Roly.

"He didn't say." Mandy fanned herself with her programme.

Her next dance was with Martin. She found him awkward and clumsy, and he admitted that he was not a good dancer.

"We're going back north again," he said. "So I don't know when I'll see you again. Will you be in Fort Johnston?"

"As far as I know. They're talking about making field dressing stations further north."

"Is Roly your, er... young man, now?"

Mandy laughed. "No, he's not my young man. For that matter, we were never really romantically attached. I suspect he's found a girl friend in Cape Town – when he was convalescing there. But he won't admit it. You see, men like to have a girl in every port."

—•—

25

Lake Tanganyika – December 1915-January 1916

Boxing Day was a Sunday, and the Commander of the Lake Tanganyika flotilla conducted a church service after the routine parade and inspection. Gavin sat with Wainwright and Dudley in the front row, wearing his better uniform. Ahead of them the lake spread in shades of blue and indigo, wind spoor drifting over its vast surface. Spicer-Simson seemed diminished by the grandeur of the great expanse of water.

Sweat coalesced on Gavin's skin and dribbled down his torso. Despite his strong Christian belief, he paid no attention the words being intoned by Spicer-Simson, reading from a small prayer book. His thoughts were about Kirsty and when he might see her again. He imagined her tending to wounded soldiers until, exhausted, she would fall asleep in the little house she shared with her sister and the matron.

There were other times when he imagined, with masochistic intensity, some faceless officer seducing her, and she, consumed with loneliness, succumbing to his blandishments. He saw the man's hands stroking the white skin and exploring places that had been denied him. In moments like this he thought he should take advantage of Lisa Steinman's open invitation.

Gavin and his fellow officers did not know that the Commander had already been informed by the Belgians that the *Kingani*, the

German gunboat, was approaching. Only after the service was completed did he order the men to get ready for action. They could now see the ship rounding a point a few miles to the north.

It was a fine sunny day, and a breeze rose to whip the lake surface into choppy little waves. Spicer-Simson took command of *Mimi,* while Lt Dudley was given *Toutou.* Gavin went on *Toutou*, as second in command. Looking back he could see hundreds of African villagers gathering on the headland to watch the two British gunboats, spectators in a minor league match between the great colonial powers.

Had it all been worthwhile? All the days of slogging through the bush, dragging the boats over the mountains. Here at last they were in their element, he thought, sleek, fast gunboats, racing towards the enemy. But he well remembered Spicer-Simson saying they could be blown to matchwood.

The crew of the *Toutou* watched as their Commander waited until his flotilla eased between the *Kingani* and her escape course back to Kigoma, sixty miles to the north. Spicer-Simson knew that the Germans' single gun was mounted forward, so she could not fire at the chasers without turning round.

Using flag signals he ordered *Toutou* to follow the *Kingani* from the lake side, while he approached from the shore side. Trailing after them was the small Belgian *Netta*, ordered to pick up survivors if one of the British ships was hit. The *vedette* also came along, manned by British ratings, and carrying reserve fuel.

The Germans soon spotted *Mimi* and *Toutou* and turned to face them, thus bringing her six-pounder gun to bear. The smaller British gunboats, with their two-pounders, did not yet have the Germans in their range. Luckily, none of the *Kingani's* shots found their target. Gavin watched with relief as the shells splashed harmlessly into the deep water.

Shortly before noon the British boats closed to within two thousand yards and opened fire.

"We've got her!" shouted Dudley, pounding the hatch with his hand.

Two lucky shots hit the *Kingani* and she caught fire. Gavin could see that one of the crew was hauling down their ensign, while an African sailor waved a white cloth. Spicer-Simson brought *Mimi* alongside, but the helmsman damaged her prow as he accidentally rammed the *Kingani*. The officers of *Mimi* jumped onto the enemy ship and soon discovered that the German skipper and two of his Petty Officers had been killed; blown to pieces behind the gun-shield. One of the ratings was overcome by the gory scene and vomited over the rail.

Spicer-Simson ordered a prize crew from *Toutou* to go aboard and fly the White Ensign from *Kingani*'s mast. The German ship was taking water as they shepherded her to harbour to the cheers of crowds on shore. No one knew which gunboat had fired the devastating shots, since both were using high-explosive shells at the time. So the officers agreed that honours should be shared.

Gavin, with his knowledge of German, was given the task of interrogating the prisoners. The engineer from the *Kingani* sat on the quay, his uniform soaking wet. He spoke fairly good English, so they switched between the two languages.

"I'm sorry about your Captain and the sailors," said Gavin.

The engineer shrugged; he looked shocked. "It was all a surprise, so sudden. We did not know you British had gunboats on the lake."

"I'm amazed," said Gavin. "It took weeks to bring them here..."

"We heard that you were bringing boats over the mountains, but we thought it was all rumours." He sighed heavily. "What will happen to me?"

"The Belgians will take you as a prisoner. I expect they will look after you well."

"I am not so sure. May I stay with your people?"

"I'm sorry, we have no facilities. Tell me about the *Hedwig von Wissmann.* Is she anywhere near?"

The engineer smiled ruefully. "I wish I could tell you, but even if I knew I would not betray my countrymen."

"And the *Graf von Gotzen*? Has she been launched?"

"I can tell you that she has. So beware, Lieutenant."

—•—

Gavin went to report to the Commander and found him composing a report to the Admiralty. Spicer-Simson listened to what Gavin said, then turned back to his writing without comment.

An hour later they buried the three men from the *Kingani*, but not before the Commander had removed the German skipper's gold ring. A guard was posted at the grave, as Spicer-Simson said that some of the local natives were cannibals. A goat found on the *Kingani* was kept as a mascot. After hauling the German boat out of the water Wainwright started the repair work. He mounted a 12-pounder gun on the *Kingani*; it had been intended for a Belgian ship.

"Isn't it a bit too big for her?" asked Gavin as he watched the work. The gun was twelve feet long, and the overall length of the *Kingani* was only forty-five feet.

"You're right, Gavin, but as long as we keep it pointing straight ahead we should be alright. If we shoot sideways it'll tip the boat over." He laughed as he imagined the debacle. "We'll put a spare three-pounder at the rear. She'll certainly be well armed. You know that the boss has christened her *Fifi*?"

—•—

The Belgians were encouraged by the British naval success and set about assembling the 1,500 ton *Baron Dhanis.* They also repaired the wrecked *Alexandre del Commune* and re-named her the *Vengeur,* arming her with the six-pounder from the *Kingani.* Meanwhile, the

British and Belgian authorities agreed that Spicer-Simson would command the Allied fleet on the lake, while the senior Belgian officer, Steinman, would command on land.

On an overcast grey day the *Hedwig von Wissmann* was sighted steaming south down the lake. Using a telescope they confirmed that she was twice the size of the newly named *Fifi*, and had two six-pounders on the foredeck, as well as a revolving Hotchkiss on the aft deck.

As they ran down to the harbour, Wainwright called to Gavin, "This might be a tougher nut."

The Allied fleet consisted of *Fifi*, commanded by Spicer-Simson; *Mimi*, commanded by Wainwright, with Gavin as his deputy; and two small Belgian boats; *Toutou* was being repaired.

The Germans were six miles away when they spotted the Allies and turned to the east to escape. *Fifi* was now carrying so much weaponry that she was too slow to catch the *Wissmann*, but *Mimi* was as fast as ever and took over the chase.

As they overtook *Fifi*, Gavin said, "I think the Commander is trying to signal to us."

"What's he saying?" asked Wainwright, not wanting to take his eyes off the distant smoke of the *Wissmann*.

"I can't read it... He's waving flags, but it makes no sense."

"Well, I'm not going to pay any attention."

Inexorably, *Mimi* closed on the *Wissmann*. But suddenly the Germans turned round to bring their six-pounders to bear. They missed a couple of times and then turned north again to flee. The manoeuvre allowed *Mimi* to gain on them, so Wainwright handed the wheel to Gavin and took over the gun, scoring several hits without doing any serious damage.

Meanwhile, Gavin could see splashes beyond the *Wissmann*. "The Commander's shots are going over her," he called to Wainwright. "They can't see from where they are. Should we drop back and tell him?"

Wainwright grunted. "I suppose so." He eased up on the throttle and *Mimi* fell back.

When *Fifi* drew alongside them Spicer-Simson started to shout at Wainwright. "Why the hell did you overtake us? I ordered you to hold back! You disobeyed me!"

Wainwright blinked and pretended not to understand. "Sir, your shots have been going over the Germans."

"Damn it!" The Commander moved ahead, but he had only three shells left for the twelve-pounder.

The two British ships drifted apart and Gavin watched through his binoculars as a gunner placed the next shell in the breech of *Fifi's* large gun, then pulled the firing lever. Nothing happened.

"Misfire," Gavin muttered.

"What?" asked Wainwright.

"They've had a misfire."

"They won't be able to take the shell out," said Wainwright. "The barrel will be too hot."

Gavin imagined the frustration of Spicer-Simson – first, when too far back he used up most of his ammunition, and now when he had the Germans at his mercy, he was unable to deliver the *coup de grace*.

The two officers on *Toutou* waited, taking it in turns to watch with binoculars as the Commander paced *Fifi's* deck, waving his arms and occasionally stopping to talk to the gun crew. It was twenty minutes before they opened the breech and removed the offending dud shell, throwing it into the lake.

Fifi's very next shot hit the *Wissmann*. It exploded in the engine room and she started to sink. The crew tried to launch the dinghy, but that sank, so they jumped into the water. Wainwright steered *Mimi* towards them and he and Gavin watched as the *Wissmann* sank bow first. They picked up the bobbing survivors, as did *Fifi*. Spicer-Simson found the German flag locker, which contained an ensign.

One of the men that *Mimi* rescued was the German skipper, visibly upset at the loss of his ship. Gavin consoled him in German and they chatted as *Mimi* steamed back to harbour. The officer revealed that he had planned a rendezvous with the *Graf von Gotzen,* though he claimed to have no idea where the large German ship had gone.

—•—

The *Graf von Gotzen* appeared on the horizon the day after the battle, probably seeking the *Wissmann*. Standing on the cliff near the harbour Dudley and Gavin watched with their binoculars, standing beside the Commander.

"May we go after her?" begged Dudley.

Spicer-Simson shook his head. "She could blow any one of us out of the water. She'll go back to Kigoma."

"But this is a golden opportunity, sir," said Gavin. "If three of our boats go after her it'll divide her fire..."

"No, Henderson. I've made my decision." The Commander turned away abruptly and walked to his hut.

Gavin looked at Dudley. "What do you make of that?"

Dudley shrugged. "I suppose he thinks that we should rest on our laurels and not take any risks."

"Is there nothing we can do?"

"He's the commander, Gavin. No, there's nothing... except we could ask Wainwright to try to persuade him."

But even Wainwright could not get Spicer-Simson to change his mind. The camp went on with their routine of servicing and testing the boats, parades, and griping about the inactivity. Then, as if to reassure them that they were needed, a telegram arrived ordering them to support the advance of Colonel Murray's land force towards Bismarckburg, at the southern end of Lake Tanganyika.

The news filtered slowly out from Spicer-Simson to his officers, and from them to the ratings. They were glad to have a task ahead, and there were rousing cheers when the flotilla steamed out of harbour at the start of their voyage. Their objective was Kituta, and it would take them two stormy days to get there.

—•—

26

Zomba, Nyasaland – January-March 1916

Many observers, including Alan Spaight, thought a higher command was needed in the campaign on the border of Northern Rhodesia and Nyasaland. He was relieved to hear of the appointment of Brigadier-General Edward Northey and soon heard that he was a career army officer, educated at Eton and Sandhurst, who served in the Boer War. In 1914 he commanded the King's Royal Rifle Corps on the Western Front, and was wounded at Ypres.

Northey arrived in South Africa in January 1916 travelling without delay to Pretoria where the British High Commissioner was in residence. He also met General Louis Botha, Prime Minister of the Union of South Africa. In Bulawayo he was fêted by the local people, and, hearing that they yearned for news of the war in Europe, he arranged to give them a public lecture lasting two hours. He repeated the address in Salisbury, where he also conferred with senior officials. However, it was obvious that all the important military commanders were at the front, and he continued his journey by train to Beira and thence to Chinde, Chindio. Limbe and Zomba.

In Zomba the General stayed at Government House. A War Council was held at the Secretariat the day after he arrived, hosted by Sir George Smith, and attended by Alan, as the Governor's military attaché, Hector Duff, the Chief Secretary, and Roly Benting-Smith, the new addition to the General's staff, who kept confidential notes. Alan was impressed by the military bearing of Northey, a man of less than medium height, exuding energy, his moustache bristling and his monocle gleaming.

Also present was Major Spratt, Northey's ADC. Alan met him before the meeting and learnt that he had served with Northey in France, coming to Africa at the General's request. To Alan he seemed to typify the upper class, born-to-the-military, supercilious officer. Short like Northey, and growing rotund, his complexion suggested over-indulgence in hard liquor.

The General looked around the table. "Gentlemen, I asked His Excellency to convene this meeting so we can discuss the strategy for our campaign. I have some ideas of my own, but I really want to hear from you who have been engaged in the war here for more than a year – in fact, from the very first days. I suggest we start with a summary from Major Spaight."

Northey had few expectations, having found it difficult to get reliable information about the campaign on his journey through South Africa and Southern Rhodesia. Now he was waiting for a tall, slender Major, who was somewhat older than himself, had also been to Sandhurst, and then served briefly in the British Army. Although not envious, Northey thought it ironic that Spaight had a CB, while he, a Brigadier-General, who had served with distinction through the Boer War and on the Western Front, had not yet received such an honour.

Alan walked over to a huge new map on the wall, then turned to face Northey. He was confident of his own views, but uncertain as to the detail required. "I will talk only about our nearest front, General; the campaign further north in German East is outside my purview."

Northey nodded to indicate that Alan should continue.

"Our information is limited by communications difficulties – of which I'm sure you're aware. We believe that the main German command, led by Colonel von Lettow-Vorbeck, has moved into our 'theatre'. His strategy seems to be aimed at tying up as many of our men as possible, thus drawing manpower away from operations in Europe – to Germany's advantage."

"His tactics are to 'hit and run', He and his officers have become adept at this. Von Lettow, as I will call him, is a wily commander and uses his limited resources to the best advantage. He's being driven south, towards Lake Nyasa, which will bring him into direct confrontation with us. This will extend the supply lines of General Smuts' army, while at the same time making demands of our resources, which also have difficult supply logistics."

"The Germans have three main routes to the south." Alan pointed to the map. "One is to the west, through Northern Rhodesia. I doubt whether von Lettow will use that option, because it's further from the Indian Ocean, which is his main potential source of weapons and ammunition. Furthermore, the local tribes in the interior are more inclined to support the British."

"The second option is in the centre, where topography limits him to Lake Nyasa – essentially he would be contained in the Rift Valley. However, we have control over the lake with our gunboats. The shore plains are narrow and not very conducive to his 'hit and run' tactics."

"The third option for the Germans is the eastern one, through Portuguese territory, where they would be closer to the Indian Ocean and supplies – if they can break our naval blockade. We expect that the Portuguese would offer little resistance to an invasion." He paused. "Perhaps I should stop at this point, sir."

"Thank you, Major." Northey was impressed. This was the first clear exposition he had received, and he thought that he was at last getting closer to the issues facing his command. "What are the tactics being used by our forces?"

"We've spent over a year containing German advances and attacks, for example at Karonga, Abercorn and Saisi – with success. However, we've done less well in our attempts to drive the Germans back from the border. On many occasions we fought them, advanced and found their defensive positions empty – they simply fled, to fight another day."

"Have you tried encircling them?" asked Northey's ADC, Major Spratt, in a languid drawl.

"We have, Major, but the local people – the Africans – are difficult to avoid. When they see us, they notify the Germans and we lose the element of surprise. It's not that the country is heavily populated – there are not many people, compared with the coastal areas. However, there are villagers almost everywhere – making it difficult for us to advance undetected to encircle the Germans. Remember, there are few roads, only tracks through the bush. When you move off the tracks the going is very slow."

The Governor asked. "Surely, as Smuts' army comes south, we could squeeze the Germans – like a pincer – force them into a battle or capitulation?"

Northey looked at Alan to answer, and he pointed to the map again. "I suspect that is why von Lettow is moving south and will enter the Portuguese colony. He wants to escape the pincer. We can try to block his invasion but we don't have enough men. We would be trying to catch him in a huge area, where there are no roads."

"Major Spaight," asked the General, "what would you propose – strategically?"

"Sir, first we must prevent the Germans from being supplied through the small harbours along the coast. I know it's a long coast line, but the Royal Navy is virtually unopposed. The blockade must be complete."

"And second?"

"As I explained, it would be very difficult to prevent the Germans moving south. We don't have sufficient manpower to make a continuous barrier from the Indian Ocean to Lake Nyasa. I think we should try to pick off von Lettow's subsidiary columns. It won't be easy, because they're small and mobile. That means we will also have to use small mobile units. Eventually, von Lettow will be left with only his HQ force. Then I suspect he would either make a grand gesture or surrender."

Major Spratt asked, "Why can't we fight them on even terms?"

"It's really because they have now become the fugitives, and we are the hunters. Up till now they were on home territory, with good knowledge of the terrain, and adequate maps. They knew the local tribes and used their well-trained *askaris*. There's evidence that, as they moved south, some tribes turned their allegiance to us. As you know, the Germans gained a bad reputation in the *Maji-maji* Rebellion. When they move into Portuguese territory they will lose much of their advantage, and we should be fighting on more equal terms."

The meeting continued for another hour, discussing logistics, including methods of moving and supplying the troops, and extracting casualties. Northey drew Alan aside when the meeting concluded.

"Thank you for your contribution, Spaight," he said. "At last I feel that I'm getting a clearer picture of the issues facing us. I trust that you will be travelling with us, so that we can have the benefit of your local knowledge."

"Sir, as you wish. Sir George wanted me to escort you and your party on the journey."

—•—

They followed what was, for Alan, a well-worn route: by car and lorry from Zomba to Fort Johnston, by steamer to Karonga, and by motor vehicle again to Abercorn. At Fort Johnston he was able to see his daughters and introduce them and Dr Sanderson to General Northey and his staff officers.

Northey took a special interest in the medical facilities, and Alan presumed that it was because the General had been wounded in France. He asked to see the hospital, and Dr Sanderson led him on a short tour, during which he asked searching questions about staffing and supplies.

When they had supper at the officers' mess, Northey told them about the carnage in France.

"We have forward clearing stations where the wounded are brought straight off the battlefield. They are divided according to the severity of the wounds and whether the limbs or abdomen are affected. Obviously they treat the most serious cases first. The numbers are horrendous."

"Our numbers are smaller here," said Sanderson quietly, "but perhaps we have more disease problems – malaria, dysentery, cholera..."

"And the nursing staff are fewer – in proportion," interjected Kirsty. "My sister and I are the only nurses north of Zomba – not counting the missions."

Northey looked at the young girl with interest. He knew from the introductions that the two girls were Alan's daughters. "What are your main problems?" he asked.

"We're too far away from the front," said Kirsty without hesitation. "If a soldier is wounded – or falls ill – he needs treatment as soon as possible. It's sometimes several days before we see them. Of course, they would have had something done for them, but..."

"Have you considered more forward medical centres?" Northey asked Dr Sanderson.

"We have, sir. But we don't know where the action will be. There seem to be skirmishes all over the northern front..."

"What about Karonga?"

Sanderson nodded. "It's perhaps too close to the front – only twenty miles south of the border. As you know, the enemy have already attacked it. They might do so again."

"Hm." Northey nodded, then turned to Kirsty. "I assure you, Miss Spaight, we'll give serious thought to the matter."

She wondered if this was his standard dismissal. Something about the little general made her think otherwise. Even so, she thought he was out of his environment, unused to the primitive conditions here, and the slow pace of life – and death.

—•—

On the three day lake voyage Alan noticed that the General spent many hours by himself, leaning on the rail and gazing at the shores to east and west. Luckily, the lake remained calm and greatly conducive to contemplation. Alan thought the General must be worried, partly because he had not been in the region before, although he had participated in the Boer War. Also, there was so little definite information about the locations of the German units. It was Alan's job to find them.

Quite to his surprise Alan saw the General walk towards him and say, "I would like to hear your story, Spaight. Sir George told me that you were a part of the anti-slavery campaign. Tell me about it."

They stood together at the rail, Alan a head taller than Northey. "I was an accidental soldier." Alan laughed. "I had been a professional – Sandhurst, the Berkshires, Sudan, and India. I resigned my commission and came out..."

"Why did you resign?"

Alan wondered how much he should say, not that he was ashamed. "My Colonel ordered me to arrange for one of my Indian NCOs to be flogged – for theft. He wanted to make an example, but I was confident the man was innocent. There was no tribunal, no evidence, and no opportunity for the man to offer a defence. Anyway, I refused to do it. The Colonel told me to write out my resignation – which I did."

"Sounds outrageous. You could have appealed."

"Yes, sir, I could have, but at the time I was disillusioned. So I decided to come to Africa and join the African Lakes Corporation; you may know that it was set up to supply the missionaries and trade in the process. They sent me north to Karonga. You'll soon see the little settlement, sir. It was much smaller then. The ALC – or Mandala, as we call it – had a trader named Fotheringham, a stubborn Scot, who was trying to establish a trading station in the face of opposition from an Arab half-caste slave trader named Mlozi. Some of us joined him to fight the slave traders..."

"Who were your group?"

"Some Mandala employees like me, and the company's managers – the Moir brothers, some administrators, like the consuls and Harry Johnston; and there were adventurers like Alfred Sharpe, who became Governor. We were a motley bunch – oh, and there were some South African mercenaries, too. But we were too few and lacking in fire-power. We were too far from Britain, and not considered at all important. By good fortune, Johnston was able to get some funds from Cecil Rhodes to bring a contingent of Sikh sòldiers from India. That turned the tide. We broke the slave trade."

"Interesting, Spaight," said Northey. "I knew nothing about the slaving here in East Africa, until I read Livingstone's journals, while I was preparing to come out here. That despite having spent three years in South Africa during the war there; I suppose we were consumed with the day-to-day minutiae of the war." He looked sharply at Alan. "By the way, you did not participate in that war."

"No. I thought the British behaviour was indefensible – a desire to brush aside the Boers and gain control of their accidental wealth. Also, to get revenge for their defeat in the previous war – Majuba Hill and all that."

Northey smiled. "You could have joined them."

"The Boers? Then I would have been fighting my own people – men like you. I didn't want that. My cousin, Martin Russell, who you'll meet – he's one of Murray's staff officers – felt much as I did, but fought on the British side."

"You missed a dreadful war, Spaight. I had little stomach for it. What about this one?"

"Hm. Strange, isn't it, sir? It's almost as if the Germans are the Boers, with their 'hit and run' tactics, and we're blundering around trying to catch them."

"I hope we don't make the same mistakes."

—•—

At Karonga Mr Webb, the Resident, gave them an account of the Battle of September 1914, and showed them the small graveyard under a huge baobab tree, where Alan pointed out to the General and his staff the markers of the two Scottish engineers who died of fever while building the Stevenson Road, and the men who were killed in the slave war, and the battle of 1914.

"Were they really 'battles', Spaight?" asked Robbie Spratt, in his languid way; Alan now knew that the ADC was inclined to make satirical comments. "Or was the first one merely a minor encounter – a tribal scrap?"

Alan smiled. "What is your definition of a battle? I remember debating the question at Sandhurst. I think the definition is 'a conflict between two armed forces in significant numbers'. The attack on Karonga in 1887 was serious affair, involving several hundred armed men..."

"Armed with bows and arrows?" Spratt's tone was scornful.

"Some with muzzle-loaders. We had rifles. I myself had a Snyder rifle and my .375 magnum hunting rifle. The 1914 Battle – by the way, my daughter was here – was also fought with several hundred on each side, and the soldiers were better armed, all with rifles; there were field guns involved, too."

Major Spratt did not seem entirely convinced, but he did not pursue the point.

That evening the General's party met with Colonel George Hawthorn, a KAR officer who commanded the South African contingent; he came to Karonga after inspecting a fortification on the border. During discussions over supper it was clarified that Hawthorn had under his command a squadron of the 1st South African Rifles, and four companies of 1/KAR, a total of eight hundred men.

—•—

Next day General Northey's party drove west along the Stevenson Road, in a Humber staff car sent by Colonel Murray. The road had been damaged in many places during the rainy season, and gangs of labourers were clearing culverts and drains, adding fresh branches to the corduroy crossings. The Germans had been pushed north, away from the border road, and were not a threat.

Roughly half way to Abercorn they stopped for the night at Fife, where Northey inspected the fortifications on the following day, severely criticising the design of the trenches. Regarding himself as something of an expert, he told the commanding officer that they were too shallow, and too straight, making them vulnerable to enfilade fire. He also criticised the buildings, pronouncing them vulnerable to artillery fire.

After three days the General continued on his way, to sighs of relief from the men at Fife. At Abercorn Northey met Colonel Murray for the first time, and was unstinting in his criticism of the fortifications. The buildings he denounced as 'flimsy Swiss chalets' and the trenches were 'just as bad as those in Fife'.

Murray and his Rhodesians were dumbstruck as they listened to this strange little British officer who had just come from Europe and, they thought, knew nothing about Africa and the local conditions.

It was evident from the start that Northey and Murray were not compatible. Northey was the archetypical upper-middle class professional officer, with service in India and South Africa. By contrast, Murray had risen from the ranks in a para-military police force, although he too had served in the Boer War. Northey had married a girl from one of South African's aristocratic families, the

Cloetes. By contrast Murray had no exalted connections; he was a true South African, though he had lived in Rhodesia for many years.

Murray hated to be criticized and thought that Northey was an insufferable prig, who knew nothing about the conditions in the African interior, which were much different to those in Europe, or even South Africa. Northey found Murray to be rather dour and unduly harsh to his junior officers.

The General was much relieved when he was introduced to Martin Russell. They had both served in India at the same time, and had met briefly in General Buller's staff during the Tugela campaign, where Martin was wounded and decorated with a DSO. Northey immediately liked Martin's demeanour and discussed with Murray the possibility of taking him onto his staff.

"It's your prerogative, sir," said Murray glumly. "But I would not wish to lose him."

"Very well," replied Northey. "You shall keep him – at least for the time being."

The General had decided that he needed a senior officer with local knowledge. His first choices were Martin Russell and Alan Spaight. He was reluctant to take away Murray's deputy, so, he telegraphed Zomba to ask the Governor if he might retain the services of Alan Spaight for the time being. An affirmative answer came the following day.

—•—

27

Zomba, Nyasaland – March 1916

The two sisters came to the farm *Khundalila* whenever they found an opportunity. Despite their pleas, often they could not come together, but on one such occasion they revelled in having two days with their mother. Mac was there, of course, but gave little interest to their presence.

Alarmed at the weight they lost, Jess prepared their favourite meals and tempted them with home-made sweets and fudge. She did think that Kirsty looked more attractive now that she had shed a few pounds, but Mandy could not afford to be thinner.

The girls spent a lot of time sleeping, rising late and napping in the afternoons. They went on farm rounds with Jess when she checked the dairy and the sheep flock. They helped her in the kitchen, and when she provided meals for her convalescing soldiers. Sometimes, they ate separately, not always with Mac present. They rode their horses round the farms, and in the late afternoons they walked with Jess, round the edges of the *dambos*.

"I do hope that you will marry Gavin," said Jess, in her soft Scottish voice. "Your father and I think highly of him. Does he write regularly?"

"Oh yes, Kirsty replied. "The problem is that his letters go through a censor – the doctor in their unit. So he can't say anything about what he's doing. I think he feels embarrassed to write endearments." She sighed. "So his letters are...well, rather bland."

"And you, Mandy?"

"Do you mean, has Roly written?"

"Yes."

"No, he hasn't. Frankly, Ma, I think he's lost interest. I don't blame him. I haven't given him any encouragement."

"And is there no one else who's thrown his cap at you?"

The girls laughed at Jess's phrase. Mandy answered: "There have been plenty of young men who have wanted a quick squeeze – or more." She smiled at her mother. "Don't look shocked, Ma. Most of them are after the same thing – aren't they, Kirst? They say their days are numbered and they want the experience before they die." She laughed to herself. "A few of them are more subtle, and a couple have been quite genuine – but, really... I don't think I want to embark on a romantic venture."

"Perhaps someone will come out of the blue," said Jess.

"The problem is, Ma," said Kirsty, " – if he does he may have to go off on some campaign – like Gavin did. It's very wearing on the emotions to have an absentee love."

"Don't I know it," said Jess.

—•—

One afternoon, when the sisters were walking along the edge of the home *dambo*, Mandy turned to Kirsty and said, "Are you really determined to stay faithful to Gavin?"

Kirsty in turn glanced at her sister, to read her expression. "I would like to. He's the man I would like to marry, but the prospect is no nearer. It's as if we're in some awful limbo, with no sign that it will change, and that we'll return to a normal life."

"But you didn't know him really well, did you?"

Again Kirsty looked at her sister. "Do you mean 'did we make love?' No, we didn't, but we feel attracted to each other, and there's a strong friendship."

Mandy sighed. “Well, I hope he’s being faithful to you.”

“What about you and Roly?”

Mandy snorted. “There was nothing between us – although he wanted it.”

—•—

28

Namema & Bismarckburg, German East Africa – April/May 1916

During April 1916 Northey made his plans to push north, now that the rains were ending. On the left flank 'Norforce' had Colonel Murray at Abercorn, with two BSAP companies and one NRP company; their objective was to attack the German fort at Namema, fifteen miles to the north of Saisi. On the right flank, based at Karonga, Colonel Hawthorn would attack Ipiana, 25 miles to the north. In the centre were Colonel Rodger and Major Flindt, each with troops from the 2nd South African Rifles. The whole force consisted of 2,600 rifles, 26 machine guns and 14 field guns, but they were spread widely between the two great lakes, and they had little knowledge of the German strength and dispositions.

After one of the staff meetings Northey drew Alan and Martin aside. "Spaight, you must be wondering whether I heard you in Zomba, and, if so, why I'm not following your suggestion of picking off the smaller German units." He smiled slightly and waited for Alan's reply.

"It's not for me to question your strategy, sir..."

"But?"

"It will be our first real thrust in strength against the enemy. I think we are at last ready. We shall see whether they fight or vanish. I suspect it will be the latter."

"Quite so. As you know, I've ordered the column commanders to try encircling the Germans."

"Let's hope they find an opportunity, sir. The spaces are vast, and the terrain is going to be very difficult when they move away from the main tracks."

—•—

Colonel Ron Murray was anxious to get his Column into action. Northey's criticisms were still smarting in his mind. He knew his men had the ability to defeat the Germans if only they had the chance. He gathered his officers and NCOs for a meeting to plan the attack on Namema. They stood around a large map table under a make-shift thatched shed with open sides. Sentries were posted outside so that no one could hear their discussion.

These men were all volunteers: farmers, miners, businessmen, lawyers, accountants. They had put their operations into the care of managers, wives, friends, or hired help, for the duration of the war, often with great financial loss. Martin Russell was a typical example, a farmer whose wife and manager were keeping the place going in his absence.

Murray started. "Major Spaight has informed me that Fort Namema is in two inter-connected sections on a bluff above the Saisi River. It's not impregnable, but will be difficult to attack. Our information is limited, so I propose that we define our tactics later, when we see what faces us. I expect the men to travel light."

"Will we take porters, sir?" asked one of the platoon commanders.

Murray nodded to Martin to answer. He was feeling unwell and knew that his temperament was unusually irritable.

"I suggest one *tenga* to every three soldiers," said Martin. "They should each take a thirty pound load of food and ammo, and a blanket for each man – no more. We must also take additional *tengas* for the machine guns and artillery pieces."

After the meeting three NCOs approached Martin. "Sir," said one of them, "the men's clothes are in a terrible state. They – we – think it's bloody unfair that the men should have to buy their own clothes. The uniforms should be provided by the Army."

Martin knew two of the NCOs, miners from Mazoe; the other was a store clerk from Bulawayo. It was obvious that their khaki shorts and shirts were worn and shredded at the seams.

"I agree," he said. "I'll talk to the CO; I expect he'll change the rules."

—•—

Martin's servant, Moses, was beginning to wonder whether he ought to have come with his boss. Even though he'd been warned about the harsh conditions, they were worse than he expected. He had made friends with Goodwill, and Alan's batman, a younger man named Josiah; they contrived to mess together.

"It's not just that there's not enough *nsima*," muttered Josiah. "It's the lack of a good relish that I miss."

The three men were sitting round a small fire, while the officers were gathered in a late evening discussion.

"You have had an easy life, my friend," said Moses. "We older men have seen hard times, and..."

"Nothing could be worse than my experiences with the slavers," said Goodwill. He stared laconically at the fire. "This is very comfortable."

"So what would you suggest for relish?" asked Moses.

"We need meat – for our strength."

Josiah gave a hollow laugh. "There is no way we can get meat."

Goodwill looked at him with sympathy, remembering how he had come looking for work at the farm, and had been selected to be a house servant, because he was polite and well-spoken. "There is no chance of getting meat from big animals, until the ration meat comes.

So, we have to catch small animals. My uncle showed me how to do it, when I was a child. I have been making traps – we can see if anything has been caught in them."

Goodwill took Josiah with him, leaving Moses to tend the fire. The older man carried a hurricane lamp, walking slowly as he went to the places where he set his traps. They found three field mice.

"One for each of us," said Goodwill, as he put them in his pocket.

"One mouthful each," said Josiah gloomily.

"They will add flavour."

—•—

It took three days hard marching to reach Namema, one of them through marshy country where the men sank to their knees while manhandling the artillery. They had to burn the leeches off their legs with lighted cigarette ends. Their exposed skin was black from the peaty marsh water, and they joked about their appearance.

Martin watched an effort to extract a field gun that had sunk to its axles in mud. Ropes were extended to firmer ground and together white soldiers and *askaris* heaved on them. He saw Drew and Goodwill encouraging the men in a variety of Bantu languages, as well as English.

"One – two – three – as you go! *Hiya!*" chanted Goodwill and the men heaved with a deep chorus of groans. Finally the gun pulled free with an obscene sucking noise, while the men fell panting on the ground, exhausted.

"They are good men," said Drew to Martin. "But they're half starved. A few mouthfuls of *nsima* – not enough. We need to give them more – and some meat."

"We can't hunt with rifles now – too much noise. Wait till we get to Namema. I've arranged for about twenty steers to be driven there from Abercorn."

"That's good. Let's hope they have some meat left on them when they get here."

—•—

They started to shell Fort Namema at first light, the explosions sending birds crying and infusing the pearly sky with smoking scarlet flares. From a neighbouring high hill the Rhodesian spotters signalled to the gunners using a heliograph, advising them about the fall of their shells. The 'May Jackson' – a 12.5 pounder named after a Bulawayo barmaid – blasted at the fort walls, knocking out chunks of rocks, but the German flag waved as if nothing had happened.

Despite the bombardment, attempts to advance towards the fort were met with fusillades from the Germans. There was a thick thorn hedge around the fort that would make a frontal charge virtually impossible.

Murray instructed his platoon commanders to place pickets around the fort, but their numbers were too small to create a cordon. They dug sapping trenches at night to get closer, but snipers on both sides were active. One Rhodesian patrol of eight men was badly shot up; three were killed and another three seriously wounded.

The German commander of the fort, Lt von Franken, ventured out on patrol and was wounded in the head. His men fled back to the fort, and the Rhodesians went forward under a Red Cross flag to bring in the severely wounded man; he died the following day.

Firing from the fort declined, and then stopped ten days after the attack started. The Germans had escaped, leaving only their wounded, and a solitary orderly to raise the white flag of surrender.

Murray was furious. "How could we let them get away," he growled to Martin as he paced up and down outside his tent. "We've heard the other columns have done well. Now we'll be seen as incompetent. I can see that little bastard Northey criticizing us."

Martin nodded disconsolately.

Murray added, "We don't even know where the Boche have gone."

"I suspect to Bismarckburg," replied Martin. "I got some information just this morning. There's a collection of canoes, and three *dhows* in the harbour there. They may be planning an escape up Lake Tanganyika, knowing we outnumber them."

Murray pounded a fist into the other hand. "We'll get them there! I want you to plan a rapid march. Send a message to those British gunboats to give us support on the lake. At the very least they should be able to destroy the *dhows*."

Martin admired his commander's energy and determination, but felt he was out of touch with the condition of his men. All of them, the soldiers and the porters, were half-starved, their clothes in tatters, sick with malaria and dysentery, plagued by flies and mosquitoes.

"The men are exhausted, sir – and we're very short of food. The *tengas* are in a bad way because their rations are so little..."

"I don't want to hear excuses." Murray turned away.

Martin heard a commotion and asked what was happening. An exultant trooper told him that a hippo had been shot and was being cut up near the river. He walked down to the crowd and saw half a dozen *askaris* butchering the animal. Hunks of meat and garlands of entrails were passed to the surrounding crowd of soldiers, who carried away their prizes to cook on open fires, now permitted.

It was Drew who shot the hippo, a young male that had been driven out by the herd and thus was on his own. Four or five hundred pounds of meat were extracted from the carcass, but almost as important was the tonic effect of the scent of cooking meat, and the prospect of adding it as relish to *nsima* cooked over a fire.

—•—

Colonel Murray called to Martin as he walked past the command tent. Without saying a work he handed a telegram to Martin, who unfolded the paper and read it.

From General Northey, Norforce, to Colonel Murray:

Prepare for active march towards New Langenburg. Advise caution as German attacks in force likely. Bismarckburg will fall to us naturally. More specific orders will follow shortly.

"What do you suppose he mean about Bismarckburg?" asked Martin.

Murray gave a characteristic grunt that became a growl. "I suppose he thinks they'll surrender when they lose all their surrounding support." He looked directly at Martin. "I intend to attack that fort."

"What about this?" Martin waved the telegram.

"Destroy it. The only man to have seen it, other than you and me, is the telegrapher, and I doubt he bothered to read it."

"The Nelson touch?"

"You can call it that. I trust you, Martin, to keep it to yourself. There's no specific command not to attack the fort."

—•—

Murray gathered his staff officers together to brief them about the attack on Bismarckburg. He was suffering from fever, though he refused to admit it. Martin insisted that an orderly ply the Colonel with mugs of heavily sweetened tea, as they stood around a makeshift trestle table, on which was spread a map.

"Here is our objective," said Murray, frowning as he pointed at the much creased paper. "The fort is on a prominence sticking out into Lake Tanganyika – obviously difficult to attack. The Germans are no fools – they chose the site well." He paused to wipe his sweating face with a handkerchief. "Martin, you take over the briefing."

Martin pointed to the map. "A water-borne landing would have to cope with the impregnable walls of the fort. The only practical route is along this road, which has to cross the Kalambo River here – it's a gorge – upstream of a spectacular waterfall. There's a bridge, but the Germans might destroy it, if they get wind that we're coming."

Martin looked around the ring of faces, sun-burned, bearded or badly shaven, weary and gaunt, the eyes sunken. They were bruised and exhausted after the battle for Namema. He was proud of them, and wished that he had words to express it.

"We know the German force is quite small – about thirty Europeans, and perhaps a couple of hundred *askaris*. The question is whether they'll make a stand against us, or whether they'll get out to fight another day."

"If they did try to escape," asked a sergeant, "which way would they go? There isn't a road along the lake side, is there?"

"Only rough tracks, which they could use, but my opinion is that they'll try to escape by boat. There's a harbour below the fort with some large *dhows* and canoes."

Murray growled. "Which is why I've asked the British flotilla to come south from Kalemie to support us. They can shell the boats in the harbour and disable them. I presume they have the fire-power?" He looked at Martin.

"They do, sir. They have a twelve-pounder and several five-pounders."

"We have to show the Germans that we're determined to take the fort," said Murray. "I don't want to get into a siege situation – which could drag on for weeks." It was easy for him to imagine Northey's disgust if the Rhodesians were bogged down.

—•—

After marching through thickly forested countryside, they reached the bridge over the Kalambo River two hours before dusk. On the far side a German guard post opened fire as soon as they approached. Martin went forward with one of his scouts and found the Germans had partially dismantled the bridge spanning the sixty foot deep gorge, leaving only a skeleton of supports for the two rails that formed the base of the platform; most of the planks had been removed.

At first sight he judged it would be impossible to take the men and guns across, but the alternative was formidable – scaling down the steep gorge, crossing the river, and climbing up the other side, all at the mercy of German gunners.

He reported back to Murray, who was attending to the blisters on the soles of his feet, pricking them with a blade of his penknife and dabbing them with a cloth wad soaked in liniment. His face glistened with the perspiration from his fever.

"We need to get the Maxim up to the crossing, to knock out that German guard post," said Martin. "Then I'll find a way to use what's left of the bridge."

"Go ahead," said Murray. "We'll cross as best we can and re-group on the far side."

Martin returned to the bridge and stood back from the skeletal remains in contemplation. Beside him were two platoon commanders, gazing in silence at the gorge and the slender remnants of the bridge.

"It would need a trapeze artist to get across," mused Martin. "He would be a ripe target, too."

"I have a man in my platoon who might do it," suggested one of the platoon commanders. "He was once a sailor in a tall ship. I'll fetch him."

The Rhodesian ex-sailor was not afraid of heights, and made successive trips across the skeleton bridge carrying the Maxim tripod, barrel and ammunition, while the remainder of the BSAP force kept up a steady fire to silence the German guard post.

Then other men went across, one by one, inching along the rails, some on their backsides, to establish the Maxim squad on the far side. They were followed by the remainder of the Rhodesians, including Colonel Murray, who went barefoot, allowing the ex-sailor to help him.

—•—

At dawn they studied their objective. The fort's tall wall faced the land interspersed with small windows from which defenders could fire; in its centre was a massive wooden gate studded with metal bolts. The approach road was flanked by trenches bristling with sharpened stakes.

Murray decided to send a white-flag party to request the surrender of the Germans. He dictated to his clerk a message that read, inter alia, *"We have an overwhelming force and wish to avoid further bloodshed. If you do not comply with my request we can blow the fort into pieces."*

Martin was drinking a mug of tea with Murray when the reply came. After reading it, Murray handed it over.

It read: *Lieutenant Hasslacher offers his compliments to Colonel Murray. I am well aware that you do not have any artillery with you, so presume that you cannot carry out your threat to blow up my fort. With all respect I deny your request for surrender and invite you to do your worst.*

"Cheeky buggers," muttered Murray.

A group of Rhodesian soldiers, under the command of Lt Ingpen, watched Murray's messenger emerge through the fort door with his white flag and assumed that the Germans had surrendered. They marched up the road, and as the main Rhodesian force watched in amazement, they knocked on the massive door. It was opened by none other than Lt Hasslacher, the commander.

"What do you want?" asked Hasslacher, in clear English – he had worked in Rhodesia.

"Oh, we're just coming in," said Dr Harald, the medical officer of the Northern Rhodesia Police, who happened to be with the Rhodesian group.

"What do you mean, 'you're just coming in'?" demanded the German.

"Well, since you've surrendered..."

"I've done nothing of the sort! Now you are my prisoners."

Dr Harald realised what had happened and shouted, "Grab him?" He had played rugby for Ireland and tackled the German to the ground. The Rhodesians then started to pull Hasslacher away from the fort.

The German defenders opened fire on the men outside the fort, apparently not concerned that they might hit their commander. Several of the Rhodesians were wounded, Ingpen severely, as they hurriedly took shelter in a ditch beside the road, among the spiked stakes.

While Dr Harald tended to Ingpen's wound – he had been shot in the hips – they discussed their options. Hasslacher offered to call off the firing if they released him, and this was eventually agreed. He stood up and waved his handkerchief, shouting to the men in the fort to cease fire, then walked back, through the door, and returned with first aid materials for the wounded men, as well as a bottle of schnapps, that was shared around, before the Rhodesians marched away, with Ingpen on a stretcher.

During the remainder of the day Murray waited for more of his men to trickle through from Abercorn. At dawn on the following day they again approached the fort cautiously. All was silent, a white flag waving from the ramparts. The Germans had gone.

—•—

Murray was livid. Martin had never seen him in such a rage, and watched him pacing to and fro in his office in the fort – formerly Lt Hasslacher's. The Colonel's brow was knotted and he swatted at invading flies with ill-temper. He was particularly upset because Lt Ingpen had died of his wounds.

"Where were the British gunboats, Martin? They let the Gerries escape! It's inexcusable. I want to see their commander. Bring the bugger here at once!"

"Actually, he's here, sir," said Martin. "Their tender is tying up now."

"Bring him here! By God, I'll give him a piece of my mind."

"With respect, sir, we don't know what his orders were."

"I do know! I have copies here!" Murray thumped his fist on the desk, where a pile of papers were scattered.

—•—

The Rhodesians had moved into the fort without delay, enjoying what few comforts the Germans had left behind. The officers now each had a room, and a communal wash-room with hot water for showers. The other ranks had spacious bunk rooms and ablutions, and the men were able to shower for the first time for two weeks.

Martin walked out to meet the British naval officers at the jetty, beside the now empty harbour. A hundred yards away were the two British gunboats, sleek and powerful, that had failed to prevent the German escape. Watching the naval officers climbing out of their tender, he was interested to see that Spicer-Simson was wearing what appeared to be a khaki kilt, his long bony legs protruding, and tattoos on full display.

The Commander shook Martin's hand firmly and introduced the two young officers with him as Lt Dudley and Sub-Lt Henderson. It was the first time Martin had met Gavin Henderson, and he was intrigued to see Kirsty's young man. He looked very young to Martin, but that was an impression often made, that he attributed to his advancing age.

He drew the Commander aside. "I must warn you, sir. Colonel Murray is not pleased that the Germans have escaped in their boats. We had hoped you would destroy them."

"It's not as simple as that, Major," replied the Commander in his usual rather haughty tone, "as I'll explain to your colonel."

Martin led Spicer-Simson into Murray's office, where the colonel was sitting behind his desk, wearing a deep frown. He did not invite Spicer-Simson to sit down, but glowered at him for several seconds.

"The Germans have escaped, Commander!" Murray barked. "How did they escape? By boat, Commander! You were supposed to support us! Where were you? Why didn't you destroy their boats? Why didn't you prevent them from escaping?"

Spicer-Simson stepped back, his face blanched. "Er, Colonel, we did not expect your attack so soon..."

"Listen, Commander, you've been here for two days. You had a huge superiority in gun-power. You could have destroyed their boats at any time. What were you waiting for?"

"We could not have got within range without coming under fire from this fort..."

Murray stood up, shaking. "Commander, are you telling me that you were afraid to come under fire?"

Spicer-Simson shook his head.

"Get out, man! Get out of my sight!"

Martin escorted a dazed Spicer-Simson from the room to re-join Gavin and Dudley, who took him to his room and left him. He had not uttered a word.

—•—

"Major Russell tells me that you're a fluent German speaker," said Murray. "How did you learn the language?"

Martin had brought the young naval officer to Murray's office.

Gavin told his story, occasionally looking at Martin for reassurance.

"You speak Swahili as well?" Murray looked fierce; he was still seething from his confrontation with Spicer-Simson.

"Fairly well, sir – from a couple of years working with labour on the coffee estate at Moshi."

Murray saw an upright muscular young man, albeit of the British upper classes that he disliked. But he recognised the value of a fluent German and Swahili speaker, and decided to test Gavin's German. He instructed Martin to find Sergeant Pieters, a Rhodesian whose parents were German. He was their only German speaker, though he had proved ineffective as an interrogator. Martin found him in the mess, and he followed in some trepidation to Murray's office.

"Talk to each other," commanded Murray, and the two men started a stilted conversation in German. They relaxed after a few minutes and were able to laugh at their misunderstandings.

"Well?" growled Murray. "What do you say, Pieters?"

"He speaks very fluently, sir" replied the young sergeant. "Much better than I do."

"Really? What do you think, Henderson?"

Gavin paused. "The Sergeant speaks native German, sir. He has a Bavarian accent, whereas I think I have a northern accent. He is perhaps a bit out of practice."

"Hm. Look, Henderson, I want you in my outfit. What do you say?"

Gavin looked at Martin, as if for help, and saw only a friendly smile. He turned back to Murray. "In what capacity, sir. I'm a naval officer. I would prefer to remain with the flotilla on the lake."

Murray nodded with only the slightest indication of sympathy. "I know, Henderson, but there are plenty of young officers with those gunboats. You would be more use with me."

"If you say so, sir."

Murray looked up at Martin. "See to it, Major."

—•—

Gavin went to see Spicer-Simson in his room and found him packing his belongings into a kitbag. The older man looked up and straightened his back. His demeanour was much different to the confident man that Gavin had known. It was as if he had been drained of all his vigour by the encounter with Murray.

"You can see I'm leaving, Henderson. The doc says I need to go home – you know, the strain of the past months..."

"I'm sorry to hear you're not well, sir." He told Spicer-Simson about Murray's request.

The Commander shrugged. "I suppose we have to appease the man. He simply did not understand the situation. It's a pity you're leaving the flotilla, Henderson. You were doing well."

"I don't suppose I have a choice, sir."

"No, I'm afraid not – nor me." He paused, then added, "I know you think I was over-cautious, Gavin, but I leave the flotilla knowing that not a single man under my command has been killed – or died. I hope you and the others realize that."

—•—

29

Zomba, Nyasaland – August, 1916

Drew Spaight was sent home on sick leave after successive bouts of malaria. He arrived at the hospital in Fort Johnston, wrapped in a blanket and shivering so violently that his teeth ached. He ate hardly anything for three days, but his companions forced him to drink water. His ragged sweat-soaked clothes were in a stinking bundle with his camping gear.

"Why did you allow the mozzies to bite you?" scolded Kirsty, as she administered foul-tasting quinine powder to her brother.

He looked up at her with bloodshot eyes. "You have no idea, Kirst – what it's like there at the front. No chance to keep them off – or the tsetses."

Mandy came to see him and lifted his spirits with stories about the men who had passed through Fort Johnston and tried to make their mark with her, some of whom could barely walk or talk. He laughed, but was so weak that barely a sound emerged. After a week his temperature fell to a normal level and he was sent south to Zomba, to convalesce at *Khundalila* in the tender care of his mother.

Jess was appalled when she saw him, though she said nothing. His long frame was gaunt and pale, his face showing the outlines of his skull. He could stand up, but could not walk unaided. He needed lots of nourishing food, and there was plenty of it on the farm; but she had to be careful not to give him too much at first. She remembered how, when her husband returned from his stints fighting the slavers, it had taken several weeks to get his weight and strength back.

—•—

"You're looking more bonny, son," she said, a few days after he arrived. "Definitely more colour in your cheeks."

He sat on the verandah, a book on his lap, and a glass of lemonade beside him. "I feel better. Nothing can compare with your cooking, Ma."

"People are asking when you'll go north again. I tell them that you need at least two more weeks before you can leave here, and then only after the doctor give you a thorough check." She brought him a slice of toast, spread with her home-made marmalade. "Are you afraid of going back to the front?"

He looked at her, wondering if there was a hidden meaning in her question. He supposed his father must have told her about his problem. "I have to explain something, Mother. One of the reasons I wanted to come back on sick leave was... because I have an unreasonable fear. Simply, I'm a coward..."

"Nonsense, Drew. Every soldier experiences fear when faced with danger. I'm sure you're no different to anyone else."

He shook his head. "No, Ma. Other men have had malaria as badly as me, and they carry on, somehow. I wanted to get away." He stood up slowly and shuffled to the verandah rail.

Jess knew that he was in no state to stay in the fighting; she'd heard that the men often marched twenty miles a day; they could manage those distances only if they were really well.

"I became a useless heap," said Drew mournfully. "Thank God Goodwill was with me when it happened at Saisi. He was able to make excuses for me, or I would be hanging my head in shame for the rest of my life. You know, Ma, men have been shot at the front in France – for refusing to go out of the trenches."

She came over to him and put her arm around him. "Have you told a doctor?"

"I told Dr Sanderson – at Fort Johnston. He promised me that he would never tell anyone, or put it in my medical records."

"Did he have any advice?"

Drew sighed. "He thought a bit like you – that I'm exaggerating the fear that all men have. He said that if I could accept that the problem stems from being frightened in childhood..."

"You mean you father telling you his war stories?"

He nodded glumly.

She hugged him. "I think it may not be as serious as you think."

—•—

Drew was surprised and disappointed that his brother seemed to stay away from him. He knew Mac was very busy running the farm; he had only Goodwill's son, Adam, to help him, and Jess to look after the animals and bookkeeping. Even so, Drew thought he would want to hear about the scraps with the Germans, and the way of life at the front.

At meals Mac only wanted to discuss farming matters with his mother, and then only sporadically, while picking morosely at his food. Drew ate his breakfast with gusto, starting with maize porridge and fresh cream, proceeding to bacon and fried eggs, and ending with toast and home-made marmalade.

Only when the conversation turned to the vehicles that were being brought into the country did Mac become animated. He had been called into Zomba a couple of times, to give advice about strengthening the cars, lorries and motor-cycles for active service with the military.

"Those people in Britain don't seem to understand that we don't have roads like theirs." he muttered. "The chassis are woefully weak, and so are the shock absorbers. It's a lot of work, trying to build up their strength. It would be much easier if they did it before sending them out here."

—•—

"I have news for you men," said Jess, one morning at breakfast. "Your cousin Clare has arrived in Zomba. You remember, I told you she was coming – Helen wrote to me. Then Clare wrote to say she's staying in the nurses' home. I went to see her yesterday – such a sweet girl; very lively."

"She's not our cousin," muttered Mac.

"Well, she's a sort of step-cousin," said Jess soothingly.

"I haven't seen her since we were at school in Salisbury," said Drew. "She must have been about eight or nine then...?"

"Let's see; I think she was born about the time of the Rebellion – in 1896. So she must be about twenty now. She looks too young to be a nurse, but that's just me getting older." Jess laughed at herself. "I invited her to come out to the farm. I said we'd bring her out for lunch, after church on Sunday."

—•—

Drew walked unsteadily into St Andrew's Church, following his mother. Mac was not there to support him; he never came to church. Drew looked around as he shuffled slowly to the family pew, seeing familiar faces, some of them looking at him with sympathetic smiles. Even so, he feared they thought his illness was a sham, and that he had escaped from the fighting to enjoy the comforts at home.

He did not see Clare, but she came in later, moments before the service started, and he recognised her. She was with two other young women; he presumed they were fellow nurses who had come with her from Rhodesia. He was struck by Clare's good looks; she was close to being tall, slender and very pretty, the young girl he remembered had become a young woman. She had been a tomboy then, keen on riding and tennis.

After the service he spoke to friends, who came to shake his hand and ask him how he was recovering from the fevers.

"Much better," he told them. "I'll soon be going back to the front."

Two of Zomba's most eligible girls came up to him together. They were the daughters, respectively of the Secretary for Native Affairs, and the Director of the Public Works Department. Although he was too shy to know it, they were both in love with him, and jealous of each other. After a few minutes Jess drew him away to meet Clare Onslow.

"Drew!" she reached up to kiss his cheek, and he noticed that her brown eyes were moist and sparkling. "You're so tall! I'm so sorry you've been so ill. We nurses see so many cases of severe malaria – and blackwater fever."

He was afraid he must look very unappetising. By contrast, Clare was an image of health, with rosy cheeks and eyes full of sparkles. She introduced her friends, who, as he had guessed, were also from Salisbury. After exchanging pleasantries they said their farewells, leaving Clare alone with Jess and Drew.

"How is Aunt Helen – and how are Flora and the boys?" he asked.

"Oh, they're fine. Of course they're very worried about Father."

Jess added, "Now they're worrying about you too!"

"Yes, but there's no need. I'm perfectly safe here – as you know. Aunt Jess, please write to Mother and tell her."

They climbed into the Wolseley and drove back to the farm, Clare sitting beside Drew, who drove. Jess sat on the back seat, thinking that they were a fine looking couple. That led her to wonder if they might fall for each other. As Mac had pointed out, they were not related, because Clare was Helen's daughter by Robert Onslow. So there would be no obstacle to them marrying.

Drew pointed out the sights to the guest. Ahead of them the expanse of Lake Chilwa, with its strange island, like a prehistoric animal rising from the water. "The Africans call it Chisi Island," he said. "But we call it Python Island."

"Presumably because it's crawling with pythons." Clare laughed in an engaging way.

"I've climbed up to the top and didn't see one."

She laughed again, and he added. "I suppose you know about Mount Mlanje, over there." He pointed to the great massif that towered up from the far end of the plain, purple and brooding, its summits cloaked in clouds.

"There are tea estates there, aren't there? Kirsty's boy-friend used to work there."

"That's right, and coffee estates."

"And have you climbed to the top?"

"I have." He took his eyes off the road to glance at her. "It was a stiff climb, but not really difficult. I did it with two friends. Mac has climbed it, too."

"Does it ever have snow?"

"The old Africans say that they have seen it, but we haven't – not yet. It's quite possible, with that height – nearly ten thousand feet."

"Where is Kirsty's boy-friend now – what's his name?"

"Gavin. We're not supposed to know. It was a secret, but it leaked out – he went to Lake Tanganyika, where some German ships were destroyed by ours. Now he's with Murray's Column..."

"That's Father's unit!"

"Exactly. So now he's with your father, and me – when I get back to the front."

When they reached the farm Clare was taken inside by Jess, while Drew put the car in the garage. He found Mac there, working on a motor-cycle engine.

"We brought Clare Onslow back for lunch," he said.

Mac looked up and grunted. "What's she like?"

"She seems a nice girl – engaging..."

"They're all attracted to you, Drew."

"Oh rubbish. Come in and get washed up."

—•—

Mac was smitten when he first saw the girl, and when she kissed him on the cheek. She was slightly taller than him, because of his stoop, and he flushed, feeling the blood rush to his cheeks. He took out a handkerchief and pretended to wipe his face.

"You're both real men now," said Clare as they sat down at the dining table. "You were just schoolboys when I last saw you."

"They're soldiers too," added Jess. "Both of them have been in the firing – Drew at Saisi, on the border, and Malcolm during the rebellion."

"I heard about that. Weren't you at one of the houses, Mac, when the rebels attacked?"

"I left before he was killed – Duncan MacCormick."

"Oh, I see." She could tell that he felt defensive.

"It must have been very frightening for you, Aunt Jess," she said, "– being here alone..."

"The only scary thing," replied Jess, "was not knowing what was happening. It only lasted a couple of days. I never felt in real danger. Some people went into town to stay with friends."

The meal was served – Drew's favourite beef curry. Jess had made sure that he was surrounded with little bowls of chopped tomato, onions and coconut, slices of banana, mango chutney and lime pickle.

"How I missed your curries," he said, mouth watering. "It's hard to exist on a few teaspoons of bully beef and a couple of dry weevily biscuits."

Clare asked after Mandy and Kirsty. "I'm longing to see them."

Jess replied. "They're both well. Drew saw them at the hospital in Fort Johnston. Mac and I haven't seen them for three weeks. They get leave to come home every month..."

"What's it like for them at Fort Johnston?"

"Hot and dusty." Drew laughed. "But the lake breezes help to cool it sometimes." His tone changed. "It's hard for the girls; really hard work, and not much to do in their free time..."

"Of which they get precious little," added Jess.

"There's a matron coming here from Salisbury – she's being sent to Fort Johnston. I met her before I left. I suppose she'll be in charge of Mandy and Kirsty – she's very bossy! I wonder what they'll think of her."

"Oh dear," said Jess. "They won't like that. They've worked directly under Dr Sanderson."

—•—

Drew went to visit Dr Thompson in Zomba, suffering from pain in his abdomen. He had no outward symptoms, but the doctor suspected he might have shingles.

"We'll soon know, if you develop a painful rash. The stress of being ill with malaria probably brought it on. There's nothing I can do."

Two days later, a sore rash emerged on Drew's waist, and Jess, who had seen it before, confirmed it was shingles.

"That will delay your return to the north," she said. "You really need to get much better before you leave here."

—•—

Clare became a regular visitor to the farm. She was given alternate weekends off, and either Mac or Drew would go into Zomba to fetch her in the car; she sometimes brought one of her nurse friends. They would ride around the farm to exercise the horses, and walk with the dogs in the early morning when it was cooler. They slept a lot, and ate more than usual from the delicious food offered by Jess.

She grew closer to Drew, thinking that she was falling in love with him. She confided to her friend Dora.

"He's such a sweet man, doesn't seem to have any vices..."

"I thought he was your cousin," said Dora.

"No. You see Father – Martin Russell – isn't my real father. My father was killed in the Boer War. That's why I'm Clare Onslow. So I'm not related to Drew at all."

"He's awfully good-looking," said Dora. "Very charming too." She looked enviously at her pretty friend. "I heard he'll soon be returning to the front."

Clare laughed. "He ought to have gone by now, but he's got shingles, poor man."

"Where?"

"Around his waist. You know, the classic site."

"No doubt you'll take good care of him?"

Clare blushed. "He's very shy."

—•—

"When will you go back to the front?" asked Clare. She and Drew were riding on the farm. "I wish you didn't have to go."

"In a week or so. You know it's not like 'the front' in France. The Germans are marauding around in the bush, and we're trying to find them, so we can attack and defeat them."

"Do you want to go back?"

He shook his head.

"Why? Is it very hard there?"

"No, Clare. It's not that. It is hard – we're usually weary and hungry. No, it's..." His voice choked.

She pulled up her horse. "What, Drew?"

He felt he had to tell her. "Will you promise not to tell anyone?"

She put out her hand and reached to touch him, but his horse moved away. "Of course I won't tell anyone – what?"

"I'm afraid..."

She laughed quietly. "Drew – everyone is afraid – every single soldier in the army. It wouldn't be normal if you weren't afraid."

"No, it's the wrong word – you see, I'm terrified."

She was dismayed to see the dejection in his expression. "Surely that's normal too?"

"No, Clare. You see, I'm a coward."

"That's nonsense, Drew..."

"No, it's true." He paused and looked around, as if to make sure that no one else could hear. "I'm so afraid that I want to run away. When we were under attack from the Germans – at Saisi – I was in a terrible state. It was only Goodwill who prevented the others from finding out."

"Goodwill?"

"Our African farm manager. He's with Pa now, at the front."

"How could he help?"

"By telling me that I was no different to anyone else – like you did. But I knew he wasn't right."

"I think he was right."

He looked at her gravely. "You see, Clare, I remember vividly the stories my father told me – when I was a little boy – about his time in the army..."

"Fighting the slave traders?"

"No, before that. He was a young officer in the British Army at the Battle of Tofrek, in the Sudan. They formed a defensive square against an attack, but the square was broken by the Dervishes – they were running at our soldiers with swords and spears – killing men all around him. It sounded horrible..."

"Perhaps Uncle Alan shouldn't have told you."

"I suppose he thought it would be interesting and exciting for us to hear – he told Mac as well. Pa survived the attack – obviously – and later he joined a Sikh regiment, and went to India for two years. He also told us about the fights against the slavers, but they didn't frighten me quite so much. It's difficult to explain – I have this overwhelming fear of men rushing at me and stabbing me with swords and spears."

"But the Germans wouldn't do that, would they?"

"Not the Germans – the Europeans – but their *askaris* use bayonets at close quarters, and so do ours. It's vicious fighting. We've heard that the *askaris* are very good at attacking with the bayonet, because it's like their tribal fighting with spears."

"Can't they give you a position away from the front?"

"Only if a doctor declares that I'm emotionally incompetent. That would be awful."

"Who have you told?"

"My parents. My father is trying to get me into his Intelligence outfit. They have patrols that go behind the German lines to find out what they're doing – that sort of thing..."

"But isn't there just as much danger in that?"

"Perhaps. But I wouldn't be cooped up in a building – or standing in a trench waiting to be overrun."

She looked at him lovingly. "Why did you tell me?"

"I don't want you to see me as – well, different to what I really am." He paused. "You see, I love you, Clare."

"Oh, Drew." She dismounted and helped him to get down from his horse. She embraced him, and said, "I don't think less of you because of what you've told me. I just hope Uncle Alan can find the right position for you. Please don't worry about it, Drew. I think you'll learn to overcome it."

They walked side by side along the farm track, their horses following at the end of their reins. Each was deeply satisfied. Clare knew that he was a fine young man, honest and charming. Drew found her much more interesting than the pretty girls who had thrown themselves at him before.

Clare now found every opportunity to come out to the farm for her weekends off. She also met Drew at social functions in Zomba, where they held dances at the club every Saturday. Drew felt uncomfortable, because he thought anyone who was well enough ought to be at the front. There were two tennis courts that were the focus of much activity in the late afternoon, and the players would adjourn to the club verandah for drinks.

Their favourite place was Zomba Mountain. Drew would pick up her up at the nurses' home on his motor-cycle, and they would ride up the narrow road to the Spaight's cottage, revelling in their freedom from the cares of the hospital and farm below.

It was always cooler on the mountain and often misty, conditions conducive to long walks along the mountain paths and log fires in the evenings.

But time was running out for Drew, since Dr Thompson could not extend his sick note any longer.

"I've had a letter from my father," he told Clare. "He says that I will be in charge of the *tenga-tengas* in Colonel Murray's Column. Uncle Martin is the colonel's deputy."

"What are *tenga-tengas*?"

"They're porters. '*Tenga*' literally means 'bring'."

"What will you be doing?"

"I'm not certain, but I think I have to organise the recruiting of the porters, and make sure that they're kept in tribal groups. We have to feed them, of course, and arrange their camps at night. Pa is going to give me Goodwill as an assistant."

"Will you be near the fighting?"

"Yes, because we have to supply the food and ammunition for the troops..."

"It sounds rather dangerous, sweetheart."

"I'll be wearing a uniform; otherwise, if I was captured I would be shot as a spy. I gather the Germans are quite civilised about that sort of thing, and they look after prisoners as well as they can."

—•—

30

German East Africa – July 1916

Murray handed the telegram to Martin Russell. It was from General Northey and instructed the column to make its way to New Langenburg.

"Fifty pound packs, sir," said Martin, handing back the paper. "I've arranged for two thousand *tengas* – Lt Spaight has done most of the work."

"Ye Gods!" Murray gave a rare laugh. "That's going to be a long column."

"A couple of miles at least. A marching square would be safer, but impractical – far too slow. We'll need good intelligence to ensure we're not attacked – and a good routine for forming up, if we encounter the enemy. We're working hard with patrols, and now we have Gavin Henderson we can grill any German we're lucky enough to catch."

"Can't we send our own men on recce patrols?"

"The problem is that we Europeans would stick out like the proverbial sore thumb. For a start, most of us can't speak a native dialect well enough to pass as an African – in the dark. There are a few exceptions – men like Drew and Alan Spaight are very fluent – and might be able to pass as natives. Then there's our physical appearance – even if we black our faces we'll always look like a musical hall act..."

"And at night?"

"We might pass at a distance, but we would be a handicap to a native tracker. Alan has lived here for years, and his son has grown up here, but we have very few with their skills."

"It worries me that we have to put so much trust in the African scouts," muttered Murray. "I suppose we have no alternative."

—•—

Their first objective was Fife, along the dry dusty Stevenson Road, much improved since the war started, but still little more than a track. Col Murray acquired a motor-cycle and puttered up and down the column, checking that the men were marching as fast as possible, and making sure they were not enjoying excessive rests. Thirst was a constant problem, as the small streams they crossed were seldom adequate for filling hundreds of water-bottles.

The Rhodesians had found a pet baboon in the fort at Namema, and named him Fritz. He walked with the column, the subject of much joking and cursing. He would hold out his small hands for morsels of food, and would cup them for mouthfuls of precious water.

At Fife they re-grouped and sent sick men back to Abercorn. The track to New Langenburg then took them over the Poroto Mountains, where the altitude reached nearly nine thousand feet. It was mid-winter, bitterly cold and misty. Each man had only one blanket, and they huddled together around small smoking fires made from damp wood. To their great relief the track eventually dropped down to lower altitudes, where the local people grew bananas in profusion.

General Northey met Murray's Column at the foot of the mountains and took the senior officers by car to New Langenburg. Martin was intrigued when he saw the fortified German *boma* on top of a hill, where Northey had established his headquarters.

"The Germans knew what they were doing when they established their colonial outposts," he said to Murray. "They chose the sites well, with good defence and water nearby."

The *boma's* main offices were built to double as forts, in case there was an insurrection. Around them were the houses of European administrators, now used by Northey's officers. Further away were dozens of smaller houses and the hospital. The *askari* barracks were at the foot of the hill, and further still the grass huts of Africans who serviced the *boma*.

The senior officers were invited to dinner with the General, including Ron Murray, Martin Russell, and the other unit commanders: Hawthorn, Rodger and Flindt. Alan Spaight, was there, now well established as Northey's intelligence officer. He and Robbie Spratt, the General's senior ADC, had recently been promoted to Lieutenant-Colonel. Roly Benting-Smith, also attended, now Northey's junior ADC. Their uniforms had seen better days and they all needed a trip to the barber, but spirits were high because they were now a combined force with some battle experience, under a seasoned professional leader.

There was still some reservation amongst Northey's officers about his understanding of the conditions under which the troops were fighting. "Too much emphasis on trenches," one of them was heard to mutter. "This isn't Flanders, for God's sake."

The relationship between Northey and Murray was gradually improving as the two men recognised their respective qualities. Martin Russell encouraged the process in subtle ways, and told them how much each admired the other.

"The Germans have an interesting approach to colonial occupation," said Northey, as the port was being passed round. "These fortified buildings suggest that they anticipated native revolts..."

"They had the *Maji-Maji* Rebellion," said Colonel Rodger. "Suppressed brutally by all accounts."

Northey nodded and continued. "Should we not expect the local populations to come over to our side? I mean, if they've had bad experiences of the Germans? What do you think, Spaight?"

Alan stroked his beard before replying. "We've had some indications of that, sir. But the Germans have kept the native chiefs well out of our way, and no doubt well paid – bribed, if you like. When we reach Iringa we ought to make a real effort to win over the main chief there."

"General, do you think the Germans will put up a fight before Iringa?" asked Hawthorn.

"I believe they will," answered Northey. "From what we know – and most of it has channelled through Alan – they will choose a tactical spot to make a stand."

"Although our intelligence suggests this, sir," said Alan, "we must remember that it's not something the Germans like to do. My guess is – when we attack them, they will quickly fragment and disappear."

"If only we could trap them," mused Northey. "Van Deventer is driving them towards us, we block them, so their choices are east and west. West takes them into the interior, where there's not much of strategic interest..."

"There are the copper mines in the Belgian Congo and Northern Rhodesia." Spratt was leaning back languidly, a cigar near his lips.

"True. Even so, I think they'll prefer to stay nearer the coast and their re-supply options – as Alan has always said."

—•—

After the best meals they'd had in weeks Murray's Column set off on the march north-east towards Iringa. There was an ever-present risk of attack by the Germans. They camped at night in squares; pickets placed outside with rotated sentry duties. Each man was on picket duty every third day. Every man in the column had to dig a rifle pit, layer grass at the bottom and shiver in it most of the night, covered only by a single blanket. If it rained he would be wet all night.

They marched from six in the morning till five in the evening, with rest breaks every three hours. Their food supplies always seemed to be far behind, carried by the *tenga-tengas*, never catching up. The countryside reminded Martin of the highveld in Rhodesia, savannah open woodland. The wild antelopes that might have supplied them with venison were nowhere in sight. "Shot out by the Germans," was the common refrain.

Meanwhile, General Northey moved his HQ to Mwaya on the north shore of Lake Nyasa. News continued to filter through to him that a strong German force was moving south towards Iringa, driven by the advances of General Smuts' army from the north, now under the command of his fellow South African, General van Deventer, a seasoned Boer soldier.

Northey now had one thousand two hundred rifles and estimated that the Germans had about the same. Murray's Rhodesians were reduced to only a hundred Europeans and a hundred and fifty *askaris*. They were well ahead and to the east of the other troops, using a very loose square formation, sometimes moving at night in bitter cold. As they approached Iringa they found the bridge over the Little Ruaha River had been destroyed, but threats of attacks by the Germans never materialised.

On 28 August 1916 the Column was greeted on the outskirts of Iringa by the Burgomeister, bearing a white flag. The Rhodesians marched into the town, tattered and battered, but in good spirits. For the first time in many months they tasted fresh fruit and fine wine.

On the following day the Union flag was hoisted at the *boma*. Gavin Henderson stood at attention watching the flag proudly. He was distinguished from the soldiers only by his battered cap which bore the RNVR emblem. His eyes scanned the Germans intently; they had been pressed into attending, almost all of them women. To his surprise and delight he recognised one of them, a tall stout woman in her forties named Helga Mueller, who had been a near neighbour when he worked on the coffee estate at Moshi. When the ceremony ended he hurried over to her.

"Helga," he said. "It's me, Gavin."

She looked at him and for a moment he thought she would be antagonistic, but she held out her arms and embraced him. "Dear Gavin!" She smelled of soap and coffee.

"What are you doing here?" he asked, in German.

"I might ask you the same question." She laughed. "I followed my husband. He's with Tafel – you know, one of von Lettow's commanders. They left two days ago, but we women had to stay here, otherwise we would have hampered their escape. Are we to be prisoners?"

"I don't know. I don't suppose so. I guess you'll all be on some sort of parole." He heard his name being called and said, "I must go. Where can I find you – so we can talk?"

She pointed down the street. "That white house opposite the church. Liesl was with me, you know. She went with Tafel's column, to be with her father."

Gavin told Alan about meeting *Frau* Mueller. "I thought I would have a meal with her – see if I can find out anything useful."

"There's no harm in trying," said Alan. "At the least you should get a good German meal."

Gavin went to the Mueller house for supper next night. It was a small white-washed house about a hundred yards from the *boma*. It once had a flourishing garden, but now there was only dry grass and wilted shrubs, full of crickets whose chorus was almost deafening. A hurricane lantern stood by the steps on the verandah, its dull light attracting a cloud of flying insects.

Helga Mueller invited him into the house and welcomed him with a beer.

"This house used to belong to the Postmaster. He was killed – while with Tafel's unit. They said I could stay here for as long as I like."

They chatted in German about days past in Moshi, where they were near neighbours.

"So Liesl has not married?" he asked, remembering the tall, strong girl, a couple of years younger than him. He had a girl friend in Arusha, otherwise he would have invited her to parties.

"No. I told you – she went with her father – with *Hauptman* Tafel. I wish she had not gone. It's hard for a young girl, marching through the bush. There are only a few other women to keep her company."

"Why didn't you go?"

"My knees, Gavin." She gave a bitter laugh. "*Mein Gott*, I can't march twenty miles a day."

"When did they leave?"

"Liesl left the day before you got here; Tafel a day before that."

They sat for supper, brought from the kitchen by Helga –. vegetable soup, roast chicken with sweet potatoes, and an apple pie. Gavin was mesmerised by the food, the best he'd eaten for weeks. He felt guilty because his comrades could not share the dishes.

Helga served coffee in the sitting room. "You can stay for the night, if you like. I'm sure you would enjoy a comfortable bed after all your nights in the bush."

He laughed. "My compatriots would not be happy. They would think I was fraternising with the enemy."

She giggled. "You could say you were extracting information from me."

"Do you have any?"

She sighed. "If I had any, I might give it to you – just to bring an end to this dreadful war. I want to go back to my farm, Gavin – to my house and my servants. When will it end?"

"I suppose only when your Colonel gives up..."

She snorted. "He will never do that – so Tafel says."

"...or the war in Europe ends."

She brought him a shot glass with peach brandy and watched him sip the fiery sweet liquid.

"It's kind of you, Helga..."

She shook her head. "We're old friends, Gavin. We should not be fighting with each other."

He downed the brandy. "It's time for me to go."

They went out onto the verandah. It was pitch dark outside. Suddenly, Gavin saw a shadowy figure at the end of the porch, and heard Helga call out in Swahili.

"Who is it?"

"It's me, Anders." An African man emerged, holding a rifle at the ready.

She turned to Gavin. "It's my husband's servant. What are you doing here, Anders?"

"The *bwana* sent me back to fetch his glasses – he left them behind."

"So he did."

"Who is this man?" asked Anders in a nervous high-pitched tone.

"He is a British..."

"The *Bwana* said I was to shoot any British I saw..."

"Don't be silly, Anders."

The African raised his rifle and fired at Gavin.

—•—

31

Zomba, Nyasaland – August 1916

Clare continued to visit the farm after Drew left for the front. The peaceful rural atmosphere was a welcome change from the clamour and stress of Zomba hospital, reminding her of the farm Long Valley, where she grew up. She enjoyed Jess's company; they talked about their families and shared news of Martin, Alan and Drew at the front, Mandy and Kirsty at Fort Johnston, and the Russell family in Rhodesia.

Mac was still managing the farm, an *eminence grise* who appeared at meals, but otherwise kept to himself, usually working on the farm machinery and his motor-cycle. He made Clare feel uncomfortable whenever they met, seeming deeply shy, frowning a great deal, and muttering greetings in a low voice. When she spoke to him he would turn away and answer so softly that she could not hear.

One evening, after Clare said goodnight to Jess, she walked along the verandah to the guest bedroom, carrying her hurricane lamp, and unlocked the door. Only then did she notice Mac, leaning against the railing as if waiting for her, the lamp-light glinting on his metal arm brace.

"Hello, Mac," she said brightly. "What are you doing here?"

"Waiting for you," he replied. "I need to speak with you."

He pushed her into her room, lit only by her lamp, which swung wildly as she tried to maintain her balance. Alarmed, she turned to face him. His dark face was in shadow and she could not read his expression.

"I love you, Clare," he croaked.

"Oh, Mac." She reached out to touch him. "I don't think you do. We don't really know each other, do we? Besides, I'm attached to Drew. You know that."

He grabbed her hand violently, and then her arm, surprising her with his strength. Pushing her onto the bed he lay down beside her. His breath smelled sourly of the cheroots he smoked in the evening.

"You must go, Mac!" she told him sharply.

"I can't, Clare." He started to kiss her and at the same time fumbled with her shirt front.

"Please don't, Mac," she gasped, trying to extricate herself. But he was too powerful, throwing a leg over her and pinning her down. He put one hand on her mouth to stop her crying out, so that the only sound emerging was a small moan. With his other hand he pulled open her shirt and rooted into her clothing with his face. He yanked at her waist band, which gave way, enabling him to pull down her skirt.

She felt powerless and decided there was no point in struggling with him. She remembered instantaneously the matron at the teaching hospital saying, 'You have two choices: put up a fight, and you'll probably be beaten; or give in and think of something else – endure it.'

He had an iron strength and seemed utterly determined to undress her. When he felt her yield he took his hand from her mouth and used both hands to pull down her skirt and underpants. Then he removed her shirt and vest so that she lay naked in front of him, lit only by the lamp.

He started to mutter endearments as he undressed, but they were so quiet that she not distinguish the words. She felt the cold of the metal arm brace when he lay on her. He was shaking as he tried to position himself, then suddenly groaned and shuddered as he ejaculated without entering her.

"Mac? Are you alright?" She was relieved, but fearful that he might take a bitter revenge on her.

"No!"

It was a wail. He rolled off her and started to pull on his clothes, his shadow looming on the wall and curtains as he muttered to himself and cursed. In a moment he was gone, slamming the door behind him. She struggled up and bolted it.

—•—

Venturing out in some trepidation for breakfast, Clare was greeted with the news that Mac could not be found.

"Have you any idea where he is? He's always up at dawn." Jess was evidently too concerned about Mac to notice Clare's demeanour. "He checks the milking and allocates work to the labourers. I went to his room and he wasn't there. His motor-cycle has gone. Did he say anything to you?"

Clare tried to show surprise and alarm, and then joined in the search of the farm buildings. She avoided talking to people, afraid she might accidentally reveal what had happened. Adam gathered some Africans who knew how to follow spoor and they succeeded in tracing the motor-cycle tyre marks along the farm road to the main dirt road leading to Zomba. They determined that Mac had turned towards Zomba.

—•—

Alan Spaight heard the news on the following day, at Northey's HQ at Mwaya, on the shore of Lake Nyasa. He went at once to the General, who was studying maps, fuelled by mugs of tea.

"Sir, my son has disappeared from the farm at Zomba," he said.

"What happened?" asked the General, looking up sympathetically. "Do you want leave to go there?"

"Yes, sir – if I may."

Northey heaved a deep sigh. "You'd better go, Spaight. I know I would need to go if it was my son. How old is he?"

"Nearly thirty..."

"Have you any idea why he disappeared?"

Alan shook his head. "No, but in a way I'm not surprised."

—•—

Alan boarded the next steamer and reached Fort Johnston three days later. During the voyage he fretted and paced the deck, frustrated he could get no news. Mac had never disappeared before. He was moody and irritable, anti-social and withdrawn, but he had always done his work, abided by the rules. He was not adventurous, and had climbed Mlanje Mountain only because his brother had done it.

Alan found Mandy at the hospital, thinking she looked far too thin. Her skin was pale and almost translucent. Her hair, escaping from under her nurse's cap, was lack-lustre, her voice unusually subdued.

"They said only one of us could go." she said. "We decided it should be Kirsty – she'll be better at looking after Ma."

Alan was fearful that Mac had been found dead. "Is there any news?"

"None." She led him to the mess and fetched him a mug of tea. "We think he may have gone to the Mlanje area – based on accounts of people thinking they saw the light of a motor-cycle on the night he disappeared. But why would he have gone there? I know he's climbed the mountain, but that means he knows how dangerous it is. I can't think of a reason for him to go anywhere – no close friends..."

"He probably wasn't thinking straight. Do either you or Kirsty have any idea why he left? Could it be something to do with Clare? Your mother says she's been spending a lot of time on the farm. She was there the night he left."

"Ma seems to think he had a crush on Clare, although he never told her so. He obviously knew she was Drew's girl – I mean he knew all along. It wasn't as if there were surprises. I suppose he might have been jealous, but why run away?"

"And Clare knows nothing?"

"She says that. I hope she didn't say something to... to hurt him." She paused, watching her father for signs of his emotions. "I wish I could join in the search. I'm not much good at comforting, which is why Kirst has gone home; but I would like to ride around the mountain and look for signs of his bike."

—•—

When he reached the farm Alan tried to console Jess while she told him as much as she knew. They both suspected that Mac's disappearance had something to do with Clare's presence on the farm on the night he left, but the girl could tell them nothing.

Alan drove to Mlanje and spoke to the planters there, most of whom he knew. They were all very sympathetic and questioned their African staff about a motor-cycle they might have heard on the fateful night, now a week ago.

On his second day at Mlanje Alan heard that Mac's motor-cycle had been discovered. It was near the footpath that led up to the Likabula Falls, at the foot of the mountain, a place where Europeans sometimes went to picnic and swim in the natural pool below the falls. Alan walked up there to see the bike, which appeared to have been left deliberately, in a small gully near the path. It seemed to have been placed there, not hidden, but in a spot where it could be found again. He surmised that Mac must have ridden up the path until it became too steep and rocky to go any further.

The planter whose labourer found the bike commiserated with Alan. "It's a pity we didn't find the bike earlier. My chap saw it by chance. We could try tracking from this site?"

"The trail will be very cold – a week old. I'll try, but I wish I had my tracker..."

"I can lend you my man – he's pretty good."

—•—

Alan spent an hour searching the bike and its surrounds for clues. The fuel tank was a third full; the panniers were empty. The depression where Mac left the bike had an obvious entrance, where tracks showed that he had wheeled it in. There was an exit at the end where the mountain slope rose sharply. Alan could see that someone had scrambled up the slope. Not wishing to disturb the scene he made a circuit to the slope higher up.

The planter's tracker arrived, a wizened old man, wearing a goatskin cloak and leaning on a long stick. His legs were thin and bare, making him look like an emaciated stork. He was a Nyanja, and Alan went through the formal introductory greetings.

"I am sorry that your son cannot be found, *bwana*."

"I need your help to find him, Kawiri. Will you help me?"

"Indeed, I will."

Alan waited while the old man examined the terrain above the depression. He straightened and took some snuff from a worn leather pouch. "There have been two showers of rain since the *njinga* was left there by your son. Most of the signs have washed away."

"Should we look further up the slope?"

"It is better."

They moved up, and Kawiri pointed to some broken twigs. A hundred yards further on they came to an overhanging slab of rock where the soil had been sheltered from the rain. There were unmistakable signs that Mac had spent time there; Alan recognised the prints of his home-made boots.

Kawiri pointed up the slope with his stick, and Alan followed him. They searched for over two hours but found no more clues.

—•—

Alan went to the *boma* at Mlanje to speak to the Forestry Officer. The great mountain massif towered behind the settlement, rising seven thousand sheer feet from the plain, its sides cloaked in rain clouds that sometimes cleared to reveal menacing dark glistening rock slabs. Mac had disappeared into this forbidding mysterious mountain.

Bill Mackay was a grizzled Scot, in his late sixties, who had come out of retirement when the younger foresters went to the war. He lived in a small brick-built cottage with a thatched roof that was allocated to the District Forestry Officer. He had heard of Alan and the disappearance of his son, and commiserated with him.

Alan told him about the abortive search with the tracker. "I think the rain has obliterated any signs."

"Aye, I expect so."

"Could my son have walked far up the path?" asked Alan.

"Aye, he could have walked for five or six miles. The path leads to our logging camp, where there's a sawmill for cedar planks. But I'm fairly sure he would have been seen. There are porters on the path every day, carrying planks down the mountain, and returning with supplies for the camp. They have all been questioned."

"Might he have branched off the path – I mean, are there other paths?"

"Some." The old forester looked at him with sympathy. "It's braw and wet up there, Spaight. Ye canna live without a fire and it's nae easy to light a fire. My natives live there, but they ha' good huts and plenty of stored dry firewood."

"Mac knows how to look after himself, but..." Alan put his head in his hands.

"Why do you suppose he went up there?"

Alan shook his head. "If only I knew. He's climbed to the summit before, and been to Likabula a few times. Perhaps he wanted to return there for some reason. Maybe he wanted to explore – but he had no equipment with him."

"We'll look out for him."

—•—

32

German East Africa – October 1916

Helga screamed in horror and saw the servant Anders run off into the night. She bent down to Gavin Henderson's body. He had dropped his hurricane lamp, which had gone out, and the light from hers was too feeble for her to see a wound. In panic she fumbled with his clothing, then stood up and screamed again.

People came running: German women from the neighbouring houses and soldiers from the *boma*. A small crowd gathered, saying they heard the shot and her screams. A Rhodesian corporal pushed forward and checked Gavin's mouth to see that his airway was clear.

He felt the pulse and said, "Good strong pulse. Let's see where he was wounded."

The corporal started feeling Gavin, starting at his head and working down. "Here it is. The bullet hit his shoulder."

Drew joined the circle round the fallen man. "That wouldn't have knocked him out."

"Probably when he fell down – he may have banged his head."

Drew bent down and felt Gavin's head. At the back was a lump the size on an egg.

Gavin was carried on a make-shift stretcher to the hospital in the compound, while Helga was taken to the duty officer, a young lieutenant, who was soon joined by Alan and the adjutant.

"Why was he with you?" asked the lieutenant, not unkindly.

Helga was weeping, and her English was poor. "We are old friends – from Moshi. I gave him supper. He wanted to ask questions."

Alan interjected. "He told me what he was doing, I suppose because I'm the Intelligence Officer."

"Who shot him?" asked the young lieutenant.

"Anders – the servant of my husband." She poured out the story, while Alan nodded and encouraged her.

The duty officer sent her home and walked with Alan to the hospital. "So you knew about this?" he asked.

"Gavin told me he would try to winkle some information from the lady. He would not have gone otherwise – I encouraged him to go."

"Do you think it was wise, sir – I mean for him to wander round the German housing, to visit a German?"

Alan shrugged. "We saw no danger."

—•—

The bullet from Anders' rifle struck Gavin in the muscle just below the shoulder joint, causing a deep flesh wound that bled copiously. He soon recovered consciousness, shaking his head like a sleepy bear.

"You're very lucky," said the doctor. "The bullet might have made a real mess of your shoulder joint – or you might have been killed. You banged your head when you fell."

"Will he be alright?" asked Drew.

"Of course. I'll sew him up and he'll be on duty within a couple of days. The greatest risk, as you know, Drew, is from infection of the wound."

—•—

It was becoming obvious to von Lettow and his commanders that they could no longer rely on supplies from the coast, where Dar-es-Salaam had fallen to the British, and the Royal Navy had blockaded most of the other small ports. The Germans had destroyed the central railway line from Dar-es-Salaam to Lake Tanganyika, and retreated south, driven by Allied forces under General van Deventer. Meanwhile, the Belgians were advancing from the west.

"They ought to be more inclined to stand and fight; they have nowhere else to go – except south," said Alan Spaight. "That's the only way they can go."

He was sitting with Northey, who was on a visit from his headquarters in Mwaya; with them were Colonels Hawthorn, Rodger, and Murray, in a circle on the verandah of the officers' mess in Iringa. Also with them, at the invitation of the General, was Martin Russell, recently promoted to Lieutenant Colonel. They had enjoyed an unusually fine supper and were smoking, and drinking local German wine.

"We interrogated a German sergeant today," Alan continued, " – at least young Gavin Henderson did. 'Sang like a bird,' he said. Seems that Tafel and Kraut don't want to tangle with van Deventer's army..."

"They may come this way," said Northey gloomily. "They probably know how few we are."

"Unless they're in a hurry," Alan continued. "If they've decided to go south-east and join up with von Lettow, why get delayed by scrapping with us?"

"Did the sergeant have anything to say about that?" asked Martin.

"No. But he did say they planned to move quickly, to get to the Mahenge area, where they think there are good supplies of food. Like us, they're often on the brink of starvation." He recognised the irony of his words after the good supper.

"We should speed them away from here," announced the General. "But we must encircle them later – if possible before they get to Mahenge. Murray, you deal with Major Kraut, and Hawthorn, you go further east to Lupembe to prevent them from occupying the Mahenge area. If there is food there we should have it for ourselves."

They discussed their strategy for another couple of hours before retiring. Colonel Murray said little; he was determined not to get into an argument with Northey, who he thought was too cautious. He feared that his views about the strategy might be influenced by his lingering dislike of the General.

Meanwhile, Martin supported Northey. He had always been caring about the condition of his men, and saw little merit in risky attacks without a foundation of reliable intelligence. He admired the General's professionalism and careful consideration for the logistical issues that underpin a campaign. He knew that Northey irked Murray, and did his best to ease the relationship between the two men.

By contrast, Alan became increasingly frustrated. Caution was playing into the hands of the Germans. Only brave thrusts towards them would engender the pitched battles that would wear them down to surrender. He made his point and knew that the General understood, then he remained silent, until the subject of capturing or destroying von Lettow was raised, by Robbie Spratt, lounging back in his cane chair, puffing on a cigar.

"Shouldn't we at least discuss it?" he proposed. "The man is uniquely dominant in their command structure – don't you agree, Spaight?"

"Yes, he is. The Governor, Schnee, has become an irrelevance. Old General Wahle commands respect, but in any other campaign would have been pensioned off. Yes, von Lettow is dominant, and if he was killed or captured – or if he died of fever – I suspect their campaign would fizzle out."

"Go on, Robbie," said the General. "What are you suggesting?"

"Would it be feasible, sir, to send a patrol with the specific objective of killing or capturing von Lettow?"

"Do you mean assassination?"

Spratt grinned. "No, sir. Of course not."

Northey turned to Alan. "What do you think, Spaight?"

"The rewards are potentially rich, sir. I think it would be worth a try. Von Lettow's main column puts out pickets, which would make in difficult for our patrol to penetrate. However, even well-spaced pickets can be penetrated... say while they're on the march. Then von Lettow could be identified and shot."

"By a sniper?"

"Yes, if that's was your tactic. If it were me, I would find an anthill and take shots as the column passed."

Northey shook his head. "That's assassination. I would not want to be party to that. What do you think, Murray?"

Colonel Murray had been listening carefully. "I don't like it, sir."

Northey nodded. "Neither do I. It would be a suicide mission, because the attackers would be unlikely to get away. The chances of pulling it off would be very small. Also, inevitably, word would get out that we'd tried to assassinate von Lettow. Imagine our reaction if the Huns tried a similar assassination of Smuts – or one of our generals in France."

—•—

Colonel Murray gazed into the hazy dusty distance ahead, trying to brace himself against the gyrations of the Wolseley staff car as it lurched along the road. The driver tried his best to avoid the potholes and gullies, weaving slowly to and fro. Whenever he was able to accelerate the surface became corrugated, and Murray winced as his back muscles went into spasm.

They left the valley floor and started to climb, the road following contours cut into a mountainside by African labourers working under the supervision of German engineers in the early 1900s. There had been no maintenance in the last five years, and sections of the road had washed away. The advanced guard of Murray's Column had made some emergency repairs, using stones and brushwood, but the road was generally in poor condition. On the Colonel's left the slope was steep and forbidding. He imagined the car rolling down, crashing through saplings, and spilling out its frail human contents.

"Where are the *tengas,* Martin?" he asked fretfully. "Shouldn't we have caught up with them?"

"They can't be far ahead," replied Martin.

He had watched the column of *tenga-tengas* wind out of the camp before dawn, munching on handfuls of *nsima* they scooped from a communal cooking pot. They had seemed cheerful enough, but he was concerned that they were underfed and sickly. Marching nearly a hundred miles in four days had taken its toll, and they carried loads of about fifty pounds each. Drew Spaight had divided them into tribal groups to generate some competition and camaraderie. There were Bembas and Angonis, Wahembe and Tumbuku, and several other tribes. They sang their own songs and shouted their own ribald jokes, but for much of the time they were silent, conserving their wind.

Beside Martin in the back seat was his cousin Alan Spaight, trying to examine a map; the draught in the open car made the task difficult. Another staff car followed several hundred yards behind, with four more officers. Behind Murray's staff cars was a lorry with the batmen and servants, towing a trailer with accoutrements of the Column HQ staff, tents, baggage, food and drink.

The cavalcade rounded a corner and came on the column of *tenga-tengas*. They were sitting or lying at the side of the road, singly and in groups, their faces dusty and streaked with sweat. Walking up and down the line was the tall figure of Drew Spaight, wearing khaki shirt and shorts, and a broad-brimmed felt bush hat. At his side stalked the equally tall and gaunt, Sergeant Goodwill, wearing the same uniform as Drew, except for the fez on his head.

Murray instructed his driver to stop and the officers climbed out, stretching their backs; Drew and Goodwill approached and saluted.

"You've made rather slow progress," said Murray. "How are the men doing?"

"They're worn out, sir." Drew stated it as a matter of fact.

"What's the problem?" asked Murray. "Are the marches too long?"

"The main problem, sir, is that they're not getting enough food..."

"It's the same for all the men."

"Excuse me, sir," said Goodwill. "These men are not getting the same rations as the *askaris*."

Murray looked balefully at the African sergeant who had spoken to him in flawless English. "The *askaris* have to be ready to fight, Sergeant."

"That is true, sir, but they cannot fight without the *tengas*. They would have no ammunition, nor food."

"He has a point, sir," added Martin.

"Hm." Murray rapped his fingers on the bonnet of the staff car. "Give me a summary of the food supply chain."

Martin took a notebook out of his shirt pocket. "The two platoons ahead have enough mealie-meal for two days. This column of porters should reach them by then, which will give all five hundred men enough for about five days. The main shortage is meat, and the cattle are about four or five days behind..."

"Couldn't we slaughter and bring the carcasses up by lorry?"

"I have a lorry load coming tomorrow. It would help a lot if we could get some fresh meat locally – an elephant or a hippo. Drew has a hunting rifle."

"And what about local crops?"

"The Germans have cleaned the place out, sir. There's very little to be found. Alan tells me that the countryside about five days march ahead is more likely to have local maize, but this hilly country has very little."

"Can we increase the *tengas* rations?"

"I think we should."

"Do it."

Drew turned to the line of *tengas* and shouted in Swahili. "The Colonel says that you will all be given more food – the same as the *askaris*!"

A low murmur spread among the men as they digested and translated Drew's words. There followed scattered laughter, as someone shouted, "Let us eat from the same pot as the *askaris*."

—•—

The Rhodesians moved south-east from Iringa and soon encountered German opposition. They advanced cautiously, digging in at night because a counter-attack was always a possibility. There were no *tenga-tengas* to carry their equipment; they were far behind, so each man had to carry forty to sixty pounds. The Germans had burnt the undercover, which made it difficult for the men to conceal themselves. Crawling through the ashes they were soon black and filthy. The guns followed, pulled by oxen and mules, on rough tracks, with much sweat and swearing. The nights were cold and misty, and the men had only single threadbare blankets to wrap around themselves. Their uniforms were in tatters, and they had no change of dry clothes.

At the end of September they reached an escarpment overlooking the Kilombero Valley. Rows of ridges, covered with almost impenetrable forest, stretched to the Mahenge plateau a hundred miles away. Though the scene was spectacular the men knew that they had days of grinding marches ahead.

Almost every day they would encounter German pickets, or the more formidable rearguard of the enemy's main column. The Germans fought from entrenched positions, carefully chosen for command of the approaches.

The Rhodesians were using rifle grenades, fired from blank cartridges. The troopers became experts at converging on the flashes of the German field guns with the explosions of their own grenades. An enemy casualty from one of the grenades turned out to be a gunnery rating from the German battle cruiser *Konigsberg*, which had been scuttled in the Rufiji Delta.

Gavin Henderson was called to interrogate the wounded sailor, who was lying on a make-shift stretcher, having suffered a broken arm.

"*Haben sie ihnen etwas zur linderung der schmerzen?* Have they given you something for the pain?" asked Gavin.

The man's eyes widened slightly. "*Ja, ich bin in ordnung.*" he replied.

"I see that you're a sailor," said Gavin. "From the *Konigsberg?* A fine ship."

"Yes," muttered the sailor. "I was sad to leave her – in the water grave."

"I am a sailor, too." Gavin pointed to the RNVR badge on his cap.

"Ah, so I see – Royal Navy."

"Reserve." Gavin laughed. "We're both a long way from the sea!"

The German laughed too, but the movement hurt him and he stopped abruptly. "How is it that you speak German?"

Gavin told him, and then brought him a mug of tea and they chatted amicably for a half hour. Without having to ask questions Gavin heard that the man had been assigned to General Wahle's army, specifically to Wintgens' column, to advise on gunnery.

"It's a pity we did not stay together – as an army," said the sailor, glumly. "I think old Wahle wanted that, but the young commanders wanted to move faster – to be more independent. Wintgens is an expert at attacking your supply columns."

"He has been quite successful," Gavin agreed.

The sailor groaned in pain. "*Ach*, what will happen to me?"

"We have no hospital here. I expect you will be sent south with our own wounded."

He smiled. "Then perhaps I will see my compatriots again, because they too are moving south."

—•—

The Rhodesians forged on under extremely difficult conditions. The roads were only tracks, and in some places so narrow that the guns slipped off. In one case a field gun dragged its two mules down a steep slope; one of them was so badly injured it had to be killed; the men were glad to cook and eat the unfortunate animal. The gun crews and *tengas* had difficulty keeping up with the troops, often arriving at the bivouac after dark and falling asleep exhausted.

On reaching the enemy-occupied mission station, on a plateau eight thousand feet above sea level, they dug rifle pits encircling the buildings, which soon filled with rainwater. The men huddled together for warmth, sharing their thin blankets.

In the morning the German machine guns opened fire on them, inflicting severe casualties. When the Rhodesians finally surrounded the German positions they found the trenches and shelters abandoned. The main building had been converted into a hospital, where they found a dozen Europeans and two dozen *askaris*, all wounded. The food store had been set on fire.

Murray was instructed to lead his column to join forces with Colonel Hawthorn. They found him at Mkapira, where the Ruhudje River was joined by a tributary. The whole area was reigned by mosquitoes and tsetse flies, and the bush riddled with the dreaded itching buffalo beans. It was early October and the heat was intense, but the troops were delighted to have a delivery of rations intended for the South Africans, which were much better than their normal fare.

A virtual siege developed, and rations were reduced as the days passed. The Germans had a seven-pounder, and its shells were a constant irritant. Tensions were high, since an attack could descend on them at any moment. One night a picket opened furious fire and all the troops stood to, but it transpired that a rhino had strayed into the sentries and had not replied with the password when challenged.

'A' Company of the BSAP planned a bayonet attack; they would advance in extended order for a thousand yards. The men wrote 'last letters' because they expected withering fire from the German pickets and the enemy machine guns further back. As the Rhodesians left their positions in semi-darkness the *askaris* of the Northern Rhodesian Police called to wish the *bwanas* well.

The troops advanced at the double, and in their excitement overran the picket trenches with little opposition. Enthusiastically jogging forward they suddenly found themselves in the main German lines. The enemy Maxims were aligned for distant targets and could not be depressed in time to engage the attackers, but three Rhodesian troopers were killed, and several wounded, in fierce hand-to-hand fighting.

From this first success they were able to enfilade other trenches, and though the Germans counter-attacked they were beaten off. The force of forty Rhodesians, with no *askaris*, had defeated twenty-two Germans and over two-hundred *askaris*, and captured five Maxim guns. The dead Rhodesians were buried together, as were the five Germans killed; a mass grave was dug for the *askaris*.

—•—

33

Zomba, Nyasaland – November 1916

Jess embarked on a programme of taking in convalescent soldiers. It started when she had a conversation with Dr Thompson while visiting the hospital with milk and eggs.

"Jess, I have these men who are recovering," he explained. "They're taking up ward space. I need their beds for post-operative patients."

"Surely we could look after them in the town and on the farms."

"That's what I hoped. Some people have guest rooms, or cottages. The patients just need a bit of supervision. It doesn't need nursing experience."

Jess offered to take two men, and later added another. Dr Thompson, grateful for her assistance, tried to give her his more interesting and co-operative patients. They stayed in the Marge's old cottage, so that the girls could stay in the main house whenever they returned for breaks.

When Alan heard about the arrangement he was not happy. "You're having a succession of strange men to stay. I don't like it."

"Why not?" she retorted. "They can't harm me. In fact it makes me feel safer, because the locals know that there are European men staying on the farm. It's silly to be jealous, Alan."

She began to enjoy the company of the convalescing soldiers, almost all officers. Breakfast was served in their cottage, but they had lunch and supper in the main house, supervised by Jess, who often sat with them. She soon realised that they had suffered weeks or even months without proper food, and delighted in the simple farm fare – plenty of meat, eggs, milk, cheese, and vegetables, all produced on the farm.

Most men stayed for a week, a few for longer. They were reluctant to leave, but Dr Thompson had strict regulations to move them on to South Africa as soon as they were well enough to make the journey.

—•—

General Northey moved his headquarters to Zomba, and Martin Russell returned there to confer with him, and the other officers who had returned from Iringa. He had wanted this respite, not so much because of the comforts of civilisation it offered, as a chance to see the Spaight family again.

He decided to contact Jess and offer news of Alan, still at the front. The officers usually congregated at the KAR mess in the evenings, but Martin drove to Zomba Club, where there were always civilians. Some had drinks on the verandah after playing tennis or golf; others rehearsed for amateur dramatics or prepared for a weekend dance, while others merely propped up the bar.

To his surprise he saw Jess on the verandah, talking to an elderly couple. He waited until she disengaged, then went up to her.

"Hello, Jess."

"Martin! How good to see you. I thought you were up north."

"I was. Came back for meetings at HQ. Alan sends his love."

Her face showed concern. "How is he?"

"As well as can be expected. It's tough for all of us, especially the older ones. He knows how to look after himself."

"Yes, he does. He's had lots of experience. You must come out to the farm..."

"Any news of Mac?"

She put her hand to her face, as if involuntarily hiding her anguished expression. "Nothing. We fear the worst, but we haven't given up hope."

"Is there any search going on?"

She shook her head. "He could have gone anywhere. As you know, his bike was found near the foot of Mlanje Mountain, so the presumption is that he climbed further and got lost. But he might have come down somewhere else and walked away. The area is too vast. Of course we've offered a reward for anyone bringing information."

"Have you any idea why he went to Mlanje?"

She sighed, and wiped her eyes with the back of her hand. "I think he wanted to get away to be on his own. He knew the place fairly well, but he might have got lost in the mist, or fallen."

Martin put his hand on her shoulder. "I'm so sorry, Jess." Then he asked. "How are Clare and your girls?"

Her face brightened. "Clare seems to be fine. Mandy is staying on the farm now, though she's teaching at the hospital while she gets over a bout of fever. Kirsty is back in the Zomba hospital."

When Martin parted with Jess he took an invitation to have lunch at the farm.

—•—

Mandy looked pale but lovely when she greeted Martin on the verandah at *Khundalila*. She was wearing a long gingham skirt and white blouse. Her blonde hair was cut short, just above the shoulder, making her look younger. He calculated that she was twenty-four years old.

"I heard you had a bad bout of fever," he said.

"I don't know what it was," she replied. "Not malaria, perhaps dengue."

"How long will you stay here?"

"Another week or so. I'm going to see to the horses; would you like to come?"

He followed her to the stables, about fifty yards from the house, in a large thatched building with partitions for six horses. There were four in residence, two belonging to people who lived in Zomba. At the rear were storerooms for their food. The strong scent from the horses reminded him of his farm in Rhodesia.

"This is Raven," she said, pointing to a black gelding of about fifteen hands. "I don't feel up to riding now, but you can take him out if you like."

—•—

The young captain hobbled along the hospital verandah towards Kirsty. He wore a white cotton dressing gown, one of dozens made by the matrons of Zomba. His dark hair was combed back from a broad forehead that glistened with perspiration from his efforts to walk.

She looked up and saw him, then frowned. "You should not be walking without support."

He was recovering from dysentery and malaria; the double dose had nearly killed him. Kirsty had watched him slowly fight back to recovery.

"How is the lovely Kirsty?" He gave her a broad smile.

"If you fall it will set back your recovery."

"I'll be careful. I saw you and had to reach you, like a drowning man striving for..." He reached the rail of the verandah and stood beside her. "What were you thinking about – as you gazed out..."

"I was looking at Mlanje Mountain." She pointed, but the massif was almost lost in veils of rain falling over the Palombe Plain. "My brother was lost there, four months ago."

"I'm sorry. I heard something about it."

"He left the farm in the night – we don't know why. His motorcycle was found at the foot of the mountain. We've found no trace of him."

"I'm so sorry," he repeated, at a loss for words. "Can I take you out – some time? I know you're busy, but..."

She looked at him compassionately. "I'm sort of engaged, Reggie."

He raised his eyebrows. "What does that mean?"

"We decided not to become formally engaged, because of the war. But we have an understanding."

As if to emphasise her words there followed a flash of lightning, and seconds later a boom of thunder. Fat drops of rain started to pound on the tin roof of the hospital, rising to a crescendo. Kirsty saw the young captain speak, but could not hear his words. She smiled and pointed to her ears.

He shrugged and turned away. A curtain of raindrops fell from the overflowing gutter round the verandah, and behind it was darkness as the storm hid the sun.

—•—

Next morning Kirsty received the news of Gavin's wounding, in the form a letter.

> *My darling Kirsty,*
>
> *I trust you are well and not working too hard – though I'm sure you are! I do miss you so much. I thought I would have a chance to see you – because I was wounded. It happened like this:*
>
> *While at Iringa I met a German frau, who was our next door neighbour when I lived in Moshi. I thought I would try to wheedle some information from her – about the recently departed German troops. So I accepted her invitation to supper (she's the same age as my mother, so please don't think I had any other motive).*
>
> *After the meal her husband's servant returned to the house, to fetch something, and shot me – in the shoulder.*

The wound was painful, but not serious. I hoped they might send me back to Zomba, but it seems my interrogation is too useful. So Dr Macrae stitched it up, and here I am, chatting to a young German sergeant who has been wounded in the leg – quite badly.

Conditions in this hospital might shock you. Poor Dr Macrae does not have any European staff, except for a couple of orderlies, who know nothing about medical matters, and are here only to supervise the native cleaners. The doctor told me he wants some nurses, so perhaps you and Mandy will come north. I think the hospital is quite safe, because it's miles behind the fighting.

Even so, conditions are very primitive. There seems to be a lot of malarial fever and dysentery, and rumours about cholera. Every now and then a war-wounded soldier appears. There's argument about whether mine is a war wound. You see, I was on official duty, having reported to my senior officer – no less than your father – who agreed to my mission. Not that it matters much, as I won't be decorated with a medal!

I long for the day when I can see you again. I would like to write more explicitly, but the censor will read it. One day we'll be together again and will be married.
Love you always
Gavin

—•—

34

German East Africa – November 1916

Njombe had become the main forward base, a German *boma* to the east of the top end of Lake Nyasa, at the foot of the Kipengere Mountains, and on the road to Songea. General Northey saw it as a gateway to the south that the Germans might want to penetrate. He agreed to locate a forward hospital there, to which patients from the front could be sent, and from where they could be shipped down the lake to Fort Johnston, and thence to Zomba.

Mandy pleaded with the doctors to be sent to Njombe as a nurse, and Kirsty opted to go with her, knowing it would bring her closer to Gavin. Both Alan and Jess made strenuous objections to the girls, to no avail.

"What concerns me," said Alan, "is that you'll be so far from medical assistance..."

"But we'll be in a hospital, Pa," countered Kirsty.

He shook his head in frustration. "I know, but if something serious happened – something you couldn't cope with there – it would take days to get you back here."

The girls were taken on the *Guendolen* to Mpanda, a small former German port on the eastern short of the Lake, and thence by a rough track that was barely passable for motor vehicles, to Njombe, where they were greeted by Dr Macrae, a South African.

Colonel Murray was assembling his Column for the next phase of the campaign. He heard that there were many troops in the hospital and decided to pay a visit. In his characteristic grumpy way he greeted Macrae and the nurses and stumped through the wards. It seemed to him that there were far too many men lounging around in threadbare pyjamas, smoking cigarettes.

He lost his temper. "Doctor, we're trying to fight a war, and half my troops are malingering here in your hospital!"

"Er, Colonel, I doubt there are any..."

"They're scrimshankers, doctor!" Murray barked, so loudly that the whole ward could hear. "I want you to get them back in uniform."

Dr Macrae approached Kirsty and whispered, "What's a 'scrimshanker'?"

She giggled behind her hand. "It means 'shirker'."

"That's outrageous! As if I would condone shirking..."

"Let it go, sir. He's an angry bear. I've heard lots of stories about him. It's his way of getting things done."

—•—

In a reversal of roles the Germans attacked Lupembe at dawn on November 13, 1916. Murray had both BSAP companies in trenches surrounding the former German *boma*, but it was all they could do to fend off the attacks. In one of them, the enemy attacked the church, and the hospital where the BSAP wounded were being treated. One of the sergeants, who was recovering from illness, took charge of the machine guns when his officer was killed, and received a field commission.

One day the BSAP scouts brought in two enemy *askaris*, who were taken to Gavin Henderson for interrogation. He found that they had a despatch from General Wahle, advising one of his company commanders to avoid Lupembe and Njombe, because the British forces were too strong.

Drew took the news to Martin Russell, at Colonel Murray's HQ. "Now that we've intercepted this message we can expect the Germans to come past here."

"Possibly." Martin perused Gavin's transcript of the message. "We should send more scouts out, to see if we can intercept their advance pickets."

"We don't have any, sir. Two are out in the bush, and four are sick."

"You could go out, with Goodwill."

"What about my work with the *tengas*?"

"They're resting today."

Later, Martin strolled over to the officer's mess, where Drew was sitting on the verandah writing a letter. Although Martin liked and admired the young man, he was concerned that if he married Clare, she would live in Nyasaland for the rest of her life, and the Russells would seldom see her.

"Writing to Clare?"

Drew stood up. "Yes, sir." He smiled sheepishly.

"Here's my plan, Drew. We think Colonel Huebener's column is coming in this direction. We need more information, about their strength and dispositions. As you told me, all the regular scouts are out of commission, for one reason or another. Could you take Goodwill out and see if you can spot the enemy?"

Drew nodded, but Martin thought he looked far from enthusiastic.

"You can take a couple of troopers, or *askaris*."

Drew smiled. "The troopers would be a liability, sir. They're good men, but they're a bit clumsy in the bush. I'll ask Goodwill if he wants *askaris* – I doubt he will."

Drew found Goodwill in the African quarters, which were steeped in smoke, and thus relatively free of flies and mosquitoes. The grizzled sergeant was whittling a piece of wood, and told Drew it was part of a trap to catch mice, many of which plundered the food stores.

"They are good to eat, *Bwana* Drew."

Drew laughed. "I would eat anything if I was hungry enough."

He told Goodwill about Martin Russell's proposition.

"I would like to go out of here," replied Goodwill. "We have had enough rest."

"When shall we go?"

"I can be ready in half an hour."

—•—

They set off in the early afternoon, along a path that ran roughly parallel to the main road from Njombe to the north. That 'road' was merely a rough dusty track, but it could be used for motor vehicles; there had been no traffic on it for several days.

Drew followed Goodwill, who loped along, stopping every few minutes to listen and sniff the air. It was easy for him to relax and leave the African to find the way and hear anything dangerous.

Goodwill was barefoot and bare-headed, wearing a tattered khaki uniform; he carried a bayonet in a sheath, and a Lee-Enfield .303. Drew wore his slouch hat – he hated the pith helmet – and khaki shirt and shorts; on his feet were worn *veldschoen*, with no socks. He also carried a rifle, slung on his shoulder, and a revolver in a holster at his waist.

For the first hour they heard nothing, but when the sun dipped down to the hills on the horizon the birds started their evening calls. Goodwill's listening halts grew longer. An hour before dark he whispered to Drew.

"We should find somewhere to spend the night. We can find a large tree."

"I'm hopeless sleeping in a tree," said Drew.

"I can tie you."

They found a large fig tree which had places where the branches abutted the trunk with ample space for a man to sit, or sleep in a sitting position. They could not risk lighting a fire, so chewed the biltong they brought in their pockets, and drank sparingly from Drew's water bottle. They found some ash from a forest fire and rubbed it on their skin to keep the mosquitoes at bay.

Drew slept fitfully and was glad to descend from the tree at first light. Goodwill whispered that he could smell smoke, so perhaps there was a camp fire up wind, to the north. They moved cautiously along the path, keeping the dirt road in sight. About an hour later Goodwill stopped and crouched; Drew did the same, his pulse racing. A few minutes later they saw movement on the road, and crept towards it, so they could see better.

It was a German soldier with three *askaris*. They were walking slowly and attentively, but with their rifles slung on their shoulders.

Drew and Goodwill decided to surprise the enemy group by sitting at the roadside, but with their rifles beside them, ready to raise. They slid into position.

Drew shouted, *"Hallo!"* and waved.

The German stopped, then walked on, calling out, *"Wie weit zum nächsten Lager?* How far to the next camp?"

Drew stood up and pointed back down the road, while bringing his rifle up to his side. The German was only a dozen paces away, with the *askaris* grouped beside him. Drew swung his rifle up and pointed it.

"Sit down!" he commanded. "We have ten men in the bush. Throw your rifles down!"

They did so, without hesitation. Goodwill quickly tied their hands behind their backs with fishing line. The German, a corporal, spoke broken English.

"We thought you were our people."

"You will not be harmed if you don't try to run away," said Drew. "We'll go back to our camp, where you will be well looked after."

Hurrying back, using the path that ran parallel to the road, they reached the camp by early afternoon, and admitted the prisoners to the wire-fenced compound. The corporal was taken to Gavin for questioning. Within a few minutes it was obvious that he was only too glad to be in the British camp.

"It is better you prepare for attack," said the corporal. "Or you should move out. Our main column has dozens of officers and NCOs, and two hundred and fifty *askaris*. Also, they have a howitzer and several machine guns."

When Gavin gave this news to Colonel Murray he decided to attack at once. A complex series of movements were made during the next few days as the column surrounded the Germans, who knew the Rhodesians were manoeuvring, and tried to shell them with the howitzer. Murray changed tactics and moved his men at night, so that the Germans could not find their targets.

When Murray had the Germans surrounded he sent envoys under a white flag aiming to make them surrender. At first Huebener refused, but he was eventually convinced that his force had no access to water. His only stipulation was that he would destroy the howitzer, which he did.

There were fifty-seven Europeans in the captured German column, four of them Afrikaners who had farmed near Mt Kilimanjaro, and had been coerced into joining the Germans. The howitzer had been on the German battle-cruiser *Konigsberg*. The Rhodesians also captured four hundred head of cattle

When General Northey heard the news of the capture of Huebener's column, he went from New Langenburg to Njombe to congratulate the troops. A parade was held and Northey gave a speech praising the men. He announced that he had recommended the award of a DSO for Murray, as well as several Distinguished Conduct Medals. Goodwill was awarded the African Distinguished Conduct Medal.

—•—

The track was cut into the side of the mountain, roughly following the contour. Barely wide enough for two carts to pass, its edge was worn and eroded by storm water, and boulders and rocks littered its muddy surface. The slopes above and below were steep and heavily wooded, the undergrowth sparse.

Two hundred *tenga-tengas* plodded along the track, each carrying a load of about fifty pounds: ammunition in wooden boxes, four gallon tins of kerosene and paraffin, and sacks of maize meal. Goodwill walked up and down the line of men encouraging them and cajoling them.

"Only another hour and you will be able to shed your load and have a meal..."

"Of what, Sergeant?" asked a scrawny man, wearing tattered shorts and a shirt that was mere shreds.

"I have arranged for some cooked *nsima* to be brought up," answered Goodwill, without much conviction.

"We will be asleep before it reaches us," said another porter. "If I don't wake up – who will bury me?"

"I cannot sleep," said his companion. "My stomach makes too much noise – it's so empty."

"Perhaps the Germans have left some food..." Goodwill had little confidence in his statement, since the Germans seldom left anything behind, let alone food.

Suddenly the enemy started shelling the road. After a few sighters they found the range. Amidst shrieks from the *tengas*, and the crackle of the explosions, Goodwill could hear boulders tumbling down the slope, unleashed by the shells, crashing through the undergrowth like rampaging rhinos. He urged the men to move into the mountain side of the road, where the bank would shield them, but they were terrified, scattering in small groups, some hurling themselves down the side slope.

A shell burst in the middle of the road disintegrating a dozen men and opening a crater that would make the road unusable. A shower of mud and stones lifted into the air, then fell over a wide area. The air was thick with smoke, stinking of cordite.

Goodwill was thrown off his feet; when he recovered, he sat up and shook his head. The scene around him was chaotic, and he realised he had to get the men off the road.

"Hurry down into the valley!" he shouted, pointing the way and pushing them. "Go down to the stream – gather below."

He waited until every man had gone over the edge, leaving only the dead, and two severely wounded men who could not be moved; they were lying side by side, and he left a water bottle between them.

He scrambled down the steep slope, shouting to the men he passed, and others he saw. "I'll call you with the *diti* sound – the ground hornbill. Keep moving!"

Another shell burst sent rock fragments flying. Goodwill reached the stream, a trifling flow between huge rocks. After taking shelter behind one of the boulders he urged the men to go further and then wait for him.

An hour later they assembled in a loose group lower down the valley, some drinking from the stream, others washing their wounds and scratches. The shelling seemed to have stopped, and Goodwill presumed that their target was too dissipated. He took a crumpled piece of paper from his pocket and started to question the men about who they had seen killed and wounded.

The German gun crew that had caused so much damage decided to lob one more shell into the valley, where they knew most of the porters had fled. It burst on a rock and threw splinters and hot metal fragments in all directions. One of them, the size of a thimble, hit Goodwill in the belly. He fell over, clutching himself, feeling a fierce burning inside his guts. He looked down and when he took his hand away blood seeped out of the hole near his navel.

One of the *tengas* crawled over to him. "Have you been hit, Sergeant?"

Goodwill groaned as he gathered his senses. "Yes. Any others?"

"I'll find out."

"Wait!" Goodwill looked at the frightened man, whose face streamed with sweat. "I think the Germans have stopped their shelling. Get the men to cut poles. Tie *nsarus* to make *machilas*. Those who are able must carry out the wounded."

The man nodded glumly and scrambled away. Goodwill tore cloth from his shirt and pressed it as a pad against the hole in his belly. The bleeding seemed to have stopped, but intense pain seared through him. He rested, waiting and wondering what damage had been made inside him. He realised that he might die, but at least he was among men he knew. He would write a note to his wife.

Ten minutes later a group of *tengas* came to him with a stout pole and started to make the webbing that would support him. They had little to work with, only strips of bark and their own clothing. Eventually, they completed a sling seat and lifted him into it. He groaned with the pain, feeling himself lose consciousness.

The *tengas* struggled downstream, awkwardly carrying Goodwill, who swung to and fro, hanging from the pole. They knew that the stream crossed the road lower down, at a shallow drift. When they reached that place they filled their water bottles, then headed down the road towards Njombe, now moving at a faster pace, and relieved that they were leaving the Germans behind.

Of the nearly two hundred men in their contingent there were only one hundred and sixty left, of whom six were being carried in *machilas* and another dozen, less seriously wounded, straggled behind the main contingent.

A motor-cycle approached; Drew Spaight with a foreman corporal on the pillion. He greeted the men and heard their story, hurrying to find the unconscious Goodwill. When he felt the man's weak pulse he ordered the *capitao* to lead the porters back to the camp, and instructed men nearby to put Goodwill on the pillion of the motor-bike and to tie him to his own back. As soon as this was accomplished he set off as fast as he could go on the rough track.

It took him three hours to reach the advance camp, where he found a lorry from Njombe being unloaded. He instructed the driver to fetch the wounded *tengas*. Meanwhile, a group of *askaris* helped him to carry Goodwill to the first aid tent, where they laid him on a stretcher.

A European orderly was drinking a cup of tea. A short, scrawny man, with huge moustaches, he jumped up when he saw Drew's pips and Goodwill's sergeant's stripes.

"What's the matter with him, sir?"

"Hit in the guts. Is there anything we can do here?"

The orderly shook his head. "Bullet – was it? If he was conscious I would suggest some morphine..."

"The porters said they were shelled, so it was probably a piece of shrapnel – or perhaps a rock fragment."

The orderly stroked his extravagant moustaches. "He'll need an operation, sir, and we can't do that here."

Drew noticed signs that Goodwill was recovering consciousness. His eyelids fluttered and his pulse was stronger. He opened his eyes but soon closed them.

"Don't give up, Goodwill." Drew spoke in both English and ChiNyanja. "We'll get you better. Just keep going a bit longer."

He could not bear the thought that Goodwill might die. He was like a second father, an example of calm dignity, and the source of all that Drew knew about the African people, their language and customs. He had taught Drew almost everything he knew about the bush and its animals.

He hurried off to see Major Stenson, the camp commander, who was in his tent writing in a notebook when he approached.

"I thought you'd gone to Mkapira," said the Major. "What's the matter?"

"The *tenga* party was shot up, sir. Shelled from the heights above the road. We lost about forty of them – the others have turned back –

they're done in – several wounded – I ordered the lorry to pick them up. My sergeant has been wounded..."

"Goodwill?"

"Yes, sir. With your permission I want to take him to Njombe. He'll need an operation to survive."

The Major sighed. "I'm sorry to hear that. You're really needed here, Drew." He looked down at the papers on his desk as he thought. "Look, I want to get this despatch off to Njombe. Why don't you take it? Can you take him on your bike?"

"I'll try. Thank you, sir...."

—•—

It took a day of hard riding for Drew to get to Njombe on the motorcycle. The dead weight of Goodwill strapped to his back exhausted him. He stopped every hour to take the wounded man's pulse and to try pouring water down his throat. He was encouraged when Goodwill regained consciousness about half way, and was able to drink, but he said nothing, his eyes half closed.

The miles and miles of dirt road unravelled slowly and painfully as Drew picked his way through the potholes and bumps, trying to minimise the jarring. He knew that the bike would be easier on the patient than the bed of a truck; a *machila* would have been better, but too slow.

On reaching Njombe he rode straight to the hospital, where two orderlies unstrapped Goodwill from Drew's back and carried him on a stretcher into the thatched building. The admission process lasted half a minute and they bore the patient into a waiting room, placing him on a makeshift table.

"Drew!" Mandy rushed up to him and embraced her brother.

"It's Goodwill," he said. "Wounded in the belly."

"Oh Lord! She went up to the prone patient and pulled aside his shirt and the cloth covering the wound. "I don't think he's lost much blood, but we must give him a saline drip. Go and find Dr Macrae. He's in that ward over there."

Drew found the doctor doing a round of the ward with Kirsty and a couple of orderlies. He quickly briefed them about Goodwill, and Macrae hurried to the patient. A young South African, large and beefy, he was a man of few words; Drew's sisters said he was an exceptional doctor.

Macrae examined Goodwill and instructed Mandy to prepare him for an operation.

"There's no exit wound, so we can presume that the shrapnel – or whatever it is – is still inside him. It was probably hot and sterile, but would have carried dirt and germs into him. We must hope it hasn't caused too much damage. Kirsty, you administer the chloroform. Mandy, you assist me."

Ten minutes later Dr Macrae was making his incision, cutting laterally across the position of the wound and opening the abdominal cavity, while Mandy clamped blood vessels and mopped up blood. Kirsty was at the patient's head with a gauze pad on which she dripped chloroform at a controlled rate, constantly monitoring his weak pulse.

"Here it is," announced Macrae, and lifted out a lump of metal the size of a thimble. "Must have been spent by the time it hit him, and slowed down by the entry. I'll excise this length of intestine and join it together. He's lucky it didn't damage any other organs – the kidneys are not far away." He cut and sutured, with Mandy passing him scalpels and needles.

"His colonic system is in shock," said Macrae quietly. "There's a very serious risk of infection. Pour in plenty of carbolic, Mandy. We have to hope that his constitution will keep him alive. How old is he? Do you know? Looks quite old."

"He was taken as a slave in the mid-80s," said Drew, standing outside the group. "He was about twenty then, so say born in 1865; that would make him fifty now."

"Hm. That's an old man in African terms. Life expectancy of these people is only about forty. But he looks tough."

After Goodwill was returned to the recovery ward they washed and adjourned to the officers' mess. Drew bought Macrae a dram of whisky and one for himself, and the girls had lemon squashes.

"What would you have done if you'd had one of your South African lads come in for surgery at the same time?" asked Drew.

Macrae looked at him through narrowed eyes. "Do you mean, would I give priority to the white man? The answer is, no, Drew. Your sisters will vouch for me. I may be a South African, but I'm not a racist. I take patients in strict priority. The wards are segregated, but that makes sense because the food is different, and they can talk to each other in their own languages."

"What are Goodwill's chances?"

Macrae blew out his lips. "He's not a young man, but he seems tough. Even so, I think his chances are less than even..."

"Father will be devastated if he dies," said Kirsty. "They've known each other for thirty years."

"I would be too," added Drew.

—•—

35

German East Africa – December 1916

The rainy season started in earnest and sometimes the BSAP troops were soaked to the skin for several days on end. Mosquitoes became more numerous, passing on malaria and blackwater fever to men who were undernourished. Colds and pneumonia were common, and the men grumbled about shortage of food, and having to smoke the coarse native tobacco.

One morning Martin Russell spotted three troopers having a heated discussion. He edged closer to hear what they were saying, but they spotted him and drifted apart. One of them, a man named Standish, was known to Martin; he worked for a newspaper in Salisbury as a compositor.

"What's the matter, Standish?" Martin asked.

The man scowled at him. "Nothing – sir."

"Come on. I could see you were having a discussion. What was it about?"

After a pause, Standish said, "The men are fed up, sir. They want some home leave."

"Wouldn't we all! You're a volunteer, man. We all have to put up with this – until it's over..."

"The trouble is that we don't know when it will end, sir. The men have been serving for over a year without a break." Standish looked at Murray with a sour expression. "We're drawing up a petition."

"That's not a good idea," said Martin. "It's too formal. Why don't you come and have a talk with the Colonel?"

"He wouldn't listen to us – would he?"

"I'll arrange for you to meet with him."

Standish shook his head. "We'll send a petition."

—•—

When Martin told Colonel Murray about his conversation, Murray growled. "Let them send me a bloody petition."

It came the next day, brought by Standish and the two other men. They handed the paper to Murray, who was seated at his camp table. He read it quickly, and his frown deepened. Then he threw the paper on the table.

"This is disgusting! I will not have you men write this sort of drivel – it's disgraceful." He looked up at Martin, who was standing nearby. "Russell, I want all the men paraded, and the men who signed this petition standing at the front."

Martin organised the parade for that afternoon. There were eighty BSAP men present, including a dozen petitioners; they waited until Colonel Murray stalked out onto the parade ground and faced them, his expression contorted with fury.

"I have received a petition," he bellowed, "asking for better conditions and home leave." He paused. "I tell you that your conditions are the best we can give you in the circumstances. We are at war – damn it! This is not some training exercise. We are fighting for our lives and for our country. I refuse to accept this petition. In fact I may send it home, for publication in the *Rhodesia Herald* and the *Bulawayo Chronicle* – with the names of the petitioners."

He threw the paper on the ground and shouted, "I'm giving you a chance to take your names off." Then he stumped away.

—•—

On the following morning Standish and four other men came to Murray and presented the petition again, with additional signatures. Martin took it to the Colonel, whose face reddened.

"Bloody hell, Martin. They are defying me!"

"I'm afraid so, sir."

"I have to report it to Northey." Murray sighed. "What a shame. Our fine reputation is being spoiled by a few rabble-rousers."

"We could send the ring leaders away," suggested Martin.

"I agree. Make a list for me, Martin. But we have to see Northey. Come with me."

—•—

General Northey was in a good mood when they entered his office. Dapper as always, he wore a neatly pressed uniform, his moustache freshly clipped, and his short hair combed down. He invited them to sit down while he read the petition.

"Dissension in the ranks, eh, Murray? Let me talk to them."

"I'm very sorry, sir," said Murray. "It's the volunteers, you see, not the regulars..."

"Well, that's good to know. Have them brought to me."

Northey received the petitioners in his office. They looked nervous, faced by the small but authoritarian figure.

"I've read your petition, men, and I understand your concerns. We staff officers sympathise with you about the poor conditions you've had to endure – and the fact that you're overdue for some leave. But there's a German column not far away, and we must concentrate our efforts on capturing it. What do you say?"

"Sir, we're not refusing to fight," said Standish. "We just want better conditions... "

"Don't we all, lads. Look, I'll see what I can do. Now let's get on with our jobs. Do you agree?"

The men nodded and muttered their assent before they trooped out.

Northey said to Murray, "You can get rid of the ringleaders, if you want. But I advise leaving them for the time being."

—•—

Moses visited Goodwill every day, deeply concerned that his friend might die. At first the patient was semi-conscious, but the orderlies said his temperature was normal, so he had probably escaped an infection.

The field hospital patients were given special rations to help their recovery. In addition to the regular *nsima* they were given broth, made from whatever meat was available.

Goodwill recovered faster than anyone expected. Within a week he was sitting up and talking, eating well, his gut working. His complexion was still grey, and he was very thin, the bones in his solemn face showing.

One morning while Moses was there, the food was brought round.

"What is this?" asked Goodwill.

"It is a soup, *bambo*," replied Moses, looking at the orderly for confirmation.

"What kind of soup?"

"Mouse soup. It will taste good."

Goodwill smiled weakly.

—•—

"We're sending you home, *bambo*," said Drew, sitting at the bedside. "You need to recover your strength."

The patient nodded. "I should argue, *Bwana* Drew, but I know you are correct – this time." He smiled. "How will I travel...?"

"You'll go on the lake steamer to Fort Johnston; they'll check you at the hospital there. Then by lorry to Zomba. You'll have a *kalata* from me and the Colonel."

Goodwill beckoned for Drew to come closer, and then to bend nearer so he could whisper.

"Will you be alright, *Bwana* Drew? I think you are not afraid now. You do not need me."

Drew gripped the older man's hand. "I will be alright. Thank you for looking after me, *bambo*."

—•—

36

German East Africa – May 1917

Drew said, "Has there been any news of Mac?"

He sat with his sisters on one of the few occasions when they were free at the same time. They sat on packing cases on the verandah of the mess at Njombe; the building had been the dining hall for the German administrators who established the *boma*. It was growing dark and scores of bats were swooping to catch insects clustering around the hurricane lamps.

"Nothing that I've heard." Kirsty sipped from a bottle of beer. "You've written to Clare about him, haven't you?"

"Of course, but she knows nothing." Drew was on the defensive. "I know that it's logical to think that it might be connected with her being at the farm, but we have to accept her word. I believe her."

"We all do," said Mandy soothingly. "It's just awful not knowing where he is. I have this vision of him lying injured, wet and cold..."

"Don't torture yourself," said Kirsty. "It's almost certain that he's died and that we'll never find him." She paused. "You know, he was never a happy soul."

"Except with his machines," added Mandy.

A young officer walked up to them and asked confidently if he might join them.

"We're having a sort of family discussion," said Kirsty. "Perhaps later?"

The officer, a captain that Drew had not met before, stood rooted, half smiling. Drew introduced himself. "And these are my sisters, Mandy and Kirsty."

"Pleased to meet you," said the captain.

"So sorry," said Kirsty. "You see, we hardly ever have the chance to meet, and our brother died recently..."

The captain's smile turned to a frown. "I'm so sorry. I don't want to intrude." He turned and walked away.

"That was a bit harsh, sis," said Mandy.

"Well, it's true, isn't it?" Kirsty replied, then said to Drew, "Have you heard from Clare recently?"

He nodded. "Got a letter yesterday. She's been moved to Fort Johnston. Says she's trying to persuade Dr Sanderson to send her up here. Do you think they'd do that?"

Kirsty shrugged. "If they're getting more Ward Sisters and nurses, they might. We could certainly use another nurse here, couldn't we Mandy?"

"For sure – more than one." She looked up and saw another young officer walking up to them, holding a lamp. "Here we go again. Are you going to say the same to him?"

The officer must have sensed that he was not welcome because he veered away.

"Where are we going? I mean what's going to happen to us?" Kirsty started to cry quietly. Between sobs she added, "It's three years now since this war started. Will it ever end? We've seen countless men go through these hospitals, with wounds and diseases. I don't know..."

Mandy moved to her side and hugged her. "It can't last forever. Sooner or later the war in Europe will end. What do you think Drew?"

"I agree. It may take a few more months or a year, but I know we'll beat them."

—•—

General Northey agreed with his superiors, Smuts and van Deventer, that Norforce was too small to invade the Mahenge Plateau until after the end of the rainy season. Meanwhile, interrogations of prisoners by Gavin Henderson and others revealed that the German forces were coalescing, no doubt restoring on better food supplies. Northey decided to withdraw his garrison at Mkapira.

Rather than sit idly during the rainy season Norforce mounted an attack on the Germans, who were now concentrated between Mkapira and Lupembe. Some of the officers likened this to looking for the proverbial needle in a vast expanse of bush, now sodden after days of continuous rain, among streams and rivers in torrents. Paths and tracks were muddy and slippery, the men always soaked, and cold at night, attacked by mosquitoes in profusion.

Colonel Murray contracted malaria and Martin took over command of the Column. Murray regarded his deputy as ‘a safe pair of hands’, and mentioned him in despatches. The men liked Martin, too. They knew he cared for their well-being and would not push them beyond their limits.

Martin asked Drew to come to the administration house, one of the few habitable buildings in the Mkapira *boma*. He waved the lieutenant to a camp chair and spent a moment appraising him. The young man’s uniform was in bedraggled condition, faded and stained, and worn at the cuffs and collar. His felt bush hat was battered and drooping. Even so, he was in no worse state than the other men.

“Drew, I won’t waste time – I want you to go out on scouting patrols. We’re woefully short of information about the enemy positions.” He saw Drew’s expression change from concern to alarm, and wondered why.

“But, sir, what about the *tengas*? Who will organise them?”

“We’ll have to find someone else.” Martin lit his pipe with deliberate movements. “You see, Drew, you’re too valuable to spend your time herding the *tengas*. You've done a great job, and you've established a system that works well, but..."

"Uncle Martin, will I be able to keep Goodwill, my sergeant."

"I thought he was sent back to Zomba, when he was wounded."

"He was, but he insisted on coming back – arrived a week ago."

"Excellent. You see, you're the best linguist we have, Drew. Everyone tells me that you speak ChiNyanja like a native, and Swahili very well, so you can interrogate *askaris* that we capture, and Goodwill can do the same. We have Gavin to question the German prisoners – he's doing a great job – but he's too busy with that to talk to all the *askari* prisoners – and his Swahili is only average."

Drew pushed his fingers through his hair. It scared him to think about changing his work from the relatively safe control of the *tengas* to the dangerous process of collecting information about the enemy. "Sir, who will give me my orders?"

"I will. You and Gavin are now equal in seniority – since he was given his lieutenancy." Martin laughed. "Strange that we have an RNVR officer and a NVR officer, working under a BSAP officer, commanded by a British general. From an admin point of view you'll be in the Intelligence Section, under your father, but he's too far away to give you orders."

"What would you like me to do, sir?"

"Hm. Well, I was impressed with the way you and Goodwill brought in those German prisoners. I would like you to probe forward, with the pickets, but even further ahead. Look, I know it will be risky, so you must be cautious. I wonder if you should take two more men, so be a team of four?"

The Column ground slowly forward but found the Germans had gone, except for a handful of men too exhausted to retreat. Meanwhile,

Col Hawthorn located the enemy and asked for support from the Rhodesians. The combined force attempted to encircle the Germans, but failed when the enemy retreated from hill to hill, leaving rearguard pickets to slow down their attackers.

Meanwhile, another column from Norforce had been sent east from New Langenburg to Songea, an abandoned German *boma*. They found two huge mounds near the town, and were told they were the burial places of forty-seven chiefs who had been executed by the Germans in the *Maji-maji* Rebellion, ten years earlier.

Murray's Column fought on; the going was dreadfully hard, and many *tengas* died from exhaustion and exposure. Sgt Evans, who had taken charge of them, was unpopular. He was too authoritarian, and the men sensed that he despised them. Word came to Murray, now recovered and in command, that Evans had forced the *tengas* to leave their dead comrades unburied. He called in Drew, and questioned him, with Martin Russell attending.

"What was your policy, Lieutenant, when you were in charge of the *tengas*?" asked Murray bluntly, while he fiddled with his pipe.

Drew cleared his throat nervously. "Sir, we always buried the *tengas* who died. The survivors made it clear that they wanted to do it – but it was sometimes extremely difficult. We had to make sure that one man in ten carried a *badza*, and they took it in turns to dig the graves. We..." He paused, thinking he was saying too much.

"Go on," said Murray.

"We always put stones and rocks on the graves..."

"They were buried together?"

"Only if they were from the same tribe."

"Yes. Go on."

"The *tengas* wanted to protect the graves from animals digging them up."

"This must have taken a long time – delayed you?"

"Yes, sir. But I though it would be worse if the *tengas* were disaffected – by leaving their friends unburied."

"Hm." Murray started lighting his pipe. "Very well, Spaight, you can go now."

When Drew had gone Murray said, "What do you think of him, Martin. Or are you biased because he's in love with your daughter?" He gave a rare fleeting smile.

"He's a white African, Ron, if ever there was one. He can talk to them, he knows how they think. He doesn't regard himself as superior to them..."

"A bit like you?"

"Yes, but I still have some ingrained prejudices."

"Perhaps you shouldn't have taken him away from the *tengas*?"

—•—

Gavin Henderson had just finished talking to a young German NCO; they were both in good humour. As he walked away he saw Drew approaching. They walked together to the mess, collected mugs of tea, and sat down at a trestle table.

"I'm coming to join you," said Drew. "Into the Intelligence Unit. Uncle Martin's orders."

Gavin patted him on the shoulder. "That's good, Drew. We need someone with your languages..."

"But it seems that I'm going to be a scout." Drew's tone was somewhat plaintive. "One consolation is that I'll have Goodwill with me. In fact, I couldn't do it without him."

—•—

The German unit under Captain Wintgens developed a threat. He had decided to move towards Fife, on the Stevenson Road, which Northey had made into a supply station. Wintgens was known for his successful attacks on Allied depots, so it seemed likely that Fife would be his next objective.

The Rhodesian Native Regiment, under Colonel Tomlinson, was brought west from Songea and put under Murray's command. Having combined his forces Murray moved them round the northern end of Lake Nyasa to New Langenburg, and then through the Poroto Mountains

Wintgens was a formidable enemy. Intelligence estimates gave him five hundred men, fifteen Maxim machine guns and two-field guns. Before the Allies could engage him he moved on to St Moritz Mission, on the banks of the Songwe River, and decided to make a stand there – the stag facing the hounds, noble, but bedraggled after three years of campaigning in the bush.

Murray invited Col Tomlinson to sit down. They had known each other for years, but there was no friendship between them. Tomlinson was tall and spare, quiet, and much admired by his men. He sat opposite Murray listening carefully.

"I want you to attack along the Songwe River, Tommy. I'll follow you, unless I go down the Bismarckburg road." Seeing Drew Spaight at the door, Murray beckoned to him.

"This is Lt Spaight," he said, by way of introduction. "I want him to go with you. He's one of my intelligence officers, and I think he and his sergeant can help you."

"If you say so," said Tomlinson without enthusiasm, though he smiled at Drew. "Have you worked with Rhodesian *askaris* before?"

"No sir – only Nyasaland men."

"We mostly speak ChiShona..."

Murray interjected, "But you have some Amandabele."

"Yes," acknowledged Tomlinson. "I keep them in a separate platoon – there's no love lost between them and the Shona."

"My sergeant speaks ChiNgoni," said Drew, "so could probably make himself understood with your men."

As Tomlinson approached St Moritz Mission his column was attacked repeatedly by the Germans, who broke through to the RNR temporary trenches, killing and wounding thirty men. The enemy fought with great determination, and were obviously seasoned troops. If they ran short of ammunition they charged with bayonets.

The Rhodesian officers gathered in a large dugout in the evening, during a lull in the shelling from the German field-guns. They began to argue with Tomlinson.

"We really should get out of here, Tommy," said one. "We can't defend ourselves properly."

"They completely out-gun us, sir," said another.

Tomlinson shook his head, and when he replied his voice was calm and steady. "We can't make an escape with the wounded men – it would be too slow and dangerous. And I have no intention of leaving them behind."

The Colonel beckoned to Drew, and put his hand on his shoulder. "Spaight, I want you and Poole to go out tomorrow with a white flag. See if you can get the Huns to exchange prisoners."

He turned away, and ordered the other officers to organise a defensive square, a *laager.* A column of about a hundred *tengas* had caught up with them, bringing supplies, and it was the only way to protect them. The porters dug shallow pits in which they lay. It was raining steadily, and their pits were soon waterlogged, so they lay on the open ground, shivering in their wet ragged clothes.

Drew was soaked to the skin. He slept fitfully, his mind preoccupied with thoughts of going out to meet the Germans, wishing that Gavin could have been here to do the job. He tried to think of ways to justify taking Goodwill with him, but Tomlinson decreed that only four men should go, including Lt Poole, who had a little German.

Next morning, the white flag party set out. Geoff Poole jaunty and confident, Drew hesitant and nervous, and two *askaris*, tall muscular Matabele men, chosen for their impressive demeanour.

A German sergeant advanced, and greeted them in English. "So? You come to surrender?"

"*Nein!*" replied Poole indignantly.

"Then what is your business?"

"We have come to request an exchange of prisoners and wounded."

"Ah. Come with me." The sergeant turned and paced away, while they followed. "You fellows made a good fight," he said, over his shoulder.

They passed through the German pickets and forward trenches, then followed a rough dirt road near the river to the mission. Typically fortified, as if to resist a rebellion of local natives, it had an impressive gate. Inside were several white-washed buildings, all flying the German flag, and a courtyard, where a field-gun was being repaired.

Captain Wintgens emerged, pale and ponderous. He was renowned as one of von Lettow's best commanders, but rumours said he was in poor health. He greeted the Rhodesian party warmly and listened to Poole's statement.

"I have your doctor, and several wounded men. You can take them back with you. But the sergeant and three of your *askaris* are too sick to be moved; better they stay with us. I am keeping two medical orderlies, because, on previous occasions, you British have not returned our orderlies."

Wintgens then wrote a letter to Tomlinson while the prisoners were brought out. Poole's party then set off back, still with their white flag aloft. Meanwhile, the RNR column had moved further away, onto a patch of higher ground, where they were busy digging trenches in a rough square. They later found a spring, and dug a lateral trench to allow them to fetch water into the *laager*.

Next day the Germans attacked repeatedly, but were held off. The Rhodesian *askaris,* encouraged by their NCOs and white officers, kept up a steady defensive fire. Attacks came at them every day, and their food supply dwindled.

Drew and his scouts ventured out at night in the hope of capturing someone. It soon became obvious that a party of more than two was unwieldy and noisy. So Drew and Goodwill went together, while the other two scouts sallied out at a different time. On one of these expeditions Goodwill discovered some small fields of maize with green cobs. He and Drew then led a larger party to gather these in, and the food shortage was partially relieved.

It was now five days since the RNR column was first attacked and still there was no sign of support from Murray's main column. At an informal meeting of the nine officers Tomlinson explained his plan.

"I've decided to send Lt Booth, to find Murray's Column and tell them about our predicament. We can't escape and leave our wounded, so we will hang on for a while. Obviously we need re-supply with food."

—•—

Two days later one of the RNR sentries spotted a signaller in a nearby hill. Using binoculars Tomlinson read the signal, then hurried to his dugout to de-code it. He emerged smiling, waving a piece of paper.

"They've arrived! But the message says 'Do not surrender. Relief tomorrow.'" Then he paused and his expression clouded. "Why 'do not surrender?' There was never any mention of us surrendering. I wonder what Booth said".

Sure enough, the advance party from Murray's column arrived next day and the Germans retreated back into the fortified Mission.

Next evening Drew and Goodwill captured a picket of *askaris* and brought them back to the *laager*. Under questioning they revealed that the Germans had plenty of food and ammunition, as well as over a thousand *tenga-tengas*, in the Mission compound. They were reported to be building a bridge over the Songwe River.

Murray decided to attack with his full Column, but each time they approached the Mission they were met by accurate machine gun fire. The Germans also used their field gun to good effect. The Colonel reluctantly held an officer meeting.

"It's fruitless and wasteful making frontal attacks – they're in too strong a defensive position. So what are our alternatives?"

"They might make a run for it," said Drew, surprised that he was the first to say anything.

Murray nodded. "How can we stop them?"

"Sir," said Drew, "we know that they'll go north – crossing the river on their new bridge."

"How can we prevent them?

Booth answered. "If we try to go up and cover the bridge they'll shoot us to pieces."

Drew held up his hand, and Murray nodded to him. "We could go upstream and float down in dugouts with explosives – blow up the bridge..."

"Do it!"

Drew formed a team consisting of Goodwill and six Amandabele *askaris* of the RNR. Keeping out of sight and range of the mission defences they worked their way round and then up the shore of the Songwe River until they reached a village. The fishermen had several dugout canoes and Drew haggled with them until he'd hired three small ones, and the services of their owners.

They planned to leave at late evening, reach the bridge at night, tie on the explosives and time fuses, and then continue downstream. They knew the bridge would be heavily guarded, and tension was high when they set off. A half-moon was rising in the east. Twenty minutes later they came round a long bend in the river, and Drew could see the high white wall of the mission. Ahead was the bridge, their objective.

"It's not there," Drew muttered to himself.

"*Eee*. Where is it?" said Goodwill, paddling behind him.

All that was left were the vertical piles. The Germans had blown up their own bridge, after crossing and fleeing north.

—•—

Col Murray was having a routine meeting with Col Tomlinson when he said, "Tommy, I've been thinking of putting young Spaight in for an MC – what do you think?"

Tomlinson pondered for a moment. "I believe he meets all the criteria, so I would support a recommendation from you. He was never enthusiastic about going out on patrol, but he went without hesitation."

"Yes, I'll send in a recommendation."

"What about his sergeant – an exceptional man."

"What would be appropriate for him? You know about the African awards."

"An African DCM."

"He already has one – he should be awarded a bar. You do that recommendation."

—•—

Murray followed Wintgens to the north-west until mid-May, when it was heard that the German commander, who was very ill, had surrendered to the Belgians; his troops disappeared to the north.

By this time Murray's column was within sixty miles of Tabora, now occupied by the Belgians. They stopped chasing, and were ordered back south to Rungwe Mission. It took them three weeks to march there, at an average of eighteen miles a day.

—•—

37

Zomba, Nyasaland – July 1917

On one of their visits to the farm Mandy and Kirsty announced that they would be moving north to the Peramiho Mission hospital, near Songea, and that Clare would go with them. They pointed to its approximate location using an old school atlas.

"I don't like it," said Jess, "but I suppose there's nothing I can do to stop you."

"We have to go, Ma," they chorused.

"Casualties are pouring in," said Kirsty. "Dr Macrae said he needs at least three nurses, working in shifts, so we volunteered. That way we can keep each other company."

"And the dangers?" Jess sounded querulous.

"It's highly unlikely that the Germans would penetrate so far south, but even if they did, they wouldn't harm us."

"What worries me," added Jess, "is that you might be sent forward to a field hospital."

"I doubt if we will," replied Mandy. "If Peramiho is so busy they won't be able to spare us."

"Clare, your father will be livid," said Jess.

"I dare say, Aunt Jess, but he can't stop me." Clare giggled. "I've been through it all with him before."

—•—

One day Jess was asked to take a young Scottish captain whose eye had been injured. She sat in Dr Thomson's office, next to the hospital, drinking cups of tea.

"He's rather stressed, Jess," said Thompson. "I would like him to come to terms with his injury before we ship him home."

"Has he lost his sight?"

"Almost certainly in one eye. As you know there's sometimes a sympathetic reaction from the other eye – and I've warned about that possibility."

"Do I have to do dressings?"

"Every two or three days – bring him in. Otherwise he can look after himself." Thompson sighed deeply. "No, Jess, it's his emotional condition that I think you can help with."

"I'll try."

—•—

"I'm glad you're a Scot," said Hamish Cameron. "Where are you from?"

"Raasay. It's..."

"I know where it is. I'm from Applecross – just across the water."

They both shared soft Highland accents. His voice was deep. She judged his age at approaching thirty, medium height, sandy hair, clean shaven. A bandage ran diagonally across his head, covering one eye; the other was an intense blue, taking in all his surroundings.

When they reached the farm she introduced him to the other patient in residence, a young lieutenant who was scheduled to leave the following day. Jess showed Hamish to his guest room and explained the arrangements for eating. He seemed to be infused with nervous energy that she found slightly unnerving.

At supper that evening they deliberately avoided conversation about the war. Jess told them stories about early days when she and

Alan came to the territory, and how they built up the farm. The young lieutenant talked about his childhood in India, and Cameron told them about his desire to become a lawyer like his father, a career that had been interrupted by the war.

The lieutenant left next day, and Jess took Hamish Cameron round the farm. He showed intense interest and asked cogent questions, but his attention was inclined to wander, mostly towards her. He asked more about her origins, her parents, her marriage, her children, her interests.

He was required to rest after lunch, and she met with him again before supper. "Have you been able to read, Hamish?"

He shook his head. "I tried, but my attention wanders. Also, it's a bit of a strain – reading with one eye – not sure why."

She gave him a beer and he settled down in his chair.

"I'm so grateful to you, Jess – for taking me into your home..."

"Och, you're welcome – an honoured guest."

"I hope I won't be a difficult guest."

"How could you?"

"Dr Thompson thinks I need to 'come to terms' with the fact that I might lose the sight of my eye."

"Yes, he told me. It would be a great pity, but... Well, there are many examples of people who have lost an eye..."

"Yes. Nelson for one." He stood up and walked to the railing of the verandah. "It will be a disability. Some people will look away, others will treat me with pity."

"I think you're strong enough to cope, Hamish. You're an intelligent man. You can make the best of your life despite the handicap."

He turned to her nodding. "I'll try to teach myself that."

"It might help you to direct your thoughts away from yourself."

He looked at her sharply. "Are you saying that I'm egocentric – or self-centred?"

She laughed softly. “No. But it might help you to take your mind away from your anxieties.” She stood up and took his hand. “Come and have some supper.”

When he left her after the meal and a glass of port he kissed her goodnight. It was more than a kiss on the check, as he held her shoulders firmly and pulled her towards him, which she found somewhat disconcerting.

—•—

Next day Jess had to change Cameron’s dressing. After lunch, before his nap, she went with him to his room, taking a basin filled with water and some Flavine. She sat him in the bathroom leading off his bedroom and unwound the bandage. A piece of shrapnel had grazed the eye, damaging the lid and bruising the eyeball.

“Hamish, I wonder if you should see a specialist without further delay?”

“Is it very bad?”

“Superficially, no. But the eye is a very special organ, and I think...”

“Then why didn’t Dr Thompson send me home straight away?”

“I’m not sure,” she replied, as she put on a new sterile pad and wound on a fresh bandage. “I think we should go into Zomba tomorrow and talk to him. From what I’ve seen of your behaviour, you’re perfectly able to make the journey.”

He laughed. “I was looking forward to spending some more time with you.”

“Och, you’ll sooner be with your family, and that’s the most important.”

He reached up and held her, as she stood over him. “But I like being with you, Jess. You’re delightful.”

“I’m also old enough to be your mother.”

“I find that difficult to believe.”

He leaned forward and put his face into her chest. She could feel his warm breath as she wondered how to deal with him. If she utterly rejected him it might bring out some bad reaction, whereas he would soon be leaving.

"Come, Hamish. Time for you to have your nap."

"Stay with me, Jess."

"I can't Hamish."

"Just stay and talk to me. It calms me when I hear your voice – I can't tell why."

"Does it?"

"Yes. Here, you can lie on the bed, while I sit here. Tell me about when you were married to Dr McPhail."

"If you think it will help you."

She climbed onto the bed and lay down, while Cameron drew up a chair and sat with his chin on his hand. She closed her eyes and tried to summon up Andrew McPhail. She had never really understood her first husband. He too had been intense, but his attention was never towards himself, only to relieving the suffering of the people.

She felt Cameron lie down beside her and opened her eyes. He put his arm over her and she started to struggle, realising that if she screamed it might bring a servant, and would look incriminating.

"It would help me so much if you... It would reassure me, if you allowed me to..."

"To what, Hamish?"

"To make love to you?"

She wriggled again, without avail, as his grip grew stronger. "You are taking advantage of me."

"I'm sorry, Jess. I'm so sorry."

He started to sob, and it took her by surprise. Her natural instinct was to comfort him, the patient, disregarding his earlier behaviour. She twisted to embrace him, rather as a mother would take a child in her arms, scarcely noticing that his upper hand was lifting her skirt and stroking her thigh.

"I need you, Jess," he murmured in her ear.

This is ridiculous, she thought. He's just a young man, not much older than my son. Why on earth would be want to make love to me. It was rather flattering, and she thought that there would be little harm if he was leaving next day. Her ambivalence was eroded by feelings of excitement as his hand stroked her higher up.

"It would help me so much, Jess. Just once, before I leave. I would be so grateful."

—•—

38

German East Africa – June 1917

By the end of June 1917 the Germans were still a formidable force with nearly two thousand Europeans, and over six thousand *askaris*. Colonel von Lettow-Vorbeck commanded the force moving south down the coastal area, while Captain Tafel led the eastern half of the force.

General Northey called a conference at his HQ in New Langenburg, attended by Colonels Murray and Hawthorn, accompanied by Martin Russell and Alan Spaight. Robbie Spratt and Roly Benting-Smith, of Northey's staff, were in attendance.

"Gentlemen, I've been ordered to engage Tafel's force. Murray, I want you to head for them – here." He pointed with this baton. "You'll be joined by two companies of the Northern Rhodesia Police under Captain Dickinson. Hawthorn, you are to move here – joining 1/KAR and 2/KAR, and the South African Rifles. Colonel Spaight, please explain the strategy, based on your scouting reports."

Alan stood up and walked to the hanging map. "We hear that the Germans are moving towards the border of the Portuguese colony. We have no evidence that they plan to invade, but they really have nowhere else to go."

"The base for our operations will be at Songea, in the German district headquarters. It has a fairly good infrastructure of buildings, not unlike this place. It can be supplied fairly easily from the little harbour at Mbamba Bay on Lake Nyasa. From Songea we can swing north to the Mahenge area, or east to support our forces on the coast. The roads are not wonderful, just basic dirt roads, but at least there's a rudimentary network to use."

Northey thanked him, and added, wryly, "We seem to be rather unsuccessful at catching von Lettow. Give us your opinion, Alan."

"I think the fox and hounds analogy is wrong, sir – he's a vicious opponent. The Germans are more like a pack of wolves that split up and re-join each other. If we are the hounds, we are no stronger, and are vulnerable to attack. Most important we're too slow – it's almost as if we're lethargic, encumbered with our weapons and porters..."

"Gentlemen," Northey interjected, "Broadly, I agree with that assessment, but what are we going to do about it?"

Hawthorn said, "The *tengas* are already carrying the minimum, sir. They can barely keep up with the troops – the poor beggars are half-starved anyway. I think our main problem is communicating with each other. We're constantly trying to think of ways to improve."

Northey smiled. "I'm not criticizing. It's just that we're casting a net – to start a different analogy – and it has huge holes in it. The Huns seem adept at finding the holes and slipping through – a classic small unit campaign. Reminds me of the South African War, when the Boers ran rings around us."

"But the Germans have less advantages than the Boers had then," said Martin, in his slow and pedantic way. "They know little more than us – if anything – about the terrain. They have no maps. The local people don't support them any more than they do us. In fact, if they move into Portuguese territory they will be mistrusted, by reputation."

Northey brought the meeting to a close. "Somehow we have to bring this campaign to an end."

The various units travelled by dirt road to Songea from Mbamba Bay. When they arrived they were impressed by the supplies waiting for them, which included new uniforms, and Lewis guns which could be carried and fired by a single man; thought to be a big advantage over the older Maxim/Vickers machine gun that generally used a team of three men. An airstrip was prepared and a spotter aeroplane duly arrived to use it, on rare occasions.

The hospital was located at Peramiho Mission, about ten miles from Songea. The newly arrived medical unit enhanced it with additional wards and staff. Mandy, Kirsty and Clare arrived and were soon on duty. They shared a bungalow, once used by the German district medical officer.

Discovering that Roly and Gavin were in Songea, they made plans to go there, on the very rough track that was barely passable to motor vehicles. A week after their arrival they were finally taken by lorry, past teams of labourers improving the road.

Mandy felt like a fifth wheel when Gavin embraced Kirsty, and Drew and Clare went aside in a huddle. She was glad to see the men, but felt a bit wistful that she was the only one without a partner.

They chided her gently when they sat on the verandah of the mess hall, where formerly German officials spent their evenings. Hurricane lamps hung at intervals, but contributed only dim light, while attracting hundreds of moths, and bats that swooped to feed on them.

"Have you not found a young man that you liked?" asked Gavin, a trifle hesitantly, since he knew that Mandy had a sharp tongue.

"Yes, what about Roly?" asked her brother.

She smiled. "I think Roly found someone else – while he was away at hospital in Cape Town. In any case, we were never really close."

"She has not been short of suitors," said Kirsty. "Almost every patient that passed through the hospital at Fort Johnston professed to love her – but in vain..."

"And the doctors?"

"They are all married," added Kirsty. "Except Dr Macrae."

"Now don't play the match-maker," admonished Mandy. "I prefer you in the other role," she laughed. "... as my defender against the suitors."

"I have to say," Kirsty went on, "the suitors have usually been at a severe disadvantage, recovering from wounds or fever. Not at their best!"

"But surely you've met servicemen outside the hospitals – like here, for instance."

"Not here," replied Mandy. "It's too far from the Mission. "We did meet men at Fort Johnston, but I always felt so jaded after a hard day's work..."

"Also, we made it known that we weren't available," laughed Kirsty. "Mind you, there were some who paid no attention and pressed on regardless. They were sometimes quite naughty at dances – poor fellows, some of them had not touched a girl for months."

"And there was me," said Gavin, "without a woman within a hundred miles, and..."

"There was that German woman – at Iringa," interrupted Kirsty sharply.

"We've been through all that, sweetheart..."

"Well, it's no different to us innocently dancing with poor lonely officers."

"Changing the subject," said Mandy, wanting to steer the conversation away from their personal affairs, "there's been a row brewing between your Colonel Murray and the doctors. It seems that Murray thinks there are too many malingerers and patients spending too long in recuperation."

"I can understand his frustration," said Drew. "He drives himself hard, even when he has malaria or flu. Sometimes I wonder how he keeps going."

Clare entered the discussion, saying. "I don't think he understands how debilitating it is to have dysentery, or some disease like that, on top of being in poor health because they haven't had proper food. I don't suppose Murray has such poor rations as his men."

—•—

Colonel Murray's original column of Rhodesians had dwindled to such small numbers that General Northey added companies of the Northern Rhodesia Police (NRP), and the Rhodesia Native Regiment (RNR), both of which had European officers and African *askaris*.

The Colonel and his deputy Martin Russell had to remain at Songea working on logistics, so the fighting column was put under the command of Acting Lt Col Jock Fair. Young and dashing, Fair had fought through the entire campaign and was much admired by his men, not only for his flair, but also because he cared for their welfare.

The objective was to destroy one of the most effective German units, under Captain Tafel and Lt Aumann, who had created a strong defensive position at Mpepo (Place of Winds). The enemy knew the Allies would have to attack and dislodge them, so they put every effort into strengthening their defences. One of their flanks was protected by the Ruhudje River, infested by crocodiles, and the Germans destroyed all boats in the vicinity.

Having found no way of crossing, the Fair Column decided to build some canoes, but the results were too heavy and were abandoned. They eventually found two canoes that the Germans thought were unusable, but the Rhodesians, with characteristic ingenuity managed to repair them and crossed the rived at night.

When Jock Fair was able to see the German positions at Mpepo, using his binoculars, he realised that his numbers were inadequate to encircle and trap the enemy. He sought out Drew Spaight, who he'd come to know and like in previous skirmishes.

"Drew, I want you to recruit mercenaries to add to our numbers..."

"Ruga-rugas?"

"Call them what you like – levies, mercenaries, *rugas* – we need about five hundred. Think you can do it?"

Drew nodded cautiously. "Do you have weapons for them?"

"Not many. If we scrape around we can find about a hundred rifles. The rest will have to use spears, and bows and arrows. You can use your wonderful Sergeant – in fact, I want to promote Goodwill to RSM."

Drew smiled wryly. "I doubt if he'll be impressed by the rank, sir, but he's the best man I can think of to recruit and train *rugas*."

Drew and Goodwill spent the next ten days walking from village to village, talking to chiefs and headmen, recruiting men for their company. They paid a handsome fee and promised regular payments, as well as food rations.

—•—

Fair's cautious approach caused Murray to question his command. One day, Fair asked Drew to join him for a mug of tea on a fallen tree and showed him a message from Murray.

"Have a look at this Drew."

> *To date very little or nothing has been accomplished. Three plans are open to you – investment, assault, or cutting off their supplies....wire me what you are doing, and get a move on.*

"Sounds like a schoolmaster," said Drew, but his smile vanished when he saw how upset Fair looked.

"I've drafted this reply. You know Murray better than I do. What do you think?" Fair handed a sheet of paper to Drew.

> *Considering the arduous work performed by myself and the troops under me during the past week your wire is most discouraging. I entirely disagree with you that*

> *nothing has been accomplished....I strongly resent the last sentence of your telegram.*

"That's telling him!"

"Well, I can't sit back and let him castigate me – unfairly."

"I agree. The problem, Jock, is that he's not here to see the situation for himself."

"Yes, but that's true of all field commanders who delegate. They have to trust the judgement of the officers to whom they've delegated command. I fear that Murray doesn't trust me."

—•—

Lt Col Fair and his company commanders decided on a frontal assault. It depended on careful timing of attack, feints, cross-firing and counter feints. On the first attempt, to Fair's disgust, it failed. The second attempt, on the following day, was little better, and now it was his turn to be furious.

Meanwhile, Drew took out a patrol consisting of Goodwill and a *ruga-ruga* who came from the locality and knew it well. Moving stealthily at night they reached a small hill behind Mpepo. Drew realised that it would be feasible to shell the German garrison at Mpepo from this hill.

"The *WaGermani* are on the hill," said the *ruga*, a piratical figure, wiry, with a wizened face, and a cloth tied round his head.

"How many?" asked Drew; they were speaking in Swahili.

The *ruga* shrugged. "Ten? Maybe twenty."

Drew contemplated going up the hill to make a more accurate assessment. He knew the German commanding the hill would put pickets around the base to warn those at the summit if attackers approached. His small patrol could easily be wiped out by such a picket.

"We'll go back to Fair," he told Goodwill, who relayed the information to the *ruga*, and they set off back to the main camp.

Jock Fair was delighted to hear about the hill, which he christened with the prosaic name Single Hill; it did not appear on any of their rudimentary maps.

"We'll take it," he announced. "Drew, I want you to show the attack force the way."

"I can lead the attack, sir."

"Absolutely not! You can lead them there, then return and report to me." Fair knew that casualties could be heavy, and Drew was too valuable to lose.

—•—

The attack on Single Hill was a success, but Lt Aumann and his Germans strenuously tried to recapture it. For the next several days the Allied force attacked Mpepo and finally succeeded in driving the German out. There followed a protracted period of ineffectual pursuit of Aumann's Column, and miscommunication between Jock Fair, Col Murray, and the Belgians.

Meanwhile, the main German force under von Lettow was being driven inexorably south towards the Rovuma River, the boundary between the German and Portuguese colonies.

—•—

"One of our patrols has been badly shot up," said Dr Macrae, walking up to the three nurses on the verandah of their mess at Peramiho. "The wounded have been brought back to a field dressing station near the Rovuma. The commander's leg is messed up – he needs intra-venous saline while he's brought back." He sighed wearily. "I would do it myself, but they've forbidden it – I mean, they won't let me leave Peramiho, even though there are no Germans in the area."

He looked at the nurses, who were watching him intently, and thought what an amazing trio they were, well-trained, capable, humorous and appealing. He guessed that they would all volunteer to fetch the lieutenant, but he could afford to let only one go. Which one? Kirsty and Clare had young men – not engaged yet, but that was only because of the war. Mandy was unattached.

"Could one of you go?"

All three raised their hands without hesitation, and he caught his breath, almost sobbing.

"Mandy, I choose you, almost randomly, but you do have a bit more experience with the saline."

She nodded, while the other two watched her. "How far is it to the dressing station? What should I take?"

"It's over fifty miles north of here. You'll go twenty miles by lorry, then about thirty miles on foot – say two days march. It may take longer to get back … but I suppose not, because he'll have to be on a *machila* – if he lives.

—•—

39

German East Africa – July 1918

Leutnant Walter Schnieder entered the field dressing station hut behind his escort of two German NCOs. Made of bush timber with a rough roof of thatching grass, it was covered with ground-sheets; this sort of structure could be built in a few hours. The sides were open, but the stench was awful, reminding him of the slaughter-house in his home town of Bremen.

Crude stretcher beds lined the sides of the hut, leaving a broad central aisle. They were crudely made of bush timber, uneven and rickety; every one of them had a wounded soldier lying on it. Many of them were swathed in bandages, like rows of Egyptian mummies.

In the aisle a group of male African orderlies were gathered round a European nurse, and Schneider wondered if they were trying to protect her, or looking to her for help. They all wore white cotton coats stained with blood, and white caps with a red cross. The nurse was incongruous, taller than the Africans, with startling white skin and blonde hair.

Putting aside his surprise, Schneider ordered his NCOs to search the hut and its occupants for weapons and to set up a guard outside. Then he beckoned the nurse forward, at once feeling a sexual tingle from knowing that she would become his captive.

Mandy extricated herself from the orderlies and walked slowly towards the German officer. He was slightly less than six feet tall, with fair hair and moustaches, pallid skin and unusually pale blue eyes. She judged he must be in his late thirties; he had a paunch, although the rest of his body was thin.

"Are you in charge here?" he asked, in a confident tone.

"Yes," Mandy replied, surprised at his clear English.

"Your name?"

"Amanda Spaight."

"Is there a doctor?"

"Not here, only at the base."

"Where? Songea?"

She nodded.

Schneider looked around the hut. It was evidently only a makeshift shelter, with no real medical facilities. "Is it your plan to take these wounded men back to the base camp?"

"Yes – as soon as they are well enough to walk, or be carried. The officer needs a saline drip during the journey."

He looked at her closely, his eyes narrowing, as if he was somehow assessing her; she felt a shiver of apprehension. "You will come with me, *fraulein*. There is no time for you to bring any possessions. We have to leave at once. Tell your senior orderly to look after the wounded."

"What about the officer? My orderly is not experienced administering a drip."

Schneider shrugged. "He will have to take his chances."

"May I say goodbye?"

"Of course. Who is he?"

"A young lieutenant. His leg has been broken by a bullet. I've been giving him saline in preparation..."

For a moment Schneider considered interrogating the wounded lieutenant, but decided against it. Experience had taught him that British officers would not reveal anything useful – unless ... the Colonel had forbidden torture.

Mandy walked down the hut to where the lieutenant lay; he was barely conscious. She bent down to speak to him. "David? Can you hear me?"

The young man nodded. He'd said he was twenty years old, but Mandy suspected he'd lied about his age, because he looked much younger. He was painfully thin, with a deathly pallor. A rubber tube led from his arm to a glass bottle of saline solution suspended on a short pole.

"I've been taken prisoner, David. The Germans are taking me away..."

The lieutenant tried to raise himself, but fell back. His deep-sunk eyes were fearful. "So sorry, Mandy" he muttered.

She stood up and turned to the senior African orderly, who had accompanied her from Peramiho. "Abraham, you are in charge now. You know what to do. You should start back early tomorrow morning. When you get back to the hospital you'll tell them what happened to me."

The orderly nodded, his expression showing his alarm at the responsibilities being heaped on his shoulders.

This had to come, thought Mandy, as she shrugged and turned to the other orderlies. It was the risk she had always faced since insisting on coming to the forward medical units. In ChiNyanja she told them to go with Abraham back to the base camp as soon as they could, carrying the wounded in *machilas*.

She knew they would not send a rescue mission. She followed Schneider.

Schneider said little for the five hours while they walked along bush paths. The pace was so fast that she could barely keep up. Because he generally walked behind her, she knew that it would be impossible to run away. Besides, she would have little chance of surviving alone in the bush.

There was only sparse conversation between the German *askaris*, and Schneider hardly ever spoke to them. They stopped to rest every hour, relieving themselves in the bush, just off the track. During these short breaks she sat on the ground and wondered what would be her fate. She knew she was a valuable commodity for her nursing skills, but was alarmed at the way Schneider regarded her. It was as if she was a possession, and he was trying to decide what to do with her.

They walked through fields and small sparsely-inhabited villages in the morning, as the heat became intense while the sun rose. It was the end of the rainy season and the maize crop was ripening, though the plants were widely spaced and stunted. It forebode hunger among the local Africans. As they passed, the men of the patrol had an atavistic aversion to taking cobs that did not belong to them, but they would not stint themselves after camping.

Feeling the sweat running down her limbs Mandy worried that she was not replacing her fluids. At noon the *askaris* ordered some villagers to produce *nsima* and fruit, as well as water in calabashes. Mandy ate some *nsima* and two bananas; she had some sodium hypochlorite tablets in her pocket and dropped some in the water.

In mid-afternoon, without warning, they arrived at the German camp, and were greeted with shouts and ribald jeers. A European sergeant came to meet them.

"*Wer ist das?*" he asked. "Where did you find her, sir?"

"*Sie versteht Deutsch,*" warned Schneider. "She was at their first aid place where they kept the wounded. We destroyed most of their patrol."

"Well, at least you have returned with a trophy."

Schneider laughed. "Yes, I must interrogate her..."

The sergeant sniggered. "Good luck, sir. Call me if you need help." He smirked and walked away.

Schneider led Mandy to his tent, the largest in the camp, pitched in the shade of a large acacia tree. He ushered her inside and she tried to adjust her sight to the dim light. A folding camp bed stood on a tarpaulin sheet that covered most of the floor. A wash basin on a folding stand occupied the end furthest from the entrance. It was surprisingly cool inside.

"You have to stay with me, *fraulein*. My men respect me, and if they see that you are with me, they will respect you. However..." he paused for effect, "if you try to escape, they will not respect you; it would be bad for you."

"Are you saying that I have to be with you all the time?"

"You could say that. Better to be with me than with them, don't you think?" He jerked his thumb to indicate the *askaris* outside.

He pulled out a metal cigarette box and proffered it to her. She refused, and he took one and lit it, contemplating the curl of blue smoke.

"I'm tired," he said. "How about you?"

"I'm very tired. I have had no sleep for a long time."

"Go to sleep then." He pointed to the camp bed. "I have some things to do; then I will come back and sleep too."

She took off her shoes and lay down, watching Schneider leave the tent. Within a minute she was asleep.

—•—

She awoke when she heard the tent flap open. It was dusk, and the lights of camp fires flickered on the tent walls. She watched through almost closed eyes as Schneider stripped off his clothes and strolled naked to the wash stand, where he used a wet cloth to wipe himself. His body was white, except where his arms, knees and face were exposed to the sun. He dried himself with a towel and put on a clean shirt and trousers, then spread a cloth on the groundsheet beside the camp bed. He lay down to sleep and soon started to snore. Mandy was so tired that the noise did not keep her awake.

—•—

It was dark in the tent when she woke again, at once feeling the need to drink. As her eyes became accustomed to the darkness she could see Schneider sitting in his camp chair watching her.

"I need to drink," she croaked.

He brought her a canvas water bottle as she sat up. While she drank he lit a hurricane lantern, keeping the flame low.

"You must bathe," he said. "Then we will eat."

She stood up cautiously, feeling the aches in her joints. "Are you going to stay here? May I have some privacy?"

He gave a short laugh. "I will stay. It's a long time since I saw a woman – a white woman – without clothing. Come on, *fraulein*, don't be shy. Remember, I am your protector."

Mandy walked over to the wash basin and started to take off her clothes, keeping her back to Schneider. She was so weary and hungry that she hardly cared what she was doing. She used a flannel cloth in the basin to wipe herself.

"Mein Gott!"

She half turned, holding the cloth to her breasts. Schneider was standing, legs astride, his eyes wide; he seemed to sway, and she wondered if he had been drinking. His expression reminded her of the half-starved Rhodesian troopers who came in from the bush and saw food on the mess table.

"Come here!" he commanded hoarsely.

"You said you would protect me."

He gestured towards the camp bed. "It is my protection. If it were not for me you would be the plaything of those *askaris* out there. Surely, you would not prefer them?"

She knew there was nothing she could do. If she fought him he would probably beat her up, and might even throw her to the *askaris*. She walked slowly towards him.

At that moment she heard a commotion outside – shouts and some laughter, and the name Schneider repeated. She picked up her shirt and started to put it on.

"Walter! *Sind sie es?* Are you in there?" A man's deep voice outside the tent; he tried to open the flap door.

"Wait a moment." Schneider went to the door. "Geisekind? What do you want?"

"You have to come now – all of you. Tafel is coming. He wants you to be ready to move out..."

"Where is he?"

"Ten minutes behind me – maybe less." Geisekind went away.

"*Verdomme!*" Schneider turned to Mandy. "Get your clothes on. Don't dare say anything to the others – or you'll pay for it." He slid sideways out of the tent door.

Mandy hurriedly dressed herself. She could hear voices outside but could not understand the rapid exchanges in German. Schneider was telling his compatriot that he had captured a British nurse and was interrogating her.

Leutnant Geisekind, a large burly man with a spade-shaped beard, laughed loudly. "Interrogating? Is that what you call it? Hurry up, man! Tafel will be here in a minute."

He opened the tent door and peered inside, seeing Mandy putting on her boots.

"*Fraulein?* Are you alright? We have to leave here. The tent has to be packed away."

"I'm coming."

She stepped out of the tent to see the whole camp in turmoil, men running too and fro as they dismantled tents and packed the camp paraphernalia. Schneider gave her a cursory glance, but was concentrating on shouting orders.

Moments later a column of over a hundred men walked into the clearing. One of them, a tired-looking officer, separated and came forward; Schneider went up to him to salute.

"We have to make a night march, Schneider" said Captain Tafel. "Get the men ready as quickly as you can." He looked at Mandy with interest. "Who is this?"

"A British nurse. I captured her. She was at a dressing station, near where we attacked that patrol… I thought she might be useful..."

"For what? For your pleasure?" Tafel did not smile, but his tone was jocular. "I hope she won't delay us." He came up to Mandy and spoke to her in perfect, unaccented English.

"My name is Theodore Tafel," he said, holding out his hand. "I'm the commander of this column."

"Amanda Spaight." She shook his hand.

"I trust you have been well treated."

"Actually, no."

Tafel raised his eyebrows. "Really. I must ask you later. If you will forgive me, now I have to get the column moving. I presume you are able to walk? If you have any difficulty I can arrange for a *machila* to carry you."

"I can walk – unless your pace is too fast."

—•—

They marched through the night for eight hours, with two stops of about twenty minutes each. Mandy was able to keep up, but she was almost dropping when they reached their destination, a clearing in the forest that had been used as a camp before. She walked most of the time near Tafel, although no one spoke, even during the two rest breaks.

It was early morning. The German officers and the *askaris* knew exactly what was needed to bring the camp to life. Mandy watched them light fires and start cooking *nsima*, with dried bush meat for flavour. They pitched tents, and brought water from a nearby stream. The ground was scraped clean of vegetation and swept with coarse grass brooms.

"You must be very tired," said Tafel. "You can use my tent, because I prefer to rest in the open."

"Will I be...?"

"Will you be safe? You have my word, Miss Spaight. Tell me what happened back there."

"Lieutenant Schneider did not treat me as an officer and a gentleman should..."

"Did he harm you?"

She hesitated, trying to choose the best words. "No. But only because you arrived at the camp."

"Hm. Well, I will make sure it doesn't happen again." He clicked his heels and left her.

On the following day they joined Captain Tafel's main column. The camp included a temporary field hospital with a doctor and a dozen orderlies. There were at least a dozen sick and wounded soldiers, and another twenty African children waiting for treatment in disconsolate groups.

After giving orders to his lieutenants and their NCOs Tafel took Mandy to the hospital and introduced her to Dr Karl Niemeyer. He was a young man, slightly built with dark hair and a couple of days growth of beard. His eyes were sunken and Mandy thought he looked exhausted. He would not shake hands with her, saying, "I must wash."

The doctor spoke to one of the orderlies and turned back to Mandy. "Let me wash up and then we can talk. I'll meet you over there, at the mess tent." He spoke good English, but with a strong accent.

She walked to the mess tent, where there were cauldrons of tea, soup and *nsima*, cooking on open wood fires. A huge German cook was supervising, his sleeves rolled up, his florid face dripping sweat. He nodded a greeting and scooped some tea in a tin cup and handed it to her. It had no milk or sugar but she did not care.

Dr Niemeyer came up to her with a slight smile. "Tafel has told me you are a British nurse." He held out his hand.

"Amanda Spaight. Yes, I am a nurse – and a prisoner."

"But not in chains." He smiled again, but wider. "Are you willing to help me? I have one German assistant, and five native orderlies, but they know very little about nursing."

He asked her how she came to take up nursing, and she told him briefly about herself.

"We must find somewhere for you to sleep. There are three German women with us, wives of soldiers; perhaps they can find room for you."

So she was billeted with the German women, who had lived on farms before the war, and were now following their men in the column. They spoke a little English and were friendly to her. One of them found a ground-sheet and a blanket, but there were no beds, since they expected to break camp within a day or two. She lay down on the ground and fell asleep almost immediately.

—•—

Mandy spent the next day assisting Dr Niemeyer. When he found that she was experienced at administering chloroform, he asked her to help him with several minor operations. They had short snatches of conversation while working, and during breaks when they took tea and a lunch of soup and *nsima*.

Karl Niemeyer had come to German East Africa five years before, to work as a government medical officer. Two years later, when the war started, he was enlisted in the *Schutztruppe*. He was twenty-nine years old.

"My first two years in Africa were wonderful," he said, in his quiet voice. "I was at a *boma* not far from Arusha, and enjoyed everything that is good about Africa. But these war years have been hard for me – so much suffering – I mean the patients. So difficult to give them proper treatment. In all the last three years I have spent perhaps only a few weeks in real hospitals – at former mission stations. The rest of the time I have been in tents or grass huts, always short of medicines – and help." He smiled disarmingly. "I don't want you to think I complain all the time."

In only a few hours working with Karl she realised that he was an exceptional doctor. He could speak Swahili quite well, and otherwise used one of the orderlies as an interpreter. He spoke calmly and confidently to the patients, in such a way that they trusted him. From observing his surgical operations she judged that he was unusually skilful. He told her that he had built up experience at an accelerated rate through working in the bush hospitals, with a great variety of patient problems.

"If I had been in a hospital in Germany," he said, "I would have been restricted to one branch of surgery – abdominal, cranial, limbs, or something – whereas here I can do everything. Furthermore, I don't have a senior surgeon to push me aside and say 'I'll do that, it's too difficult for you'!"

—•—

Mandy was introduced to the other women, one of whom was Liesl Mueller, though she was unaware of the German girl's connection to Gavin, when they were near neighbours in Moshi. Liesl was tall and strong-boned, with a wide face and high cheek-bones. She had a cheerful demeanour as she showed Mandy the tent where the women slept. There was another girl in her twenties, a friend of Liesl, and another wife; both were in their forties.

Tafel's column moved almost every day, using well-practised routines. There were few orders shouted because everyone knew their role – packing the medical equipment and cooking utensils, pulling down huts and removing the ground-sheets that roofed them. Forward pickets left first, followed by Tafel's command group, then the main body of askaris, the medical group, the civilians, and finally the rearguard.

During the marches between camps Mandy often walked with Karl Niemeyer, and sensed that he enjoyed her company.

"How did you learn to speak English so well?" she asked.

"My father was a doctor – he studied in England. We went there several times before he died. My mother was a music teacher; she died when I was ten years old. It's such a shame that our countries are at war."

On another occasion she said. "You don't seem like the typical German."

He laughed. "What is a typical German?"

"Oh, your nation has a reputation for being rather serious and... arrogant... authoritarian. We've heard stories about the harsh treatment meted out to Africans in your colonies."

He frowned, and she was afraid she had offended him. "I understand our reputation, but of course it is a generalisation. I am not the general type, I suppose. As for the harsh treatment of natives – it is true. You are probably referring to the *Maji-maji* Rebellion and the Hottentot Rebellion in South-West Africa. But you British have also been harsh in your reaction to rebels, not only in Africa – such as the great Mutiny in India. Did you not have a rebellion in Nyasaland? Many natives were shot or hung, with little or no judicial process."

"Hanged," she said.

"Bitte?"

"We say – meat is hung, but men are hanged."

He laughed for a long time. "It is such a difficult language – even for a German."

She liked the way he talked freely with her. He was not opinionated, but he had strong views. She asked him when the war would finish.

"I don't know enough about the situation in Europe," he replied. "Here? Well, von Lettow wants to carry on. If he were not in command – who knows? There might not be the skill, or the determination to continue. It's amazing to me that you British have not captured or killed him, because he is the crucial factor in our campaign. Don't you agree?"

"I don't know, Doctor..."

"Please call me Karl."

"Very well, Karl. Are you saying that there isn't any other commander who could take over?"

"Yes, that's what I'm saying. He has capable officers, like Wahle, Tafel and Koehl, but do any of them have his expertise, his determination, his ability to command loyalty? I think not."

She noticed that he sang while he operated. She could barely hear him, even though they were a few feet apart, but she could see his lips moving, and sometimes caught the sounds.

"What are you singing, Karl?"

He smiled. "Oh, did you hear? Schubert – my mother used to sing his songs to me, and I learnt them later – *'Heidenroeslein', 'Gretchen am Spinnrade', 'Die Forelle'*. She never sang the dark ones, like *'Der Erlkoenig'* and *'Der Tod und das Madchen'*. He turned serious. "I hope that death does not come looking for you, Amanda."

—•—

One evening, when Niemeyer had performed an emergency appendectomy, he sat with Mandy by the camp fire, long after most of the Germans had retired. Only the duty officer was walking around the sentries and pickets to ensure they were awake.

He said, "Sometimes I think I am dreaming when I see you, Amanda."

"Why don't you call me 'Mandy'?"

"I like 'Amanda'. It's a woman's name, whereas 'Mandy' is a young girl's name."

"Am I not a young girl?"

He laughed. "Of course, but I think of you as a woman."

He sipped from his mug of tea, looking at her over the rim. "It seems to me, Amanda, that you have been sent to me as a gift from heaven. Not only are you a very competent nurse, but you are also skilled at anaesthesia. You are also very lovely."

He held up his hand when she started to protest. "No, no, let me finish. I've watched you at work. Even when you are tired and work-stained your beauty shines through."

She blushed, but he could not see it in the dark. "You flatter me, Karl. It may be because you have been so long away from civilisation. I'm just an ordinary girl."

—•—

40

Zomba, Nyasaland – August, 1917

News of Mandy's capture by the Germans filtered back, starting with her medical orderly Abraham, who successfully brought to Songea the lieutenant and other wounded. Dr Macrae was informed, and broke the news to Kirsty and Clare.

"It was bound to happen," muttered Kirsty, wiping tears with her sleeve.

"I wish we could be with her." Clare was sobbing uncontrollably.

"I've sent a telegram to Colonel Murray," said Dr Macrae. "I'm afraid that any attempt to rescue her would be impractical – if only because we don't know where she is."

He urged the girls to go to the mess and have some tea and something to eat, and went with them.

"My mother will be devastated," said Kirsty. "She's still grieving after Mac's disappearance..."

"Always will," added Clare. "One of us ought to go back to the farm to be with her."

Macrae shook his head, and for a moment the girls thought he would refuse. Then he said, "I suppose we could manage without one of you."

"I would be the best person to go", said Kirsty.

"The Germans are quite good at sending us news about prisoners. What about Drew?"

"He could go, but I doubt Colonel Murray would permit it?"

—•—

It was agreed that Kirsty should be the one to go back to Zomba and break the news to Jess. She was able to travel down the lake on the *Guendolen*, and then was given a ride in an army lorry from Fort Johnston to Zomba. It was three days after Mandy's capture that she found her mother at the shop, where she was delivering milk and butter.

"Darling! What a lovely surprise!"

Jess looked radiant, wearing a check pinafore over her white cotton dress, her dark hair tucked under a broad-brimmed sun hat. Kirsty drew her mother aside, and Jess's expression changed to concern.

"Ma, I've bad news. Mandy has been taken prisoner."

Jess's hand flew to her mouth. "Is she safe?"

"We think so. We only know because her medical orderly saw it happen. She was at a forward dressing station..."

Jess groaned. "I thought you girls were not to go to those places – because of the risks."

"They needed a nurse to use a saline drip for a wounded soldier. They thought there were no Germans in the area. Her orderly saw her taken away, by a German officer. Pa says the Germans send a message about once a month, listing the prisoners of war – and we do the same – so we ought to hear soon."

They walked out to the small truck that Jess used for delivering produce from the farm.

"Kirsty, I can't bear it. First Mac, and now Mandy." She started to weep.

Kirsty put her arm round her mother's shoulders. "We haven't lost her, Ma. She'll look after herself. We'll get her back when the war ends."

"When the war ends." Jess repeated the words bitterly. "I've heard that so often; in fact, ever since the war started. We've been fighting for three years, and there's no end in sight."

—•—

They drove out to the farm and went about routine tasks, Kirsty staying by her mother's side. They supervised the afternoon milking, and talked to Adam about a sick cow. Jess held a clinic for farm workers, and Kirsty helped her to dress small wounds and administer treatments such as cod-liver oil and aspirin.

For supper they joined two men who were convalescing, both young officers. Dr Thompson did not send other ranks, unless they were settlers in the NVR, thinking that they might feel uncomfortable dining together; he had another farm family that took only NCOs and enlisted men.

Jess introduced her daughter, and both men struggled to their feet. They were not wounded but were recovering from malaria. One was Scottish, the other South African.

"Your mother has been so kind to us," said the Scot, a lieutenant attached to the KAR. "We haven't eaten food like this since we left home a year ago."

"True," added the South African. "It will be difficult to drag ourselves away."

"You'll be dragged away by your commander," said Jess.

—•—

41

German East Africa & Portuguese East Africa – November 1917

Colonel von Lettow-Vorbeck was facing a difficult decision. Determined to continue fighting, his column of troops, porters and camp followers was handicapped by the wounded and sick; he was also short of ammunition. About a third of his riflemen were armed with old weapons that used 'smoky' cartridges, which gave away the position of the firer. The wet season was about to start, and food would be difficult to find until the harvest season in the winter of 1918.

Meanwhile, the Allies were bringing in fresh troops, who were constantly re-supplied with food and ammunition from the coastal ports, while the Germans had to scrounge food from local villages; their ammunition was mostly captured from Allied supplies.

Von Lettow decided to reduce his strength to two thousand rifles, most of whom were Europeans. Two hundred Germans and six hundred *askaris* would be left behind to surrender at the hospital at Nambindinga. His difficult decision was exacerbated because many of those being left behind wanted to continue fighting. The Colonel hoped that his smaller, leaner, force would be better able to continue the campaign.

On November 25, 1917, the German advance guard crossed the Ruvuma River into Portuguese East Africa. The river was over a thousand yards wide, and the men waded across in chest-deep water. They brushed aside the Portuguese army outpost that was supposed to stop them.

—•—

Meanwhile, Captain Tafel was about a hundred miles away, and had not been able to communicate with von Lettow for nearly two weeks. At one of their rest places, near midday, he beckoned to Mandy. As she approached him she realised that he was so exhausted he could barely speak. Iridescent droplets of sweat beaded his forehead as he fanned himself with a folded map.

"Miss Spaight," he croaked, "I plan to surrender."

Surrender? Mandy instantly became excited. She would be able to rejoin her own people, see her father, and take leave to go to Zomba. It would mean leaving Karl, but that might be the best thing for both of them. She beamed at Tafel, waiting for him to continue.

"I suppose you would like to stay with me and thus join your compatriots, but I regret I cannot give you back. You are too valuable. You must go with Lt Baumann to join the Colonel's column."

Her smile faded as she shrugged. "Captain Tafel, I feel like a sort of pawn. I have to go where you command." Then she added. "You know I will do my best as a nurse."

He stood up and shook her hand. With great sincerity, he said, "Thank you, Miss Spaight. Believe me, if it was my own decision I would give you back to the British."

She walked despondently back to the ward, where Karl was washing, bending over a canvas basin, his torso bare, splashing water on his face and chest. She put her hands on his thin back.

"You didn't tell me that Tafel was going to surrender."

He turned to face her, his eyes anxious. "I knew it was a possibility, but..."

"Tafel wants me to go with Baumann." Her tone was urgent. "Baumann is not giving up; he's going to try to find von Lettow." She told him what Tafel had said. "What will you do, Karl?"

"I don't want to surrender – not yet. I will go with Baumann." He put his hand on her cheek in an affectionate gesture. "Are you disappointed?"

"You know I would like to return to my people. But I also want to stay with you. Will Baumann take you?"

"He has said he wants me, and I want you with me."

—•—

They left at first light, a small group of two dozen Europeans, fifty *askaris,* and the same number of porters. Baumann, a taciturn young man, surmised that von Lettow was heading south, but had no idea whether he was moving south-east towards the coast, or south-west towards Lake Nyasa. He made his own decision to move down the centre, thus keeping his options open. He had no way of knowing where to find the Colonel, and his two scouts were not familiar with the country. The local Africans fled when they approached, but Baumann guessed they would not know much about events outside the environs of their villages.

He set a target of fifteen miles a day, and would have preferred twenty, but the *tengas* were half-starved, and the *askaris* were too weak to carry more than their rifles and ammunition. The countryside was flat and featureless, the vegetation open savannah, stunted *Brachystegia, Uapaca and Acacia.* They seldom saw any large antelopes, only duiker and bushbuck, and shot a few for the pot.

It was ten days before they had any news of the Colonel's column. A young African strolling towards them suddenly saw them and tried to run away. The *askaris* caught him, and, terrified, he explained that he had been visiting his uncle, when a party of *azungu* and *askaris* appeared and stole all their food and crops. From his descriptions they guessed that it was von Lettow's column, about twenty miles to the east. Elated, Baumann led his force in that direction.

Two days later a scout from the main column found them and led them to the Colonel's headquarters. It was early evening; von Lettow was sitting at his travelling desk, under the flap of his tent, writing his journal. He stood up and walked unhurriedly to greet Baumann, embracing him.

"You good fellow," he said. "We heard that Tafel had surrendered. I don't blame him, but we cannot afford to lose so many men. You were right to seek us out." He ordered food and drink for them.

Baumann introduced Dr Karl and Mandy. She was surprised that the Colonel was so modest in stature and demeanour. He was somewhat below average in height, with pallid skin, sparse hair and a short-clipped moustache. A monocle dangled on a ribbon at his chest, beside his Iron Cross. She noticed that he seemed to have a problem with his eyes; one of them was half closed, while the other was watering.

He took a particular interest in the young nurse. "I'm sorry you are a prisoner, Miss Spaight," he said is perfect English. "If times were different we could enjoy a social relationship. Even so, you are my guest, and I will try to ensure that you are as comfortable as we are." He laughed. "Of course, we are on the march, camping at night, and often fighting for our lives, so do not expect The Ritz!"

He went on, "There are six other women in the Column, wives and widows. None of them is a trained nurse, but they assist when they can. We have two doctors – and now a third – and they are always busy. Sadly, they can perform surgery only when we are in camp, which restricts their time. Besides, they are usually exhausted after the march."

Regarding her with an astute expression, he asked. "I'm sure you are aware of the circumstances. How long have you been a prisoner?"

"About three months."

"So you have covered many miles. You are English?"

"A mixture of English and Scottish, but I've lived in Nyasaland all my life."

"How is that?"

"My father is a farmer – near Zomba."

"Indeed. Our travels might take us there. Well, we are fortunate to have a trained nurse in our column. Dr Karl has told me that you are expert at administering anaesthetics."

—•—

Mandy learnt that the Colonel had divided his column into three; he commanded the main column in the centre, while old General Wahle was in the west, and Captain Koehl followed the coast. News came that Koehl's column was attacked near Medo, and he was retreating inland to join with von Lettow.

The routine for the Column was to march after an early breakfast, rest at midday, march again in the afternoon, and camp at about five. An armed party went ahead and chose a camp ground, preferably near water. The sick and wounded were carried on *machilas*, and Mandy and the German women walked near them, so that they could administer medicines to those who needed them. A hospital hut was erected as soon as they camped, and an operating hut nearby. The doctors did as much as they could before the evening meal.

The hospital was a mere wooden frame, made from bush timber, with a roof of ground-sheets, laid overlapping, like huge tiles. A team of labourers was employed specifically to erect the hospital, the operating room, and the mess. They were adept at cutting the poles in the bush and tying them with bark thongs. Within half an hour of arriving at the camp site the buildings were ready to use, aligned so that whatever breeze prevailed would cool them.

The two older doctors were in poor health and were usually so tired after the march that they contributed little. The burden of work now fell almost entirely on Dr Karl, assisted by Mandy. Two German women, wives of officers, volunteered to assist at the hospital tent. One of them was a friendly young woman, the other was older; she kept her distance, and refused to have anything to do with the African patients.

—•—

One day Mandy was asked to come to the Colonel. She found him under the flap of his tent, sitting barefoot on his chair, with a basin at his feet. An African orderly was teasing jigger larvae out of his big toe. He looked up as Mandy approached.

"Forgive my appearance, Miss Spaight. Damnable things, these insects. Do you have experience of them?"

"Oh yes, I've had them in my feet. The Africans are very expert at removing them." She noticed the orderly was using a sharpened stick, and she spoke to him in ChiNyanja. To her surprise, he answered her in the same language.

"It would be better to use a sterilised needle," she said to him.

"Where can I get that, *dona*?"

"I will fetch one."

She came back, and showed the orderly how to cauterise a needle in the flame. "Where is your home?" she asked.

"Near Nkhata Bay, *dona,*" he replied. "I went to work at an estate near New Langenburg. Then I became an *askari* when the war started." He looked at her with some suspicion. "How is it that you speak ChiNyanja, *dona*?"

"My home is near Zomba."

"Ah." He nodded as if this explained everything.

The Colonel interjected. "I'm sure this is a very interesting conversation. Perhaps you would include me. By the way, Miss Spaight, I'm impressed that you can speak the native language so fluently. Many colonists do not take the trouble to learn the local languages properly."

The orderly left when he finished removing the jigger larvae, bowing to the Colonel, and to Mandy.

"Have a look at my eye, Miss Spaight," said the Colonel. "A few days ago, a grass stem stuck in it. I fear it must have done some damage; it has been very painful."

She could see that his eye was watering, and went to fetch a magnifying glass. When she returned she examined the eye and could see that there was a small wound in the white of his eye which had not healed. She explained that it would be better if he kept the eye closed for at least some of the day.

"My problem, Miss Spaight, is that the other eye was damaged in the Hottentot Rebellion. Have a look at it."

She turned her attention to the other eye, where she could see an older wound that had affected the cornea.

The Colonel gave a rumbling laugh. "One bad eye was a nuisance, but I remembered your Admiral Nelson was not unduly inconvenienced. But with both eyes damaged I can barely see what I am doing."

"I'm sorry, sir. You will have to depend on your aides."

"Yes. I will manage. Thank you."

—•—

A couple of days later Mandy was having her breakfast when she heard her name called, and one of the Colonel's aides came to fetch her. Von Lettow was sitting under the flap of his tent, drinking a cup of coffee. He held his mug up as she approached.

"*Guten morgen*, Miss Spaight. We were lucky to bring some good coffee from Moshi," he said. He put the mug down and picked up a piece of paper. "Have a look at this."

It was a letter from the Allied commander, General van Deventer, requesting von Lettow to surrender, 'to avoid further unnecessary bloodshed'. She handed it back, trying to gauge his attitude from his expression.

"I will reply." said the Colonel, "thanking him for his suggestion, but declining his offer. I have no intention to surrender."

"Isn't it rather pointless?" suggested Mandy. "What can you achieve? You're virtually surrounded."

"On the contrary. I think we can achieve a great deal, despite our reduced numbers. Our activities detract from the British efforts in Europe."

"Yes, but by how much? Is it really worth all the hardship and suffering? I don't mean just you and your men, or me and the wounded. What about the African villagers who have had their crops stolen or destroyed?"

She could see his expression change. His eyes narrowed slightly, and she was afraid she's angered him. "Miss Spaight, you have to understand that I am the military commander of German East Africa. I am under the orders of the High Command in Germany. They know that we have made a valuable contribution to my country's war effort and want me to continue the fight, even though we have left our territory – temporarily. As for the villagers – war brings suffering, both to the military and civilians. It is the nature of war."

Mandy knew that there was no point arguing with him. His tone had been determined and pedantic. It was much easier to discuss these things with Karl, who could see other points of view.

—•—

Mandy knew that she and Karl would become lovers if only the opportunity came. While the column was marching and camping overnight there was no way that they could be alone for more than a few minutes. She spent the nights with the other women, crowded into a single tent, with a watchman standing guard outside. Karl had his own small tent, but she could not visit him without everyone in the camp knowing.

In mid-December the column arrived at Chirumba, which had been the headquarters of the Portuguese merchant company that administered the northern region of the colony. Situated near the Lujenda River, it had extensive brick buildings, offices and accommodation for officials. Along the banks of the river were orchards with different varieties of fruit, such as mangoes, papayas, oranges and mulberries.

The Colonel decided to spend some time in Chirumba, to accumulate supplies of food and to organise patrols. The officers were billeted in small houses that were formerly used by Portuguese officials, each surrounded by a garden, soon made neat by the column's labourers. One of these houses was allocated to Karl. It was swept clean, but had no furniture, so his servant soon made a bed from bush timber and bark thongs. About a hundred yards away was a three-bedroom house allocated to the women, where Mandy shared a room with Liesl, the young German who had been with her in Tafel's column.

The two women had not spoken much before, mainly because Mandy spent most of her time in the hospital huts, and with Karl. Also, Liesl's was shy about speaking English, even though she was fluent. Now that they occupied the same house, Mandy made an effort to talk to her.

"My father is leading a patrol," said Liesl. "I always fear for his safety."

Mandy asked her where she lived before the war.

"We had a coffee estate near Moshi," she said. "On the lower slopes of Mount Kilimanjaro. We had a good life, with nice friends. It all came to a halt when the war started. We had a choice: to be interned by the British, or to go with my father in the *Schutztruppe*. So my mother and I went with Captain Tafel..."

"Where is your mother now?"

"She decided to stay in Iringa – to become a prisoner. You see, she had difficulty on the marches, because she has... sore joints?"

"Rheumatism?"

"*Ja*. I could have stayed with her, but she wanted me to look after my father. We were lucky to escape from Iringa. We ran from the town the day before the British captured it. So, my mother is now a prisoner. She is quite well – I had a letter from her, passed from patrols."

Liesl looked shyly at Mandy, then emboldened by their conversation, she asked, “Is Dr Karl your... your boy-friend?”

Mandy smiled. “Yes, I suppose you could say that. Neither of us is married. We are getting to know each other.”

Liesl sighed. “I’m glad. I had a boy-friend in Moshi, but I don’t know where he is. I have not had a letter from him for two years. It is possible that he has been killed, or has died of some illness.”

—•—

A large dining room had been used by the former Portuguese officials, and this became the mess for the Europeans in the column, discreetly divided between officers and NCOs. The huge kitchen was soon brought into action, and the neighbouring villages were scoured for pigs, chickens and guinea fowl, while hippopotami were shot in the river and the meat used to feed the *askaris* and camp followers.

“We hear this is a good area for food,” said Karl, while he was working with Mandy in the hospital. He laughed quietly. “The Colonel is cheerful – that’s good.” Then he looked at her seriously. “Would you visit me – in my little house?”

She tried to interpret his expression. “Is that a proposition?”

“I don’t know what you mean. My English is not so good.”

She smiled. “When a man propositions a woman he is making an advance, but verbally.”

“Oh.” He laughed quietly. “Well, I suppose I was making a proposition.”

“Is it safe? Liesl will know if I leave the room, but she won’t say anything.”

“There is a sentry, but he will not pay any attention. Of course, I might be called to the hospital. Then you could follow me.”

—•—

There were several wounded British prisoners who travelled with the Column; most of them could walk, but some were carried in *machilas*. At Chirumba they were interned in a large warehouse, which was clean and surprisingly cool. They knew that, if they escaped, prospects of survival in the bush were slim. Even so, one of them, a young lieutenant named Peter Simmonds, told Mandy that he was planning to make a run for it.

"It's only my arm that's holding me back," he said. He had a bullet wound in his forearm. "I reckon I can make ten miles a day. The villagers will give me enough to survive."

"But you don't know where to go."

"True, but if I follow this river it will bring me to the Rovuma, and then I can walk downstream to the coast. Besides, the troops stay near the rivers so that they can get water. I'll soon meet our patrols."

She thought his plan was desperate and impractical. "You would be more likely to meet Germans than British."

"I would take that chance."

"Where would you sleep at night?"

"In trees."

She laughed. "Seriously, Peter? Have you ever slept in a tree before?"

He grinned sheepishly. "No. But it would be safer – I mean, from wild animals." He looked at her yearningly. "Come with me, Mandy."

She had considered escaping many times. It would be much more difficult and risky for a woman alone. In fact she had long ago ruled it out. With a man her chances would be better, but Peter had no experience in the bush, and was incredibly naïve.

Also, wanting to stay with Karl held her back. It would be much easier to stay with the Column until the war ended. Then they could decide what to do; whether to get married, or at least try to live together. He was determined to return to Arusha, but she would prefer him to come to Nyasaland.

—•—

Light from a half moon lit the compound, enabling her to find her way easily to Karl's house. The shadowy shape of the sentry drifted towards her, making her spine tingle.

"*Wer ist das?*" said his deep voice; the *askari* knew some basic German.

"Going to call the doctor," she replied in Swahili.

He lifted his hand in acknowledgement and she walked on. A candle guttered in the small porch of Karl's house, surrounded by moths that had burned in the flame, or drowned in the melted wax. She tapped on the door and he opened it, drawing her in.

He gave her a tour of the house. It had two main rooms, a living room and a bedroom. There was a small bathroom behind the bedroom with a tin of water and a hole-in-the-floor toilet. In the living room was an upturned crate that served as a table, and two wooden stools, made by local craftsmen. The bedroom had only the bush pole bed, with a mosquito net.

Karl hugged her. "Thank you for coming."

She felt awkward, having only kissed him on a couple of occasions. Their liaison had been so furtive, and, now they had an opportunity to be alone, she was nervous.

"We will be here for at least a week," he said. "If you wish we can just talk."

"We could, but I'm always aware of the dreadful things that can happen in this war. I don't want to lose this time with you."

"I'm glad you feel the same way as me."

—•—

Colonel Northey moved his headquarters to Zomba, expecting the von Lettow would move south, and therefore nearer the southern part of Nyasaland, which was considered at risk. The railway to Chindio was seen as a plum that the Germans might wish to pick.

The original two BSAP companies had been severely reduced in numbers, through battle casualties and sickness. The remaining men were absorbed into other units, mostly as machine gun crews and officers in a new battalion of the RNR. At the same time Colonel Murray became ill and was invalided out on 27 January 1918. When he left Songea there was no farewell ceremony, but Martin Russell and the other officers shook his hand and wished him well. As he drove away, he saw a roughly chalked sign that read 'Farewell scrimshanker.'

—•—

42

Portuguese East Africa – March 1918

"We must try, Mandy. Don't you see? It's our duty to escape, so that we can be with our own side..."

"You wouldn't be much use – with your wound. You would be sent south to a hospital."

"True, but when I recover, I would come back to the front. It's even more important for you to escape. You're actively helping the Huns..."

She laughed. "And also the British prisoners – like you."

She was dressing Peter Simmonds' bullet wound. It had a persistent sepsis and she had to clean it every day. If she was too busy administering anaesthetics, she checked that one of the orderlies had done this work properly.

They were apart from the other patients and whispered to each other, Peter excited by their proximity.

"It's Dr Karl, isn't it?" he said. "If it wasn't for him you would come with me."

"You can't go on your own, Peter. You know nothing about survival in the bush. You can't speak a word of any native language."

He shrugged petulantly, like a little boy. He was only twenty-two, but a lieutenant, and she had grown fond of him. He was usually good humoured, and she enjoyed his obvious admiration for her. He had tousled fair hair and pink cheeks; she often thought he looked too young to be an officer.

"I think about it all the time," he said. "I imagine us sheltering at night beside our fire. We would sleep together, to keep each other warm..."

"I thought you were going to sleep in trees."

"Only if I have to go alone. If you come with me we can build a fire and keep watch. Besides, we couldn't make love if we were in a tree." He looked at her as if surprised that he'd made such a bold statement.

"Peter! I'm shocked." She laughed quietly. "If I came with you, you would have to promise to behave like a gentleman."

"Oh, I would. So you will come with me?" He gave her an engaging smile.

"I've been thinking about it." She fastened the new dressing and patted his hand. "Now go and find some tea to drink. Keep up your fluids – very important."

He left her, reluctantly, and she moved to the next patient, a German corporal with a wound in his chest. The bullet had passed through his lung and exited his back. She feared the track had become septic, because his temperature had risen.

As she worked she thought deeply about Peter's proposal that they escape. Of course he was right; it was her relationship with Karl that held her back. Ironically, it was also one of the major reasons that decided her to leave. She felt disloyal having a love affair with one of the enemy. Much as she loved Karl, she would have to put it behind her.

She often thought about what would happen to them after the war. Could she introduce him to her family? He who had been on the other side for over three years. Admittedly he was not a combatant, but he was a loyal German.

She had composed a letter to him in her mind, and that night she wrote it.

Dearest Karl,

You will never know how difficult it has been to make my decision to escape. I love you, but my conscience tells me that I must try to re-join my own people.

You deserve someone better than me, and I hope you find her.

I will always remember you.

Amanda

She assembled a few things in her sling bag, the one she had with her when she was captured. There were disinfectants and bandages for Peter's wound, a knife and a scalpel, a water canteen, and Vestas for fire lighting. She was cautious about collecting and stowing the items.

Only one thing was missing – a weapon. She decided to steal Karl's revolver. He once showed it to her, so she knew where it was kept: in a tin valise under his bed. He told her he had never used it, and never would. That evening, when he fell asleep, as he often did after they made love, she quietly pulled out the valise, which was unlocked, and took out the Luger, which he had wrapped in an oily cloth. It had a long barrel and she remembered how her father admired the model. Back at her hut, she checked that the chambers were loaded – there were six cartridges.

The next time she dressed Peter's wound she asked him what he would bring.

"A canteen of water. I would like to bring some kind of weapon, but you know that's not possible. When will we go?"

"Tonight."

"Tonight?"

"Yes. There's enough moon. It comes up at about nine."

"So we'll be walking in the dark?"

"Yes, silly. Well, in moonlight. We can't walk during the day, at least at the beginning, because of patrols. Besides, we need several hours start, otherwise they'll send a search party for us."

"Do you think they'll do that?"

"No. Not for two of us. That's why I've always said we shouldn't take anyone else. They plan to break camp at dawn, with a long march ahead, so they won't be bothered searching for you and me. I know the way to the river."

—•—

She wept when she left Karl. He was asleep when she went to his tent, after an exhausting evening operating. She left her note in the tin valise, then hurried back to her own hut, collected her bag and stumbled along the path to the latrine area. There was no one in sight; most of the camp occupants made sure they relieved themselves before dark.

She gave a low owl call and Peter emerged from a moon shadow. Leading the way, she walked as fast as she could, though sometimes stumbling because it was so dark. It was the path to the river, used to fetch water for the camp, threading through trees for about a hundred yards, then breaking into open grassland along the river side. She turned off the path, to the east, following the tree line.

From years of walking round the farms Mandy knew that there was often clear ground between the tree line and the longer grass, sometimes with a foot path or an animal trail. If there were sand rills they showed white in the moonlight. Now, she found a foot path and they made a good pace along it.

"I'm tired," groaned Peter quietly.

"So am I. We have to keep going."

She slowed her pace and checked to see that he was following. She tried to stay alert because there might be wild animals about. They would come out of the forest to drink in the river pools, and return the same route. Predators would wait for their prey on the same paths.

Two hours before dawn she stopped and led Peter into the trees. Knowing that it would be difficult to find something for him to climb, she looked for a very tall ant-heap, eventually found one, and hauled him up by his good arm. He collapsed, exhausted, at the summit, about ten feet above the forest floor, and soon fell asleep. She cut some bushes down and tried to fashion a patch of shade.

She was surprised at the silence. Apart from some persistent babblers and a pair of mourning doves, there were no sounds when she awoke late in the afternoon. Peter was still fast asleep. She rummaged in her shoulder bag and pulled out two maize-bread rolls, ate one and drank a few sips of water. Then she shook Peter and woke him, fed him, and made him drink.

"We'll do the same as soon as it's dark," she said.

"How far did we walk last night?"

"Perhaps ten miles. I think we averaged about two miles and hour, but it might have been less."

They walked slowly through the next night, using the same strategy. Once they startled some large antelopes – Mandy thought they might have been elands; they ran off, crashing through the undergrowth. Later they had to cross a tributary, but it was merely a deep gully with stagnant pools. She knew the water would be far too dirty to drink.

As dawn approached Mandy decided they could walk a little further, because they could see better and move faster. They were following the verge of the *dambo*, with open forest on their right; the river was a couple of hundred yards to their left. Most wild animals had drunk at the river during the night. Visibility increased quickly and had reached the fullest extent when they entered a clearing and saw the buffaloes.

There were a dozen of them – cows and calves, and two bulls, one old, the other not quite mature. They all faced the walkers, some of them snorting in alarm, about thirty yards away. Mandy's attention was riveted on the bulls, knowing they could be extremely dangerous. She assessed the situation in seconds, realising that any of the adults might attack to defend the calves.

"Don't move," she said quietly. "They might go away."

Peter said nothing, but Mandy could hear his quiet high-pitched moan of fear.

The older bull came forward a couple of steps and snorted. He raised his massive head, then lowered it and pawed the ground. His black eyes gleamed with what Mandy perceived as fury. His horns spread from a central boss like a grey wig, out to black points that gleamed with menace.

The bull charged, moving with incredible speed. Mandy pulled the sling bag from her shoulder, thinking she could use it as a rudimentary matador's cape. Behind her, Peter turned and ran.

Attracted by the movement, the bull followed the man, ran him down, smashing him down with the massive horn boss. Then it hooked its horn into Peter's body and flung him up. He spun in the air like a rag doll and landed in a heap, inert.

The bull stepped back and looked at Peter's body, as if wondering what it was. The other buffaloes were a passive audience, though alert.

Her heart pounding, Mandy ran quickly into the trees, where she found a fig tree and clambered up in terror, skinning her shins. She could almost feel the great horns raking her down. When she was twenty feet above the ground she sat in an elbow and looked down, gasping for breath.

The bull was looking in her direction, but soon returned to his herd, shaking his massive body proudly, while the other buffaloes stood facing the place where Peter's body lay on the ground.

She wondered whether he could still be alive. Either the butting or the goring could have killed him. She pulled the revolver from her belt and checked the breech. It would be pointless to fire at the buffaloes, unless they came back to attack Peter. Better to let them move away.

She stayed very still, knowing that the beasts would eventually move off to find grazing and water. It would be too dangerous for her to get down while they were anywhere near. She would have to see them move some distance away before she would dare to climb down.

She had about a half cup of water left in the canteen, and one bread roll. It would have to last all day, if necessary. Her main concern was that she might fall asleep and drop out of the tree. Very slowly, hanging on with one hand, she removed her trousers; one leg she tied to her belt, the other round a branch above her. It would be enough to hold her for crucial seconds if she nodded off.

She dozed and missed seeing the buffaloes move away, so she had no idea where they were. Several vultures had descended onto Peter's body, squabbling for position. Two jackals ran up and the vultures moved away, impatient to resume their scavenging. In an elaborate dance the jackals defended their position, while the vultures circled round, waiting for the right moment to dart in.

Mandy fired her revolver, and the vultures rose with clattering wings and angry cries; the jackals fled. The kick from the revolver made her lose her balance, and she clutched wildly for the branch. For a sickening moment she thought she would fall. Steadying herself, she untied her trousers, pulled them on, and scrambled down the tree trunk.

Walking cautiously towards Peter's body she thought the buffaloes must have gone, but hyenas might be around, attracted by the activities of the vultures. Scavengers could be dangerous, especially as a pack, and she felt terribly vulnerable.

Peter lay in a pool of congealed blood; she guessed the goring had ruptured a major artery. She felt in vain for a pulse and signs of breathing. At least he must have died without knowing much. She started to weep. Poor lad, he was so determined to escape, despite his inexperience. She started to castigate herself for failing to look after him.

The dreadful fright from the buffalo charge and her physical exhaustion combined to drain what little strength she had left to bear Peter's death. As she wept she felt helpless, wondering what her father would advise her to do in this circumstance. She imagined him telling her to climb back into the safety of the tree, but she could not stay there for ever. Sooner or later she would have to move on.

Besides, she could not bear to watch the vultures and jackals devour Peter's body. The great ugly birds were descending to the edge of the clearing, and started to hop towards the body, jostling each other.

At that moment she heard voices and hid behind a tree. It was a line of five *askaris,* walking along the path towards her. Were they German or British? Their uniforms were so similar. They would pass within twenty yards of her. She decided she had to call them.

"Halloo!"

The *askaris* stopped and un-shouldered their rifles, looking around. They saw the vultures and one of them went to investigate, causing the birds to fly off.

"Halloo!" She waved, and they saw her.

"*Wer sind sie?*" called an *askari.*

"*Fraulein* Mandy," she said. "From the Colonel's column."

They came towards her, cautious because they had heard her shot and knew she was armed. They were thin, and their uniforms were ragged; they seemed menacing.

"Do any of you speak ChiNyanja?" she asked.

"I speak it, *dona*," answered a short *askari*, who wore sergeant's stripes. His huge shorts came half way down his shins.

She was nervous of them and kept her hand on the revolver. She told the sergeant that she was a nurse and had seen the patient run away; she had followed him, knowing that he was mentally unstable.

They all nodded, and it seemed that one them recognised her. They walked over to Peter's body. She sobbed when she again saw the pitiful remains and asked the sergeant if they could bury the body. He looked at the sun and shook his head. Their camp was an hour away, but he said they would return next day, if the officers agreed.

—•—

She was taken first to the Colonel. It was well known that she often attended him, and the young officers led her to his tent. He was sitting at his camp table, under the flap of his tent, and looked up myopically as she approached. She felt ashamed of her appearance, her clothes in rags, her feet caked in mud and scratched, her hair like a birds nest.

"Miss Spaight?" He looked at her quizzically, then pointed to a canvas chair. "You look exhausted."

She nodded. "I'm terribly thirsty."

He instructed one of his aides to fetch her some water. "So, you decided to leave us?" He was smiling wryly.

"I felt it was my duty, sir."

"Hm. Well, I don't blame you for that. As you have found, escape is not really practical. Tell me what happened to the officer who went with you – by the way, he was on parole."

She recounted the story, her voice dry and weak, while he listened attentively. The aide brought a canteen of water from which she drank, and her voice became stronger.

"A sad story," said the Colonel. "Were you in love with the young man?"

"Oh no."

"I thought not. Well, you must get some rest. We leave at dawn tomorrow." He sighed. "Another long march."

She walked slowly to the hospital tent. Karl was bending over a patient and looked up as she came near. For a moment his expression changed, lighting at the sight of her, then reverted to his customary tired smile.

"Did you read my letter?" she asked.

"No. Where is it?"

"In your tin trunk. I took your Luger. The *askaris* have it. I told them to give it back to you."

He nodded and turned back to his patient. She stood for a while, watching him, then walked to the women's tent to sleep.

—•—

They crossed the Lurio River on June 1, 1918. The Column was not in good shape, receiving flank attacks, and their stock of quinine almost exhausted. Yet they struggled on south, and headed for Namacurra on the Lugella River, where there was a sugar factory. The Portuguese garrison had been strengthened by the KAR, but was attacked by the Germans on the following day.

Many of the Portuguese soldiers were asleep and the Germans made rapid gains, capturing some machine guns and artillery. Both Portuguese and British troops were trapped against the river and over a hundred of them drowned when trying to swim away, including the British commander.

The Germans indulged in an orgy of feeding and drinking. They plundered over four hundred rifles, hundreds of thousands of rounds of ammunition, and three hundred tons of food. It was characteristic that they slipped away before the Allies could bring reinforcements into action.

—•—

43

Fort Johnston, Nyasaland – March 1918

A small crowd gathered on the parade ground at Fort Johnston gazing into the sky. Most of them were Africans, soldiers and their families, living at the base. A few were British and South Africans. They had been told that an aeroplane might fly in that afternoon.

"I can hear it."

"Is that it up there? The *ndege*, the big bird?"

Goodwill was standing next to Alan Spaight. "There it is, sir. Like you told me, a big bird."

"Yes, I can see it now. I hope the landing field is long enough. They told us two hundred yards, but we've made it longer than that. It will come in pointing into the wind – not that there's much wind."

"Is it difficult for a man to fly it?"

"More difficult than driving a car, Goodwill, and more dangerous. There is an engine in the plane – you can hear it now – similar to the engine in a car. If it stops, the plane can glide down, but if there's no landing field it will crash."

"Surely it cannot fly in a storm?"

"You're right. It would break into pieces."

For years Alan had read with fascination about the development of the aeroplane: the Wright brothers' first sustained flight in 1903, and the New Zealand farmer, Richard Pearse, who flew before the Wrights, but with less control. He was also enthralled by Louis Bleriot's crossing the English Channel in 1909, and the exploits of the Royal Flying Corps in Europe, and the Royal Naval Air Service spotting the *Konigsberg* in the Rufiji Delta.

The sound of the engine was much louder now, and they could make out the details of the biplane, its coffin-shaped fuselage, the disc wheels and flimsy fish tail. They could see that there were two men in cockpits, wearing helmets and goggles.

The Africans who had gathered muttered, gasped and exclaimed. This was something magical, a machine flying in the sky like a huge noisy bird; it was enthralling and frightening. As it swooped lower to land they fled. Left behind were three RFC mechanics who had arrived on a lake steamer a few days earlier.

The plane swooped down on the landing field, and Alan noted that it stopped within a hundred yards of touch down, the propeller throwing up a cloud of dust. The engine subsided to a powerful throb as the plane taxied towards the shed, where the stores were kept. It stopped with a final cough and the two men clambered out. They were wearing khaki overalls, and peeled off their leather helmets and goggles. To Alan they both looked very young, like schoolboys. He walked forward to greet them.

"Lieutenant Peter Hendrie, Royal Flying Corps," said the pilot. "This is Archie Forbes, my observer." Forbes wore sergeant's stripes.

Alan introduced himself. "How was the flight?"

"Long!" Hendrie laughed. "We carried extra fuel, but it was only just enough."

"Is this a BE-C?"

"Yes, sir – a BE-C 2. Great kite, but a bit slow – though that doesn't matter, because we're using it for reconnaissance."

Alan took Hendrie to the officer's mess, while Sgt Forbes joined the RFC mechanics to secure the plane with ropes and chocks. Hendrie asked if he could strip off his overalls; he wore old threadbare shorts and a short-sleeved shirt underneath.

"It can get very cold up there," he explained. "Feels like a Turkish bath down here!"

Hendrie was soon joined by Forbes, and they were plied with beer at the bar. Several officers gathered round to ask questions, and to hear about their exploits in German East Africa. Later they were shown a room where they could bathe and change their clothes.

Alan invited Hendrie and Forbes to join him for supper at the officers' mess, which was near the lake shore and often enjoyed a breeze, relieving the oppressive heat. They were joined by Kirsty and Clare, still in their nurse's uniforms. A mess servant brought beers for the men and lime squashes for the women.

Kirsty, Clare and Dr Macrae had been withdrawn from Peramiho as the Germans moved south in PEA. It was now easier to bring the sick and wounded overland to Fort Johnston and then to Zomba. The two airmen were astonished to meet attractive women, claiming not to have seen a white one for at least six weeks.

"There are three other nurses," explained Kirsty. "We work in rotation..."

"What do you do?"

"We mostly assist at operations and administering anaesthetics. The ward nursing is done by African orderlies."

Alan told the airmen that his elder daughter had been captured by the Germans. "We know she's safe – or as safe as one can be in a campaign. She's with von Lettow – somewhere in PEA, to the east of us."

"You want us to find von Lettow, don't you?" asked Hendrie.

Alan nodded, and glanced around, as he did habitually, to see that no one was within earshot. "We have two units trying to engage him. But he's elusive, and it's difficult country to work through. We thought that an aerial reconnaissance might be the answer. What sort of range can you cover?"

Hendrie, a quiet young man, with a serious expression, replied. "Depending on conditions, sir, we can stay up for about three hours.

Our cruising speed is seventy miles an hour, so we can do only a couple of hundred miles. However, we can double that if we carry petrol cans and re-fuel in the air."

"Isn't that a fire risk?" asked Kirsty.

He smiled ruefully. "It is. The exhaust pipes are hot enough to ignite the petrol, so we have to be extremely careful..."

"It's my job," added Forbes, with a broad smile. He was more outgoing that his officer colleague. "Smoking a pipe is out of the question, more's the pity."

"So you would be able to fly a couple of hundred miles east, and then turn back?" Alan asked.

"Yes," replied Hendrie, "but that would not allow any lateral observations, so perhaps we should aim for a hundred and fifty miles."

"Would it be practical to establish a landing field in PEA?"

"Oh yes. But it would have to be supplied overland with fuel. Did you have somewhere in mind?"

"A couple of places. There are no roads, but we could use porters to carry the petrol there – and they could clear a landing field."

"Essential," added Forbes, laughing. "Preferably without anthills or ant-bear holes."

Hendrie gazed out over the lake, watching the sun sink behind the Kirk Range. "This is a beautiful place. What a pity we're engaged in a war and can't enjoy it."

"Would you take me up in your aeroplane?" asked Clare suddenly.

Alan was about to admonish her, when Hendrie replied, quietly and seriously. "I wish I could, but we're not permitted to take civilians."

"Oh well." She shrugged and smiled.

"One day, after the war, there will be opportunities, I feel sure."

Alan said to Clare, "I would be very nervous if you went up in that plane." He turned to the pilot. "Do you have parachutes?"

Forbes laughed. "They're not allowed."

"Why not?" demanded Kirsty.

Hendrie answered. "The high-ups don't want us to have them. They say that it would reduce our fighting spirit. It's not common knowledge, but my father works in the government in London, and that's what he heard – made him mad!"

"It's ridiculous," said Alan. "I've heard that the German pilots now use them."

"Our balloonists use them," added Hendrie. "But it's easier for them. I think it would be quite difficult for us to use a parachute; it could so easily become entangled in the rigging."

Forbes added, "We would have to have a system whereby you jump first and then open the parachute when clear of the plane."

—•—

Sgt Forbes developed a fever next day. Hendrie went to see Alan, then conferring with General Northey, who had driven up from Zomba. Alan introduced Hendrie, and Northey asked some questions about the capabilities of the aeroplane.

"What are the implications of your observer's sickness?" asked the General.

"There's no sense in going on my own, sir. I need to concentrate on flying the plane..."

"Is there anyone else you could take?"

Hendrie scratched his head. "One of the mechanics. But, frankly sir, I don't think any one of them would be much use. It would be better to wait until Forbes gets better."

"We don't have the time. He might be ill for days." Northey walked over to the map table with his customary brisk stride; the others followed him.

"Our two units are here." The General pointed to the map. "You think von Lettow is here, Alan?"

"Yes, sir. Based on reports from our scouts they're moving closer. We think they'll stay near the river, because it's dry country and they need the water."

"So, if we can confirm that – from the air – we could signal to Barton to move to block him – here. What do you think, Alan?"

"We ought to try, sir. But he's wily. He probably won't fight; he might turn west, towards us, and we could tackle him. If he turns east towards the coast we'll lose him."

Northey twisted his moustache as he pondered. "Somehow, we need to convince him to turn towards us. How can we do that?"

"You could set fire to the bush?" suggested Hendrie.

Alan shook his head. "They know how to back burn. They've had lots of experience. We could to send a message for them to intercept..."

"How can we do that?"

"We could set up a chain of heliographs," said Alan, "in the hope the Germans would see one of them."

"But they would normally be sent in code, so we would have to assume that the Germans can break the code. If we sent in clear the Huns might smell a rat."

"We could let the Germans intercept a messenger, rather than a message?" offered Alan.

Northey's expression brightened, then clouded again. "The message would be in code."

"Yes," replied Alan, but the messenger would be questioned and could give away information."

"Would the messenger be treated as a spy?" asked Northey. "We couldn't send someone if we knew he would be shot."

"I really don't think the Germans would do that, sir. Not if the man was wearing a uniform. I know of no cases where that's happened."

"Do we have anyone in the area?"

"I have two scouts, sir – about here..." Alan pointed to the map, then walked away as he cogitated, while Northey watched him. He turned back. "They could allow themselves to be captured..."

Northey thumped the map with his fist. Then he said to Alan. "But you would lose your scouts."

"We would sacrifice them – I mean, when they're taken prisoner. I don't like it, but..."

"We could drop the message to them," offered Hendrie. "Could you find them – if you came with me?"

Alan tried to collect his thoughts. It would be a great experience to go for a flight with Hendrie. But was it a foolhardy, risky enterprise?

"The scouts knew that we might send a reconnaissance plane over their area. If they see it, they should signal to us, and it would then be easy enough to drop a canister with a message. They can both read."

Northey interjected, "We could put two messages in the can. One, which they would destroy, would tell them to move towards the enemy and allow themselves to be captured. The other message, which they would keep for the Germans to read, would be intended to get them to advance towards Barton."

Hendrie clapped his hands, evidently impressed with the General's plan. Northey looked enquiringly as Alan, who stroked his beard as he thought about it.

"A problem, sir, as you mentioned earlier, is that we would normally put a message like that into code. If the message is in 'open text' the Germans might suspect it. Instead of a message, we could simply ask the scouts to tell the Germans about a large mythical unit to their east – behind them."

"Could the scouts carry it off?"

"I think so."

"I like it." Northey beamed.

"Our scouts wear proper uniforms. I make them carry a card with name, rank and number, and a request that they be treated as legitimate combatants. By the way, sir, I'm the only one who can locate the scouts. I would go with Hendrie."

"Out of the question! I can't allow you to go, Alan." Northey shook his head vehemently. "You're too valuable to risk."

The General walked to his desk and lit up a cheroot. "Hendrie, you'll have to take one of your mechanics. Colonel Spaight can show him what to do." He paused, thinking. "We must also inform Barton about our ploy. He'll then be prepared for von Lettow marching towards him. Send a message."

—•—

An hour before dawn Alan walked with Hendrie to the plane. Forbes' fever had grown worse, and he had been moved into the hospital. Reluctantly, Hendrie had chosen a mechanic named Monty to take over as observer for the flight, knowing that he would have difficulty identifying landmarks in the bush.

As they approached the plane, they could see the two RFC men checking the fuel and oil, and testing the rigging. One of them came forward, wiping his hands with an oily cloth and wearing a worried expression. He saluted the officers.

"Monty's sick, sir," he said to Hendrie.

The pilot groaned in frustration. "What's the matter with him?"

"Don't know, sir; vomiting 'is guts out. We put 'im to bed."

Hendrie turned to Alan. "What do we do now? There's no time to brief someone else. Besides I need these two men on the ground. I want to get going while it's still fairly cool. Could you come?"

"You heard what the General said." Alan looked towards the lake, where the first light created a pale opal sheen on the surface. A waft of cool air drifted over the airfield, picking up swirls of dust.

"I can ask him."

"Either that or we abort the flight, sir."

"I'll speak to Northey." Alan turned abruptly and walked quickly to the officers' quarters, where he saw Northey's batman cleaning the general's boots, a Cockney corporal who had been with the Northey in France.

"Please wake the General, Hobbs. It's urgent."

The batman nodded and went in, while Alan waited outside. He could hear voices and guessed that Northey must have been asleep.

The door opened and the General stepped out, barefoot, wearing an old pyjama top and shorts. His short hair, always brushed immaculately, was dishevelled. "What's the matter, Spaight?"

Alan told him, adding, "It ought to be a straightforward mission, sir."

"I know. But it's strange how things go wrong." He paused, rubbing his eyes. "Very well, Alan; you had better go."

—•—

"As you know, sir, your cockpit is the forward one," instructed Hendrie. "You have no controls – just a belt to hold you in. I advise you to use it; the bumps and pockets can be severe, and you don't want to be thrown out – with no parachute." He laughed. "Also, it'll be very cold. Evans' suit is too small for you, but you can use his helmet and goggles. I see you've brought a sweater and jacket – that's good."

"What do you take in case you have a forced landing?"

Hendrie looked at him with a hesitant smile. "Nothing, sir. We fly light."

"You mean, not even a first aid kit?'

Hendrie shook his head, almost guiltily.

"A gun?"

"No. I have a pocket knife."

Alan laughed and shook his head in disbelief. "Water?"

"There's water – hot water – in the radiator."

Alan walked around the plane. It looked so fragile. Sticks and cloth, he thought. Of course the frame had to be light for it to fly, carrying an engine, fuel, and two men. How could it withstand the strains from air pockets and the strong wind gusts accompanying storms?

He said to Hendrie, "I brought my revolver and my own first aid kit."

They had to carry extra fuel, and Hendrie showed Alan where the cans were stowed, in a bay that was designed for bombs. Accessed through a hatch at the observer's feet, the two four gallon cans of petrol could be pulled up by the observer to replenish the main fuel tanks. In emergency, or when empty, the cans could also be released in the same way as bombs.

"You have to hold the petrol can up, like this," said Hendrie. "Then put the spout tube into the filler hole of the main tank. Be very careful because any spillage could catch fire on the exhaust pipes."

It was six o'clock, and the sun was rising behind the hills to the east; the cool breeze wafting off the lake stirred the windsock, but failed to fill it. A flight of egrets soared past and settled in the reeds along the shore. Alan knew it would be a glorious day; a tad too warm, perhaps, but no storms in the offing.

The mechanics were checking the plane, making sure that everything was functioning, the rudder and ailerons, the wheel bearings and the instruments. There was nothing complex, yet every simple piece of equipment, every wire and strut, was vital.

"Time to go." Hendrie glanced at his watch.

Alan climbed up to his cockpit, helped by one of the men, awkward in his heavy clothing. There was little room for his long legs. He pulled on his leather helmet and goggles, then fastened the waist strap, watching one of the mechanics move to the propeller, while the other held the tip of one wing.

Hendrie tapped Alan on the shoulder and held up his thumb. The mechanic swung the propeller and the engine coughed, then started a guttural roar that increased to a crescendo. Before Alan could catch his breath the plane swung round and taxied to the end of the runway. The pilot increased the engine revs and they set off, gathering speed down the runway, bumping, then lifting.

Fighting nausea in the pit of his stomach Alan looked down. The plane soared up and he could see Fort Johnston and the shimmering blue of the lake. There was the outline of the old fort, and he remembered Harry Johnston and Cecil Maguire discussing the design, and how to fend off attacks from the slavers. That was thirty years ago, and here he was, in the air above, defying gravity.

To their left the deep blue lake stretched away for three hundred and fifty miles, the horizon lost in lapis lazuli haze. Hendrie followed a compass bearing that took him due east across the bottom end of the lake, then across fifty miles of Nyasaland, before entering Portuguese territory.

Below them opened a vast panorama of savannah woodland, interspersed with fingers of grassy treeless *dambos*. There were no roads; the widely scattered villages were linked by footpaths. Alan thought to himself that it would be virtually impossible to land a plane without a prepared runway. In emergency it could be put down in a *dambo,* but he knew that the grassy surface was usually pitted with burrows, or scattered with small anthills.

Warm air lifted above the land as the sun rose higher, creating the pockets and bumps that were the bane of the aeronaut in Africa. At first the little plane wobbled slightly, but a few minutes later it rose in a stomach-churning bump, and Alan wondered how the slender wings could withstand the stress. He looked round anxiously at Hendrie, who raised his thumb, grinning.

The landscape below was surprisingly uniform and Alan realised that he would struggle to find the hill ranges and rivers to locate their position. The map on his knees was rudimentary. His scouts had told him about a pair of *kopjes* near the Lujenda River, though it was by no mean certain that they would be on the line of flight. The river ran from south to north, a tributary of the Ruvuma; they had calculated it to be near limit of their endurance.

Half an hour passed and to Alan the engine seemed to be running smoothly, a healthy growling sound passing through the exhaust pipes on either side of the fuselage. His calculations showed that Barton's column would be below them in about five minutes. Using his binoculars he scanned the bushveld below.

There they were! An ant-like group of soldiers who waved. Turning to Hendrie he pointed down and the pilot nodded, putting the plane into a shallow dive, which brought them down to five hundred feet. The column of troops was much more visible now. As they passed over, Hendrie waggled the wings in salute, then circled back to drop a canister, with ribbons trailing behind it, carrying the message for Barton.

They continued flying east and ten minutes later the river came into view, a dark line, with strips of grassland on either side. A mile beyond were the two *kopjes*, each about a couple of hundred feet high, jumbles of tumbled boulders. The scouts were supposed to have left the vicinity of the *kopjes* that morning, heading for the river and then Barton's column.

Alan signalled to Hendrie to turn and follow a line back towards Barton's column, a manoeuvre they had planned. He saw vultures circling and thought there might be a lion kill below. The pilot took the plane a little lower.

Suddenly Alan saw a dark shape hurtling towards them. Instinctively, he ducked and heard a loud thump ahead, and felt a jarring bump. The plane shuddered as he looked up and saw the propeller slowing down, at a crazy angle. The engine ground to a stop.

An eerie silence followed, broken only by the whistling of the wind through the wire rigging. He turned to look at the pilot. Hendrie lay back in his cockpit, like a man asleep in an easy chair, but his helmet and goggles were covered in blood.

Alan realised at once that they had hit a large bird, probably a vulture. Its body had come past the propeller, and then hit Hendrie in the face.

The plane was gliding, but nosed down at too steep an angle, wind screeching through the wire rigging. Alan leaned back to the rear cockpit and shouted to Hendrie. There was no response. The pilot's head was bent back at an abnormal angle; he was either unconscious or dead.

He was alarmed to see how far they had fallen. Remembering the petrol cans, and the risk of fire if they crashed, he pulled the lever that released them. Losing eighty pounds of weight altered the balance of the plane; the nose came up slightly.

He looked down again and judged they were about a hundred feet above the trees. The open forest stretched ahead as far as he could see, the tree tops almost uniform in height. As the plane came lower the upper branches rushed past. Alan knew then that he was about to die.

—•—

44

Portuguese East Africa – March 1918

The seconds unfolded in slow motion. Tree branches thrashed the nose and propeller of the aeroplane. One of the wings sheared off and the wire rigging twanged and pinged as it snapped. Alan bent forward, his arms protecting his head. Then followed an almighty crash and he lost consciousness.

When he recovered, it took him a few seconds to realise where he was. He detected a strong smell of petrol and guessed that the plane's fuel tank had ruptured. There was also a foul odour which must have come from the vulture that caused the crash; its blood, viscera and feathers were scattered all over him and the cockpit. A fierce pain shot through his left arm when he moved it – broken.

Grimacing with pain he used his right hand to pull off his helmet and goggles and unfasten his belt. The plane was entangled in the middle branches of an acacia tree, about twenty feet from the ground. The fuselage was more or less horizontal, but the remaining wing was pointing down.

He managed to turn and reach back to Hendrie's head, lifting it gently. It was loose and reminded him of a doll his sister owned that had a broken neck. He felt for a pulse and could not find it.

What shall I do now? he pondered. He could stay in the plane, but had no food or water. He could climb down, though it would be difficult with only one arm functioning, and could try to find water.

The arm was broken and he would have to fashion a sling or splint. He chose to go to the ground, and gradually worked his way down the rigging on the drooping wing.

He was half way down when suddenly a wire that supported him snapped. He fell about eight feet, twisting his ankle and falling on his broken arm. He lay for a moment, badly winded, before the pain in his arm and ankle forced him to sit up. He knew the ankle was badly sprained, perhaps broken. Blood was oozing from the fractured arm. He crawled in agony to the bole of the acacia tree and leaned against it, almost passing out.

He knew that the scouts must have heard the plane and would wonder why the sound ceased suddenly. Was there some way he could direct them to the site of the crash? He could fire a shot, but it would probably be a waste. He could light a fire, and that would also keep wild animals away. Barton's men would be puzzled if the plane did not return. Would they send a search party?

Around him was the endless *miombo* forest, as far as he could see, perhaps a hundred yards in any direction, and, he knew, for hundreds of miles beyond. Working slowly but steadily for an hour he gathered firewood, mostly dead branches fallen from trees, light enough for him to drag as he crawled on all fours, two of them useless. He lit the fire with a Vesta from his jacket pocket. Smoke drifted up, though not enough to attract attention. The sun was high; it was about midday.

Lying near the fire he drifted in and out of consciousness, woken by the pain in his arm and ankle. By late afternoon he had almost given up hope of being found that day, knowing that the scouts would not move at night. He managed to light his pipe with one hand, and that gave him much comfort.

He wondered whether Kirsty would have alerted Jess by telegram, or would she wait until tomorrow. Poor Jess; he was sorry to put her through this, especially after Mac's disappearance, and Mandy's abduction. What would she do if he died? Would she re-marry? He doubted it, imagining her saying, 'Twice is enough.'

He took his Webley revolver out of its holster, congratulating himself for bringing it, and again contemplated firing a shot. Gunshots were notoriously difficult to pinpoint, but it might draw attention to the smoke from the fire.

—•—

It was an hour before dark when he saw two Africans approaching cautiously. He called to them and they hurried forward – they were his two scouts, Tobias and Mlati. After ritual greetings he told them what had happened. Mlati, the younger of the two, gathered more wood for the fire, then went half a mile to a *dambo*, to re-fill a canvas water bag from a pool of water.

The elder scout, Tobias, put Alan's arm into a sling, following his instructions, after bandaging the broken skin where the fractured bone protruded. Tobias was one of Alan's favourite scouts; intelligent, good-humoured, and reliable. He was small and stocky, but had a presence that commanded respect from the younger scouts.

"The Germans are moving this way," said Tobias.

"Are you sure, Tobias?"

"Sure, *bwana*. We heard them talking in their camp. We were close enough to hear – in the dark."

"Where are they?"

"Two days march." He pointed east.

"That's good. Major Barton will be waiting for them. Why are they coming here?"

"Water, *bwana*. There is little water east of the Lujenda River." He looked up at the plane and pointed. "What shall we do with the dead man?"

"You two men could bring him down and bury him, but you have no *badza* to dig a grave."

"We can leave his body up there and cover it with branches."

Alan agreed that this was the best option. The branches would keep scavenging birds away from the corpse.

"Can you walk back to Major Barton, *bwana*?" asked Tobias, looking doubtful.

Alan knew that he could only hop, and every step would be agonising. "I could wait here, while you get help."

"We could carry you."

"It would be too slow."

"Mlati can go to Major Barton. I will stay to take care of you."

"Thank you, Tobias. You know, we had a plan for you and Mlati to allow the *WaGermani* to capture you, so that you could tell them our soldiers are coming from the east. We thought the *WaGermani* would head this way. Then Major Barton would fight them."

Tobias smiled. "That was a clever plan." Then his face clouded. "But the *Wa'Germani* might have shot us?"

"Not if you were wearing uniforms. In fact, they probably would have released you, because it's too much trouble for them to keep prisoners."

"There is no need now. They are coming."

—•—

It was on the second day that help came. By then Alan had a fever, suspecting that his arm wound was infected. The rescue party, guided by Mlati, was led by a young lieutenant, Paul Johnson, plainly nervous about the proximity of the Germans and the ever-present dangers of the bush.

"Do we know where they are, sir – the Germans?"

"Not exactly, Johnson. My guess is their advance patrols are within a few miles. How far is your camp?"

"It's twenty miles, sir. A full day's march if we set off at dawn. We have a *machila* for you."

“We can’t wait here. But first we must bury the pilot.” Alan pointed to the plane.

Johnson grimaced. “We’ll do it now.”

It took four men half an hour to bring the body to the ground. Alan asked the lieutenant to confirm that Hendrie’s neck had been broken. However, Johnson could not endure the odours from the putrefying body and collapsed in a paroxysm of vomiting. So Alan made the examination himself.

They dug the grave at the base of the acacia tree in which the remains of the plane rested. Johnson started to carve a simple inscription on the trunk, following Alan’s instructions, but Tobias had to take over, because the lieutenant was too slow:

Here lies Peter Hendrie, Lt RFC,
died in the service of his country. 6/3/18

“You’re burning up, sir,” said Johnson. “I wish there was something I could do.”

“You’re here, Johnson. If you can get me to Barton, what medical unit do they have?”

“A couple of orderlies. There’s a doctor and nurse further back near Mahua.”

Alan felt light-headed. “Who are they? Do I know them?”

“It’s Dr Clements, sir, and the nurse is Kirsty – pretty girl.”

He sighed. “She’s my daughter.”

—•—

Kirsty had asked for an interview with Dr Thompson at the hospital in Zomba. She sat waiting on the verandah, thinking about what her father said. Ahead of her were the treetops of the lower slopes of the mountain, interspersed with green-painted tin rooftops of civil servant houses. Many of the trees were ornamental, flamboyants and jacarandas, fuchsia-coloured bougainvilleas, frangipanis and oleanders.

"I absolutely don't want you to go, Kirsty," her father had said. "The bush in Portuguese East is not the place for women. It would be a different matter if you were on a camping trip with me. But now it means travelling mostly on foot, perhaps fifteen or twenty miles a day, sleeping in the open, sometimes with your clothes wet, and an empty stomach. No cups of tea, no servant to bring your breakfast. It's very difficult to work under those conditions. Dr Macrae told me he felt exhausted most of the day, and it was all he could do to stay awake while he operated on wounded men."

"Pa, that's precisely why I want to go – to help doctors like Macrae. I think I can cope with the conditions..."

"But you would be the only woman."

"I'm sure they would respect me and look after me." She put a conciliatory hand on his arm. "Besides, Mandy is doing all those things."

Alan had sighed in exasperation. "I know, Kirsty. I don't know how I could face your mother if anything happened to you."

"I told you both – before I came here – that I was aware of the risks. You didn't stop me then..."

"Because we thought you would stay at the hospital in Fort Johnston. Then you went to Peramiho, despite my objections. But this is a totally different matter – you going off into the bush where the fighting is. The Germans are ruthless."

"Well, I'm going to ask Dr Thompson."

Now, she looked further out at the view from the verandah, always impressed by the vista, but drawn to the Mlanje massif. She wondered if Mac was there, still alive, or had his body rotted in some hidden gully, washed away by the incessant rains.

An orderly came to lead her to the doctor's office. Dr Thompson invited her to sit down on the other side of his overloaded desk. His usual good humour was strained by his load of work, administration on top of surgery.

"I've considered your request, Kirsty, and I've spoken to Dr Clements about it. He and I both think you would be valuable in a field hospital, but we're concerned about the poor conditions that you'll have to endure. Clements says he'd do his best to look after you. He spoke to Colonel Barton, who has agreed – he even cited your sister Mandy's contributions at Karonga. What news of her, by the way?"

"She was still with von Lettow when they started moving back north. We're hoping she's safer now she's with the main column."

"Your father is adamantly opposed to you going."

"Yes, but I'm an adult, Dr Thompson. I have the right to make my own decisions."

"Hm. That's a debatable point."

"Do you mean whether I'm an adult?"

Thompson laughed. "I won't argue that, Kirsty. Look, you can go. Just be careful."

She clapped her hands in a way that he thought girlish and belied her earlier claim to adulthood.

—•—

At sundown next day the rescue party reached the Barton column encampment. Dr Clements and Kirsty had come up to the camp from Mahua and were waiting for Alan, now delirious, as he drifted in and out of consciousness. An orderly cleaned the patient from head to toes, while the doctor and nurse examined him.

"So, this is your father?" muttered Clements.

"Yes. He's a farmer – or was before the war – near Zomba."

Clements shook his head to Kirsty, then said to Alan, "Your arm has signs of gas gangrene. I'm afraid I have to take it off."

He could see that the patient did not absorb the statement, and turned to Kirsty. "Look, you can see it's in there. Prepare him. You have to do the anaesthesia. I'll take it off below the elbow, if the infection hasn't gone any higher."

She felt nauseous seeing her father's condition, and hearing about the planned operation, wondering whether she could cope with watching her own father under the scalpel.

"What about the ankle?" she asked.

"It seems stable. It can wait till we get him back to Fort Johnston."

—•—

Clements was a colonial medical officer, but at the age of thirty-five had plenty of surgical experience. He had never performed an amputation, but tackled it with his usual confidence. He found gangrene in the elbow, so cut the arm off between elbow and shoulder. After two hours he had sutured and sewn, then wearily stripped off his gloves and gown.

"What do you think, Kirsty?" he asked. "Are you alright?"

"Amazing. It wasn't easy to watch, but – sort of fascinating. It's a good thing I'm not squeamish. Pa seems to have held up well. Pulse is good."

"You'll stay with him?"

She nodded and he went out of the operation tent. She found a cloth and wiped the sweat off her forehead. Her father's face, the only part of him exposed, was deathly pale, but she was not perturbed. He would regain consciousness within an hour, but nausea was always a problem with chloroform, and she would stay with him when he vomited, to make sure he didn't choke.

Although she was in love with Gavin, a fact that she did not question, she found Dr Clements very interesting. There was something about his demeanour, his assurance and confidence, that drew her to him. He had not given any indication that he was attracted to her, and that surprised her a little. She knew that she was desirable, and had been approached by dozens of men, mostly army officers, who wanted to take her out. But Roger Clements was absorbed in his work, and otherwise spent his time reading novels.

She sat beside her father as he regained consciousness. She supported him as he retched into a metal basin, groaning and coughing. She held a tin mug of water for him to drink before he sank back, exhausted. His body was bathed in sweat and smelled sour, so she called an orderly to wash him again, and change the sheets. Then she went to find Dr Clements.

Clements was anxious to return to Zomba, where his bachelor bungalow waited for him, with his books and his records. He was determined not to take any risks, and presumed that the field hospital would be well behind the firing line and thus comparatively safe. He was relieved that there had been no firing at all. The enemy was known to be elusive. However, the two scouts who brought in Alan Spaight reported a German patrol not far away.

—•—

45

Portuguese East Africa – March 1918

Drew was on the march, east from Fort Johnston, in company with Lt Col Charles Barton, DSO, commander of 3/1 KAR, the same officer who, as a captain, had been the commander at the Battle of Karonga, three and half years earlier. His second in command was also the same as at Karonga, Lt Col Alexander Griffiths, DSO. Their objective was to establish the line of communication from Namweras, on the eastern border of Nyasaland, to Mahua, in Portuguese East Africa, essential in the process of intercepting von Lettow's column as it moved north. They had thirty-five British officers and NCOs, three hundred *askaris*, eight machine guns and over eight hundred porters, carrying food and ammunition.

"Unwieldy," said Drew, to Griffiths. "Why aren't we in smaller faster units?"

"The problem with a small mobile unit is that, if it encounters the German column, it lacks the strength and the fire-power, to do anything effective."

The large numbers of *tenga-tengas* was a reflection of the poor quality of the tracks and the lack of motorised transport. The route they now marched had been widened to take motor vehicles, but was extremely rough. The column encountered many streams and swamps that had to be bridged. Although the two colonels had a staff car, they usually preferred to walk.

Drew had a motor-cycle, but he also walked. He was the Intelligence Officer for the column, recently promoted to captain, and had twenty African scouts under his command. They were carefully selected NCOs with campaign experience and ability to survive on their own in the bush. One of Drew's tasks was to ensure that the column was aware of any German presence.

"I'm very concerned," said Barton, when briefing Drew. "We certainly don't want to meet any German raiding parties."

"I agree, sir. I'll have a screen of scouts ahead. But it will be easy to miss German raiders and pickets, because of the nature of the country. Also, it's difficult for my scouts to get the information back to us in HQ. The most reliable method is for them to come back to us on foot, but that's rather slow."

"Couldn't we use heliographs?"

"I've thought about that, sir. The pocket heliographs have a very limited range – about twenty miles, and only if the scout can get onto a *kopje*. There are many areas where it's too flat for helios."

When they camped that evening Drew joined the other officers at the mess table, a crude affair made of bush timber, around which they arranged their canvas camping chairs.

"Well, Drew," said Barton, as they started the meal. "What do you have to tell us?"

Drew had always found Barton intimidating. Ostensibly he had a mild manner, but there were hints of simmering impatience. Everyone knew that the officers and other ranks under his command were new and not adequately trained, but the need to defeat von Lettow was paramount.

"Sir, we've seen no evidence of a German presence ahead. We will, of course remain vigilant."

There was a round of guffaws from the other officers, and Drew blushed. "It's my duty to warn you all, sir. We have to be careful during our night camps. The Namweras district is known for its man-eating lions." He looked around the faces and was pleased to see that the younger officers suddenly looked nervous. For most of them it was their first excursion into the bush.

"Why is that?" asked Griffiths.

"The local people say that the main diet of lions in this area is bush pig, but at this time of year the pigs move into swampier country, seeking water, and are more difficult to for the lions to find – so they turn to easier prey. The villagers here never venture out after dark."

"So what precautions do you advise?"

"Sir, I suggest always stay near a fire. Lions don't like fires, although it's not a guaranteed protection. Frankly, the men who are most at risk are the sentries. I also urge you to beware of hyenas. They have been known to drag a man from his tent."

"Are they that strong?" asked a fresh-faced lieutenant – he'd arrived from England two weeks before. "I mean, it's just a big dog, isn't it?"

"They can be very large – up to about 170 pounds, and their neck and jaws are immensely strong," replied Drew. "Don't confuse them with dogs. The hyena is a different biological family. In many ways they behave like the cat family. There are only four species – one of the smallest in nature."

"But surely they're scavengers, Drew?"

"They do scavenge, even dead humans, but they kill most of their prey. Here in Nyasaland, they are known take children or women from villages."

—•—

The 3rd battalion KAR established a camp at Mahua and probed eastward. A small but fierce battle followed at Kariwa, with casualties on both side. The British wounded were brought back to the field hospital at Mahua, where Dr Roger Clements was in charge, assisted by Kirsty Spaight, with several African orderlies. A Royal Army Medical Corps officer, Lieutenant Cobb, was designated to go forward with the troops when they attacked.

Most of the wounded were *askaris*, but three were European officers. Kirsty administered the analgesics and anaesthetics, under the instructions of Dr Clements. Because of her training in Salisbury and experience at the Zomba hospital she was highly effective.

At the end of the operating session Dr Clements said, "Well done, Kirsty. I'm glad Barton agreed to have you come with us." He smiled. "I wasn't aware that your brother was in our unit."

—•—

In fact, Kirsty had seen Drew only twice since she came up to Mahua, and then only briefly. She was entitled to use the officers' mess – a mere large elongated hut – and knew that they would sometimes meet there. A few of the officers resented her presence, saying that it inhibited their male conversations. However, the majority welcomed her as a reminder of homes and families. Besides, she was pleasant and interesting to talk to.

That evening at dusk, as she was returning from the hospital tent to her own small one, she saw Drew's tall figure approaching. She ran up to him and hugged him.

"Can we meet later?" she asked. "Are you very tired?"

"I am, but I want to talk to you."

"I'm going to shower," she said, "then have supper. I'll see you at the mess. Then we can take a walk round the compound and talk."

Later, they walked side by side, before the evening meal, when they knew that a private conversation would be impossible.

"I've heard that you were recommended for a Military Cross," said Kirsty. "I hope you get it."

Drew shrugged. "Sometimes these awards cause envy and bad-feeling. There are so many deserving soldiers who go unrecognised."

"But they say it's good for morale."

—•—

A concerted attack was planned when a German presence was identified by Drew's scouts. The enemy were encountered at a village named Nakoti and this is where a vicious battle ensued, with many casualties on both sides. At the end of the first day the KAR force dug trenches in the thick woodland, licking their wounds and trying to eat some food.

Next morning the KAR companies advanced, clashing with German pickets. They came under heavy machine-gun fire and had to retreat, losing several of their own Lewis and Maxim guns. At midday the command group was hit by machine gun fire and Barton's adjutant, Captain Granville was killed. A bullet hit Barton in the mouth, knocking out his front teeth. He collapsed, but recovered, and, though he could not speak, gave written orders through Lt Col Griffiths.

The Germans tried to surround the KAR position, but were unable to maintain contact with each other because of the thick bush. By nightfall the KAR men had run out of ammunition because the porters had run away. However, a German orderly was captured and found to have a message to Major Kraut from von Lettow, ordering a retreat. Evidently they had suffered too many casualties and were short of ammunition.

The KAR companies then withdrew, but had to leave their wounded with Lt Cobb. Seven officers and fifty askaris had been killed, and eleven officers and a hundred and twenty askaris were wounded. The Germans had lost a quarter of their fighting strength. Four DSOs were awarded, including bars for Barton and Griffiths.

—•—

46

Khundalila Farm, Zomba, Nyasaland – March 1918

Alan reached Zomba hospital after a long journey, by *machila* to Namweras and then by lorry. He was taken directly to the recovery ward, where Dr Thompson checked him over.

"Clements seems to have done a good job," he said. "Neat stitching. I hear that Kirsty assisted."

"She did," said Alan. "I wasn't *compos mentis* at the time. What now, Tommy?"

Thompson sat on the edge of the bed, facing the patient. "We need to be sure that there's no infection, by checking your temperature regularly. Jess can do that. We have to sort out the sprained ankle – I don't think it's broken. Other than that – it's for you to adapt to life with one arm; others have done it successfully – Lord Nelson for one."

"Was it his right arm? I can't remember."

"It was. Hit by a musket ball. He refused to be helped onto his ship when they took him back. I believe he was giving orders within half an hour of the operation."

Alan laughed weakly. "He was made of sterner stuff than me."

"In time – you should consider getting fitted with a prosthetic limb. There's a man I know in Salisbury who makes those things."

—•—

General Northey came to visit Alan in the hospital. He was no stranger to the place, and Dr Thompson showed him into the ward. He smiled sympathetically at the patient.

"Well, Alan, I'm sorry you've had such a serious injury. I hear you've made a good recovery."

"Thank you, sir."

"I had some sort of suspicion that something might go wrong with your flight. Perhaps that's what made me reluctant to let you go. At least you can be satisfied that the German came into our trap. We'll never know what prompted them."

Alan nodded. "It sounds as if Barton's column gave them a bloody nose."

"Yes. But we have to be sure they won't retaliate."

—•—

Jess came to the hospital to fetch Alan, greeting him tearfully.

"Thank God, you got back safely," she sobbed. "Even if you had to lose an arm – you're here, and I'll look after you."

"I can't hold you properly," he said mournfully. "I'll have to get used to hugging you with one arm. How are you?"

"Well. All the better for having you home."

On the drive back to the farm – he let her drive – he told her what had happened. "When the war started I could imagine dozens of ways I could be wounded or killed, but I never thought it would be an aeroplane crash. It may not have been worthwhile. We wanted the Germans to move closer, so that Barton could engage them."

"Will you wear a … a false arm, or something?" asked Jess tentatively.

He laughed. "I might. I wish Mac was with us. He would have made something."

"There are specialists in these things."

"Yes. Tommy says I should go to Salisbury and get fitted with something."

"You could go to South Africa?"

He shook his head. "I'd rather go to Rhodesia. I could buy some things for the farm – see what they're doing with their tobacco."

—•—

It was a couple of days later that he drove to Zomba for the first time, relishing his ability to do something by himself. He went to the post office and opened the mail box, No 10. Taking the small pile of letters and a newspaper he returned to the car. He hoped to find a letter from Kirsty, although she seldom wrote, or even an official missive about Mandy.

Among the letters was one that he did not notice was addressed to Jess. Holding the envelope with his teeth, he carelessly ripped it open.

It read:

Dear Jess,

I arrived home yesterday. They had a good look at my eye in Cape Town and said I could make the voyage. Have an appointment to see a specialist tomorrow. Let's hope they can do something.

Have thought so much about you and your kindness. Please forgive me for taking advantage of it. I feel very guilty. I was not really myself – it was all a bit of a shock. I feel much better now and realise how badly I behaved.

I hope all's well with you and your family. I expect the war will end one of these days and they'll all come back to your lovely farm.

Take good care of yourself. I'll always remember.

Love from

Hamish

—•—

He tossed the letter onto the table where Jess was sewing. She picked it up and her face turned pale as she read it. Then she blushed deeply.

"Who is Hamish?"

She bowed her head, then looked up at him. "A patient who stayed here. He went back to Scotland..."

"Did something happen between you?" His voice was harsh and insistent.

"He had an injured eye – he needed some kind of reassurances..."

"So what happened, Jess?" His voice rose. "I have a right to know."

"He forced himself on me. I ..."

"You couldn't prevent it?"

"I wasn't strong enough. I couldn't scream – I thought about it, but it would have brought the servants."

He paced the room, feeling numb. He looked at her, sitting contrite, and found it difficult to blame her. But she must have given him some encouragement, or at least placed herself in a vulnerable situation.

"Where did this happen?"

"In his guest room."

"How many times?"

"Once. I insisted he leave the next day."

"Why were you in his room?"

"I was changing his dressing..."

"You could have done that here. Why did you go to his room? Surely he must have given you some hints that he might misbehave."

"Darling, he did not." She stood up and walked towards him. "I'm so sorry it happened. I hoped you would not find out. All I can say is that I did not want it to happen."

Alan told himself not to be angry, but he felt aggrieved. Yet knew that he could not blame Jess – if she was telling the truth. He had always trusted her, and there was no reason for him to lose this trust.

—•—

47

Portuguese East Africa – April 1918

Von Lettow's cheerful demeanour was tested by the losses at Nakoti. Chastened, he moved his column further north, hoping to avoid a large-scale confrontation with Allied forces.

Mandy was resigned to her life on the march. No measures were taken to guard her, but the experience with Peter Simmonds had convinced her of the futility of trying to escape. She felt physically drained by the long marches and the hours of assisting Karl with his operations. Exhausted, she fell asleep within seconds, and awoke wishing she could have several more hours.

Opportunities to talk to Karl were limited, since all their waking hours were spent either moving from camp to camp, or operating on patients.

She had some idea of the direction of their movements because the orderlies spoke about it. She knew that they were moving north, back to the Rovuma River. They said that the Colonel was returning to the former German colony, even though it was now occupied by the British. There was speculation about his objective; some said he would return to Tabora, others surmised that he would head for Dar-es-Salaam. Only a few suggested that Northern Rhodesia might be his target.

One evening, when Mandy was treating the Colonel's eye, he said, "You know, Miss Spaight, I was thinking of invading Nyasaland. What would you think of that? We would move into your home country."

She looked at him carefully, wary of his changing moods, not wanting to upset him. "I suppose they would have strong defences to prevent you."

"Of course, but it is the road and railway infrastructure that I covet. I am weary of marching through the bush. I'm sure you are, too."

She inserted into his eye some drops of a solution of boric acid and sodium hypochlorite, concocted by Karl. "It has been a long hard slog. I hope you think it has been worthwhile."

"Oh, I do. I'm confident it has been of great value to my country. But, as regards invading Nyasaland, the point you made is a valid one. My enemies would find it easier to defend Zomba and Blantyre, because of the transport infrastructure that supports them." He sighed. "I suspect that my column is now too small. Besides, the country between here and Zomba is not at all easy to traverse, full of lakes and marshes."

"So will you move north?"

He gave a short laugh. "Your compatriots would like to know, but you have no means of telling them, do you? So, I can safely tell you. Yes, we will continue to move north."

When she finished he stood up and smiled at her. "I thank you, Miss Spaight. One day I will find a way to reward you for your services."

—•—

Walking beside Karl on the long marches she often mused about the future – 'when the war ends.'

"What will we do, sweetheart? Will we spend the rest of our lives in a little colonial *boma*, tending the sick?"

"Perhaps. It's a calling, isn't it? For me." He glanced at her fondly. "I know you would like to live in Nyasaland..."

"To be near my family."

"Hm. I wonder if the British would have a German in their colonial medical service."

"Why not? You haven't been a combatant."

"I suppose it's possible."

She shifted her shoulder bag, from one calloused shoulder to the other. "We could raise a brood of children."

He laughed. "That would be fun. As many as you like."

—•—

48

Long Valley Farm, Salisbury, Rhodesia – June 1918

Helen looked up from her sewing as she heard a car come down the driveway. She put down her needle and walked down the verandah steps to greet the visitor, soon recognising him as Alan Spaight. As he stepped out of the car and came towards her, a half smile on his face, she noticed that his left sleeve was empty.

"Alan! What a pleasant surprise." She hugged him, sensing the emptiness where his arm should have been. "What happened?"

"Didn't you get my letter?"

"No."

"I'm sorry – oh, well. I must have overtaken it." He laughed, then waved his empty sleeve. "This is the reason I'm here – in Salisbury – to see if I can get some kind of artificial arm."

She led him into the house, while he told her about the plane crash, then she sat him on the verandah and brought cold drinks and sandwiches.

"You poor thing. What a horrible..."

"I survived, Helen."

"Thank heavens. Where are you staying? Do you want to stay here?"

"At Meikles. It's kind of you to offer, Helen, but it will be easier if I stay in town. I have to go to the clinic every day. They fit and modify, then fit again and try – constantly adjusting."

"And what will you get at the end?'

"I hope an arm with a sort of hand that can hold things." He laughed. "I don't expect to play the piano."

—•—

"When did you last see Martin?" she asked.

"Must have been about a week ago. I was in Zomba – taking my leave of General Northey and the staff, and he came there to liaise with us. When did you last see him?"

"I haven't seen him since August 1915 – nearly three years ago."

Alan shook his head in sympathy.

She sat back with her tea. "How was he – when you last saw him?"

Alan looked up. "Quite well. He's tough, isn't he?"

"How is Clare?"

"She seems well. Drew is besotted with her – like I've never seen him with a girl before. I think she likes him well enough, but she's much younger."

"She's told me about it in her letters. She seems quite serious about being in love with him. I must say I'm very pleased, Alan."

"Yes, it's good that our families can be linked by marriage..."

"I'm sure Drew is a fine young man – I haven't seen him since he was a schoolboy, of course."

"He is a good fellow. By the way, Helen, he's been decorated with an MC – a Military Cross."

"Heavens, what an honour!"

"Yes, and well deserved."

She brought him a cup of tea. "They say that serving in the war matures men and women – do you think that's true?"

He pondered before answering. "Yes, I do. It seems to have changed Drew. He's more self-assured now. Clare, too, is more serious. I don't mean to say she's lost her liveliness. But she's worked very hard and made a reputation for efficiency."

He sighed. "This war does drag on. We seem no nearer winning it than we did a year ago." He looked around at the garden. "This is a lovely place, Helen. You don't look after the farm by yourself, do you?"

"I have a farm manager. He has very poor eyesight, so was not taken into the army. The boys help me, but they're weekly boarders in Salisbury. I have an old family friend staying here – Betty Martin – though she's away now. And my husband's partner, Tom Ellsworth – you met him – drops in occasionally."

"When Martin heard I was going to spend time in Salisbury he asked me to come and see you, so here I am."

"Thank you for coming. How do you find Meikles?"

"Oh, it's alright. A bit lonely. I have a few other contacts, but there's not much to do. I'm supposed to be eating lots of good food – to build up my strength."

"When do you return?"

"Another week – or so." He gave a short laugh. "My boss – General Northey – has been appointed Governor of British East Africa."

"Look, Alan, would you like to stay and have some supper? I'm on my own, and I don't have anything special laid on, but..."

"That's very good of you, Helen. I would be delighted to have supper with you – if it's not inconvenient."

"No, not at all." She went to the kitchen and called for the cook, then gave him instructions about preparing a cottage pie. When she returned to the verandah she found that Alan was standing on the lawn, looking up at the roof.

"That's a fine thatch," he said.

"Yes, it's ten years old."

"It was good to see something of Clare. Lovely girl."

"How was she?"

"Well. They work very hard those nurses. We owe them a lot." He looked at her. "Where's Flora?"

"She lives in the town. She's a junior school teacher. She comes her for weekends."

"You must look forward to having her and the boys at the weekends."

She sighed. "I wish they lived here all the time – especially as Betty is away. Her mother is ill, so she went down to South Africa to look after her."

"Do you feel safe here – on your own?"

"Oh yes." She laughed. "We've had the servants for many years. Would you like to see the cattle sheds – I need to take a brief look."

"Delighted." He fell in to walk beside her.

—•—

By the time they sat down to supper Helen was enjoying his company, since they had a lot in common. He had always found her extremely charming, an intelligent, well-travelled woman that was easy to talk to. It occurred to him that she was rather lonely, and the flow of her conversation suggested that she was enjoying his company.

After the meal they adjourned to the sitting room and she gave him a glass of port, to follow the good South African wine he'd drunk during the meal. He began to feel a little queasy, and thought it might be the effects of the wine and big meal on his rather debilitated constitution.

"I say, Helen. I'm feeling slightly out of sorts." He explained his suspicions about the reason.

"Well, you had better not attempt the drive back to Salisbury. I'll have the guest room made ready for you."

He held up a hand in protest, but she was already walking out to give instructions to the servants. She returned and took him to the room, found him an old pair of Martin's pyjamas, and made sure that there was hot water for him to bathe.

"It's very kind of you," he said. "I feel better just knowing that I can drop into bed."

—•—

He woke up and looked at his watch, but it was too dark to read, so he struck a Vespa – awkwardly with his one hand – then noticed a hurricane lamp on the floor, with the flame so low it was almost invisible. He turned up the light. He must have been asleep for a couple of hours; he felt much better. He went into the bathroom to have a pee, felt thirsty and decided to look for some drinking water in the kitchen. Bumping along the corridor he accidentally hit Helen's door.

"Alan? Is that you? Are you alright?" Her voice was coming closer, and then the door opened.

"Helen, I'm so sorry. I feel a bit groggy."

She was wearing a white nightgown with embroidery at the breast. Her hair was loose, her eyes large in the subdued light. Without thinking he put the lamp on the floor and caught her in his arms.

"Alan! You must not do this."

"No, you're right. I'm sorry. I couldn't help it."

Her first impulse was to feel sorry for him. She knew he was an honourable man... "Really, Alan, you'd better get back to bed."

"May I talk to you, Helen?"

She indicated the sofa, and lit the fire, then went back to her room, returning wearing a dressing gown. She poured him a tumbler of brandy, generous in the hopes that it would help him to sleep.

He told her about what had happened to Jess. "What do you think? Should I be outraged...?"

"Certainly not! Look, Alan. If she is to be believed, it was not her fault..."

"But she should not have put herself in a situation where he could take advantage of her."

“Perhaps, but that’s a counsel of perfection. Look at us now. You could argue that I should never have invited you to stay. And you should not have stayed. But we are both married and in an extended family, so no one would assume that we would fall into bed together.”

—•—

He came out to the farm at the weekend and again met Flora and her three brothers. Relaxed, he ate his fill, watching with admiration the matron with her children. Occasionally, she would glance at him in a questioning way.

When they were alone, he said. “I’ve had my marching orders. I leave on Tuesday – train to Beira, and then on home.”

“You must be glad.”

He smiled wryly. “I am, but I would have liked to spend more time with you.”

—•—

49

Portuguese East Africa – September-October 1918

At the end of September 1918 von Lettow's column crossed the Rovuma River, thus returning to the former German territory, now administered by the British, but with only a few scattered officials. As the Germans marched north they lost more and more porters, who defected to return to their villages. This attrition was a constant worry for the Colonel, since his own Europeans and the remaining *askaris* were weakened by long marches, shortage of food and fevers.

It now became apparent that a respiratory infection was spreading through the column, having the same symptoms as influenza. Von Lettow asked his doctors about it during the evening meal.

"Is it normal to have such a widespread infection," he asked, "or is it because our people are so debilitated?"

"We don't know much about it," replied the senior doctor. "Some news has come through about similar epidemics in Europe."

"Is it influenza – or pneumonia?"

"We think influenza, sir."

Karl held up his hand and von Lettow nodded to him, inviting him to speak.

"This pathogen seems particularly virulent, sir. We are observing a higher than normal mortality rate..."

"That might be because of the condition of the men," interjected the Colonel.

"Perhaps," said Karl. "But the mortality seems worse in young adults, compared with the children of our followers, who ought to be more vulnerable."

The other two doctors shook their heads, evidently not agreeing with Karl.

"That's interesting, Dr Niemeyer," said von Lettow. "Please keep me informed. We cannot allow the sickness to slow down our progress. Those who cannot keep up have to be left behind, with as much food as we can spare."

"Their prospects will be dire," said Karl.

His older colleague doctors frowned in disapproval of their young colleague.

"I'm aware of that Dr Niemeyer," said the Colonel. "We have no alternative, if we are to continue our campaign. I have no intention of abandoning our march to take care of the sick people."

—•—

Karl was about to operate on an African woman with a suspected ectopic pregnancy; she was the wife of an *askari,* and had walked for hundreds of miles with the column. He spoke to her in Swahili, in soothing tones.

"The *dawa* will make you go to sleep while I see what the problem is. *Dona* Amanda will ask you to breathe the *dawa*. Do not be afraid."

He nodded to Mandy, who dripped chloroform onto a cotton pad and held it gently to the woman's face. Only her frightened eyes showed above the pad, then closed as the anaesthetic gradually made her unconscious.

Karl started to sing quietly to himself, as he made his incision in the woman's abdomen.

"*Vorubert, Ach Vorubert,*" he sang, and Mandy recognised the opening words of *Der Tod und Das Madschen*. At the end of the first verse he stopped and looked up at Mandy.

"I hope death passes you by, Amanda. There are so many perils."

"I thought you were singing about this woman."

He shook his head and smiled. "You know the words now, don't you? No, I was thinking of you."

"We are both vulnerable – treating the infectious influenza patients – in constant exposure to their fluids."

"Especially as we are young adults."

"What will happen to this woman?" she asked.

"She will be left behind – presuming she recovers from the operation."

"That's almost like a sentence of death."

"Her husband must look after her."

She shook her head. "He's an *askari*. The Colonel won't allow *askaris* to stay behind."

"Unless he has influenza." He looked at her directly. "I will certify him as unfit to march."

"You're a good man, Karl."

—•—

"Do you know where we're going?" asked Karl as he marched alongside Mandy. "You seem to have von Lettow's ear."

She laughed, "I don't know about that. He tells me only what he wants me to know."

"He doesn't tell me anything, so you know more than I do."

"I'll ask him."

She moved up the column, a long line of men and women, all carrying loads of some kind. The Colonel was near the front, in a *machila* chair carried by four men. He seemed to be dozing, but opened his eyes when she walked up alongside him. He smiled and beckoned her closer.

"I feel unchivalrous – sitting in this contraption, while you have to walk."

She shrugged. "Fortunately, I'm able to walk. I've been wondering where we're going."

He laughed lightly. "I think most of us have guessed that we're going west."

"Really?"

"It's the only option for me."

"Are we to continue for ever? Are we a sort of terrestrial version of The Flying Dutchman?"

The Colonel laughed heartily. "By the way – one of my favourite operas. Do you like Wagner's music? Well, you may not know, Miss Spaight – we have some captured newspapers. Regrettably, we have lost Cambria, St Quentin and Armentières, but they may be strategic withdrawals – who knows. At any rate, we will continue to fight here in Africa."

—•—

After a particularly long march, during which they were drenched with rain, Mandy and Karl prepared for their evening clinic. There were no operations, but plenty of patients with sores, malaria and influenza to be treated. They selected those who would have to be left behind. Later, they fetched mugs of tea from the makeshift kitchen and sat side-by-side on a log. She touched his arm, then sucked in her breath in alarm.

"You have a temperature, my love."

"I'm afraid so." He looked at her with a wan smile. "If it is influenza you will leave me behind."

"Never! I would not let him force me to do that. It may be malaria, so take some quinine at once."

"I think not, Amanda. I can feel the inflammation in my lungs."

"At least change into dry clothes."

—•—

Next morning Karl's fever was worse and he was unable to march. Although he asked to be left behind he was put in a *machila* at the orders of the Colonel. It was another long and arduous march, with the Livingstone Mountains looming to their left, shrouded in clouds, and generating showers that soaked their clothing.

When they reached the evening camp-site Mandy hurriedly changed Karl into dry clothes, his only other set, and laid him under the shelter of a tent. He was delirious, muttering German words that she did not understand.

Surgeon-Major Kraute came to see him. "I fear he has the influenza. He cannot travel tomorrow."

"Sir, we can't abandon him here."

"We have no alternative, Miss Spaight. As you know, the Colonel insists that we go forward. He will not stop for a single day."

"Then I will stay with him..."

"It is not permitted."

She broke into tears for the first time. "I will speak to the Colonel," she sobbed.

"As you wish."

—•—

Von Lettow sat at his folding table looking at maps, using a simple magnifying glass. He looked up at her, bleary-eyed, as she approached.

"How is he, my dear?"

"Not good, sir. We think he has influenza."

"I see." He paused, looking at her with a sympathetic expression. "I'm so sorry – we have to leave him behind."

"I want to stay with him."

He looked at her steadily, then back at his maps. Finally, he stood up and called for his *aide de camp*. "Miss Spaight, do you remember that I once said I would find a way to repay you for your dedicated nursing? Well, the time has come. My re-payment is to permit you to stay with Dr Niemeyer."

His ADC, Lt Herman Weikert, came up to the tent and saluted, nodding to Mandy.

"Weikert, I want you to assist *Fraulein* Spaight. As you may know, Dr Niemeyer is too sick to travel tomorrow – he has to remain in this camp until he recovers. I have given permission for *Fraulein* Spaight to remain with him. Please advise Dr Kraute, and the other medical staff. Also, arrange for three *askaris* to stay behind with them. Choose trustworthy men, and, if possible ChiNyanja speakers."

He dismissed Weikert and said to Mandy. "My dear, we need to consider two outcomes. One – that Dr Karl recovers – you can then follow our route, though I doubt you would catch up with us – we move quickly, as you know. At any rate, you would find camp-sites and perhaps some food. Second – if the doctor should succumb – you should bury him and hasten to find us."

When Mandy started to sob, he held up his hand. "I'm so sorry, but we must face these things. You should do your utmost to find either my column or a British unit. Do you promise me?"

—•—

50

Former German East Africa – November 1918

Mandy stood outside Karl's tent at dawn, watching the Column march away. Colonel von Lettow-Vorbeck waved to her as he passed; Dr Kraute raised his hand in a salute that said, You should not have been allowed to stay behind.

With her were three sentry *askaris*, two other African soldiers who were too sick to march, and their wives. They had enough food to last three days, all that the Column quartermaster could spare. There was a village a mile away but the column had already stripped it of all its food.

She returned back into Karl's tent. His fever was raging, his body radiating heat. She used a wet cloth to wipe away the perspiration, and muttered words of encouragement that she knew he could not hear.

She spoke to the *askaris,* all of whom knew her. The senior man was a corporal, with whom she could speak fluently in ChiNyanja. He had joined the KAR as a young man, but when his regiment was disbanded before the war he walked north and enlisted with the Germans. His name was Abel, a Christian, educated at a mission near Nkhata Bay. He reminded her that Karl had incised a boil on his leg, and that she had dressed the wound.

"We must gather firewood, Abel," she instructed. "I would like a central fire for boiling water and cooking, and three outer fires to frighten off wild animals."

"*Inde, dona,*" he replied. "Also, I will send the women to fetch water." The column had left a cooking pot and a ladle. Each of them had a jam tin for drinking and a tin plate.

"I need to attend to the doctor and the sick *askaris*. You take charge of guarding the camp, and make sure the women boil the water and cook enough *nsima* for today."

"*Inde, dona.*" He saluted and left her.

—•—

By evening she knew that Karl was dying. She tried to make him drink water, but he had no strength to swallow; it dribbled down his cheek. She barely noticed the fall of darkness and the emergence of guttering firelight. Abel brought her *nsima*, and she ate it with one hand while holding Karl's with her other.

Near midnight she noticed he had stopped breathing. She checked for his pulse and could find nothing. She sat on her heels and allowed herself to sob, then kissed him and covered his face with his thin blanket.

"Goodbye my darling Karl. Perhaps I will come to join you soon."

—•—

She went out to the fire and found Abel squatting there, gazing into the low flames. He stood up.

"He has died?"

She nodded.

Abel bowed his head. "I am sorry, *dona*. He was a good man. All of us knew he wanted to care for us."

"Yes, that was what he wanted to do. Please ask the men to dig his grave in the morning."

"Where shall we dig it, *dona*?"

She wiped the tears off her face with the back of her hand. "We must find a large tree. When this fighting is finished I want to come back and find this place – to find his grave and put a proper – you know, Abel – a large stone."

"I know, *dona*. We will find a big tree. The village near here is called Chipembere's."

"*Chipembere?* Rhinoceros?"

He smiled. "Yes, *dona*." He used his hand to describe the curve of a rhino's horn. "The chief must have been a big strong man."

—•—

At dawn she went with Abel to find a grave site. There were no outstanding trees in the *miombo* forest, but they found a stately *mukwa (Pterocarpus angolensis),* with a pleasing shape. Abel fetched the other men, those who were able to walk, and they dug a grave. Fortunately the soil was sandy, but she stopped them when it was three feet deep because they were exhausted.

They carried Karl in his blanket and laid him in the grave. Mandy instructed the men to fill it with earth, and then tamp it down. There was an area nearby with small rocks and stones that were ideal for covering the grave, to prevent wild animals from digging it up. She borrowed Abel's bayonet and carved a cross in the bark of the tree.

"Which direction is the village?" she asked. They pointed and she muttered, "Nearly due west. So I will find Chipembere's village and walk east and find this tree. How far, Abel?"

Abel consulted the others and they agreed the village was about ten minutes walk away. She nodded.

"Time to get ready."

—•—

When they returned to the camp site they discovered that one of the women was running a high fever. She was coughing and when Mandy checked her with Karl's stethoscope she could hear the gurgling of fluid in her lungs.

Mandy said to Abel, "I think she has the same illness that killed Dr Karl. Can we carry her?"

Abel looked doubtful. "We are not strong, *dona*."

"Then we must stay here."

"It will be more difficult to find the Column if we stay longer."

"It can't be helped."

Abel looked sheepish. "The other two *askaris* want to go to their homes..."

"But the Colonel..."

"I know, *dona*. But they have been away from their homes for over a year. They know that if they run away there is no one left to go after them."

"Should I speak to them?"

"You can try, but I think they will leave today."

—•—

Before Mandy could speak to the two *askaris* they had gone. She spent the remainder of her day looking after the sick woman and the other patients. The woman was barely conscious. Mandy concentrated on making her drink, and wiping away the perspiration from her fever.

It was almost dusk when she noticed that the woman had died. She checked for vital signs, then called for Abel.

"It is too late to dig her grave. We will do it tomorrow, at first light." She looked at him, trying to judge his mood. "I hope you will not run away, Abel."

He was vehement. "I will not. After we have buried this woman we will try to find the Column."

"What about the two sick *askaris* and their wives? Can their wives take care of them? The one with the bad leg will soon be able to walk. The other has malaria, and he is past the crisis."

"Yes, we can leave them and hurry to join the Column."

"Abel, if we meet a British patrol, what will you do? I don't want you to fight them."

He laughed. "I will not fight, *dona*. I will surrender. What will they do with me?"

"They will make you a prisoner, and you will be looked after, until the war is ended. Then you will be freed."

"After the war, will they keep me in prison because I fought with the Germans?"

"Oh, no. Only if you committed a crime, and you haven't done that, have you."

"No, *dona*."

—•—

They buried the woman in a grave near Dr Karl Niemeyer. Mandy was relieved to see that his grave was undisturbed. It took them an hour to dig the new grave, taking it in turns to wield the small *badza*. She carved a second cross on the tree.

Back at the camp they left almost everything with the two *askaris* and their wives, packing only their personal possessions in their shoulder bags. Mandy was filling her water bottle when she saw Abel raise his hand to command silence.

She heard voices. They would not be villagers in the forest. Whether they were German or British she wanted to meet them. She thought about firing her revolver, but the sound would cause alarm and would be difficult to locate, so she decided to wait.

The voices came nearer; it sounded like a large group.

"Halloo!" she shouted.

The voices went silent.

"Who are you?" she shouted.

"Who are you?" came back – an African speaking English.

"We are..." She could not think what to say.

"Send a man with a white flag so that we can know who you are."

"Yes," she called. "Wait."

Mandy turned to Abel. "I will go forward. You wait here. Put your rifle down." When he hesitated, she explained, "If they are German soldiers you will not need it. If they are British soldiers they want to see you unarmed."

She took her handkerchief that was barely white, and tied it to one of the tent sticks. "I'm coming now!" she shouted and started to walk towards where the voices came from.

There was no path, but the grass was sparse between the trees. She had a fright when a dove flew clattering up from near her feet. Then the silence became ominous.

"We are here," said a voice, not far away.

She saw a figure beside a tree. A rifle was aiming at her.

"I am unarmed," she called, her voice shaking.

"Come forward, slowly."

The man emerged, an African soldier with a fez and tattered khaki shorts and shirt, with sergeant's stripes. "Who are you?" he demanded.

"I am British. I was a prisoner of the Germans."

He lowered his rifle. "Are there others?"

She told him and he beckoned her forward. Other *askaris* emerged from the scrub, about a dozen.

"My name is Amanda Spaight," she said. "I am from Zomba, and I speak ChiNyanja."

The sergeant smiled. "*Muri bwanje, dona.*"

"*Ndiribueno, zicomo,*" she replied. "*Kaya enu?*"

They exchanged salutations, grinning in the relief of tension. Then the sergeant said, "My lieutenant is coming. I have sent a soldier to tell him."

—•—

She was talking to the sergeant when the main body of British soldiers arrived. They were all Africans except a young white man, with a second lieutenant's single pip on the epaulettes of his khaki tunic. He was short and rotund, his puttee-covered legs stumpy and thick. He removed his pith helmet to reveal a balding head, shining with sweat. He stuck out a beefy hand.

"Rogers," he said. "Derek Rogers, First KAR."

She introduced herself. "I was taken prisoner in September last year. I was with von Lettow's Column until three days ago."

His eyes widened. "Good Lord! Where are they now?" He looked around, as if expecting to see them.

"They will be fifty or sixty miles away." She explained how she had been left behind with the doctor and *askaris*, and the women.

She led them back to the camp. Abel was nowhere to be seen. She asked one of the sick *askaris* where he was and he replied that Abel had run away, saying that he did not want to be taken prisoner.

"How come you speak the lingo?" asked Rogers.

She explained, then added, "What shall I do now? There's only me and these sick people."

Rogers frowned. "My orders are to patrol – for another two days – then return to Fife..."

"Fife? Are we near Fife?"

"Two days march."

She burst into tears. After a moment, when she recovered, she apologised. "It's been a long haul. We've walked over a thousand miles."

"I'm sorry, Miss Spaight. You must be exhausted. Under the circumstances I will ask my sergeant to continue the patrol, while I escort you back to Fife."

—•—

As the Rogers patrol approached Fife they could hear sounds of rifle fire and the explosions of mortars. He ordered a halt and beckoned to Mandy.

"Before I left camp they were expecting an attack from the Huns. Seems to have started. You had better wait here. I'll try to find out what's happening."

Mandy noticed that he gave all his orders in English through the sergeant, and when she mentioned this, he said, "I've only been out here for five weeks – haven't had time to learn the lingo."

"I can help you."

He looked at her dubiously.

"Derek, I was a prisoner of the Germans. Don't you trust me?"

"Of course." He smiled sheepishly. "Well, I'll ask for your help if I need it. I've sent some men to find out what's happening."

They sat down to wait, and Mandy fell asleep. She woke to the sound of voices. The small patrol that Rogers sent had returned with a prisoner, a German *askari*, who had been slightly wounded. Because the lieutenant could not interrogate he asked Mandy to help.

The prisoner had a flesh wound in his thigh, and she used Rogers' first aid kit to clean and dress the wound.

"What tribe are you?" she asked in ChiNyanja.

"I am Angoni," he replied, cautiously.

"Do you understand me if I speak ChiNyanja?"

He nodded.

"Were you with the main *WaGermani* column – with the Colonel?"

"I was, *dona*."

"So was I. I was a prisoner."

"I know. I saw you in the clinic. Did you escape?"

"No. I was left behind with sick and wounded. Then we were found by this patrol. Where is the German column now?"

The man looked over his shoulder. "We attacked Fife, *dona*, but the British were too strong, so we were told to march to Mwenzo Mission."

"So, where is the Column going?"

"They did not tell us, *dona.* I heard officers talking about marching to Kasama. They said it was the main depot where supplies were stored, so it would be a good place to raid."

Rogers was growing impatient. "What's he saying?"

She told him.

"My God! Kasama?" Then he started shouting to his men to get ready to march. He turned back to Mandy. "Thank you, Miss Spaight. We must hasten to Fife."

—•—

The patrol was welcomed by several pickets to whom they shouted passwords, before reaching the entrenchments on the outskirts of Fife. Mandy's heart was pounding as she saw European officers, who came forward to shake her hand. She was led to a surprisingly young Lt Col Hawkins, who plied her with tea and biscuits.

"There's a Captain Spaight here," he said. "Any relation?"

"Drew?"

"Yes. That's him."

She burst into tears, burying her face in her hands, as she heard the Colonel send for her brother.

—•—

The German column had indeed headed for Kasama, reaching the town on November 12, 1918. There von Lettow received a telegram, carried by a despatch rider with a white flag.

> *To be sent to Colonel von Lettow Vorbeck. The Prime Minister has announced that an armistice was signed at 0500 hours on November 11 and that hostilities will cease at 1100 hours on November 11. I am ordering my troops to cease hostilities forthwith, unless attacked, and of course I conclude that you will do the same. Conditions of the armistice will be*

forwarded to you as soon as I receive them. I suggest you remain where you are to facilitate communications.
Signed: General van Deventer.

On the following day the Colonel received another telegram:

13.11.18: Send following to Colonel von Lettow Vorbeck under white flag: War Office London telegraphs that Clause 17 of the armistice signed by the German Government provides for unconditional surrender of all German forces operating in East Africa within one month from November 11th.

The telegram went on to say that all prisoners should be handed over, and that the German forces should proceed without delay to Abercorn.

—•—

Drew was among the officers who gathered in Abercorn for the surrender ceremony. When he had an opportunity he went up to von Lettow and introduced himself.

"Colonel, I wanted to thank you for looking after my sister..." When von Lettow looked puzzled, he added, "Amanda Spaight, a nurse, she was captured and walked with your column."

Then the Colonel smiled. "Of course. Miss Spaight. How is she?"

"She's well; she recovered from her influenza. I'm sorry – your Dr Karl died."

Von Lettow shook his head. "Poor Niemeyer. A good man. The influenza epidemic is no respecter of people; it strikes hard at those who fight it. Thank you, Captain."

They saluted each other.

—•—

51

Long Valley Farm, Salisbury, Rhodesia – July 1919

The year 1919 was an auspicious one for the Russell and Spaight families. Drew Spaight and Clare Onslow married at Long Valley Farm, near Salisbury, Rhodesia, thus further uniting the two families that were already related to each other. The ceremony was held in the Presbyterian Church in Salisbury and the reception at the farm.

Colonel Martin Russell, DSO and bar, watched the guests assembling on the lawn and remembered his birthday in 1914, his forty-eighth. Now he was fifty-three, greying and gaunt from his years of campaigning. In a country full of former soldiers his record was outstanding – the Matabele War, the Mashonaland Rebellion, the Boer War and finally the Great War – the war to end all wars.

It was the time for speeches. Over a hundred guests gathered round the steps leading up the verandah, on which Martin Russell stood. The best man had spoken, followed by the groom. Now it was the turn of the father of the bride.

"Most of you know," he said, "that after Clare and Drew have honeymooned they will go to Nyasaland to start their new life together. Both our families will be making a motor trek, through Portuguese East to Nyasaland. Helen has insisted that our family should go – they want to see some of the places that Clare and I have been to, during the war years."

"It's a four hundred mile journey, on roads that are rough or almost non-existent, and we have to cross the Zambesi River at Tete. We will have three Thorneycroft lorries, for the twelve of us – plus two servants – and, of course, the newly-weds will have plenty of baggage." He paused for laughter.

"When we reach Zomba, we have another wedding to celebrate – between Gavin Henderson and Kirsty Spaight." He noticed the couple standing together and pointed them out, to great applause.

Everyone knew about the impending journey. It had even distracted the families from their wedding preparations.

"I think you're more interested in how to get those lorries to work than you are in the wedding," Clare had accused, only half joking.

The men, who were less interested in costumes and procedures, talked endlessly about mileages and fuel, and about what spare parts to take.

—•—

"A penny for them, Martin," said his cousin Alan, coming to join him after the cake was cut. "Your thoughts, old man."

"Oh, I was thinking of our trip – what else. It's going to be an adventure, Alan, something I'll really enjoy."

"Are you sure you haven't had enough of trekking and camping?"

Martin laughed. "This will be different, I hope – the two families together, three lorries – it ought to be great fun. We'll have Moses and his son to look after us. No time constraints." He laughed. "Most important of all – no enemies to attack us."

"Just mosquitoes and the tsetse flies."

They both laughed, and a few heads turned.

"What do you think we can average, Martin?"

"Ten miles an hour? At that rate we would take thirty-five hours, say four days – if we don't take a day off in Tete..."

"If we don't break down." Alan drank some of his beer; he did not care for champagne, even the expensive stuff that Martin provided for the wedding. "Actually, it would be fun to spend a day or two in Tete. The place has a lot of history."

"The only stretch of the journey that concerns me," said Martin, "is between Nyamapanda and Tete. When I went prospecting with Tom Ellsworth, before the war, we crossed the border at Nyamapanda, and it was just a rough track through the bush. I've heard it's improved since then."

"Let's hope so. At least there'll be no rivers to cross, until we get to the Zambesi."

Martin laughed. "My boys are so excited they can hardly contain themselves. They talk of nothing else. Speaking of the devils – here they are."

Ben, Richard and David came to join the two men. They were now sixteen, fourteen and twelve. All were tall and gangling, dressed in long trousers for the reception, but longing to shed their ties and change into shorts.

"Dad, Ben says we may see lions on the trip," said Richard, "but I said they only move around at night."

"Well, we may see lions, because, although they generally do their hunting at night, they usually lie up in groups – prides – in the heat of the day. So we'll be looking out for them."

"And," said Ben, "David is afraid the lorries may sink in the Zambesi River."

Martin smiled. "It would be bad luck if all three sank! We'll take them over on the ferry one at a time – to make sure. You see, the Portuguese have built a pontoon ferry, large enough to take a lorry – plus some people. If it tips over, which is very unlikely, we'll swim."

"What about the crocs?" piped David, whose voice was breaking.

"They prefer smaller rivers," replied Alan soothingly, "where animals come to drink."

David looked doubtful, and ran off to eat more cake.

Ben said, "Dad, I heard one of your friends say there may be another war."

"I wonder who said that. Well, son, there will always be wars. It's in man's nature to fight wars. Men will always find a reason, whether it's religion, or wealth – like the Boer War – or territory – like the Matabele War. So I think there will be more wars. I just hope you do not get involved. What do you think, Alan?"

"I agree with you. It's inevitable, but let's hope it won't be on a scale like this one."

—•—

Mandy and Kirsty, with Clare the bride, stood together watching the guests. Mandy drew their attention to Martin, Alan, and the Russell boys.

"Look at them; what's the betting they're talking about cars, or shooting..."

"...or the journey to Nyasaland."

"Of course. Men! Well, you've got a long journey starting very soon, Clare. Looking forward to it?"

"Oh yes," replied Clare. "The best thing is that, although I'm leaving my home, I'm not leaving the family. It's so good that they're all coming with us. I'm looking forward to showing them the farm, and our house, and Zomba, and the mountain..."

—•—

Helen was the one who had spent least time thinking about the journey, because she had planned the wedding. Like most mothers of brides she had mixed feelings: happy to see her daughter with an admirable young man, but sad to know that she would be moving to another country. Helen knew that one of the reasons for the road trip was to show everyone that they would not be so far apart.

She knew she had aged during the war. It had been hard running the farm while Martin was away, even with a manager, and advice from Tom Ellsworth. She had worried constantly about her husband and her daughter, hearing news of the casualties, and seeing the sick and wounded at the hospital in Salisbury, where she and Flora had visited the wards.

She noticed her husband in animated conversation with Alan, and was glad that the two cousins shared such a strong brotherly friendship. Had Martin been faithful to her during the war? Their only contact had been weekly letters, and he had not mentioned any women, other than Jess and her daughters, and of course Clare.

She glanced at Jess, who was talking to Drew. Surely Martin would not have had an affair with Jess. She was pleasant enough, short and dark, with a lively demeanour. But Jess was so obviously in love with her husband. How about Mandy? There she was, talking to her sister and Clare. She was less a girl and more a woman, but that had made her even more alluring, Helen thought. She had lost weight, no doubt due to her privations as a prisoner of the Germans, and her bones were evident in the structure of her face, but that gave her more character. She was not just pretty, she was beautiful.

There were stories of Mandy having an affair with a young officer who was wounded. She'd heard mention of a German doctor, but that did not seem likely – people did gossip.

The younger sister, Kirsty, had also become more good-looking, having lost most of her teenage plumpness. She seemed to have a keener mind that her sister. Nevertheless, she had noticed Kirsty putting her husband down on more than one occasion. He'd taken it in good part, but surely she wouldn't have done that if she'd had a genuine affection for him.

—•—

Drew and Clare drove off in Martin's car, towing tin cans and old boots, waving in response to the well-wishing cheers of their families and friends. They spent the first night of their honeymoon at Meikles Hotel in Salisbury, before setting off for the Russell's cottage at Inyanga, in the Eastern Highlands. The journey took five hours, along the five thousand foot watershed to Rusape, and then rising another thousand feet to the misty purple mountains.

Before the road reached the tiny settlement at Inyanga it branched south on a track leading to the Mtarazi Falls, where a stream plunged in a slender spectacular drop into the Honde Valley.

They arrived at the cottage in the early afternoon. It was already starting to grow cold, and they hurried to unload the car and stow in the cabin the things they had brought with them. While Clare cooked a pot of curried chicken and vegetables on a portable gas stove, Drew built a fire in a pit about ten yards in front of the cabin, in the centre of the clearing.

After supper they sat together, hand in hand, in front of the fire, talking sporadically. Sparks flew up into a sky spangled with stars. They both felt the immensity of their location, far from other habitation. They also sensed a certain loneliness and apprehension. Their isolation contrasted so much with the warmth and companionship of their combined families.

Next morning, as soon as they woke, they walked to the edge of a gorge and looked down at the Pungwe Falls, where the river, a thousand feet below them, plunged over a cliff and along a narrow gorge. The air was scented with wood-smoke and from the pine forest around them. The cries of kites echoed in the gorge, swirling up to them. It was a primitive African scene, full of primeval beauty.

They spent the morning cleaning up the yard – it was three months since the Russells' last visit. Some broken branches were added to the woodpile, and weeds pulled out. Drew chopped more firewood from the plentiful supply of dead branches in the forest nearly.

After lunch they drove the three miles to the Mtarazi Falls, When Drew first visited the falls with the Russells, as a schoolboy, he asked how high they were.

"About two and a half thousand feet," replied Martin.

"That must make them one of the highest in the world?"

"The Angel Falls in Venezuela must be higher..."

There was not much water in the river now, it was more like a large stream, and its falling plume was light enough to be blown into clouds of spray, watering the plants clinging to the glistening rock face. The cliff had been scoured over the centuries, as if some giant hand had scraped it clean.

Although at weekends a few visitors came to admire the view, the place was now deserted. They walked upstream from the falls, where a succession of pools lay among rocks. The surrounding valley was grass clad, with no trees, and only a few clumps of aloes.

Sitting on a rock they enjoyed the warmth of the sun and watching the water cascading through the rocks.

"Let's have a swim," announced Clare. "See who's the quickest into the water." She looked back up the slope to the road, which was several hundred yards away, then pulled off her shirt and shorts.

"Don't stop there," said Drew.

She shyly took off her bra and underpants and stepped naked into the largest pool, then backed away.

"It's freezing!" she squealed.

Drew admired his young wife's body as she prodded the water with her toe before wading in and sinking down into the deepest section of the pool. She rose in a shower of droplets, her skin pink, and hurried towards him.

"Your turn."

"Do I have to?" he asked.

"Yes, you do." She smacked him playfully. "But I warn you – it's icy cold."

After his almost painful immersion they lay side by side on the warm rock, glancing occasionally to check that no one was nearby. They did not to speak much, but knew they were deeply in love.

—•—

52

Rhodesia to Nyasaland – July/August 1919

The convoy set off on a cold winter morning at the end of July. Each of the three Thorneycroft lorries carried four people. One vehicle belonged to the Russells, and the other two were newly delivered for the Spaights to take up to Nyasaland. They were Type 'J' four-ton lorries of the kind that had been used extensively in the war. The six litre internal combustion engine gave ample power, and the transmission and suspension were well-proven in all conditions. The solid rubber tyres meant that punctures were not an issue; they had double wheels at the rear.

Martin and Alan had spent several weeks modifying the vehicles. Each had well-padded front and rear bench seats, on which passengers could sleep at night. The main bed of the lorry was fitted with a canvas roof over wire cage walls. This would enable additional passengers to sleep in the back, safe from marauding animals.

They had to carry twenty gallons of fuel, enough for two hundred miles; more would be purchased in Tete for the second half of the journey. Water was carried in double canvas-skin bags. All three lorries were fitted with front-mounted winches.

During trials they were reminded of a problem experienced during the war. The air often eddied into the bed of the lorry, so that the passengers choked on the exhaust fumes, and contents were soon coated with dust. The two cousins experimented with baffles to divert air from the front of the vehicle, creating enough draft to prevent the suction phenomenon. They also turned the exhaust pipes upwards to vent well above the canvas roof.

—•—

They planned to set off as early as possible, but the farewells and last minute remembered tasks meant that the convoy rolled out of Long Valley Farm just after nine o'clock. They lunched at Mrewa and spent the night at the travellers' hotel in Mtoko, where they booked several rooms.

The three lorries parked side by side in front of the hotel. Moses slept in one, while his son, Petrus, slept in the other, somewhat to the amusement of the hotel's night watchman, who thought the Africans ought to be in the servants' quarters provided by the hotel. Martin slept in the front of the middle lorry; the three boys and Gavin were in the rear. In three hotel rooms were Drew and Clare, the newly-weds, Helen, Mandy and Kirsty, and Alan and Jess.

It was a bitterly cold night; the water in the hotel night-stand basins froze. The air was redolent of wood smoke from cooking fires, faintly tinged with the odour of petrol from the lorries. The boys were so excited that it was a long time before they fell asleep.

—•—

The next leg of the journey took them to Nyamapanda, on the border between Southern Rhodesia and Portuguese East Africa. Here the road changed from a graded gravelled surface to a rough sandy track that wound through the scrubby bush, roughly following the watersheds. It was over a hundred miles from Nyamapanda to Tete, and slow going.

They stopped for lunch, and again for the night, making camp beside a stream. Martin and Alan were nervous about sparks igniting the petrol stored on the lorries, so they built the fires twenty yards distant, one central and three satellites to ward off animals. They had a half-drum grill and used embers from the main fire to fuel it, cooking steaks and sausages.

They all slept in the lorries, secure in the cabins and wire-caged rears. Moses and Petrus were in one lorry, with Martin and his sons, Drew and Clare shared another with Kirsty and Mandy, while Helen and Jess were with Alan and Gavin in the third.

—•—

"Is that a lion?" Ben nudged his father.

"Yes, I think so. Moses?"

"Inde, bwana?"

"Nkanga?"

"Inde, bwana."

"Moses thinks so too."

The lions were hunting together. Martin imagined the lionesses communicating to each other with their coughs, as they slunk though the bush, circling their prey in tightening rings of threat until one of them pounced for the *coup de grace*.

"Could they come here, Dad?" asked David in a querulous tone that made Martin smile.

"They wouldn't come here," he said, "because of the fires..."

"Unless they are very hungry," added Ben.

—•—

By midday they reached Tete and saw the great Zambesi River. Here it flowed majestically, half a mile wide, through wide floodplains, cultivated by the local Africans, who lived in scattered villages of grass huts. The town was a strange mixture of villas, tin-roofed sheds and African huts. It had been a Portuguese settlement since 1531, becoming a market centre for trade in gold and ivory.

They drove straight to the bank to investigate the ferry, a large metal pontoon, buoyed with forty-four gallon oil drums and powered by a diesel engine.

Alan drove the first lorry down the steep bank and onto the two wide wooden planks that spanned the gap onto the ferry, moving cautiously across, watched by all the others. Only when he'd parked the lorry at the further end of the pontoon and chocked the wheels did the passengers board. Priority was given to the Europeans, but an additional dozen African passengers were permitted to board, carrying their baggage, some of it produce, including gourds and vegetables, bananas, and chickens in baskets.

It took thirty minutes for the ferry to cross, aiming upstream to allow for the drift downstream caused by a strong current. The bank on the far side was steep and sandy, and Alan feared the lorry would not be able to climb off the ferry. He paid the ferry operator to wait while Moses and Petrus gathered branches from dead trees along the bank that had been washed down in floods. They laid the branches as a corduroy to give the lorry's wheels traction. Alan revved the engine and rushed the lorry off the pontoon and up the bank. Relieved, he left it in the charge of Moses and Petrus and returned to help with the next crossing.

It all went without a hitch until the third lorry stalled on the steep bank on the far side. Alan hauled on the hand-brake, while Gavin, Drew and Martin placed chocks behind the wheels. They then attached a wire hawser to the winch of a lorry above the bank, re-started the engine and hauled the vehicle up the bank.

It had taken four hours to get the convoy across the river, and they were well satisfied. They drove for another hour, to get into sparsely inhabited countryside before making a camp.

—•—

That evening, sitting around the camp fire, they discussed the day's events.

"The Portuguese are quite different to us, aren't they?" said Drew. "What do you think of them, Pa?"

"They are different," replied Alan. "The Germans ran right through them when they invaded their territory. They had no stomach for a fight – just turned tail and ran. Mind you, the types they send out here are not the same calibre as our administrators. But don't forget," he added, in his quiet conciliatory way, "they came here two hundred years before we did. They had the seafarers, the navigators and the know-how, to find the Zambesi and explore it, right up here to Tete, and beyond."

"Why didn't the British push them out – at least along the river?" asked Kirsty. "Then Rhodesia and Nyasaland would have had access to the sea."

"Rhodes wanted to," replied Martin, "but it would have provoked international disputes and war. We were too late – as Alan said, they got here first."

"What's that?" squeaked Richard. He had been looking beyond the firelight, and had seen a pair of eyes.

Everyone stopped talking.

"*Nyama ndi chiyani?*" asked Alan of Moses, who was sitting nearby.

"*Kaya. Kapena fisi.*"

"He thinks it might be a hyena."

A few seconds later they heard a lion cough. It was perhaps half a mile away, and was answered by another.

"*Nkanga,*" said Moses.

"Shouldn't we get in the trucks?" asked Helen nervously.

Alan stood up. "Yes. Better to be safe. We don't know their predilections in this area." He picked up his rifle, which was beside him.

"*Ukachula nkanga kwera mtengo.*" said Alan. As the Nyanja say, 'If you mention a lion, climb a tree'."

They took their belongings and moved quickly into their allotted places in the vehicles, Alan and Martin last, facing outwards with the rifles at the ready. The coughing, interspersed with an occasional short roar, came closer.

"Are you sure they can't get in here?" asked Richard plaintively.

"You're quite safe. Just listen to them. They're talking to each other – probably youngsters herding some buck towards the lionesses, who will do the killing."

—•—

The last two days of the journey were comparatively uneventful. The formalities at the Nyasaland border post were minimal. Thereafter, the graded dirt road wound through hilly country into the Shire Highlands. In places it was quite steep, but the traction was good.

They spent the last night at Cholo, with the Williamson family, for whom Gavin worked before the war. It was they who had notified him about a nearby estate, and he'd put in a bid for it, using funds sent by his parents in England.

"It's a fine little tea estate," said Jon Williamson, a portly Yorkshireman who had been a tea planter in India. "Just large enough to have your own factory, but not too costly."

They sat on the verandah after supper, looking out towards Mlanje Mountain. The women were unpacking, tired and ready for bed, but the men wanted a last pipe and a whisky before turning in.

"What are the markets like?" asked Alan.

"Not bad. Of course our quality will never be as good as India's or Sri Lanka's..."

"... and Kenya's?"

"They have a better climate too. No, we must go for yields, to compensate for the lower quality. We can do it."

"There's something very special about a tea estate," said Alan, musing. "I suppose because you're usually higher up in altitude, with more rain, and the pruned bushes are so attractive."

"There's always that tea aroma," added Gavin. "It spices the air. I'm really looking forward to having my own place. I know I'll get lots of help and advice from Jon."

"All of us here are delighted that you're joining us," said Williamson.

—•—

They reached *Khundalila* farm in the early afternoon, tired but triumphant after the long road trip. The lorries had been reliable and economical, and all the passengers enjoyed themselves, especially the three Russell boys, who soon ran up to the water tank to swim. Mandy and Kirsty went to the stables to check on the horses, with the Ridgebacks in tow. Alan and Martin drove the car down to the Likengala River, to see how the seedbeds were progressing. They took Goodwill with them, and he told them about the happenings on the farm during the month they were away.

At supper that evening they toasted their safe arrival and made plans to take the visitors for a trip up Zomba Mountain.

—•—

53

Zomba, Nyasaland – August 1919

"Guess who's coming to the wedding," Jess announced as she was reading her mail.

They were all sitting round the dining room table, drinking tea and coffee after breakfast; it was a time to their make arrangements, when they were all together.

"It's Roly." She read: "'Major Roly Benting-Smith, DSO, has pleasure in accepting your kind invitation to the wedding of Gavin Henderson and Kirsty Spaight."

She read from the letter:

> *Dear Alan and Jess,*
>
> *I married Emily Fountaine in June. I had known her for years. We decided to visit mutual friends in South Africa – thought about a trip to Nyasaland, and then received your kind invitation.*
>
> *H.E. has kindly invited us to stay for a week – Lady Smith is an old friend of my mother.*
>
> *We look forward to seeing you soon.*
>
> *Your old friend*
> *Roly*

"You remember her, Drew," added Jess. "Sir George brought Emily here to shoot before the war. You took them out didn't you?"

Drew swallowed uncomfortably. "Yes, I remember. She came to Zomba with her mother."

Jess continued: "I remember Roly saying that his parents were friends of the Fountaines – Emily's parents. That was how he got the position of ADC to the Governor in 1914. Emily's father was some high-up in the War Office – they were in Cape Town when Roly was in hospital there."

"Everyone is getting married except me," said Mandy brightly.

"Well, you keep turning them down," remarked Jess. "All those dashing young officers – right through the war. Even the man in question – Roly..."

"There was never anything between us," said Mandy. "I felt rather sorry for him, especially when he was wounded. Besides, it wasn't a good time for marrying..."

"But it was for making plans – as Drew and I did," added Clare.

Mandy sighed. "You're right. I suppose I let my chances pass me by. Now Kirsty is beating me to the altar."

—•—

Gavin and Kirsty married in St Andrew's Church, Zomba. Kirsty's bridesmaid was her sister; Gavin's best man was Drew. The reception was at *Khundalila* farm, attended by about two hundred guests, including many of the planter families and senior civil servants. Gavin's parents came out from England.

It was a fine winter afternoon, a cloudless sky and warm sunshine, as the guests gathered on the lawn in front of the house. Trestle tables were laid with sandwiches and cakes, and the servants circulated with trays of champagne and wine. Moses manned the bar table, dispensing beer and whisky.

The wedding cake was brought out by Goodwill, resplendent in his KAR uniform with campaign medals. Then Drew made his speech as best man, nervous, but well rehearsed and not needing prompting from Clare.

He alluded to Gavin's background, welcoming the parents, who had travelled all the way from England. He told about Gavin's exploits on Lake Nyasa and Lake Tanganyika.

"He may be unique...," said Drew, "well, of course he is, but I mean that he took part in actions on both lakes. He was also our interrogator in the Murray Column, and was wounded at Iringa. He received another wound, but... Anyway, I'm proud to have such a fine man as my brother-in-law. I only wish he could play his rugby for Zomba and not Cholo!"

"My sister Kirsty has proved a wonderful daughter to my parents, and I'm certain will make Gavin a superlative wife. As most of you know, she served as a nurse throughout the war, and was promoted to the rank of Ward Sister – she tells me that she'll continue nursing at Limbe Hospital. Mandy and I could not have asked for a better sister – a great friend and valued counsellor."

Gavin followed with a short speech thanking the bride's parents for the wedding, and his parents for coming out from England.

"I'm glad Kirsty and I have been able to show my parents the farm that we are buying – with their generous help. They now know that we have a good way of life here. It's different from England, and we lack some of the civilisation and culture of my home country. But this country makes up for it, with its fine climate, its opportunities for people like us to farm – and we have a good social life. Most of all, we enjoy the fellowship of our fellow planters and all those who live in this fine country."

—•—

Mandy was slightly alarmed when Roly and Emily approached her. She was interested to see how he had changed. His youthful ebullience had matured into a calmer self-assurance that she liked. She even wondered if she would have found this man more to her liking. Not that it mattered, because he now had a wife on his arm, pretty, and proud to be with her tall army officer.

"So, Major Benting-Smith," said Mandy. "When do you expect to be made a colonel?"

He laughed, the bray now muted. "It takes longer in peace time, Mandy. If there's no war it might take another ten years."

"Surely not as long as that," interjected Emily.

"Perhaps." Roly glanced round the throng of guests. "This has been a fine wedding. I'm so glad that we were able to attend. We've enjoyed meeting old friends and acquaintances, haven't we, Em?"

She nodded. "We haven't spoken to your brother and his wife yet."

Mandy caught Clare's eye and beckoned to her, who in turn caught Drew's arm and led him over. Mandy introduced Emily to her sister-in-law, and added, "Of course you and Drew met before the war."

"We did indeed," said Emily, thinking that the young man was even more appealing than she remembered.

Clare appraised Emily, wondering what, if anything, had transpired between her and Drew. He had not mentioned her, but she had discovered that Drew had many casual girl-friends before the war, so she was not jealous of this young woman on Roly's arm.

"So sorry we couldn't come to your wedding," said Roly. "We couldn't get up there in time."

—•—

54

Nyasaland/former German East African/Portuguese East Africa – January1920

Mandy begged her father to take her to the place where Karl was buried. Riding with him one afternoon, a week after the wedding, she felt unusually nostalgic, enjoying the fading light and the sounds of birds settling to their roosts.

"I need to go back to put a proper grave in place."

Alan nodded. "I know you wouldn't ask if it wasn't important. Was he very special?"

She burst into tears. "I was in love with him, Pa. He's the only man I've ever truly loved."

For the first time she told her parents the whole story, that evening. At times she watched them closely, to gauge their reactions; otherwise she stared out of the window, watching the flickering lightning of a summer storm.

"I know you'll think it strange – even unpatriotic – to fall in love with a German, but he was a very special man. You two would have liked him; you especially, Ma, because I think he was like Dr McPhail – from what you've told me about him. Karl wanted to heal people, to cure people. He didn't care who they were, or how he lived. Do you think badly of me, for falling in love with a German?"

"Of course not," said Jess. "It's the man that's important, not his nationality..."

Alan added, " – or the accident of history that put our countries at war with each other."

—•—

They voyaged on the *Pioneer* lake steamer to Karonga, Mandy and her father. It gave them ample time to reminisce about the war, and Alan's campaigns before that. Mr Webb had moved on, and there was a new District Commissioner, who arranged for one of his officers to take them across the border to Chipembere's village, in the new territory of Tanganyika. They purchased a bag of cement in Karonga, and hired a man to carry it, and another two porters to bring their camping gear.

The chief's son was living in the village, a young man who professed antipathy towards the Germans and friendship to all Britons. Alan was certain that he expected a handsome gratuity. He led them to the grave site, which was known to the village elders.

As they walked through the bush in single file, searching for the *mukwa* tree, the forest and its sounds reminded Mandy vividly of her months with the German column and her relationship with Karl Niemeyer. The long marches had passed as nothing because she had his company.

"There it is," she exclaimed, and ran to the tree, touching the carved crosses on the trunk.

The piles of stones lay undisturbed on the graves. Alan arranged with the chief's son for a stonemason to come from a neighbouring village. Meanwhile, he and Mandy, with the help of the porters, made a camp nearby, and were brought food and water by the villagers.

They spent the following day gathering more stones, placing them on the graves in such a way that the mason was able to make a cohesive covering. He had only the one bag of cement, which he mixed with sand and water at the stream.

Mandy wrote with a stick in the wet cement the words:

Doctor Karl Niemeyer
(1890-1918)
loved by Amanda Spaight

On the other grave she wrote:

Unknown woman
victim of war and influenza
(1918)

Alan took the members of the party a short distance away, to leave Mandy to grieve for a while. He waited while the others returned to the village. When Mandy rejoined him, he looked at her carefully to judge her mood.

She gave a heavy sigh, then laughed. "It was a long way to come. I'm so grateful to you, Pa. You understood how important it was for me to come here. Karl's parents are dead, and he was an only child, so I don't suppose his family will want to know about the grave."

"Your previous departure was all too rushed. You needed this time to close the episode, to give it some finality."

"Yes, that's exactly what I needed." She hugged him.

—•—

It was the dry season of 1920, two years after the end of the war. The Spaights had been playing tennis at the club; Drew and Clare – four months pregnant, Alan and Jess. They were sitting on the verandah of the clubhouse drinking beer and lime squashes, when a young man approached, wearing a police uniform with Inspector's rank. He was clean-shaven and came up to them with assurance.

"Hello," he said, "my name is Neville Hendrie." He proffered a hand and Alan stood up to shake it, then introduced the others. He invited Neville to sit down and join them, beckoned to a waiter, and ordered more drinks.

Hendrie coughed, and said to Alan. "You knew my brother, sir. Peter Hendrie – at least you were with him in the crash, when he was killed."

Alan's mouth dropped. "So you're Peter's brother?"

"Yes. I'm in the Colonial Police – was in Kenya – and they posted me here – almost by chance."

"We never met Peter," said Jess. "Alan always said what a fine young man he was."

Neville frowned for a moment. "He loved flying. It was terribly sad that he could not have done it for longer – after the war." He sipped his beer. "I'm very glad to have met you all. You see, my parents are coming out from England. They were hoping to go to the site of the crash – to see the grave. You remember; you wrote to them, sir – offered to take them there."

"So I did." Alan stroked his beard.

"You were badly injured, sir?"

Alan pointed to his sleeve. "Only my arm. I was lucky."

Mandy was appraising the young man. She judged him to be about thirty years old, quite tall, dark hair cut short. He had a military look about him, something to do with his bearing, and the smartly pressed uniform.

"I remember Peter telling me that you were in the East Africa campaign," said Alan.

"Yes, sir. I was called up from the Metropolitan Police and sent out to Nairobi. When the war ended I decided to join the Colonial Service, and stayed up there – until now. This was a promotion for me."

"Well, the offer's still open," said Alan, "to take your parents to the grave site. It will not be easy – there are no roads, so one has to walk some of the way. Would your parents be up to it – with the heat?"

"I think so, sir. They're both keen walkers and very fit. Of course, we would depend entirely on you, but they would pay all the expenses. We realise that it would be a great imposition. "

Alan shook his head. "I would like to go back. We could make a proper safari. Jess, you would like to go?"

She nodded. "I won't be left behind."

"Drew, you and Clare – you'll take care of the farm."

Clare patted her belly. "I couldn't go in any case."

"Mandy?"

"I'll come – definitely. After you took me to Chipembere's, the least I can do is come with you."

—•—

The Hendries, Geoff and Moira, turned out to be friendly and easy. The Spaights invited them to stay on the farm, and they soon started to enjoy each other's company. Neville was a frequent visitor, enjoyed riding, and fell in love with Mandy.

One day Jess said, "I see that Neville has taken a fancy to you." She was watering her vegetable garden, while Mandy picked tomatoes.

"Do you think so?"

Jess laughed. "You know he does. Moira alluded to it yesterday, very discreetly. I dare say he said something to his parents."

"He hasn't said anything to me."

"It's not easy for a young man," said Jess. "You give the impression that you don't suffer fools gladly."

Mandy shrugged. "I'm sorry if I'm so intimidating."

"Give him an opening – if that's what you want. What do you think of him?"

"I like him – what I've seen. But it's a big step to go from 'liking' to the next plane."

—•—

Alan was delighted to organise the expedition, but he was concerned about finding the crash site. His memories were clouded by his injuries and dominated by his efforts to survive. Goodwill was commissioned to find Tobias and Mlati, the two scouts. Within a couple of days he returned with news that Mlati had gone to South Africa to work in the mines, but Tobias had joined the police, and was now a sergeant based at Dedza. Neville was able to negotiate some leave to join the expedition, and arranged for Tobias to be released as their guide.

Goodwill asked Alan if he could come with the expedition, and raised a team of a dozen porters. Alan used his Government contacts to get permission from the Portuguese provincial authorities for them to enter that territory, and politely declined their offer of assistance.

They held a meeting on the verandah at *Khundalila*, when Alan set out the plans for the expedition.

"We'll take the two lorries on the dirt road to Namweras, near the border. There's a District Assistant there, and a police post – we've notified them. We can travel a further thirty miles on rough tracks. Then we'll continue of foot, leaving the lorries under the care of a couple of local policemen. I estimate it will take three days to reach the crash site, so, assuming we spend a day there, and three days for the return walk, we'll be away from Namweras for about a week."

He explained what personal equipment they would take, in addition to the usual camp gear.

Geoff Hendrie, a dapper retired accountant, spoke up. "Alan, you must be sure to tell me how much all this will cost, so that I can reimburse you. Moira and I, and Neville, are very conscious of the time and effort you and your family are putting into this expedition..."

"There's not much out of pocket expense," explained Alan, laughing. "It's mostly time, and we won't charge you for that!"

—•—

It took the best part of a day to drive to Namweras. They slept in the lorries – the Spaights in one, the Hendries in the other. There was accommodation only for African staff in the *boma*; the district was notorious for its man-eating lions. By lunch time next day, when they had to leave the lorries and walk, they saw ample evidence on the dusty tracks – huge pug marks. Next morning the cool morning air was redolent of the scent of the animals.

Alan and Neville carried rifles, and Geoff Hendrie a shotgun. Tobias led, following the track used by Barton's column when it marched from Namweras into Portuguese territory. Goodwill brought up the rear, making sure that the porters did not lag behind.

They encountered a few villages, where Tobias sought confirmation that the track was leading to the Lujenda River.

"There were two small *kopjes*," said Alan, when they camped that night, "but they have no known name, and it's a common formation around here."

"It's so good of you to bring us here," said Moira Hendrie, small and cheerful.

"Oh, we enjoy the bush – don't we, Jess and Mandy," replied Alan. "It's one of our favourite things to do. Of course it's better when you have food and water, servants and porters. In the war we were wet and hungry most of the time – sleeping under the stars."

"Peter loved the bush," said Moira, "although he didn't have much experience." She turned to Neville. "And you do too, don't you."

Her son nodded. "That's why I joined the Colonial Police. There's something very special about this continent."

—•—

They pitched two large tents at night, one for the men, and the other for the women. The Africans slept under the stars. All were protected from wild animals by a thorn bush fence, with log fires inside.

"What do you think of Neville?" asked Jess.

"Me?" replied Mandy. "He seems nice. Easy to talk to. He's not a typical Pom, like Roly – more like a Rhodesian; I suppose because he's spent a long time in Kenya. He had a tough time in the war, like us."

"Surprising he hasn't married."

"He's had girl-friends. He probably thinks it's surprising that I haven't married."

"What have you told him?"

"Enough for him to know that there are no big skeletons in my cupboard. I've told him about Karl..."

"What did he say?"

"Just that he's sorry it ended like that."

—•—

They found the crash site with ease; Tobias had an eye for the landscape, an instinctive tracker. Alan pointed out the big acacia, which still bore the engine, propeller and wheels, and a few tattered remnants of the aircraft's fuselage. He showed them the carvings on the trunk, and then found the grave. The stones and rocks had moved a little, but the grave was still intact.

The Hendries stood side by side, he with his arm round her shoulder, while the Spaights withdrew. After a while they started to collect more stones and rocks, piling them on the grave and making a defined ring around it. The parents had brought a steel cross with an inscription, and they placed this at the head of the grave, secured by the heaviest rocks.

Next, Geoff Hendrie read a prayer, and Moira tearfully thanked all those who had brought them to the grave site.

"We are so grateful to you, the Spaight family. We can now return to England knowing that our beloved son is securely buried. We can remember this spot for the remainder of our lives."

—•—

The Spaights drove the Hendries to Limbe for the start of their long journey back to England; Kirsty and Gavin met them at the hotel for lunch before they left.

On the drive back to Zomba, Alan said to Jess, “I hope Mandy marries Neville. He’s a fine young man, don’t you think?”

“I agree.”

“If they do, I hope they have a time of peace to enjoy their lives together – and Drew and Clare – and Gavin and Kirsty.”

“And us too.”

—•—

Epilogue

Neville Hendrie and Mandy Spaight did in fact marry, and Neville's parents came out to Nyasaland again, this time for a wedding. The young couples: Drew and Clare, Gavin and Kirsty, and Neville and Mandy, started families, children born in Nyasaland, grandchildren for Alan and Jess, and Martin and Helen. No trace of Mac Spaight was ever found.

Martin was prominent in the campaign to resist the amalgamation of Rhodesia and South Africa in 1923. He was a revered elder statesman when he died in 1938.

The Spaight and Russell children and grandchildren enjoyed twenty years of peace before another great war erupted in Europe. This time, the southern part of the continent was spared, but North Africa was engulfed in 1939-1943. The families were all drawn into the conflict, and their stories will be told in a forthcoming novel.

—•—

Colonel Paul-Emil von Lettow Vorbeck (1870-1964) did not believe at first that Germany had surrendered and that the Kaiser had abdicated. His column was considerably reduced in numbers, but still well-armed and active. The Europeans were interned at Dar es Salaam for several weeks, and most of the *askaris* at Tabora; the Spanish flu took its toll in both locations. The Colonel reached Germany in February 1919, and was fêted as a hero. He survived WW2 though both his sons were killed in action.

Major-General Sir Edward Northey, KCMG, CB (1868-1953) commanded a brigade in France at the beginning of WW1. He was wounded, and in 1916 was given the command of the Nyasaland-Rhodesia Field Force (NORFORCE). He was awarded a CB in 1917 and was knighted in 1918 when he was appointed Governor of British East Africa (later Kenya). In 1922 he left to be High Commissioner of Zanzibar. He retuned to the army in 1924 and retired in 1926.

Colonel Ron Murray, DCM, DSO (1874-1920) commanded the Rhodesian Column. When he left the front in ill health he reached Salisbury, but left immediately for Cape Town. There the Murrays bought a farm, but had to sell it to move to England. Murray died on June 29, 1920, aged 46. Throughout the long campaign he never avoided a fight, never lost one, and never lost a gun.

—•—

Place names, past and current

Abercorn	—	Mbala
Bismarckburg	—	Kasanga
Belgian Congo	—	Democratic Republic of Congo
British East Africa	—	Kenya
Cholo	—	Thyolo
Elizabethville	—	Lubumbashi
German East Africa	—	Tanzania
Inyanga	—	Nyanga
Marandellas	—	Marondera
New/Neu Langenburg	—	Tukuyu
Northern Rhodesia	—	Zambia
Portuguese East Africa	—	Mozambique
Rhodesia	—	Zimbabwe
Rusape	—	Rusapi
Salisbury	—	Harare
Umtali	—	Mutare

Acronyms

ADC	Aide de camp
ALC	African Lakes Corporation/Company ('Mandala')
B&EA	Blantyre & East Africa (Company)
BSAP	British South Africa Police
CB	Companion of the Most Honourable Order of the Bath (members belong to either the Military or Civil divisions)
CPO	Chief Petty Officer
DC	District Commissioner
DCM	Distinguished Conduct Medal (awarded for gallantry to NCOs)
DO	District Officer
DSO	Distinguished Service Order (awarded since 1886 for distinguished services during active operations against the enemy)
GEA	German East Africa (now Tanzania)
HE	His Excellency
HQ	Headquarters
KAR	King's African Rifles (regiment raised since 1902 in British territories in east and central Africa)

LEGCO	Legislative Council
MC	Military Cross (award for gallantry, generally for younger officers)
NCO	Non-commissioned Officer
NRP	Northern Rhodesia Police (a military and civil police force started in 1903)
NVR	Nyasaland Volunteer Reserve (military reserve started in 1901)
PC	Provincial Commissioner
PEA	Portuguese East Africa (now Mozambique)
PWD	Public Works Department
RFC	Royal Flying Corps (the flying branch of the British Army during WW1; merged with the Royal Naval Air Service in August 1918 to form the Royal Air Force)
RNR	Rhodesia Native Regiment (formed in May 1916, with white officers)
RNVR	Royal Navy Volunteer Reserve

Glossary

alonda	watchman (ChiNyanja)
anguru	Yao immigrant to Nyasaland from Portuguese East Africa (ChiNyanja)
askari(s)	African soldier(s) (ChiNyanja and Swahili)
azungu	Europeans, white people (ChiNyanja)
badza	digging hoe, with wide blade and wooden handle (ChiNyanja)
bambo	father (ChiNyanja)
boma	enclosure, protected area, fort, government complex (ChiNyanja)
bundu	African bush, bushveld (Southern Africa Bantu languages)
capitao	headman, boss (ChiNyanja, from Portuguese)
chambo	Tilapia (bream) fish species from Lake Nyasa (ChiNyanja)
dambo	open (wet) grassland (ChiNyanja)
dagga	mud
dawa	medicine (Swahili)
dhow	Arab sailing ship (Arabic)
diti	ground hornbill (ChiNyanja)

donga	gully (Southern African bantu languages)
fisi	hyena (ChiNyanja)
kalata	piece of paper, note, letter (ChiNyanja)
khundalila	dove's cry/song (ChinNyanja)
kopje	small hill (Afrikaans, from 'small head')
laager	camp/protected by wagons/fences (Afrikaans)
machila	conveyance, usually for one person, consisting of a hammock slung between two poles, carried by bearers (Portuguese)
miombo	forest consisting of Brachystegia/Uapaca species
msasa	tree, Brachystegia spp (ChiShona)
muti	medicine (South African bantu languages)
mvu	hippopotamus (ChiNyanja)
mzungu	European/white person (ChiNyanja)
nagana	animal trypanosomiasis – parasite disease (East African bantu languages)
ndege	literally 'bird', also aeroplane (ChiNyanja)
ngona	crocodile (ChiNyanja)
njinga	bicycle (ChiNyanja)
nkanga	lion (ChiNyanja)
nkwali	francolin species of bird (ChiNyanja)
nsaru	cloth (ChiNyanja)
nsima	maize porridge (ChiNyanja)
patsagolas	snacks (ChiNyanja)
pombe	beer brewed (from millet/maize) in the village (ChiNyanja)

ruga-ruga	armed levy, mercenary (East/Central African bantu languages)
samosa	triangular savoury fried pastry containing spiced vegetables or meat (Hindi)
Schutztruppe	Defence Force (German)
tangata	tenancy with rent paid by labouring (ChiNyanja)
tenga-tenga	porter (East/Central African bantu languages)
ulendo	journey (ChiNyanja)